WHERE THE LIGHT DIES

THE BLOOD OF EITH, BOOK FOUR

GILLIAN GRANT

This is a work of fiction. All of the characters, organizations, and events portrayed in this novel are either products of the author's imagination or are used fictitiously.

www.GillianGrant.com

DEDICATION

For Connor. Thanks for being biased.

PRONUNCIATION GUIDE

People and Creatures:
- Sahar Al Fazil: Sa-**har** Al **Fuh**-zil
- Nerezza Quill: Ner-ehz-uh
- Drystan: **Drih**-stan
- Eirunn: **Ai**-roon
- Keres: Keh-**ruhs**
- Mortova: **Mor**-tow-vuh
- Ikedree: **Ike**-dree
- Evren: Eh-v-r-eh-n
- Gyda: **Gee**-da
- Sorin: Sor-en
- Abraxas: Uh-**brak**-suhs
- Arke: ar-**kuh**
- Solri: Soul-**ree**
- Viggo: **Vee**-go

Places and Countries:
- Etherak: Eh-ther-ahk
- Vernes: **Ver**-nes
- Terevas: Ter-eh-vahs
- Boreal Sea: **Baw**-ree-uhl

- Melkarth: Mell-karth
- Gratey: Grah-**tay**
- Orenlion: **Ore**-ren-lee-on

Things:
- Xirstine: Zir-stine

Terms:
- krevas: kruh-**vas** - a dwarven term for dishonored one, coward or traitor
- levenya: lev-en-**ya** - elven word for family, clan, or group
- foya: **foy**-ah - Ikedree term for father

The Banished Faith:

Once a nearly universally worshipped religion, the Banished Faith is now solely clung to by those in Etherak and few others. Once, the Divines were able to give their closest worshippers great power, and their absence has left the once powerful kingdom of Etherak crippled.

- The Banished Divines:
  - Haphion, God of Light and Flame
  - Nutvian, Goddess of Ice and Order
  - Vuhione, Goddess of Honor and Justice
  - Holtia, Goddess of Love and Healing
  - Emion, God of Music and Dance
  - Mandros, God of Knowledge
  - Elos, God of Change and Freedom
  - Eitrix, Goddess of Industry and Money
  - Roania, Goddess of Nature
  - Zelmis, Goddess of Darkness and Chaos
  - Nomien, God of Wrath and Fire
  - Mituna, Goddess of Tempests and Seas
  - Vyone, God of Death
  - Nuris, Goddess of Illness and Envy

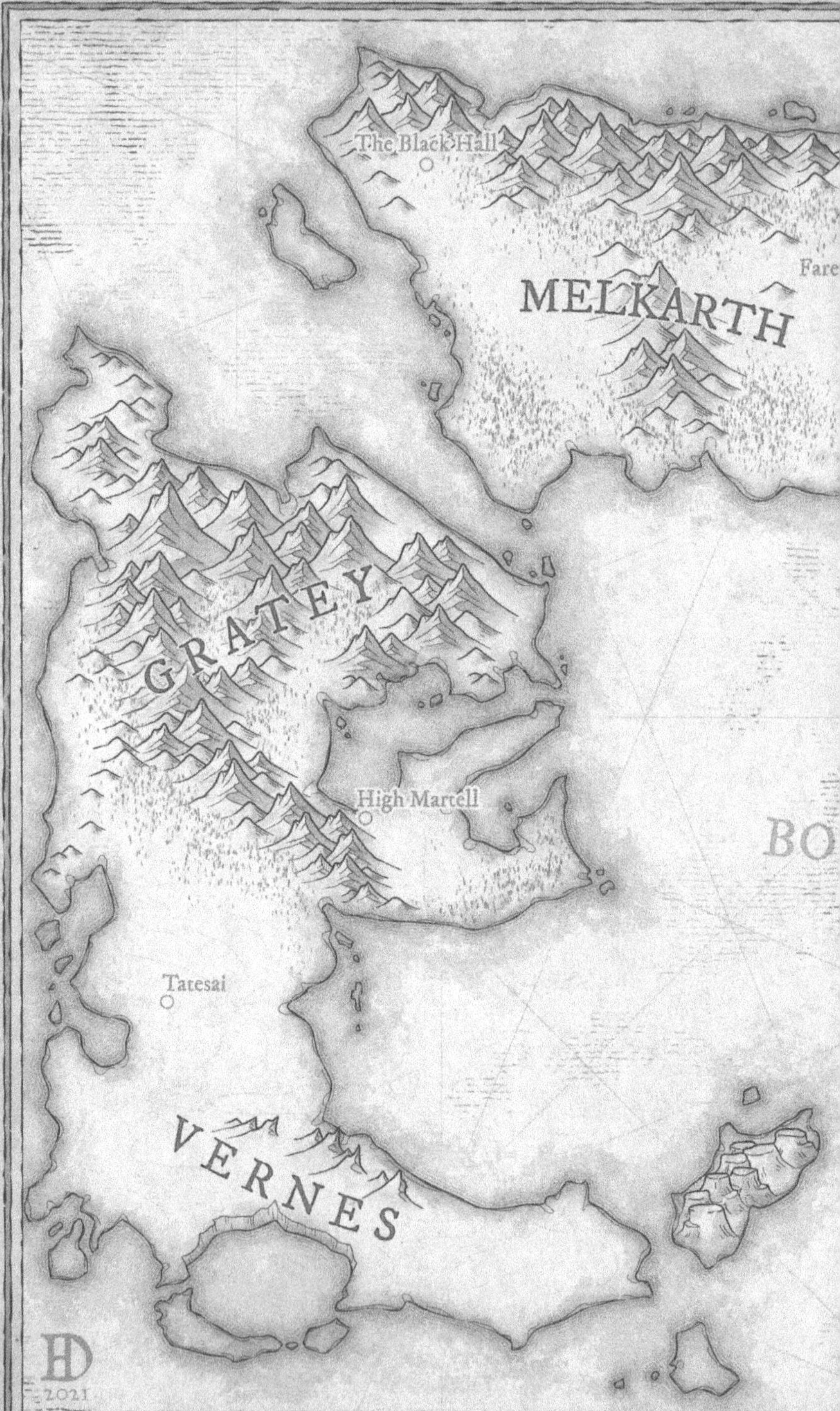

The Black Hall
MELKARTH
Fare
GRATEY
High Martell
BO
Tatesai
VERNES
HD
2021

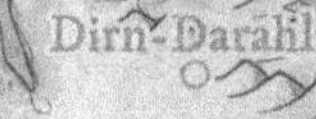

Dirn-Darahl
ETHERAK
Linston
TERERVAS
Rhienwall
SEA
AMRUTHAN
EITH

1

Abraxas

Eith was blanketed in a dismal silence.

The soft, heavy kind in the grey of dawn. The kind that deafened even the blood rushing in his ears. There was no end in sight to the vast grey fog, nor the damp quiet it enraptured. Even the dark waters of the Boreal Sea were still and calm, barely lapping against the great wooden hull of the *Crooked Wrath*.

The Vasa ship was old. Her hull had been visibly patched with different colored woods, and the salt-worn deck showed how vicious a mistress time could be to those who refused to die.

Like their ship, the *Wrath*'s crew had fought like demons for every last breath. And, in the end, their fighting had been useless.

Abraxas gripped the railing of the ship with bloody hands. He was staining the wood with every desperate thrum of his finger. His eyes ached from staring into the unending grey in front of him. He hadn't known a fog this dense and enveloping so far out at sea. He'd never seen in all his many crossings the water so calm. The Boreal Sea was rage and chaos, the physical embodiment of the goddess who had once drawn her power from it.

Mituna. Young, prone to fits of violence and cruelty to get her way. Daughter of Nomien and every bit as evil in nature. Whereas her father was calculating and patient in his evil acts, Mituna was anything but. Her actions were as unpredictable as the sea itself. The Vasa who made their home on her waters were at her mercy more than any other, but in all his years he'd never found one who willingly worshipped her.

The Boreal Sea hadn't been safer once she'd been banished with the rest. If anything, the frequent storms, monsters, and waves as high as mountains had gotten even worse without her there to control them.

But Abraxas had to remind himself *when* he was, just as much as *where*. It was still difficult for him to wrap his mind around, that in the moment that should've been his death he'd sent himself to a different time entirely. The first time he'd questioned someone, after they stopped gawking at his bloody form, they'd told him and he'd been too stunned to even attempt fighting the next three days.

He'd sent himself, with Nerezza as a passenger, one hundred years into the past.

His bloody nails dug into the smooth wood. The fog remained unchanging.

One hundred years. The gods were still in Eith. Etherak was fifty years into its hundred-year occupation of Vernes, Gratey, and Terevas. The Wandering Sols, save for himself, had yet to be born.

Abraxas tried to breathe through the weight that constricted his lungs each time the truth of what he'd done hit him. But the humid air did little to expand his lungs. No matter how hard he tried, he still felt like someone had their arms around his chest in a deadly squeeze he couldn't break free from. No amount of air was enough.

The hairs on the back of his neck prickled, and Abraxas fought the urge not to shiver as a dull scrapping sounded on the deck behind him. He knew what he'd see, but he couldn't help but turn around anyway.

The crew of the *Crooked Wrath* milled about the deck in a shambling but well-organized manner. No orders were shouted and no shanties were sung. The deck was quiet except for the scraping of bones and the slapping of rope on wood. Several of the crew swabbed blood up from the deck, blood he'd spilled. More still climbed the rigging missing limbs. The navigator of the ship stood at the wheel, his jaw missing and his eyes glowing blood red. The whole crew shared the same magic now, one that wouldn't let them rest beyond the death he'd brought them.

The grizzled woman who'd once been the captain shuffled past him, tripping over her broken leg with every other step. Her salt-and-pepper hair, shorn close to her weathered skin, was caked with dried blood. The wound where he'd caved in her skull with the pummel of her own sword had finally stopped bleeding. That same sword dangled from her belt where he'd carefully put it back after her death. She'd fought well, despite being clumsy and self-taught. He respected her drive to protect her crew, fruitless as it had been.

She was just like them all now. A corpse puppet, driving her murderers for home.

Abraxas's fingers twitched for the sword as she walked past, reeking of salt and sea-laden rot that had started to take hold of the whole crew. He could end it for them. Run her sword through her heart and every single one of her crew. He could lay them to rest the way Sorin had taught him back in Direwall, although he'd long forgotten the song he'd sung. It felt like a lifetime ago when he'd stood by the Vasa's side on an icy shore, sending a boy monster's body into the cold depths with a song and a prayer.

Divines, Abraxas missed him. He missed them all. He imagined a future where he succeeded in freeing the Vasa. He laid them and the ship to rest. He sunk himself and the witch behind it all with him. Whatever horror Mituna had waiting in her depths he'd gladly take and drag Nerezza there, too.

The captain passed by him, once again tripping over her own ankle as she lugged an armful of rope. Abraxas reached his hand toward her belt, the sword's pummel still splattered with its owner's brain matter waiting for him. His fingers brushed the metal, grim in their determination, until pain seized him.

His muscles spasmed and then locked up. His bones crackled under the weight of a familiar agony. But no matter how used to the feeling of boiling blood and quaking marrow he was now, it still brought him to his knees. His vision swam as the pain was leashed back like a rabid dog. He shook, still feeling it there, waiting to be unleashed.

Abraxas never understood how Evren seemed to draw strength from pain. All it ever did was make him want to die.

Abraxas was still gasping for air when his vision started to clear. He saw the deck, crusted with salt and gore. He saw his own murderous hands keeping him from collapsing. And then a pair of boots stopped just shy of his fingertips. The ashen grey of the robes fluttered to a stop over his wrists and he jerked back. He drew as much venom and loathing to his expression as he could manage and lifted his chin.

Nerezza stood over him, as cold as she ever was. Her black eyes were voids he could discern nothing but contempt from. And she was staring down at him with an unhealthy dose of it now.

"I thought we were past such self-sacrificing ideas," she mused.

He sneered. "I don't know what you're talking about."

"Don't play the fool, Abraxas. You've never been good at it."

He shifted uncomfortably on his knees. She couldn't have known what he'd planned. He'd *just* thought about it after being at sea for over two weeks. He'd made sure to be as quiet and complacent as she expected him to be. When she ordered him to kill the crew a mere day ago and take the ship, he hadn't even protested. When she infected the dead with her necromancy, he'd bit his tongue and looked away. He'd thought he'd played the perfect, obedient attack dog. Unless she could control his mind as well as his blood . . .

Abraxas shuddered then and struggled to keep eye contact with her.

"You can't read minds," he said with more confidence than he felt. "You have nothing but your own paranoia."

"Oh?" She cocked her head to the side. "Is that so? Then enlighten me. What did you want our dear captain's sword for when you couldn't get it out of your hands quick enough yesterday?"

Abraxas opened his mouth and then shut it again. A lie would be useless. He didn't have Sol's talent for manipulation. He was an open book to Nerezza. She could read his motivations as if he'd written them in blood across his face.

No, lying would be useless and would likely just cause more pain. And Divines, he was so tired of hurting.

He bowed his head and heard Nerezza chuckle.

"That's what I thought. I'd hoped we were past this point, Abraxas. You learned weeks ago that fighting is useless."

He had. He'd fought Nerezza every step of the way out of the dragon's carcass, through the roads of Terevas and to the port city of Noxcairn. He'd almost gotten free there. The city was seated on the delta of the River Nox and had canals instead of streets. Abraxas knew them well enough from his time stationed there at the beginning of the war. He knew the bridges to take, the alleyways that had secret passages for smugglers, and which gambling dens would hide you for a time depending on how much you paid.

But the black waters of the canals didn't save him. The masks and parades didn't hide him. In the end, he'd stumbled into a small temple the occupying soldiers had built. Empty and damp, smelling of rotting fruit offerings and burnt incense. It wasn't built for Haphion, instead for Eitrix, the shapeshifting God of Wealth. It was the only god the people of Noxcairn readily accepted, from merchants and gamblers to politicians and thieves. Eitrix was a fickle god, and not his, but he prayed anyway. He was met with silence, but stubbornly stayed until Nerezza found him again.

The pain had been severe then. Enough to keep him in a daze for the next day. He hadn't even remembered her booking their passage on the *Crooked Wrath*, and he'd been too exhausted to ask why.

But now, after murdering an entire crew full of innocent people, he had regained his senses.

Abraxas looked her dead in her black eyes again. "I was going to take her sword and kill them all over again. I was going to wrench their dead hearts out of their chests and leave you with nothing. Then I was going to sink this whole ship and bring you down to death with me."

Nerezza blinked, her face unreadable as she took in all the hatred he was throwing at her. She seemed to relax a little, as if him saying it had confirmed something for her. And then she smiled.

"You're welcome to try. But, Abraxas, if you wanted a sword, all you needed to do was ask."

She said it in a soft, crooning voice. Like he was a child who'd tried to steal a cookie instead of asking her for it. He bristled and pushed himself to his feet.

"I don't *want* a sword." He hissed, and his muscles were already tensing for another wave of pain.

But Nerezza smiled at him, amused. The fingers of her

remaining hand stayed loose and calm at her side, and he struggled not to watch them. One curl of her pinky would have him writhing at her feet again.

"You wanted one just a few moments ago," Nerezza said. She flicked her white braid over her shoulder and then snapped her fingers. Abraxas flinched, and she chuckled. But it wasn't for him. The captain tossed her rope down and lumbered back to Nerezza like a bored but obedient pet. She stopped just shy of Nerezza's outstretched fingers.

In any other circumstances, the differences between the two of them would've been laughable. Nerezza was thin and pale, like pieces of bone held together by gossamer grey robes. The captain, in life, had been a tall woman built with thick, corded muscle and more scars than Abraxas could count. She had been more pirate than sailor, which made sense as to why Nerezza picked her ship. No honest sailor would've taken them without the proper papers and authority during a time of war.

The captain of the *Crooked Wrath* could've snapped Nerezza in two in life. But in death she was nothing more than an extension of the mage's will.

"Your sword, captain." Nerezza said.

The corpse unsheathed it, uncaring of her own blood coating the blade, and handed it over. Nerezza regarded it closely, then gave a wordless command. The captain tore off part of her linen shirt and used it to wipe the blood and gore from the blade, and when she was done it still shone pink.

She held it out to him. "Here."

Abraxas didn't move. He eyed the sword, once a lifeline, like it was a waiting snake.

Nerezza rolled her eyes. "Oh please, it won't bite."

"You might."

"You don't want it? Fine." She shrugged and then hurled the sword over the side of the ship.

Before Abraxas even knew what he was doing, his hand

shot out and grasped the hilt before it could fall into the dark sea. Nerezza laughed behind him as he stood frozen over the railing with the sword in his hand. He squeezed his eyes shut, trying to will his fingers to let go of the hilt and let the sword go. This was a trap. This was playing right into her games and would just end in more pain. He should let go.

The worst part was this was entirely *him*. Nerezza's compulsions came in waves of agony. His own reflexes had saved the sword, and it was his that refused to let it go.

Eventually, he brought himself away from the edge with the sword in hand and stood before her. Shame colored his cheeks, and he didn't know why. But he clutched the hilt tightly despite its power meaning nothing to him now.

"Why?" he croaked.

"My Champion needs a weapon." Nerezza said.

He flinched again. "I'm not your Champion. That service belongs to one."

"Ah yes, Haphion. How is he, by the way?"

Abraxas kept his mouth shut again. This time he knew the shame that burned well.

"Stop this, Nerezza," he said instead. "Please."

"You'll have to be more specific."

He gestured to the corpse crew. "Them. Me." He pointed furiously at himself. "All of it!"

She blinked, letting his voice echo across the foggy waters for what felt like ages. Then, she stepped closer. Just one step, but it was enough for him to recoil as if he'd been hit.

"Do you know how to sail a ship this size by yourself?" she asked.

He gritted his teeth. "No."

"Do you know how to navigate the Boreal Sea?"

"*No.*"

"Then stop complaining," she snapped. "These weren't good people, so stop acting like I killed a bunch of orphans."

"They're still people, Nerezza," he argued. "This is wrong."

"This is practical," she corrected. "I need them to get me where I'm going. And if the captain hadn't threatened to slit my throat if I didn't pay her triple our agreed fee, then they'd all be alive. I'm not entirely malicious. My cruelty has purpose."

"And me?" he asked, already dreading the answer. "Why do you need me for this insane quest of yours? I'm more trouble than I'm worth."

"Oh, don't sell yourself so short. You're exactly what I need. A shield to keep me from harm. A sword to kill when I can't. And a guide for the journey ahead."

"If you wanted a guide, you could've had anybody."

"True." She smiled again, and this time it sent chills down his spine. "But only you know war-torn Vernes well enough to guide me through."

Vernes.

No.

He couldn't go back. The mere thought of it sent panic and bile climbing up his throat. His sword shook in his hand, and he must've looked terrified because Nerezza's face softened. She let out a sympathetic noise and cupped his face with cold, thin fingers. He shuddered under her touch but couldn't find the strength to get away.

Nerezza brushed a damp strand of hair out of his face. "Vernes will not hurt you this time. If you believe anything, believe that. You are coming back stronger than your past self, more openminded. You will finally give that wretched place the reckoning it deserves."

Nerezza stepped away, and he found himself strangely still. But his mind was a storm, and he couldn't grasp a single thought. Long after night had fallen and he laid in his swaying cot, he clutched the sword as if his life depended on it, his fingers digging into the leather grip until he could feel it breaking.

Abraxas prayed to Haphion with fear coursing through his veins. He poured all his desperation and pain into every uttered word. He prayed like he did every night since Haphion had been banished. And, as with every other night, he was met with silence.

Thick, dismal, blanketing silence.

2

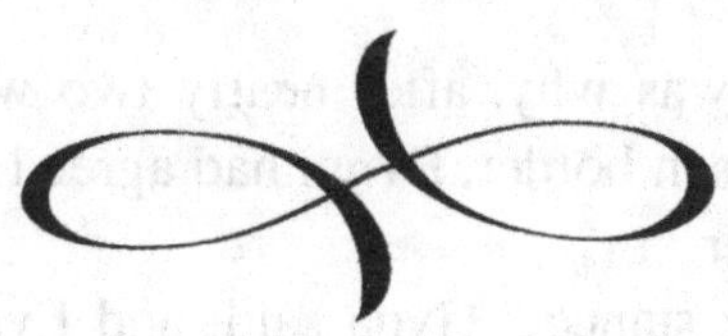

Evren

The thin mountain air did little to keep the hot sun from beating down on Evren's bare shoulders. She rolled them under her sweat-soaked tunic and tried to remember how to hold her quarterstaff as she faced her opponent.

Across the courtyard, Gyda was tightening her scarf around her hair again, tucking a strand of blood-red hair back from where it'd flown out during their last round. The act was methodical and slow, which made her sudden grab for her quarterstaff all the more terrifying. Evren's muscles instinctually stiffened, half ready to bolt and half ready to take another searing blow.

Gyda merely grinned.

"Jumpy this round, hm?"

Evren shrugged, keeping her staff in a guarded position in front of her. It still felt awkward using it. The wood was deceptively heavy, thick enough to break bones and crack skulls if used properly. In her hands it felt clumsy and awkward. In Gyda's it looked too small compared to the massive sword the warrior usually wielded.

But Gyda was far more comfortable with the quarterstaff. In fact, over their long weeks of travel, Evren had come to find that Gyda was comfortable with all forms of weapons so long as they let her do some personal damage up close. The greatsword was her favorite, but she fought like she needed it to breathe.

Maybe that was why, after nearly two weeks waiting to cross the Terevasan border, Evren had agreed to let Gyda beat the shit out of her.

"Widen your stance," Gyda said, and Evren immediately obeyed with a scowl on her face. "Don't make that face. I would've snapped your kneecap if you stood like that."

"I know how to stand," Evren muttered, but did as she was told. Mei had done her best to train her with spears back during the hopeful months training to be a Khama, but the instruction never stuck like archery did. Quarterstaffs were close enough that Evren didn't make a fool of herself often, but she didn't have the prowess Gyda exuded.

"We can always take a break."

Evren narrowed her eyes. Her burning muscles would love that and, frankly, her pride was smarting more than her skin from these sparring sessions. But the offer was a test. Gyda would always offer because she knew Evren would always take it as a challenge. It was something she did often now, and Evren could feel the thrill that raced through both their chests.

"Not a chance."

Permission granted. That was all Gyda needed.

The warrior lunged forward at a frightening speed. Evren had just enough time to shift her defensive stance to catch the blow. The crack of wood against wood snapped through the quiet courtyard, the first blow of many.

Evren threw Gyda's staff off her own, bringing the other

end to sweep her legs out from under her. In a blur of light wood, Gyda blocked her.

Everything after that was a blur. Their frantic dance of swift footwork and arching wood was an elegant back and forth. Action, then reaction after reaction. A chain of hits, a string of feints smattered with healthy bit of dirty play. The same game they'd played out every day for the past four weeks, just different moves.

Gyda had reach and strength. Evren had speed and a whole lot of luck, and that was all that kept her on her feet.

Evren would be lying if she said she didn't enjoy it. Whether it was Gyda's heart beating a steady rhythm in her chest or the thrill of being this close to her, she didn't know or care. Every successful block was a victory. Every time she darted out of the way and felt the staff woosh past her hot skin made her smile. No matter how hard she was pushed, how many times she fell or lost, there was a stark difference between how she felt before and during the sparring. She'd drag her feet until Gyda goaded her, but after that she was golden.

She was still grinning like a fool when Gyda's staff smacked against the back of her knee, successfully pulling off the same move Evren had attempted to open the fight. The pain was bright enough that she didn't feel herself hit the ground, and there were still stars in her eyes when she brought her staff up.

Just in time. Gyda's next blow slammed right between Evren's hands. Evren's fingers ached from the aftershocks, and the staff gave a little in the middle.

Both women eyed the splinters cautiously. Gyda with a look of apology. She hadn't meant to hit so hard, Evren realized. Unblocked, that blow could've done some serious damage.

"You've been pulling your punches," Evren panted.

Gyda frowned down at her. "And yet, you're still on your back."

"Best two out of three?"

Gyda had barely given a nod before both of Evren's feet were on her chest and kicking her off. The warrior stumbled back, dazed but smiling.

Evren kicked again, this time at her staff. The wood broke clean in half. She rolled herself back, getting to her feet swiftly enough to cause her head to spin. In her hands the two halves of the staff were similar to daggers, and she grinned as Gyda eyed them warily.

"Do you ever play by the rules?"

"Since when are there rules, love?"

Evren's heart stuttered in her chest, as it did every time she called Gyda that. Perhaps it was cheating since it left her dazed for a moment. But it still gave Evren a thrill.

She didn't give Gyda a chance to recover. Evren was on her in a flash, putting everything she had behind her blows. The first two landed on flesh before Gyda's staff snapped up and the dance resumed.

Evren's reach was shorter now. She had to stay closer in Gyda's range. But the split staff was lighter in separate hands. She was quicker. She spent less time recovering from Gyda's hits and more time spinning into her next attack. The danger was there, even if it wasn't *true* danger. Gyda wouldn't intentionally hurt her. This wasn't a fight to the death. But having her so close, a breath's difference between a block and a hit, sent a thrill through her.

They traveled through the whole courtyard, trading hits and darting from one wall to another. They were feet away from one another, far too close for Evren's comfort, when Gyda stopped pulling her blows. She needed to get them back in the open but, before she could dart away, Gyda's next move was looming over her.

Evren caught Gyda's overhead blow by crossing her

staves. Her muscles smarted painfully at the jarring impact. Gyda growled from the back of her throat and shoved her back. The warrior put all her force behind the push and Evren's own staves slammed in her face.

A spark of pain. A crack of cartilage. Evren was falling backwards. Even temporarily blinded, she could feel her balance failing her.

But with pain came strength. With blood came clarity.

Evren threw herself into the fall, arching back into a backflip. Her extended foot caught Gyda's chin, and the warrior was still cursing as Evren landed on her feet, licking the copper from her teeth.

Her blood was thrumming. Her vision clear and all fatigue gone from her muscles. Gyda was still shaking off the head blow. Evren could end this. She could *win*.

She took her chance and ran. Not towards Gyda, but towards the stone wall of the courtyard they'd pushed themselves against. She picked up just enough speed to jump and run along the wall itself. For a few glorious footfalls, she was walking on the wall, arching her back to direct herself for the final finishing blow.

But it was the sight of Gyda that made her falter.

She was on her knees, her staff on the ground, forgotten, clutching her chest.

Evren dropped to the ground and left her broken staff behind her as she raced to Gyda's side. All the adrenaline was gone, replaced with cold, numbing fear. She skidded to her knees in front of her, taking her face in her hands.

"Gyda? What is it? Are you hurt?"

Even before she answered Evren knew she wasn't. None of the hits she landed would've been enough to do more than bruise. Gyda had suffered far worse than a foot to her face. But still, she shook under Evren's fingers.

"No," Gyda rasped. "I just . . . I felt . . ."

She couldn't finish, but her hands were still fisting the

shirt at her chest. Evren enveloped them with her own smaller ones. She could feel her racing heart mirrored in her own ribcage, but through her shirt and skin it was barely beating. The scar, another mirror to Evren's, was icy to the touch.

Weak.

That was what Gyda couldn't say. She felt like the life was ebbing out of her, and it was a feeling Evren knew well.

"Oh, fuck," Evren said, horrified. "Gyda, I'm sorry. I didn't think. I didn't mean to use it."

Gyda shook her head, lacing her fingers through Evren's. She looked down at her, still shaking. "Do not apologize. We knew this might happen."

It still made Evren sick. She hadn't used her Blood magic since the fight with Nerezza in Orenlion. There hadn't been a need, and she was still waiting for Arke to finish the custom runes and spells for her to try.

But she'd known there would be a cost to Gyda's sacrifice. She might give up half a heart and be able to live, but the consequences had plagued Evren's nights. They learned quickly that Gyda had no Blood magic of her own, but no magic came without a price. And now, by sheer accident, they'd found it.

"I shouldn't have. It was just instinct—"

"Evren, I know," Gyda said softly. The shaking had subsided, as had the strength in Evren's limbs. She found herself exhausted and burning with new hurts, but not nearly as fatigued as she'd been in the past. Gyda, having regained some color, still looked more ashen than normal. While guilt and regret swirled like a deadly storm, Gyda squeezed her hand and grounded her.

"You don't have control," she said. "We will learn."

Evren shook her head. "I won't use it again. I don't need to."

"You will."

"Gyda—"

"I won't have this weakness hanging over us." The warrior pressed further, iron leaking into her voice. "We will handle this together, as we have before."

There was no arguing with Gyda now. Or ever, really. Evren was one of the few who could get away with it, and she mentally noted to start this conversation at a date where they were both in better form and health. For now, she'd just have to take Gyda's word that she was all right.

Evren stood up and helped Gyda to her feet. She was unsteady at first but found her balance easily enough. Whatever weakness clung to her bones, she did her best to shake it off.

"So . . . who won?"

Both women spun around to the source of the voice. One man out of the dozen who stood at the far end of the courtyard watching. Evren's ears burned with embarrassment. How much had they seen? Judging by the pieces of gold exchanging hands, they had to have seen most of the fight.

Gyda's hand fell on her shoulder. "This round belongs to her."

A small, squirrely man hugged his gold as a handful of others tried to take it. "Its two out of three! You heard them. Fight's not done yet."

"Yes, it is," Evren said. "No more show today."

The small crowd grumbled and started to exchange gold in earnest before shuffling back through the doors. Evren couldn't blame them for their disappointment. There was very little to do waiting to cross the border, and all travelers had to wait an obscene amount of time before being let through. Before Evren and Gyda, there had been a bard that sung himself hoarse to keep the people entertained. He'd left without being able to speak above a whisper. Before that, there had been a traveling magician who made animals from paper.

Vanguard was what stood between anxious travelers and

another kingdom. Evren glared over the courtyard walls at the massive fortress. The grey stone was carved from the mountains that surrounded it and it nearly blended in with its surroundings. If it wasn't for the massive wall that circled it, it might've looked like an extension of the mountains themselves. But there was nothing pretty about Vanguard. An Etherakian fortress built to control flow to and from Terevas, as well as act as a defense should either side try to invade, it was built for war. She could barely make anything out behind its massive walls. Occasionally she could see patrols along the ramparts, and the warm flicker of candles from behind the small, gated windows. But she didn't get to see beyond the massive metal gate that shut the fortress up. The drawbridge that connected Vanguard to the small encampment travelers waited at had yet to come down and bridge the ravine that separated them.

Evren tore herself away from the fortress and busied herself picking up her broken staff and the one Gyda had abandoned. Gyda tossed her a fresh cloth and she gladly wiped the sweat from her neck.

"They're getting worse," Evren mused as she saw the last of the audience leave.

Gyda snorted. "They're bored."

"I'm not getting beat up for their entertainment. At least the bard got paid for his trouble."

"I don't doubt Sol is collecting gold on our behalf."

"Sure, but this is ridiculous. How long do they expect us to wait?"

Gyda looked up at Vanguard with the same impatience Evren felt. "We were warned that it would take a while to get through."

"It's been too long." Evren pointed at her with her staff. "I don't know which side is responsible, but when I find out, I'm going to beat them—"

"Lady Evren, we're finally leaving!"

A bright, cheerful voice stopped Evren's tirade before it could truly start. She turned back to the entry of the courtyard. Once again, it was not as empty as she thought, but instead of a crowd of bored bettors, she was greeted with the sight of a teenage girl bouncing up to them, cheeks brightly colored with pink joy.

"Morning, Dagny," Evren said carefully as the human skidded to a stop just before them, slightly out of breath. "What have you got?"

Dagny was grinning from ear to ear already, but she somehow managed a wider smile when she pulled a piece of parchment from the pocket of her dress.

"Official approval for us to cross the border!" she squealed. "Isn't it great! We're supposed to be at the bridge by noon."

Evren blinked, staring at the parchment. After nearly two weeks of waiting, she didn't believe it. She took the paper from Dagny and hastily opened it. The writing was curt and to the point, very clearly written by a soldier who couldn't care less about the orders they were carrying out. But it was exactly as Dagny said—a way out.

Evren tried to stamp down her smile as she handed the paper back. "Well, I guess you better start packing."

"Oh, I already am! I've hardly removed anything from my bags just in case this happened. But I can hardly believe it! Can you?"

"I'd all but given up hope."

Gyda nodded to the paper. "Have you shown the others?"

Dagny shook her head. "Not yet. I'll go find them now."

"Good," Evren nodded. "And don't be too loud. We don't want to rub salt in the wound for those who still have to wait."

"I won't! I'll be very quiet. See you at the bridge." And then she was running off again, her blonde curls flying from her hasty bun as her excited steps tore through doorway.

"I suppose you'll have to finish those threats in person," Gyda smirked.

"Very funny." But Evren was beyond relieved. She needed to get out of Vanguard's shadow as quickly as she could. There was plenty in Terevas she had to do, but more than anything she was ready to just move again. All this sitting still had made her antsy. And it left too much time to think.

Evren and Gyda put up their equipment and took the time to put Evren's broken nose back into place. She was still staunching the bleeding as they walked out together. The soft dirt of the courtyard turned to hard stone, and shade overtook the bright sunlight. Evren blinked until her eyes adjusted, relieved to find it empty.

"Dagny was so excited she didn't even notice my nose." Evren chuckled. "Remember when she fainted over Sol's broken ankle?"

Gyda hummed in agreement. "I'd say she's getting better, but I think she's just blind to all she doesn't wish to see. I still don't understand why she's here."

"She needed help across the border. It's not an easy crossing."

"She didn't ask us for help."

Evren squirmed under Gyda's knowing look. They'd had this conversation before. No one in the Wandering Sols knew why Dagny mattered, but they hadn't argued much when Evren had asked to take her with them to Terevas. They only resisted when Evren said it was for free.

But they didn't need to worry because it wasn't their burden. Truly, it was no one's but Evren's. Even Dagny didn't know why Evren had offered to help her set up a new life in Terevas. Her dream life, one she hadn't told anyone before meeting them. Only Evren remembered the young soldier who fought to save every piece of gold so his sister could have the life she wanted. She'd snuffed Chayne's life out, erased him from time itself. Even Dagny didn't remember him. But Evren did, and it was the least she could do to make up for his sacrifice.

She'd see Dagny's dreams fulfilled so Chayne wouldn't have to.

"It's just a favor for a friend," she told Gyda with a smile. "Don't worry about it."

~

"My LORD, you cannot take wild beasts across the border with you."

The monotone of the clerk's voice was a direct contrast to Sorin. Standing at the massive, metal gates of Vanguard, the only thing that stood between the Wandering Sols, Dagny, and freedom, was a squat round man whose droopy eyelids gave the effect that he was half-asleep. He sat behind a wooden desk stacked neatly with papers, all carefully hidden from the sun and sudden gusts of wind by a little alcove in the wall. He wasn't even looking at Sorin, who was holding his worg puppy—now nearly as tall as he was up on his hind legs.

"Excuse me." Sorin huffed and looked between the worg's ears down at the clerk. "This is my purebred war hound."

"My lord, that's a juvenile worg."

Evren put her hand on Sorin's shoulder and shook her head. All his arguments got bottled back up and he let the worg down on all fours as Evren turned to face the clerk. He wasn't looking at her either, instead rifling through what looked like blank papers.

"The worg is going with us."

The clerk signed, dropping his quill. "My lady, the rules state that no wild animals, companions or otherwise, native to Etherak may cross into Terevas through unnatural migration patterns. Such actions would damage the local ecosystem—"

"We're not setting him lose in the fields."

"I'm afraid that doesn't matter. You have my sincerest apologies."

Evren had the feeling she did *not* and frankly didn't want them if she did. She rubbed between her eyes and tried not to let the frustration get the best of her. She'd faced monsters, armies both living and dead, and had fallen through time itself. She could handle a customs clerk without losing her calm.

"Listen." She tried to make her voice as smooth as possible. "You know who we are. You know we come with a letter from Prince Barrion himself that lets us pass with all the members in our party, and with no trouble."

"I'm aware, my lady. The letter includes all members of your party, including a tag along miss Dagny Verrec." He finally looked up at her, frowning terribly. "I should also mention that your letter allows the passage of a goblin, something previously not allowed. But since you have friends in high places, I must turn a blind eye. All that is included in the Prince's letter. The worg was not."

Evren had had it. It was one thing to ignore them, make them wait for weeks for no reason, and then insult their dog. It was another thing entirely to insult Arke.

He'd been in the back of the party the whole time, pulling his cloak as tight as he could to hide himself. At the clerk's words, he shrank back even more.

Evren gritted her teeth. Arke hadn't hid since he'd first come to Dirn-Darahl with Sorin. As an adventurer, he didn't have to. He stood before the Sovereigns of Orenlion and their venom gazes proudly. He hadn't wrapped himself in anything oversized since they left the mountains because he wasn't cold. Seeing him so withdrawn when she knew he was anything but, set her blood on fire.

She turned back to the clerk. "Do you really think it's smart to insult a member of my party?"

The clerk's ruddy cheeks paled. "Uh, in-insult, my lady? I don't remember . . ."

He trailed off as she put her hands on his desk and leaned forward. "His name and his deeds were listed on that letter. Remind me of them."

His eyes went wide. "My lady?"

"Go on," she urged. "Remind me of what he's done."

The clerk shuffled through the papers with shaking hands. It took him too long to find Barrion's letter. Evren spied the neat, elegant handwriting long before he had taken it in his hands. He held it before him and cleared his throat, hesitating only long enough to see if Evren would call him off before speaking,

"Tamed and contained a prison riot. Expertly used magic to evade Alkimos the Great Worm of the Deep. Successfully thwarted a war and eliminated the corruption in Dirn-Darahl's leadership. Aided in the killing of Mortova the sea serpent. Destroyed waves of undead at the siege of Direwall that saved hundreds of lives. Ended the undead threat in the Reino Terminan. Survived and befriended a previously hostile race of intelligent . . . g-giant spiders. Traveled through time . . . ? My lady, I think this has been tampered with."

"It hasn't. Keep reading."

"Of course. Traveled through time. Faced a battle with the undead, a dragon, and a necromancer, and singlehandedly held said necromancer at bay while dragon and undead were contained. Obtained peace between Etherak, Orenlion, and Hisrachi parties."

The clerk set the paper down on the desk, hands still shaking in time with his jowls. Silence fell over them, and Evren could see Arke peeking out from his cloak out of the corner of her eye.

And then Sorin tapped on the desk. The clerk nearly jumped out of his skin and eyed the Vasa's devious grin as if it meant his dismemberment.

"Don't forget that he's the greatest mage on this continent. Self-taught too."

The clerk nodded quickly. "Of course."

Sorin blinked. "Well, go on."

"I'm sorry?"

"Say it too."

The clerk looked like he'd prefer dismemberment at this point. He sighed heavily. "He's the greatest mage on this continent."

"Very good! And what's his name? Say his name."

The clerk gritted his teeth. "Arke. Arke is the greatest mage on this continent."

It might've been too much, Evren and Sorin both bullying the man for just doing his job. But Evren had faced enough racism in her life. Small comments or straight up refusal to look her in the eyes, it was all the same. She could at least stand up for Arke as they were about to step back into his home country.

"That still leaves the matter of our war hound," Evren said.

"Juvenile worg," the clerk corrected weakly.

Evren shrugged and pushed off the desk. "Sol?"

Nearly hidden behind Gyda, Sol broke away from her animated whispers with Dagny. She peeked around, eyes bright, and her smile widened when she saw the scene before her. It wasn't a hard thing to read the clerk's discomfort and Sorin's irritation, but Sol could see motivations deeply buried behind surface emotions. It was what made her so good at picking people apart, whether with words or knives.

"Oh, so soon?"

"Unfortunately."

The clerk's body went from miserably melting into his seat to rigid fear, and those droopy eyes locked onto Sol's bouncing form as she scooted to the front of the group and elbowed Sorin out of the way.

Sol looked like an enigma. Dressed in dark leather armor and armed with four different daggers, that were easily seen, she held herself like a hired assassin. But her smile was easy. The sunny expression on her face made even the surliest of people want to be friendly towards her. The clerk was torn between smiles and knives, relaxing and fearing for his fingers. He went for fear as Sol dug into her bag and didn't relax until she set down a clinking sack of gold on the table.

"That should be enough to cover our hound," Sol said cheerfully. "And plenty extra for yourself. I doubt the pay here is all that great, huh?"

The clerk blinked at the gold, and then at Evren, and then back to Sol. "You're . . . bribing me?"

"Of course." Sol frowned. "Isn't that what you wanted?"

"I-I don't take bribes."

"Oh, you do. You pull a tiny detail that holds up whatever party or group of travelers you're dealing with from going through. Something small that they could definitely live without, but you know they won't let go of. You argue until someone gets desperate enough to drop coins on the table. Any is enough really. Extra gold to pocket away for the hair oil you're using or those brand-new boots. Drake-hide?"

He shifted in his seat. "Yes."

"Excellent taste. Be careful with how much conditioner you use though, too much softens the leather and it'll scuff at the slightest thing."

"Right . . ." the clerk drew out, looking at all of them. "You're just okay with this."

"Normally, no," Sol said, with the same sunny voice. "But we've places to go and I'm not in the mood to clean up another mess. I take it that gold will suffice?"

With more frantic nods and scribbles of approval on their papers than Evren thought was possible, the gold was taken off the desk and their papers returned neatly folded. Evren pocketed them as the clerk stuffed the gold in a hidden drawer and then rung the little brass bell nailed into the wall above his head.

What she expected to be a tinkling chime turned out to be a dominating, deep toll that echoed through the mountain air. Three tolls, each as shocking as the last. And on the last one, the gate lifted.

The rattling of chains and metal on metal overcame the echoes of the last bell toll easily. As the Wandering Sols watched it climbed higher, the clerk started to fold away his papers and desk. Evren blinked, watching as the sturdy wood turned to paper. The documents wiggled themselves securely inside the desk paper, like they were encasing themselves into an envelope. The chair joined it too, turning to paper as if it hadn't been holding up an adult human the entire time.

It could've been rune magic, although Evren hadn't seen any on the table or papers themselves. And if it was, it wasn't like any rune she'd ever seen before.

The clerk caught her staring and got a smug look on his face. "Fey charm," he shouted over the rattling gate. "Better get used to it where you're going."

His desk and chair went into his pocket vest. He rang the bell again, this time only once. As the gate ahead of them came to a stop above their heads, the drawbridge at their backs started its ascent.

"Better move quickly," the clerk ushered them in. "Last folks who stayed and watched lost a leg when they couldn't get through in time. Come come, surely you don't need to see Etherak anymore."

They didn't, but Evren was still strangely torn as she walked away. She glanced over her shoulder, catching a glimpse of the stone compound she'd called home for the past couple weeks, the Vanguard Mountains she'd climbed previously, and just beyond that the sliver of green land that belonged to the oldest kingdom in Eith.

Etherak was many things. A center of magical learning, a subject of contempt, and once the seat of the Divines. But, for Evren, it had been the first place she'd seen after leaving Orenlion. It had been the kingdom she and her friends had crossed after every adventure. They'd befriended the future King, had seen him marry his future queen. The wild, unapologetic land had a way of sucking Evren in, no matter her feelings on its history.

Etherak wasn't home, but it was the closest the Wandering Sols had so far.

Evren turned her back on it and followed her party into Vanguard. The drawbridge shut with a final boom, and the air itself seemed lighter.

The clerk didn't chat as he led them through the dark gatehouse. Evren spotted another portcullis hanging from the ceiling just as sunlight streamed through again. As she stepped back into the light, blinking, the sheer size of Vanguard hit her all at once.

The fortress was a dominating form amongst the peeks of the mountains, so much so that she couldn't see them over the walls from her spot on the ground. Four sentry towers rose high above them, marked with narrow flags in Terevasan blue and yellow. Great stone stairs curved around the large courtyard. Evren craned her neck as they walked past, glimpsing wide-open doors and a great hall filled with workers. That upper level of the fort had another, smaller courtyard, where wood and materials were stacked neatly, sorted by workers who milled about them like ants. Before she could see more, the clerk urged them forward.

"No time to dawdle, come come."

There really wasn't time to dawdle. But there was plenty to gawk as he led them through the fort. They passed a kitchen brimming with cooking food which smelled divine. They passed mostly empty barracks and a completely gutted armory being repurposed for cleaning and medical supplies.

The clerk didn't take them up to the ramparts, but Evren itched to see the view from there.

"What's all the construction for?" Sol asked.

The clerk waved her off. "Hard work taking a military fort and making it into a waypoint between countries. Her Majesty wants it more hospitable."

"This place reeks of war," Gyda said. "Where are the soldiers?"

"Well, there are no soldiers. Terevas doesn't have a standing army."

The warrior scowled. "That sounds weak."

The clerk laughed heartedly. "We have no need for an army. We didn't when we got our independence from Etherak, and we don't now. Clever words often trump sharp metal if you give them a chance."

Gyda grumbled something under her breath, less than impressed. Arke elbowed her leg as he walked beside her.

"Get used to it, they're all like that," he muttered.

"I can see why you left."

"Yeah,"

The goblin grew quiet then, still huddled under the cloak. He didn't say anything else as they walked. Evren made a mental note to pull him aside once they'd left the fort proper.

Halfway through, the biggest part of Vanguard showed itself.

Off the main hall, which was several stories tall, rose a thick tower twice its height and size. Evren had seen it from her time waiting on the border, but being so close that it blocked the sun was another thing entirely. It had no windows, and the rounded stone gave the impression that it was bigger than Evren could see from the ground. Likely bigger than the hall of the fort.

Sol gaped up at it, her eyes sparkling. "What's this for?"

"Huh?" The clerk turned around, irritation flickering bright across his face. "That? That's what we call War Mage extravagance. Useless to us now, so it's just a big tower in the middle of the fort. Decent lookout spot, I guess. Or would be, if we could get in."

"No door?" Sol asked.

"None. Damn mage that built it didn't think he needed it if he could just teleport to the top."

"What did he use it for?"

"I don't know, I'm not a historian." He threw his hands up in the air. "Some magic bullshit most likely. Can we please keep moving? I have a whole day of appointments with the likes of you."

"The likes of us?" Evren frowned but started walking. One by one her party followed her, although Sorin had to pry Sol away from the tower. "What do you mean?"

"Oh, adventurers all over have been showing up. Rhein-wall's yearly celebration for heroes of the Collective. A parade and all that for those still alive to make it. Most take the easy route through Noxcairn and up the river, but more than I'd like get stuck like you through Vanguard."

Sorin sighed wistfully. "A parade is nice. Think Sahar will go?"

Sol snorted. "Her father oversees the Collective. She'll have to go."

"Right, like anyone can force that woman to do anything." Sorin shook his head and looked over at Evren. "Can we go?"

A parade and celebration sounded crowded. And from what Evren had heard of Terevasan cities, they had more people living in them than most countries. Better quality of life and such so close to more people, if the rumors and Dagny were to be believed. Direwall had been enough to send Evren's skin crawling, and the idea of more people packed one on top of the other, watching them and a celebration in their honor did little to help the sudden swell of anxiety.

"Let's see what Sahar thinks when we meet her. Collective rules have bitten us in the ass before, remember?"

"Yeah, I know," he grumbled. "It'd be nice though, to just celebrate being alive, you know? All our parties happen after everyone is dead or something horrible has been narrowly avoided. No offense, Gyda, that was a hell of a party. But I'd like to dance and drink just *because*, you know? Not after I've saved a lot of lives from impending doom."

Everyone, save Dagny who was blissfully confused, nodded in time with his words. That was a sentiment they could all share. Besides, they deserved a rest, didn't they? After everything they'd lost, a break would be nice.

After *who* they lost.

Evren struggled not to look at the space where Abraxas should've been. Even now, months after his death, the Wandering Sols unconsciously left an empty spot of air where he would normally walk. As if, at any moment, he'd just appear beside them. Evren never had the heart to close that little gap, foolish as that hope might be.

His silence had never been true silence. Abraxas always had a heavy air around him, filled with words unsaid and past regrets. Evren hadn't even realized she could miss that heavy, shadowed, feeling until it was gone. There was nothing but a memory left.

She looked away from it. "We can go, Sorin."

She expected a little dance of joy, maybe a laugh of triumph. But it was like he felt her thoughts and where they led. He just nodded, smiling sadly. "Thanks."

They walked the rest of Vanguard in silence. By the time they got to the other side, the double portcullises were raised and the doors were wide open. The grey stone gravel turned to a partial dirt road that had several feet of level packed earth before a steep decline. The mountains on either side of the path were smaller, and Evren could see the end of the range easily.

As they stepped past the gates, Terevas bloomed at their feet. Rippling waves of grass and rolling hills. Green as far as the eye could see. Puffs of pure white clouds dotted the bright blue sky, and the sun was warm on their backs. Not too far in the distance, a great black lake glittered under the sun and at its shore was a city built for beauty.

Evren let out a heavy sigh and adjusted her bag on her shoulder. "One step closer. Shall we?"

She looked at Arke, the question simple but layered for him. He shook off his hood, squinting at the rolling fields and grasslands. A soft breeze came from the south, carrying the freshest air they'd smelled in their travels. His ears flew back a bit from the wind and he looked back at Evren.

"Welcome to Terevas." He shrugged. "Home to Fey, goblins, and all the shit in between."

With Arke in the lead, they all took their first steps into Terevas. A queendom that promised to look towards the future. A land brimming with beauty and possibility.

A place for a new beginning.

3

Evren

"**W**here will you go?"

Night was settling over the soft, rolling hills. Wildflowers brushed Evren's shins, dusting golden pollen and petals on her boots. Overhead, the sky was a calm grey, and stars were beginning to open their shining eyes. Beside her, Dagny stood fiddling with her bags.

"Well, I don't know yet," Dagny said. "Rheinwall will swallow me whole, but a few travelers talked about the little farming towns in between. I could work my way through there, get down to Noxcairn in time. I know it's not Tal-Mashad, but a port city is what I'm used to. There's always jobs to be had on the docks."

She flicked a nervous glance to Evren. "I can do it on my own. You don't have to escort me anymore."

Evren should've, could've, insisted on doing just that. But Dagny was right. She was young, barely nineteen, and excitable. But she was Etherakian. There was an iron in her blood unique to her people. She wielded a sword decently. She was tough enough to survive on her own.

Yet those eyes, a mirror to a brother she never had, made Evren pause. She'd treated Chayne poorly, and then she'd done worse by erasing his existence entirely. Didn't she owe it to his sister to guide her to her dream?

No.

No, because Evren couldn't give Dagny her dream. Because, in the end, their paths should never have crossed, and Evren had done enough just by getting her across the border. If Dagny wanted her new life badly enough, she'd fight for it, and she wouldn't need outside help. Iron blooded or not, the future bowed to no one.

Finally, Evren nodded. "I know. You've got quite the journey ahead, however. Is there anything you need before you go?"

Dagny shook her head, laughing. "Divines, no! You've done plenty. Truly, Evren, I can't thank you enough. I would never have gotten enough gold together to leave Tal-Mashad on my own, let alone cross the border."

"It was nothing."

"It was everything," Dagny insisted. Then she reached over and took Evren's hand in her own, her bright eyes earnest. "I don't know why you helped me. Divines know you didn't have to. But I'll be forever grateful. And I can never repay you for such kindness."

Evren smiled thinly and kept her hand still. She didn't deserve this gratitude. She didn't deserve Dagny's look of admiration. But she couldn't shake it off without an explanation, and the one she had would make no sense. So, she let Dagny pour her heart out, and despised the woman she'd been in the Deep Wood the whole time.

"There's no need to repay me," Evren said. "I know your people work in debts, but I don't. The only payment you need to worry about is finding yourself safe where you love."

Dagny chewed her lip, thoughtful. "All right, I can do that. But before I go, I'd like to give you something."

"Uh, gifts aren't necessary. Please—"

"No, I insist."

Evren shut her mouth and nodded. There was no use in arguing with her. Quickly, Dagny let go of her hand and fished out a leather corded necklace from under her blouse. She lifted it over her head, the iron pendant flashing in fading light. Even before Dagny had pressed it into her still hovering palm, Evren knew the symbol. She'd traveled with it emblazoned on black armor for months. It was seared into her mind.

Still, her hand shook as Haphion's symbol rested in her palm. The iron dragon wasn't polished, but was exquisitely crafted. She could make out the individual scales on his body, and the many flames of the sun he carried in his claws.

"I know you're not religious," Dagny said hurriedly as Evren stared at the pendant. "But I'm of the mind that symbols have power. Even if he's not here now, Haphion has protected me through that necklace, just as he will with you."

Evren's throat closed up and she struggled to speak. "I can't take this,"

"You can," the girl said firmly, and Evren's eyes snapped up to her. "This isn't an attempt at conversion, Evren. I'm not so crude as that. This is simply my way of thanking you. I believe that pendant will protect you on your next journey, wherever that leads you. And from the stories you told and the scars that tell more still, you'll need it."

Dagny picked up her bag and slipped both arms through it so it rested squarely on her back. Her eyes gleamed like mirrors of starlight as she looked south, towards her dream.

"Our paths diverge here, but it's truly been a dream knowing you and your friends," Dagny said wistfully. "Adventurers really are the best of Eith. Maybe I can live an adventure of my own." She looked back just enough to wink. "Farewell, Evren of the Wandering Sols."

Evren smiled and raised her hand in goodbye. "Farewell, Dagny of Terevas."

She giggled. "That does have a nice ring to it. Well, off I go!"

With a bounce in her step, a girl with her whole life on her back and a dream in her heart walked deeper into the fields of rolling flowers. Evren watched her go until she couldn't see her form past the swells of hills. The silver moon hung low in the sky by then, and she was still clutching the iron pendant with a grip strong enough to leave indents in her palm.

She lifted it up until the dragon's eyes met her own. Cold iron and nothing more, yet Dagny's words made her shiver. Casual or devout, every Etherakian she met clung to their faith. Once, she'd thought it had been for the power the Divines gave them. But now she wasn't so sure. People, especially the common folk of Etherak, craved comfort more often than power.

Evren had wielded a piece of her people's history. She had firm evidence that the Elders, the beings that made the elves of Eith, existed. But they'd also died, torn themselves apart, and disappeared. How were they any different than the mortals of Eith?

Banished Divines, dead Elders, absent giants—Evren's world was filled with pieces of a tragic history she could barely fathom. And she'd *lived* parts of the past. Some of the future as well.

Evren pocketed the necklace. True, she didn't worship Haphion. She didn't even see the appeal of him, nor the rest of the pantheon. But a gift was a gift, and this one reminded her of Abraxas. It stung, but she endured and turned her eyes to the stars.

Her father, Mei, and Aster looked to the stars and saw the beauty of the Horizon Walker. Evren never had. Gyda's people and Sorin's both saw the stars as the souls of their dead, eternal watchers and guides for the living. There was a beauty in that belief that kept Evren looking up every night, as if she could pick out which star was her friend.

But if either Gyda or Sorin found comfort in the idea of Abraxas watching over them, they didn't say. And every night after his death felt more and more normal. She didn't want to forget how to miss him, she didn't want to stop hurting. But more and more the stars were nothing more than pieces of light in the vast blackness of night.

Evren didn't feel Abraxas's soul in the stars, no matter how hard she tried.

She tore herself away from the sky and buried the ache in her chest before she walked back to camp. Nestled between two hills and under the branches of a lone tree, her party had cleared enough grass to safely make a fire. The tents had been set up, and Gyda was stirring something in the pot above the fire as Sol and Sorin talked animatedly.

"You have to give him a name at some point," Sol said, jerking her thumb to the already dozing worg. He'd curled up at Gyda's feet, his snout still twitching in hopes of fallen scraps.

"Why does he need a name?" Sorin asked.

"It's annoying to not have something to refer to him as."

"I dunno, you've been doing fine for months . . ."

Sol let out an exasperated sigh. "That's not the point! He deserves a name of his own."

Evren patted Sorin's shoulder as she passed, making him jump. "She's got a point."

The Vasa held his hand over his heart. "Walk a little louder next time, would you? And names aren't that simple. They have to have meaning. I can't just saddle him with something mediocre and live with myself."

Gyda frowned into the pot. "So, it's not that you won't name him, it's that you can't."

"Fine, yes!"

Sol's frustration ebbed away, replaced with soft concern. "You could always ask us for help."

"Uh, no?" Sorin looked at her dumbfounded. "I found him, he's my responsibility."

Evren shook her head at him. "Isn't he the party's war hound?"

"My puppy! Not yours."

Evren held her hands up in surrender. "All right then, I see there's no point in arguing. Where's Arke so he can wrangle some sense into you?"

Sorin looked under his arms and the blanket he was sitting on. Then he poked his head into Arke's tent before coming back out, shaking grass from his dreads. "Not here. Funny, I thought he was sitting right next to me . . ."

Evren's mental alarm bell tolled when Sol shrugged her shoulders. "I haven't seen him since we set up camp. I thought he was with you."

Gyda's gaze drew Evren's with nothing more than its weight. She'd pulled all their bowls out of the bag, fingers still fumbling over the extra one before putting it back with a grim set of her lips.

"He went for a walk." Gyda nodded past the tree. "Needed to clear his head."

Sorin's face fell. "Fuck, I've been an idiot, haven't I?"

"You'll have to be more specific, sea rat."

"He's back home. It's gotta hit hard, you know? He didn't exactly leave on good terms."

One by one, a hushed silence fell over them. They all had pasts they'd rather not talk about. Hells, Evren was still trying to get Sorin to open up about his life at sea and how he'd lost his crew and ship. But out of all of them, Arke was the quietest about his reasons for staying away from home. He talked about Terevas with disdain, true, but he did that with most things. He was loud in his opinions, and Evren cursed herself for letting him be so silent for so long.

Sorin started to get up, but Evren lightly pushed him back down. "It's all right, I'll talk to him."

His golden eyes were pleading as he looked up at her. "Evvie, I completely forgot. I have to talk to him."

"You will," she promised. "But there's something I've got to say first. And when we're done you can grovel for his forgiveness."

Sorin settled back down, a pained expression on his face. "You're going to talk bad about me to him, aren't you? And I won't be able to stop you."

Sol pushed a bowl of stew into his hands, followed by a spoon clattering into the wooden bowl. "Don't be ridiculous. They'll always do it to your face. It's just more fun like that."

Sorin grumbled his reply, mostly around his spoon as he shoveled food into his mouth. Evren gave his shoulder a squeeze, nodded to Sol and Gyda, then walked back into the night.

Worry nagged her steps. Less for Sorin. As fragile as he was, he'd be okay waiting for a while. And he had Sol and Gyda to keep him company. But Arke was another matter entirely.

She should've talked to him earlier, when they were climbing down the last of the mountain trails. Pulled him back and let Gyda lead while they talked. Oh, he would've fought. Pulling a heartfelt conversation out of the goblin was like pulling teeth at the best of times. But he'd been there for Evren in her worst moments, and she hadn't imagined the understanding in his eyes when she slipped to darker thoughts in Orenlion.

She'd never have the connection with him that Sorin had. Or the quiet coexistence that he and Gyda shared, founded on a strange mutual respect that had been firm from the moment they met. Evren would never have Sol's ability to make him snort with laughter, or pull his hair out with her long-winded monologues about her current architectural fascination. But Evren and Arke had connected over one small thing before, and it had held them together ever since.

It was far easier to be on their own. Their cold demeanors and sharp words hurt only themselves then. They learned to rely on themselves, and it was so much better than trusting someone else. Survival was a game they mastered in a world that punished those who stood alone. And yet, against all odds, they found themselves unwilling to leave each other.

The fire had faded away behind her a while ago and Evren was walking half-blind through the shadowed meadow. Up one hill and then down another. She cursed every time her toe got caught on a root she didn't see. How far had the goblin gone?

"Arke?" she panted into the night as she started climbing another hill. This one wasn't as steep and as she got to the top she could dimly see the ground leveling out to a flatter plain. "Arke, you better not be fucking with me. If you're hiding, I can and will find you. You know I will."

"Might take you a good hour in this light, but sure, kid."

Evren stifled a scream and whirled around. The field of grass and flowers around her appeared empty, simply swaying like waves in an endless, green lake. It wasn't until she saw the blades a few feet from her rustle and part, revealing two glowing eyes, that she relaxed.

"You're hiding." She combed her fingers through her short hair to play off her embarrassment.

"Nah, I'm standin'. I'm just short."

"Oh. Okay then. Listen, I came out here to talk—"

"Got somethin' better. Come on."

The trail of parted grass abruptly turned around and started moving in another direction. Evren stared after him, a little too perplexed to move, before willing her feet to follow. It only took a couple of long strides to come to his side, and from this angle she could clearly see his face and large pointed ears underneath the white cloud of hair sticking up in the air.

"Arke, we're all a little worried," Evren began.

"Huh?" He twitched his ear towards her. "'Bout what?"

"Well, we know it can't be easy coming home. You never told us why you left . . ."

"Nope."

They trudged through more grass, hiking up another shallow hill as she waited for him to elaborate. When he didn't, she sighed.

"I guess we're just trying to make sure everything is okay with you being here. Just so we're prepared."

"Well, I ain't a halfblooded noble missing a vital organ. Don't got an army of deadies after me. Not caught up in a secret lover's bullshit to claim more power and fuck me over so . . ." He shrugged. "Nah, I'm good."

Evren grimaced. She should've expected that. "Well, that's a relief, believe me. We just thought with the way you were in Vanguard that—"

"Had lots of time on my hands there, by the way. Whipped up some new glyphs for you to try when you're ready. Should be stable, but I'd stick on the safe side with them."

Cold dread pooled in her stomach. She hadn't told him about Gyda's incident while sparring. She just never found the time after packing and leaving. She couldn't try them out without hurting her, and she didn't want to risk it just to see.

"About that—"

"Shut up!" he hissed. "I almost missed it."

Evren's mouth snapped shut before she could point out that she hadn't said more than two words, not nearly enough to distract him. At that point they'd crested the hill and the first argument died on her tongue. The next struggled to get out at all as she stared at what he'd found.

"Arke, how in the hells would you miss this?"

"Seems like everybody has." He snickered. "Good thing you hate usin' roads or else I'd never have found it."

Under the starlight and the rising moon, dragon bones gleamed like silver. A full skeleton, mostly intact, from what

Evren could see, sprawled at the bottom of their hill. The wingspan was shattered and twisted from the death throes, but still gloriously massive. Wildflowers and weeds grew through the broken ribcage. A young tree had started to grow out of its mouth, roots tangling through the eye sockets to get to the soil and new green leaves fanning out over the broken jaw.

Evren scrambled down the rest of the hill, Arke right at her heels barking curses for her going too fast. They reached the skeleton together, laughter bubbling up their chests.

"Old beast," Arke wheezed, eyeing the claw bigger than himself.

Evren nodded and placed her hand gently on the forearm. The bone was smooth asglass, and up close she could see it wasn't white or cream but a glittering bronze, as if fire was trapped inside the dead marrow. It still felt warm to the touch.

"They never stop growing, you know," Evren said as she walked towards the head. She let her fingers brush every bone, imagining how beautiful the dragon had been in life. She'd only seen two before, and they'd both tried to kill her, but there was something so fascinating about them that her mind looked past those terrifying memories. "They start off the size of a cat and grow until they die."

Arke grunted, sniffing at a knuckle bone. "Don't sound healthy for anyone else."

"Not all dragons are evil." She reminded him. "They're intelligent beings, capable of being as good or evil as we are."

"Yeah, but I could do significantly more damage if I was this big."

Evren snorted a laugh and continued her slow trail up the neck. Arke busied himself with the knucklebone, digging it out with his claws and some tools from his robe. Evren was half tempted to tell him that a tooth would be easier, but as she rounded the head she stopped.

She knew that skull.

Visions of Orenlion under the feet of the dead Storm of

the Wood flashed in her mind. Her and Saros careening through the air. Gouging at eyes that weren't there, spitting acid at bone that wouldn't melt. She saw Nerezza's undead monstrosity as clearly as she saw the live one Gyda had pulled through time.

Just as clearly as she was seeing her now.

Evren snatched her hand away, all wonder melting into cold confusion and fear. "Arke."

Her voice must've betrayed that same feeling, because Arke immediately jumped away from the half-pried knuckle-bone. He frowned at her, glowing eyes searching for the reason behind her change in tone.

"What?"

"I know what dragon this was."

He laughed nervously. "You ain't that good of a hunter. You only know one well enough to *know* her."

"I know," she said and his smile slipped. "I'd know her anywhere. This is Storm of the Wood. I'd stake my life on it."

Arke stared at her and then the dragon. His mouth flapped open and closed as he struggled to find a way to prove her wrong. But he was seeing the same thing she was. The same curve of the wings, the same crest of horns at the head, half buried in the dirt. The same horn on the nose, chipped with time but no less damning.

"But . . . how?" He shook his head. "The Archdruids said they destroyed her. Nerezza and . . . everyone with her. This skeleton is old, kid. It ain't a few months dead."

"So how is it here?" she asked, half scared of the answer.

She shouldn't have been, because Arke didn't know and Storm of the Wood wasn't giving up her secrets.

4

Abraxas

"When I asked how you planned to deal with a stolen ship full of undead, this was not the solution I meant," Abraxas hissed as he adjusted his cloak.

From his spot on the beach, he could see the *Crooked Wrath* on its side, beached on the reef Nerezza had ordered them to run into. From this distance, he could still make out the corpses hanging from the deck. Some had already slid into the water, finally still since their death. The rest had yet to fall.

The ship wouldn't sink. It would be pushed and pulled as the waves pounded it into the reef repeatedly until it resembled the dozens of others strewn about like dismantled skeletons. Aside from the rowboat they'd used to escape, the *Crooked Wrath* looked like any other shipwreck—so long as no one looked too closely.

Nerezza worked the thin fabric of her shawl over her hair and ears, not giving him a passing glance as she tucked in every last bone-white strand. "You said that we couldn't dock at one of the port villages, as they would be controlled by

Etherak soldiers. You also pointed out that our papers wouldn't hold up against them, and no smugglers would work with us if we showed up in a boat full of corpses." She cocked an eyebrow at him. "What would you have had me do?"

He'd hoped she would've braved the docks and gotten them killed on the spot. But he didn't say that. Instead, he worked his fingers into a familiar pattern, taking off the fabric of the cloak he didn't need and fastening it into a turban.

He hadn't imagined he'd ever need to wear one again. The trick he'd picked up from the local rebels to keep the sun from destroying his skin and dehydrating him had been one he would've gladly forgotten.

Already the heat rising in his chest threatened to choke him. The sand at his feet was damp with sea water, but familiar all the same. He'd turned his back on the landscape behind him. He'd kept his eyes down since sighting land.

He should've drowned himself weeks ago instead of allowing himself to step foot on this cursed land again.

"It's just a place, Abraxas." Nerezza scoffed. "The land itself isn't out to kill you."

Only he knew that it very well would, if given the chance.

It was a dim hope that the same sun and sand that Abraxas had seen kill warrior and mage alike would claim Nerezza as well. Perhaps a brighter one was that they'd run into pieces of the war being fought all over the country and she'd be caught in the crossfire. The rebels wouldn't hesitate to kill anyone that wasn't their people. The Etherakian soldiers would mow down any and all necromancers.

Abraxas felt her hand on his shoulder, and he was forced to turn away from the sea and look inland. Nerezza's surprisingly strong grip never left him as they stared out at the seemingly endless golden dunes together.

"Does it frighten you to be back here?" she whispered.

"Yes," he answered, with no small amount of difficulty. "This place was my undoing."

"Somewhere in those distant sands, you're already there. Which city are you burning, I wonder? What man or woman are you beheading in the name of your god?"

He wrenched his shoulder out of her grasp. "Let us pray you don't find out."

Nerezza frowned, although she wasn't unhappy. There was a spark in those deep eyes of hers that he longed to snuff out. "What? Don't like the idea of your past self being a zealot?"

He rounded on her, fingers inches from her neck and practically spasming in the effort to not choke the life from her. She remained stock still, amused, as he raged. "I, more than anyone, know what I am capable of," he seethed.

A dry wind from the desert swirled sand between their legs. They were statues standing at the precipice of two deadly halves of the world. They simply stood there for a time, staring at each other as the sun watched with merciless curiosity.

"You were a monster," she said. "And make no mistake, you still are, beneath all that honor and posturing. You were raised to destroy and then had that stripped from you. Such a beautiful monster turned to hated fiend. You and I . . ." she faltered, something cracking her confident, smug expression. Before he could pry it open more, it had sealed shut. "It takes monstrous people to reshape the world, Abraxas."

"A monster doesn't make a god," he told her. "You upset the very nature of things with your quest."

"To live is to upset those who oppose me. And I think you'll find that all gods are monsters."

When had his hand fallen to his side? He could've killed her while she was talking. He could've *tried*.

Instead, he allowed her to walk around him unharmed. "Come now, let's make the most of daylight. I've been dying to see the part of Eith everyone bled so much over."

~

SOMETHING ABRAXAS HAD ALWAYS FOUND funny was how Vernes was described by people who had never been there. They heard desert and immediately thought of sand dunes. It wasn't a lie, but Vernes was not simply a sea of sand. The Moving Sea dominated most of the central and eastern parts of the country. Farther north, near Gratey's border, was rocky and flat. He remembered vividly the plateaus to the south, so large and vast that the cities built at their tops touched the clouds. He remembered how the jagged red mountains to the west bled into the sand during the wet season and how much like blood it looked. But the thing burned into his mind the most was Tatesai.

Vernes's capital city, in the most arid part of the country, had eluded him his whole campaign. The worst part is that it had seemed straight forward at first. The great city was built inside the walls of the biggest canyon the country had. The shade and the water from the deep river flowing through it gave the rebels life, and they defended it well. If it had been as simple as following the Godeset Run, then the capital would've fallen quickly. But the rebels found ways to drain the water and leave traps in the shallows that destroyed their boats. Marching on foot was too slow and left them vulnerable, and too many were lost to flash floods. The land surrounding the canyon was so hostile that those who made it to the city were little more than husks in armor to be cut down.

Vernes protected its people, and it had turned the sand around Tatesai, and many other cities, as blood-red as the mountains.

Regardless, the dunes were Abraxas's least favorite kind of desert. Only an hour into it and already his boots were full of sand. He wanted nothing more than to turn back and dunk himself into the Boreal Sea. He endured the sand instead.

Behind him Nerezza huffed. "It's impossible to move fast in these sands."

Abraxas considered letting her talk to herself. She didn't deserve his conversation. But his next step sent more hot sand pouring into his sock and he *needed* to think of anything else.

"The campaign in this part was slow at first," he said. "It took our commanders weeks to realize that the dunes were more of a threat than the sun. Heavy armor and many feet don't move fast in these conditions."

"Fascinating," she grumbled. "So you all died."

"No. We watched the locals."

"I thought you killed them."

"Different locals." Even as he spoke, he shuddered. The sand on his teeth tasted like blood. "The dunes are home to more than just elves and humans. Dragons, elementals, djinn, giant scorpions. And the Dra'Nacti."

"You're going to make me ask?"

He shot her an irritated look over his shoulder. "I was taking a breath."

"Oh, then please continue." She waved him on.

He scowled and turned back. "The Dra'Nacti have been in Vernes longer than anyone else. They claimed to have been born from the sand and the blood of dragons."

"Did you believe them?"

"The few I saw. They make you believe. Regardless of what you think, their connection to the land and creatures is undeniable. It changes their very bodies. They know how to move to create the least amount of resistance as possible. They're nomads as well, and we saw them moving in great sand ships driven by the wind or beasts of burden."

"So you built your own."

He nodded. "Not as elegant at first but they got the job done. Eventually the skiffs were the fastest way to get anywhere. And as spread out as the war was, speed was essential for troops as well as messengers and spies."

Abraxas walked for a little while in silence, just breathing. He squinted angrily at the dunes ahead. "I could use a skiff about now."

"Well," Nerezza huffed, "don't look at me. Unless you want it made of corpses."

What decent mood he'd had soured immediately. Not that talking about war made him happy, but he'd always liked the idea of the skiffs. He'd been fascinated by the Dra'Nacti at the time. Even still, there was so much more he wanted to know about them, to learn from them.

The problem was he liked to tell stories, and he'd done it so often with the Wandering Sols that he'd forgotten for a moment that Nerezza wasn't a friend. She wasn't even an ally.

She was one of the worst things walking the sand at their point in history. One of, because Abraxas knew better than to think he was aware of all of Vernes's evils. The sand hid shadows darker than any in the Yawning Deep.

He couldn't stop the stinging words that left his mouth next.

"Do you ever wonder how your party would react to seeing you like this?"

A heavy pause, and then a poison-laced answer. "You don't get to speak about them as if you know them."

"I knew Sahar."

"Shut up."

"I thought I knew you."

"ENOUGH!"

Abraxas braced for the pain, but the force with which it washed over him drove him to his knees. He was only dimly aware of the hot sand on his knees, or the raw feeling in his throat as he screamed. By the time it ebbed away, Nerezza had his chin in her rough grasp again, forcing him to stare through the glaring sun at her.

"You know nothing!" she hissed. "You think because we fought together in Direwall that you have a piece of me? That

I'm a book you can browse whenever you so choose? I am so much more unfathomable than you can imagine. You can't touch me. Do not pretend to know me."

He couldn't help the weak laugh that bubbled past where her fingers squished his lips together. "I may not know you, but I know that Drystan would've turned against you the moment he saw what you became."

Her fingernails pierced his cheeks and lip. He tasted blood, felt it dribble down his chin, as she leaned in close enough to eclipse the sun.

"Apologize."

It wasn't a request, he knew that. Nerezza never had never been a woman who asked for anything. She simply took, and what had been admirable before was now killing him.

"No." He wouldn't apologize for the truth.

Nails scraped bone. His toes curled inside his boots with the sand and a weak groan of pain escaped his lips.

"I said," Nerezza breathed ever so softly against his burning skin, "apologize."

"You'll have to kill me if that's what you want."

"If you think—"

Nerezza stopped, her grip loosening on his face enough for her nails to slip out of his skin. His gasp of relief wasn't hidden, but as he struggled to keep his sandy fingers from clutching the wounds, he froze too.

"You hear that?" Nerezza asked.

He had. Pain and wounded pride all but forgotten, Abraxas was on his feet with his stolen sword drawn before he took his next breath. With a flash of sickening arcane energy, Nerezza had changed her face back to the features he knew in Direwall, but he hardly cared about her appearance.

The slightest shift in the sand sent adrenaline coursing through his veins. His blood pounded hot and heavy in his ears. His left arm felt weightless without his shield to ground him. In that moment, he was prepared for anything to burst from the dunes. A rebel ambush, or a Dra'Nacti hunting party. Perhaps a young drake looking for a challenge.

What he didn't expect was a teenage boy.

A spray of sand trailed in the boy's wake as he teetered down the dune. He was all gangly limbs and billowy fabric that swallowed him in an effort to protect his tan skin from the sun. He carried no water, no bag except the small leather pouch clutched in his hands. His sandals had been lost, his burnt feet covered in blisters.

When he caught sight of Abraxas and Nerezza, he skidded to a stop. The fear in his brown eyes was familiar and sickening. But sand didn't allow such abrupt stops. The cascade pooled around his ankles, calves, and knees until he was tumbling the rest of the way down the dune, landing mere feet from the two of them.

"Huh." Nerezza's stiff posture melted. "Interesting."

The boy was gasping instead of screaming. The raw panic in his eyes made Abraxas's stomach turn. He'd seen that look before. Over the course of a hundred years, he'd cut down many with that same expression. Some young, some old. In the end it was always the same. Panic before the dimness of death overtook them.

The boy's chest was rising and falling too fast. Peeling lips gaped open and closed in a voiceless cry, over and over. Abraxas knew that word too.

Mercy.

"He's asking for mercy," Abraxas said, lowering his sword. "He thinks we're Etherakian soldiers."

"Good for him that we are no such thing."

Nerezza brushed past Abraxas and towards the boy. He tried to scramble away but his obvious dehydration made him too weak for his fear-addled limbs to work properly. All he ended up doing was kicking sand at her, which she disdainfully ignored.

A spike of fear went through him. "Nerezza, don't."

He didn't know what she'd do to the boy. All he did know is that there was only so much he could do to stand in the way before she had him on his knees again, utterly useless.

She spared him a dirty look before turning her back on him entirely and kneeling in front of the boy. He was a wheezing, exhausted mess. Even as he struggled to get away from her, he was moving more sand than himself.

"Peace," Nerezza said and held up her hand in surrender.

The boy flinched, croaking out another desperate plea for mercy.

Abraxas winced. "He doesn't understand you. Core isn't taught much in Vernes."

"Then translate."

He bristled at the command. But, flicking his gaze to the boy, he felt himself soften. Drudging up a language he'd tried to forget, Abraxas let the Vernesian language roll off his tongue with one simple word. One he knew but had rarely used.

"Peace," he said, in the boy's native tongue.

The look of sheer terror didn't go away, but he stopped trying to get away. Abraxas held one hand up as he sheathed his sword. He knew what the boy saw when he looked at him. A heartless ghost from a heartless kingdom hellsbent on destroying his way of life. Abraxas couldn't change that any more than he could wipe the centuries of blood from his hands, but he still tried.

It seemed like a lifetime ago that Evren had looked at him with a similar shine in her eyes. More disappointment than fear as she stood between him and Keres. He'd been so sure of the enemy then, of what was evil and what was good. He still wasn't sure which Keres was, but he also knew what he wanted to be.

He wanted to be better. Forgiving. Compassionate. A healer not a butcher. And if it started with one boy in the middle of the desert, then he'd take his sign for redemption and run with it.

"Peace," he said again, lowering himself into the sand. "We mean no harm."

"Please . . ." the boy croaked. "Do not kill me. I'm no threat. Please just let me go."

His eyes were welling with tears his body couldn't afford to lose. They cut rivers through the sand dusted on his cheeks and got caught on the faintest whiskers of a young mustache.

He was so young.

"We're not going to harm you," Abraxas said slowly. "We're just travelers. We have no side in the war."

"Rebellion," the boy snapped, with a surprising amount of strength.

Nerezza looked at Abraxas questioningly. "What did he just spit out?"

Abraxas didn't break eye contact to look at her. "He corrected me." He switched back to the boy's tongue. "Many apologies. I meant no disrespect. My companion is going to give you some water. She'll drink some, too, if you'd like to be cautious."

The boy hesitated before nodding.

Abraxas turned to Nerezza. "Take a drink of water, then give him some."

Nerezza scowled. "You don't give the orders here."

"As translator I do. He's scared and dehydrated and I promised him no harm."

"Fine," she bit out, then took out her water bladder. She took a small sip before handing it to him.

The boy grasped it so quickly some spilled out. He licked it from his fingers before drinking deeply for many long seconds. Neither Abraxas nor Nerezza had the heart to stop him. When he finally put the bladder down and wiped his mouth, the fear had ebbed from his eyes.

"Now," Abraxas began, softly as to not scare him. "Can you tell me why you're running?"

"I'm not running," the boy whispered.

"You're holding that pouch very closely. You're not dressed for travel. You're running from something."

His bottom lip quivered, and he tried to suck it against his teeth to still it. "My village was attacked. We live in the Ovor Oasis not far from here. We don't have rebels. We were just simple traders." He teared up again. "My brothers . . . they were fighting in the north. Came home with this." He raised the pouch. "They thought they weren't followed, but a War Mage had tracked them. The night came and . . . the fire came as well. My brothers fought. My parents, too. They weren't anymore when I ran."

Abraxas translated all of this solemnly to Nerezza. She frowned between them. "Is this common?"

He shrugged. "Depends on what the boy has. War Mages are elites. If one of them was following the brothers, then whatever they had, and he has now, they'll want it."

Nerezza swallowed the silence. "What is it?"

Abraxas didn't have to ask. He simply glanced back at the pouch and the boy curled around it.

"No!" he wailed. "It's all I have. I have to take it to Cuskhe!"

Cuskhe.

Abraxas's blood went still. One name and he was back in those streets, drenched in blood and carving through an army of rebels. He heard the screaming again. He stepped over his fallen brothers and sisters. Over his head the Etherakian flag soared from the highest tower in the city. The signal of victory didn't stop the battle, it had inflamed it.

Blood on his sword. Blood on his teeth. He was inhaling too much smoke. A wound in his side screamed with every jolt of his armor. Behind him, civilians screamed as they were caught in a mage's spell.

Cuskhe still stood. He was too close to it.

The echoes of battle didn't leave his ears. Instead, it was another scream that snapped him back to the present. The boy's, as he cried over the spear through his chest.

"Nerezza!" Abraxas shouted a warning, but the mage was already on her feet. He stood with her, sword flashing in the sun, as they turned their back to the dying boy and towards the new enemy.

Abraxas knew them before they tore through the sand. He knew the style of spear, and he knew the number of soldiers who'd be escorting the mage. Five in total. Three lightly armored and quick, two built like metal mountains for defense. And the mage behind them. He just didn't believe they'd catch up so fast.

He didn't see the mage yet, just the five knights. That was their miracle.

"Blood magic only, no necromancy," he growled to her, then charged.

It had barely crossed his mind that a lifetime ago these had been allies. Did he know the soldiers behind these helms? Did he care at all now? They'd murdered a *boy*. One who hadn't been armed.

Abraxas had always chastised Gyda for letting her emotions get the better of her during a fight. This time he let his rage overwhelm him.

A spear cut through the shimmering air. Abraxas knocked it aside with force enough that it would've broken in two if he'd had his old sword. The soldier that threw it was one of the faster ones, their eyes widening marginally under their helm as he rushed towards them. They pulled out a short sword, parried and traded blows for a few seconds, before Abraxas cut them down.

The rush of killing didn't feel good. Sinking the clumsy blade into the soldier's chest made vomit crawl up his throat, but he shoved the feeling aside.

The sun blocked from his vision for a moment, and Abraxas barely sidestepped a massive blow from one of the bulkier knights. The man was cursing him, but through the helmet and the rush of blood in his ears, Abraxas couldn't understand him. He dodged another blow, rolling in the sand to try and get out of his reach.

Then he felt a blade tear through his calf.

He bit back a cry, dropping to his knee out of his leg's sudden weakness rather than the pain. Without thinking, he flipped the hilt of his sword in his hand and stabbed it back through the gap between his arm and torso. A long shot, but he felt a sick twinge of satisfaction when the blade hit flesh he and heard a cry of pain.

He twisted the blade and jerked it back out. The heavy knight was on him again. Abraxas saw his end in seconds. Skull cleaved open, blood staining the sand. An end, finally.

But then the knight froze mid-swing, his eyes bulging. Abraxas watched in horror as blood started to leak from those eyes. A trickle at first, and then it was pouring out of him so fast that Abraxas couldn't see the whites of his eyes anymore. It took seconds, but he felt like the suffering went on for ages before the knight collapsed. From behind his body, Nerezza shook out her hand, her face grim. "End this," she ordered, and it was the one order he had no problem obeying.

He took the short sword from his calf and ignored the wet flow of blood coating his foot as he stood. A stolen sword in each hand, he faced off against the rest.

It was not going to be a fair fight. As strong as Nerezza was, she was strongest in necromancy. And Abraxas was wounded. Against three armored and well-trained foes they would have had trouble.

Against three armored and well-trained foes *plus* a War Mage, they had no chance.

Still, he fought. Slicing and parrying around Nerezza's crude magic, he wished now more than ever for Arke's clean, elemental spells. Fire burnt impurities. Ice was crisp and simple. He spilled enough blood to not need to see magic from it.

But her magic was the only thing that even somewhat leveled the playing field against the three knights. Whenever they tried to lash out at her, he'd block their blows. Whenever they overwhelmed him, she'd lash out with blood-red magic. For a moment, he thought they might win.

Then the air changed. The temperature dropped dramatically. He felt his ears pop and his fingers go cold.

He turned to Nerezza, a word of warning on his lips that was silenced as a shrill cry pieced the air. The sand between their feet gathered like a small tornado, sucked in by an invisible force, Abraxas and Nerezza with it, the air sucked out of their lungs. He felt his skin screaming from the pressure as the shriek built to an earsplitting crescendo.

All at once it stopped, and the sand exploded outward.

His eardrums broke. His body flew backwards, peppered with sand like tiny knives and that same cold force. He hit the opposite dune with enough force the sand exploded out around him. He felt his ribs crackle on impact. He felt his skull crack like an egg.

He laid there, dazed. The pain was nothing, one thing he could thank Nerezza's conditioning for. Was that more blood he felt trickling down his neck? Why couldn't he breathe properly?

The blue sky was darker now, despite it being well near noon. Abraxas tried to blink the black away. When he did, a figure appeared above him. Their face was too blurry to make out, but he knew those crimson robes well enough.

Just as he started to slip into the black, he thought he heard their voice.

"What are you doing here, Abraxas?"

5

Abraxas

Abraxas dreamed of a boy in a temple.

The stones at the boy's bare feet were white and glittered like opal in the bright light that shimmered in the air. Incense, sweet and heavy, coiled in his nostrils, nestled inside his lungs. Outside the temple walls the city was loud, boisterous in their celebration. But away from it all, the boy found blessed silence.

He padded across the warm stone, hope blossoming in his chest. But more than that, excitement. The feeling never faded, no matter how many times he ventured inside.

The temple was empty and the boy was relieved. A part of him was still a little embarrassed, although he had no reason to be. It felt too personal and private to share with other people. While the priestesses and caretakers knew, they'd never *watched* him. That was something else entirely and he wasn't ready for it.

At the center of the temple rose a great oak, ancient as the city itself, with a trunk and branches made of stone, leaves pulsing with Divine fire. The light from the open roof cascaded through the twists of branches, shading the boy as he knelt between the roots.

As always, he squeezed his eyes shut. He kept his hands tight against his chest until his breathing calmed. There was nothing to fear. He was safer here than anywhere else in Etherak. More than that, he was chosen.

"Are you there?" the boy whispered.

I am, my child, a hallowed voice replied.

~

WATER WAS BEING PRESSED to his lips. Abraxas, barely conscious, drank it greedily. The crisp, clean liquid washed a path through the dry grit in his mouth, and with every swallow he felt a little less like death itself was sitting on his chest.

The water was taken away when he opened his eyes. He grimaced at the light sending spears of pain through his eyes and he turned away from it. He took a couple deep breaths, feeling his ribs ache a little but not nearly as much as they should. He flexed his leg, finding no pain at all. If he explored the back of his head he was sure the part where his skull had cracked would be completely fine.

"One of the new initiates tried their hand at healing you. How'd they do?"

Abraxas looked up, squinting past the shaft of dusty sunlight streaming through the window to the woman standing beside it. She was, by far, the most striking thing in the bare room. And yet the bare stone walls and dirt-packed floor suited her. Gone were her long red robes, and instead she wore simple leggings and a red jerkin, structured with sharp angles and black leather accents to show her status. It swept low down her back, ending just behind her thighs in a sword-like point. In the front it ended at her waist, leaving her legs free for more practical use in wartime.

Everyone in Vernes knew what that red uniform meant. Fewer knew the purpose behind the swirls of arcane ink tattooed across nearly every inch of her skin.

"Divara Rimel." His throat dried up again as he stared up at her. "It's been a while."

Divara stepped into the light, straight-backed and serious. His heart lurched a bit. The last time he'd seen her, at the end of the war, she'd looked worn and broken. But the mage in front of him was far from that. There seemed to be steel under her skin instead of bones. Youth was still obvious in her warm brown cheeks and her black hair, twisted into many short knots along her head that wasn't yet threaded with silver.

She arched a brow in a silent question, the tattoo of intricate knotwork that framed her eyes rising with it. "It has. You look like death."

A little laugh escaped his lips. "I feel like it."

This was bad. Never mind that Divara's powers rivaled his own back when he had them, she was the most intelligent person he knew. Her strategy in battle had given their soldiers an edge against the guerrilla attacks from the rebels and had earned her a place at General Loghain's side as his second in command. In Vernes, Divara had power in both the arcane and in political force. She was the last person he should've wanted to see.

She knew him. She knew the old Abraxas that was fighting the same war. Out of everyone from his past to crash into, why did it have to be her?

"You look . . . different. Older," she said, frowning.

"I am," he said without thinking, then cleared his throat. "Metaphorically, anyway."

She narrowed her eyes at him. They were stilled ringed with the remnants of black kohl they used to keep the glare of the sun at bay during battle.

"Abraxas, you killed three of my men. You maimed another two."

He winced. How could he explain this? When he'd fought so hard with so much pent-up anger? She'd seen that. She'd put him and Nerezza down as a result.

He looked like a traitor, and he was.

"I don't . . ." he struggled to speak. "Divara, I can't explain."

Her eyes softened marginally. She took a measured step and then knelt beside him. "I don't understand any of this. But I trust you and that's why I've kept you free of chains. You must know how this looks."

He shuddered. "More than you know."

"Then tell me."

He shook his head. "It's not that simple. You wouldn't understand."

Anger flashed across her face, and he knew he'd said the wrong thing.

"I've endured my whole life of men telling me what I can't understand. You have never been one of them," she said coldly.

"You know I didn't mean it like that."

"Then *explain*," Divara pressed. "I lost good men to your sword. The mage you travel with has magic I've never seen, and you were seen aiding the enemy. Give me an explanation to fit the man I know."

He couldn't. Because he wasn't the Abraxas she knew. He was a shell of himself, empty and lost and angry. Still reaching to the heavens and grasping with empty fingers. Still looking for the Divine beauty in the world and finding nothing. Never before had he wished to be his old self so badly, just so he could relish in the trust and pride that Divara used to give him. They left Vernes the same, broken and hollow, but for different reasons. Now that he was shoved back in time, face to face with a woman he admired above all, he didn't know what to say.

But it couldn't be the truth. Not all of it.

"We weren't aiding the boy," he said carefully. "We'd just stumbled on him when you attacked."

"Where were you going?"

He hesitated. "I can't say."

She growled. "Abraxas,"

"It's not my place to say," he snapped. "I can't."

Partly because he didn't know. Partly because he didn't know what Nerezza would do to him if he told Divara everything.

"Because of the mage?" she asked. "Who is she?"

He licked his lips. "Terevasan. I was told she could help end the war, but not how."

Divara frowned. "A Terevasan mage? I thought we'd stopped taking troops from there."

He offered an apologetic shrug. "I did too. Her magic . . . it's horrible, Divara."

For a moment, Abraxas nearly broke. He wasn't a good liar and Divara was an ally. She could help him break this spell of Nerezza's that kept him chained. She could free him and then he could . . .

What? Live the next hundred years over again? Fight in Vernes again? Endure the loss of the Divines anew and then wait even longer for the Wandering Sols? That was no future, even if it was free. He couldn't wait that long and still be the same person for his friends.

But what was the alternative? Abraxas couldn't see a way out.

Divara put her hand on his shoulder. He hadn't even realized he was shaking until she stilled him. Her dark eyes were wide with concern, lips parted as she sucked in a steadying breath. "I saw. Divines know I don't understand it, and I'll make her pay for the lives she took after your mission. But no matter her magic, you were sent to guide her because you are stronger." She squeezed his shoulder. "You have a god on your side, my friend. That is something she can never hope to beat."

Oh, if only she knew.

"I'm sorry about your men," he said. "I thought . . . I've been away from everyone else for so long, all I saw was an enemy."

"This war destroys us all," Divara said. "I can't promise there won't be repercussions, but it sounds like Loghain sent you on an important mission, and I can't get in the way of it." She stood up, dusting her hands on her jerkin. "You'll stay the night. The spell I put on your mage will have her in a deep sleep and won't wear off until morning. You can leave the city then."

Abraxas pulled himself to his feet, his head spinning enough that he had to brace himself against the wall. When the dizziness passed and he could stand on his own, he looked her square in the eyes and asked a question he dreaded the answer to.

"Where are we?"

"Cuskhe."

All the air left his lungs in a horrible gasp. "No."

Divara frowned at him. "Yes. We seized the city three months ago. The civilians have been cooperating ever since."

He knew this story. Cuskhe was taken, feigned obedience and became a hub for the Etherakian army for months. It built up its rebel force in secret. It learned their tactics and weaknesses. It waited until Etherak had become complacent and then it butchered everyone inside the walls that did not belong.

Abraxas, a hundred years ago, had been part of the army that fought to take Cuskhe back. He'd thought that the sheer size of their force would be enough to subdue the civilians. Rebels? No. But the common folk never wanted to fight before. But Cuskhe was different. Everyone fought then. There was no surrender.

Abraxas killed so many people that day. So many that wore no armor and had no weapons. In the end, Cuskhe had nothing more than a bloody grave.

"We need to leave," he blurted without thinking, *again*. "Get out of the city."

"Cuskhe is a safe haven for our troops crossing the Moving Sea." Divara argued. "It's the closest city we have to the sea. This city is the key to the rest of the country. Why would we leave?"

"Divara, please listen to me." He grabbed her shoulders, suddenly aware of how weak he felt compared to her stiffening muscles. But she didn't push him away. "This city is not friendly. The civilians don't want you here."

"We liberated them." She argued. "They helped us push the rebels out."

"It's a ruse! A trick." He wanted to shake sense into her but knew better. "They're going to turn on you and it'll be a bloodbath for both sides."

Finally, she shoved him off. Her jaw was tight and her hand went to her belt where she normally kept her spellbook clipped. "Cuskhe is my victory."

"Cuskhe isn't a victory!" He tore his hands through his hair. "It's a ploy, a mistake we never recovered from."

"What are you saying?"

"I'm saying that we shouldn't have come here, and we need to leave. Not just Cuskhe, but the whole damned country."

Abraxas hated silence. He hated even more how Divara looked at him. Some mix of fury and confusion. And, worse, pity.

Her thumb was still looped in her belt when she took a step closer to him, her voice deadly soft. "I don't understand. Where is this coming from?"

He swallowed roughly. "I've always thought like this."

"Worgshit," she snapped. "I could understand feeling this

way when we took Gratey, or even Terevas. Hells, I questioned our fight then. But here? Now? Abraxas, this place reeks of evil. Its crawling with the undead and necromancers who have no respect for the souls that need to pass on. They treat their people like slaves based on what time of year they're born, and there's no hope for escape. This country is dark, and lawless, and festering. We need to be here."

Abraxas let the truth crawl out of his bones, up his throat and out of his mouth. "No, we don't. Vernes will be our doom and it'll be our fault."

Divara stopped short. He hadn't realized until now that the shaft of light from window was all that stood between them. A shield that would break as soon as one of them had the courage to cross it, forever dividing two souls who had once been of like mind.

The irony wasn't lost on him.

"I don't know you," Divara finally said. "Whoever you are, you are not Abraxas Kain."

"Far worse," he croaked, "is the knowledge that I am him."

Abraxas surged forward, breaking the light with shadows and frenzy. He had only one thing in his favor; Divara had neglected to bring her spellbook, making her weaker than normal. All he had to do was overwhelm her and escape, and he could figure out the rest later.

Her arms went up to protect herself, but last minute Abraxas changed his footing and jammed his elbow right under her ribs. The breath rushed out of her in a crackled gasp, and she fell to one knee.

That was all he needed. Abraxas left her on the floor gasping and bolted to the door. It took no time to get to. The room was small and his run was so frenzied that he slammed into it with his whole body instead of stopping. He grasped the handle, cold iron biting into his palm, and then he froze.

He tasted iron on his tongue and felt a chill settle all over his body. Divara's magic always felt like the stinging bite of winter. He tried to pull his hand away and found he couldn't so much as move a muscle. He could barely glance over his shoulder as shame roiled in his belly.

Behind him, Divara got up calmly despite the sheen of sweat on her face and the murderous look in her eyes. In her hand something was smoking.

No, she was burning.

Abraxas watched in horror as the tattooed combination of runes spread along the soft flesh between her thumb and forefinger shriveled and burned as bright as embers. The smell of burnt hair and sizzling skin filled the room, and behind the rage in Divara's eyes was a measure of pain.

"Did you really think I'd leave the door unlocked?" she hissed. Her smoldering hand twisted sharply, as if she was wrenching bone from a piece of meat, and another wave of magic engulfed him.

This time he felt the iron of the door latch crawling up his arm. He didn't need to look at it to know what the rune was doing. He'd seen her do it to prisoners before, turning men of flesh into statues of iron.

The rebels called her *khet ameksu*, Iron Witch. He'd been a fool to forget what she was capable of, and even more of one to think she would ever leave herself defenseless.

Abraxas couldn't move. He couldn't beg, even if he wanted to. He waited until the iron was sealing his lips, then he let out a breath and closed his eyes.

6

Evren

Sahar Al-Fasil's family manor wasn't built inside the city proper of Rheinwall. Instead, the sprawling house was sitting on many acres of lush farmland and orchards. The smell of apple blossoms was heavy in the air, and waves of growing crops swayed in the warm breeze. Workers moved about the fields, chatting happily. One sang a song as she worked, and those around her groaned until they too began to sing along.

The path the Wandering Sols walked was wide enough for two carriages and lined with perfectly symmetrical trees that formed a canopy of green shading them from the sun. Through the trees Evren was beginning to glimpse the manor in all its glory, and she couldn't help the bubble of nerves in her chest.

"We should go back," Gyda said.

Evren bit her lip. She didn't want to have this argument again. Instead, she focused on the way the gravel at her feet crunched like snow. Luckily, she didn't have to worry because everyone had heard Gyda.

"We searched the whole carcass, Gyda," Sol said gently. "There was no sign of him."

"We should've looked harder," she snapped. "We missed him."

"It might not have been the same dragon," Sorin said. "Right? I mean . . . Evvie, your father said that the Archdruids' spell destroyed her—Nerezza, Abraxas, and dagger included. There's no way she would've ended up here, looking like she's been dead for years. It's a different dragon. Has to be."

He sounded like he was trying to convince himself as well as Gyda, but the warrior shook her head firmly.

"I know that beast. It was her."

Evren wanted to deny it because it felt easier than dealing with this new wound, but she couldn't. "She's right, it's the Storm."

"Then we go back," Gyda said. "Sahar can wait."

Without waiting for approval, she turned sharply on her heel and walked back the way she came. Sol stared at her, dumbfounded, before starting to go after her. Evren held her back.

"Don't."

Sol looked between them. "Evren, we can't go back. We spent two days searching that dragon. Why can't she see that he's not there?"

"She hasn't moved on." The answer came easily, and Evren hated it. "Not really. You all go ahead, and I'll talk to her."

Arke grunted, already walking away. "She's less likely to take your head off than ours. C'mon, kid."

He yanked Sorin's coat to get him to follow. The Vasa spared Gyda's retreating form one last look before giving in and following him. But Sol hesitated, anchoring herself and Evren between their split friends.

"She's hurting," Evren said. "But she'll be all right."

Sol's face contorted with worry. "I worry about her. Losing Abraxas hit all of us hard, and there's not a day that I don't miss him, but I've never seen Gyda so . . . shaken. Even after the White Cairn she was stronger than this."

"She can't be strong all the time," Evren reminded her. "But that's what we're here for."

"No, that's what you're there for." Sol lightly pushed her in Gyda's direction. "Lover and all that. Well, go on. I'll make sure the boys are playing nice until you get back."

"We won't be long," Evren promised, already backing away.

"You can take all the time you need." Sol winked and walked away.

A familiar burn tipped Evren's ears, but she ignored it and jogged to catch up to Gyda. No matter what she told Sol, she was worried about Gyda, too. Death wasn't something anyone was practiced at accepting, but every night seemed like a fight between what Gyda knew and what she wanted to believe. And Evren knew she was supposed to be the one to help her through this, but she didn't know how. She didn't exactly have the best record of moving on herself.

It took a while to catch up to her. Gyda was stiff-backed and surefooted, moving at a pace Evren could barely keep up at with a jog. She watched as the warrior's head twitched in her direction, hearing her footsteps on the gravel, and she slowed down.

Evren breathed a huff of relief. A few moments later she caught up and circled around Gyda, then stopped entirely.

Gyda nearly ran into her, biting back a hiss of frustration as she took a step back. "What are you doing?"

Evren panted. "Attempting to talk to you."

"We can talk as we walk, come on."

She tried to walk around Evren, which normally wouldn't have been a problem because of the size difference between them, but Evren sidestepped her, blocking her way again.

"Is this a game to you?" Gyda asked.

"We're not going, Gyda."

"Hells we aren't."

"We didn't miss anything." Evren put her hands out in front of her to act as another barrier. "He's not there, love. We would've found him."

Gyda didn't move for a bit and stared right Evren. Or through her, she couldn't tell. Their heartbeats were steady and calm, completely opposite to the energy crackling between them.

"You really won't move?" the warrior asked, and there was something like a test in her tone that Evren couldn't quite pick apart. She felt like she was walking into a trap. Under normal circumstances that same tone might've excited her.

She thought out her answer, and then confidently said, "I'm not moving."

Gyda shrugged. "Fine." And then picked Evren up by her waist and slung her over her shoulder.

Evren was too stunned to even fight her for a moment. Then Gyda started walking and the ground was lurching beneath Evren's head. She had the sick feeling that she was going to fall even with Gyda's arm securely around her legs.

Finally, she snapped out of her stupor and smacked the warrior's back. "Gyda!"

She didn't flinch. "You wouldn't move."

"Put me down."

"I thought you liked when I carried you."

Evren scowled, shoving her sword out of her face. "Not like this. I'm trying to have a conversation with you."

"You can talk while I walk."

Evren was half tempted to give up and just let Gyda carry her all the way back to the dragon. But she wasn't in the mood for that and, damn it, she had a point to make.

Evren pushed herself up off Gyda's back, feeling the arm around her legs tighten in warning. But she didn't care. She wasn't going to put up with this. She watched the woven branches pass by her head, now so much closer thanks to Gyda's help, and waited for the right one. When she saw the perfect one, she reached out and snatched it in her hands.

One minute she was caught between a horrible tug-of-war between Gyda and the tree, and the next she was twisting and wiggling her legs out of Gyda's grasp. She slipped one leg out, and then the other.

Gyda cursed, swinging around to snatch her leg back, but Evren had already pulled herself up onto the limb entirely and tucked her feet underneath her.

Gyda glared up at her. "So you're hiding now?'

"Well, you can see me so . . ."

"Evren."

"You started this!" Evren pointed out. "My feet were firmly on the ground before you tossed me over your shoulder like a sack of grain."

Gyda folded her arms across her chest. "Come down."

"Only if you talk and stand still at the same time."

Hesitation flitted across the warrior's features. She looked down at her feet, shuffling them through the gravel. Half of her body was angled towards the exit, as if she was ready to run. The other half was stock still.

Evren chewed her lip and when Gyda made no move, she started to climb down, not just jump down to land in the middle of the path. She moved down the branch itself towards the trunk of the well-manicured tree, easily slipping from one crook and knot to the next branch. She found one closer to the ground than the others and sat down on it, swinging her legs in the open air.

"Gyda, come over here."

She held her hand out and, after a moment's debate, Gyda walked over and took it. Their battle calluses were as different as the weapons they wielded, but Evren relished the feel of their hands clasped together. She pulled Gyda closer to the branch until Gyda was shuffling between her swinging legs. With the tree branch, Evren was a little over eye level with her and she smiled.

"That's better."

Gyda grunted, her eyes flicking back down to her boots, and Evren's smile faded.

"I know you're not ready to let him go," Evren began softly. Gyda stiffened under her touch, but she kept her close. With her other hand she lifted Gyda's chin gently so she could look her in the eyes. "None of us were as close with him as you were. It's okay to need more time."

"It's not like that," Gyda said, and her voice was so small that it took Evren's breath away. "I know he's gone, I do. But it's happened to all of us."

"What has?"

"Death. All of us have been at death's door before. Some of us have passed that threshold. We've all come back. I keep waiting . . ." She took a shuddering breath, her eyes closing. "I keep waiting for one of his miracles and for him to be there again. The dragon . . . I thought . . ."

All the words Evren had planned stuck in her throat. What could she possibly say? Of course, Gyda would hope for that miracle. They'd seen so many already that it felt natural, ingrained. And it was uncharacteristically soft for Gyda to be the one to take Abraxas's love of miracles to heart when the rest of them had tried to think practically. Evren had just assumed Gyda did, too.

Evren let her hand fall away from Gyda's face, a little numb. Without her support, Gyda's head bowed and rested on Evren's shoulder and, despite the painful conversation, a part of Evren loved having Gyda lean on her.

"I did, too," Evren whispered. "When Arke and I first found it, I thought there was a piece of another puzzle I had missed. I don't know how she got there, but dragons aren't built like the rest of us. We don't know what my father did to them, but I don't think we'll find him there, Gyda."

"It just doesn't feel like he's gone." Gyda's breath whispered on her skin.

Evren knew that feeling well. She squeezed Gyda's hand. "Can I show you something?"

Gyda's head lifted, her eyes red from unshed tears. She nodded firmly.

Evren didn't let go of her hand but rummaged in her pocket with the other one until she found what she was looking for. Her fingers hooked around metallic wings and leather, and she pulled out Dagny's gift.

The dragon's scales glinted in the spring sun. Evren let it rest on her knuckles, making sure Gyda saw it clearly.

Her eyes widened a little. "That's his."

"Kind of," Evren admitted. "Dagny gave it to me as a parting gift. It's the symbol of his god. She said it would protect us from harm like it did her." She fell quiet for a bit before softly adding, "Like he did for us."

Evren held it out to her and Gyda took it with barely trembling fingers. It laid against her palm and Evren swore the dragon was winking at her, or the sun was playing tricks. The warrior's thumb smoothed over the iron scales.

"It's not him," Gyda finally said.

"No."

"I don't believe in his gods."

Evren shook her head. "Neither do I, but that's not the point. What do you think of when you see that symbol?"

She furrowed her brow, the knot that Evren loved so much forming between her eyebrows. "Abraxas."

"See? It's not Haphion's symbol to us. It's something else entirely. Something more."

Evren curled her hand around Gyda's and closed her fingers around the pendant. Gyda's eyes snapped up to hers, brimming with questions and a storm of feelings. Evren smiled down at her.

"Everyone grieves differently, but we all have to take the pieces he left and carry on. You're not alone in this Gyda, you don't have to grieve alone, either."

Gyda pressed the pendant to her chest, her mouth wavering between a firm line and a frown. "I need to be strong. They need me to be. So do you."

"No, we don't."

This time she did frown.

Evren said, "We need you to just *be*, Gyda. You don't have to be the sword that stands between us and danger all the time. I certainly don't want that. You're allowed to let yourself rest."

Gyda shook her head. "I can't—"

"Yes, you can." Evren forced some strength into her voice that took even her by surprise. "Not only can you, but you need to. A tired pack of wolves doesn't hunt nearly as well as a rested one. And I need you in every form. Strong or weak. A bulwark in battle or leaning on me like this. Do you understand?"

Slowly, with small movements, Gyda nodded. "I think so, yes."

Evren wanted to melt in relief, but she had to drive it home. "Do you remember in Orenlion when I pushed you away and was killing myself by generally being a fool and refusing help?"

"Vividly."

"This is similar." Evren tapped Gyda's chest, just above the pendant and where their mirrored scars were. "Grief is an illness that takes time to recover from. Don't let it infect you because you're too stubborn to take your medicine."

Gyda blinked, her eyes clearing as if she was suddenly seeing it all laid out in front of her for the first time. "Since when did you become so wise?"

Evren grinned. "I learned from the best. Also, I did refuse to accept my father's death and as a result nearly killed myself in the process. I'm a bit of an expert on it at this point."

"It'll take me time, Evren," Gyda cautioned. "I can't lock him away and forget about him."

"And none of us are asking you to. We all carry guilt over what happened. Talk to us, any of us. That's what we're here for. Protecting and supporting each other on and off the battlefield. Understand?"

She nodded, this time surer. "I understand."

Evren had never tried to put a name to whatever she and Gyda were. There were forces in Eith that were strong enough to never need names or titles, to simply be accepted for what they were. A small part of Evren raged against that, while the rest slipped into something akin to acceptance as she sat there, spring breeze tousling her hair, with Gyda's hand in hers. Whatever this bond was, whether simple love or an effect of Gyda's sacrifice, she didn't care. She'd loved Gyda before and she loved her now, and hundreds of years into the future her soul would still love Gyda's for quiet moments like this; where the words were easy and the touches were soft, and the rest of Eith didn't matter so long as it was just the two of them sharing the same air and heart.

In truth, it might've scared the old Evren at how quickly she'd come to that conclusion. But the rest of Eith traveled quick paths of destruction and rebirth, why couldn't her own feelings find a similar road?

The rumbling of carriage wheels on gravel broke the peaceful moment. Gyda stepped away, slipping the leather cord of the pendant around her head and tucking the dragon away as the disturber came into view.

The carriage was massive, taking up the entire path she'd originally thought was for two. An ornate, gilded thing, it was pulled by a team of six beautiful black horses. Their coats shone like oil, their manes and tails perfectly braided back.

The carriage driver didn't even have to pull at the reins to get them to stop, all he did was click his tongue and all the horses immediately obeyed, drawing the carriage to a stop right before Evren and Gyda.

The door jerked open, and an elegant hand of tanned skin and manicured nails kept it open.

Sahar grinned knowingly at them. "Well, don't just stand there. We have a parade to attend."

7

Evren

Even with all five of the Wandering Sols and Sahar in the carriage, it wasn't cramped. There was space enough between Evren and Sorin that their legs didn't touch, and the only one who looked uncomfortable was Gyda, who scowled with every jostle and bump and had to hunch to keep her head from brushing the roof.

Sorin and Sol flanked Evren, all stewing in the awkward silence of the ride. Sahar sat opposite of Evren, graciously sitting between Arke, who was pressed against the window, and Gyda's hunched form. And she didn't look the least bit bothered.

Evren had gotten used to Sahar's way of looking put together and poised even covered in blood and dirt back in Direwall. But it was something else entirely to see her utterly devoid of those things. She carried herself like a lady, but only now did Evren see her wearing it like armor. Gone was the sharp cut coat and polished boots, and instead she wore a dress unlike anything Evren had seen. The snug bodice was wrapped in light blue satin but looked as sturdy as any armor.

It seemed to keep her back straight, as if she ever slouched, and accented her waist where the rest of the dress pooled out in a flow of fabric that dominated the legroom between them. She wore no jewelry besides a pair of pearl studs in her ears, and her hair was pulled back in a similar, albeit more intricate, updo.

She was a Terevasan lady through and through, Evren just hadn't realized how different those ladies were from the ones she knew in Orenlion or Dirn-Darahl.

"You cut your hair." Sahar broke the silence.

Evren touched the shorter ends brushing her ears. "It was time for a change."

"And you don't look nearly as dead. Sol said that had something to do with the ruckus Etherak and Orenlion are putting up with their alliance?"

She shrugged. "We helped that along, got a few things in return."

The smile slipped and Sahar's eyes turned to a darker shade of pity and understanding. "As well as losing someone."

If she hadn't just been talking to Gyda about it, Sahar's bringing it up would've been like a punch in the gut. But she took a deep breath and found the words easier to say than before.

"Abraxas didn't make it, no. It's been . . ." her eyes flickered around the carriage at her friend's faces and then back to Sahar. "Well, you know how it's been."

Sahar nodded. "I do. You have my deepest regrets. Abraxas and I were never close; indeed, I can't remember sharing more than a few words with him during that adventure, but he was a fighter. He didn't need to fight so hard for me and mine, but he did. And for that, I will forever be grateful."

"I think he would've appreciated those words far more

than you know," Evren said. "I know he respected you a great deal."

"Perhaps, although fate has made it so we'll never know for sure, the cruel bitch."

Evren almost laughed. She'd forgotten that beneath all the charm and poise was a woman who captured fire in glass bottles and had saved Eith from three different disasters. A foul mouth was seemingly necessary to stand between Eith and its monsters.

Sol nudged Evren. "There's something else we should tell you. Abraxas wasn't the only person we lost in Orenlion."

Sahar's already dark eyes widened a bit but, outside of that, her body was as still as one could be in a rocking carriage. She let the silence permeate the air for a moment, before looking at all of them in turn.

"Tell me."

And so they did.

Evren was relieved that the story traded off and it wasn't just her telling it. They started with Barrion's quest, Evren's dilemma, and the stakes. Evren bared the truth about the figure she was seeing, which had ended up being Nerezza. Gyda took over with the Hisrachi, and Arke butted in with Neri and her story. Orenlion was a tale traded between Sorin, Sol, and Evren, and she found it surprisingly hard to talk about Aster. The attack on Orenlion, Evren's father, the wedding, and the race to the Eternity Keeper's dagger flew out of their lips faster and sounded stranger than they experienced it. There was no extra flair, no grandiose retelling. It came out numb, just the facts the closer to the end they got. And when the end came, it was on Evren to tell Sahar that Nerezza was gone, taken by the same magic as Abraxas and the dagger. That there was nothing left of her friend to bring home.

The carriage rocked quietly for a while. No one dared to speak a word. Finally, Sahar shifted in her seat and leaned toward Evren. The fire in her deep brown eyes was brighter now, when Evren expected grief to douse them.

"Nerezza isn't dead."

Arke's head snapped away from the window so quickly his ears whapped against the walls. Gyda stiffened. Sorin let out a sound that could've been a laugh but died before it made it past his throat as he stared at her, dumbfounded. Sol was counting her breaths.

Evren, in true fashion, blinked twice and then said, "What?"

"She's not dead. I'd know it."

That flicker of maybe started to fizzle out again. She didn't necessarily want Nerezza dead; there was certainly a lot less death and destruction in her absence, but it wasn't that idea that brought her so close to Sahar their knees were touching.

If Sahar survived, then maybe so did Abraxas.

"Tell me you have proof," Evren said, and couldn't keep the hope from her voice.

"Proof? No." Sahar shook her head. "Evren, you just told me that I lost her."

Evren's heart sank. "So, this is just denial."

Sahar's eyes flashed. "No, it's a gut feeling. I would know if she was dead. I would feel it."

Evren sat back, swallowing her disappointment. The air in the carriage seemed a lot more suffocating now, and every one of the Wandering Sols had withdrawn on themselves. Sorin patted the worg's head and plastered on a rueful smile.

"Sahar . . ." he started.

She snapped her gaze over to him. "Don't."

"What?"

"Don't patronize me. I've spent every day since I got back home dealing with sympathies and false smiles from everyone I crossed paths with. I've had mere strangers telling me to move on with my life, I do *not* need to hear it from you."

"I'm not trying to be patronizing," he said. "You've lost more than we can even wrap our heads around."

"But not her," she said, leaning back against the cushioned seat and looking away. The conversation was over.

~

THE REST of the ride was silent and awkward, but Evren knew without looking out the window when they'd arrived in Rheinwall. The city assaulted her senses, but it was her ears that suffered the most. People shouted over each other, to the point where she couldn't pick out the different words between them. It took her a minute of focus to realize that it was partly because she didn't understand most of the languages being spoken. Elven and Core, yes. But the Dwarven was so fast she couldn't even snatch the words Sol had taught her. Orcish popped up more than she expected. Even Vernesian words were there. It was like a dozen different symphonies playing different songs at once.

Add in the marching of hoofbeats, the rumbling of carriages, frenzied music playing at every corner, and the sound of street food being cooked, it was chaos.

The carriage lurched to a stop and after a few moments the driver had opened the door and was waiting for Sahar with his hand ready. She took it, lifting her skirts around Arke and stepping into the bright street. The rest of them had no choice but to follow, stepping into the streets of Rheinwall one by one.

If hearing it was a shock, seeing it was another. Evren had never seen a city built so *tall*. Orenlion had used the trees for height, Andovine and Dirn-Darahl the stone around them. But Rheinwall used nothing but its very own buildings. The ones nearest reached up ten stories above her head, others even higher. Their architecture was the same ornate and extravagant style as Sahar's carriage, but amplified. Roofs and steeples so steep even the birds couldn't rest on them. Wrought iron fences and stained-glass windows. Archways with so much detail and filigree that her eyes crossed trying to look at them.

The road at their feet wasn't dirt or mud, it was even and well-maintained cobblestones that fit together so perfectly there was barely a crack between each stone. The streets were crowded with people of all heights, races, and colors. Evren watched with a bubble of amazement as a grey-skinned orc passed out flower crowns to passing children. Ladies in skirts far larger than Sahar's flitted about with hair resembling beehives and fans fluttering away at their faces. Crowds parted around passing carriages before swallowing them back up. Over the street, ropes lined with colorful flags and streamers were tied back and forth, and an acrobat balanced gracefully while doing a number of tricks in the air that made Evren's stomach twist.

Rheinwall was chaos. Rheinwall was beautiful.

Sahar snapped until she had everyone's attention, and then fluffed out her skirts while she talked. "The parade will be just down this street. Simply follow the crowds and you'll find it easily."

"You're not coming with us?" Evren asked.

Sahar's mouth twisted into a frown. "I have people to visit here. Even while celebrating, the Collective never rests. Besides, a lone adventurer with no party puts a damper on such a good day. You'll be fine without me."

Sorin was staring up at the acrobat with wide eyes but looked away just long enough to speak. "They'll let just anyone into the parade? Or are we just allowed to watch?"

"You'll be walking with the parade. Believe me," Sahar looked them up and down. "You look the part. Besides, word has already spread of what you've done. Orenlion is the icing on the cake."

Sol gasped. "Cake sounds wonderful. Let's get cake."

"Do enjoy yourselves. I'll find you when it's done." She started to leave, but with a woosh of skirts turned around so fast Evren had to back up. "By the way, it goes without saying to be careful, right? Rheinwall is a civilized, progressive city, but this is still Terevas."

"What do you mean?"

Arke growled loud enough for a few passersby to give him a wide berth. "She means Fey. They like shit like this. Revelin' and such. Pays to be careful. Don't take food or drink from strangers. Be polite but don't thank no body. Don't give your name."

Evren floundered. She'd never messed with Fey before, but she knew Terevas was full of them. But they weren't inherently bad creatures so far as she knew. "Isn't all of that rude? Won't we just piss off normal people?"

Arke barked a laugh. "This is Rheinwall. Ain't nobody normal."

"Not helpful, buddy," Sorin chided.

"Unfortunately, he's right," Sahar said. "Terevas has had centuries to develop a culture and system to where we live peacefully amongst the Fey. It's not something you can learn in a day. But Arke has the basic rules down and you're smart people. Have fun, just not so much that you die from exhaustion."

She waved a goodbye, whirled her skirts around again, and disappeared in the opposite direction of the moving crowd.

The driver watched her go and then turned to the party. "I'd recommend leaving your weapons inside the carriage, my lords and ladies. You could cause quite a fuss armed to the teeth so openly."

Gyda finally spoke, glowering at him. "You expect us to walk into a strange city with no weapons?"

He snorted and Evren noticed how hooked his nose was, like an eagle's. "Heavens no! This is still Eith, my lady.

Concealed weapons are highly encouraged. I have extra available if you do not."

Evren could barely contain her smile. "That won't be necessary. We have plenty to go around."

"Very good, my lady."

The Wandering Sols unpacked their weapons and stashed them inside the carriage. Gyda reluctantly pried her fingers from her hilt and set it down gently on the cushioned bench. Evren laid her bow and arrows beside it. Sorin's sword and three of Sol's biggest daggers were stashed as well. Arke kept his spellbook on him, and not even the driver recommended otherwise. They each hid a dagger somewhere on them, straightened their clothes, bid the driver farewell, and merged into the river of people flowing forward.

A moment of panic, however brief, threatened to overwhelm Evren as the press of so many bodies threatened to overwhelm her. She ran into shoulders and elbows, tripped over skirts and boots. The smell of a dozen different perfumes, food, and sweat clogged her nose. Just as she was about to give up on breathing all together, Gyda's hand found hers.

It wasn't that the air was instantly cleared or cooler, making it easier to breath. It wasn't that the people weren't so close that she could see the cracks in their makeup and lose threads of their shirts. No, all that remained. Now she had an anchor, someone to lean on when things got too much. She was so grateful she could've melted.

The crowd started branching out as they reached another, larger street. This one had garlands of blossoms laced between the buildings. Thick crowds of people waited along the sides, cheering and throwing flags, parcels of food, trinkets, and flowers at the passing parade.

Evren wasn't sure what she expected, but the procession still took her by surprise. Adventurers of every kind walked down the wide street. Some were on moving, decorated platforms pulled by a mage in the front with just a wave of their hand and the burning of a page. Others were riding armored horses. Most were simply walking. Some waved, others danced and passed out sweets to children. Others stared ahead, bored or tired, Evren couldn't tell.

A party of four dwarven mages tossed sparkling coins in the air that turned into bees when they got close to the ground. A half-orc wearing a mantle of golden thread so light it floated through the air as if it weighed nothing at all blew kisses at every lady he saw, and his human companion rolled her eyes and ignored everyone as she tugged him along. Tarnished sellswords laughed and drank ale as they walked. Elves wearing armor made of glittering dragon scales watched the skies with every third wave of their hands.

"Well," Sorin shouted over the din of the crowd. "This is our stop. Arke, may I?"

"Eh, whatever. Wait, what are you doin'—"

Sorin scooped Arke up by his armpits and hoisted him on top of the worg's broad shoulders. The worg didn't even budge, but his butt wiggled happily as Arke grabbed onto his fur to stay on.

"There!" Sorin said cheerfully. "Now you've got a horse of your own and look quite fearsome."

Evren had to laugh. The goblin did look like something straight out of a storybook on top of the worg, all quivering ears and bared teeth. But Arke slowly started to relax, still scowling but trusting Sorin.

"If this thing throws me off, I'm eatin' your sheets." He pointed a claw at Sorin.

"Fair bet to me. Ladies." He turned back to the rest of them and swept his arm out into the parade. "Shall we?"

Evren didn't give herself a moment to doubt. She grabbed Sol's hand and tugged her and Gyda forward. With Sorin and Arke behind them, they joined the river-like parade as easily as putting on a pair of well-worn boots. They slipped behind a group of magicians, and they were seen.

The same bunch of nerves was there, only now Evren was being watched. Children pointed her out by tugging on their mother's skirts. A bard at the corner winked at her and tried to throw her a rose before it was snatched by one of the magicians in the front. He scowled as the magician stuck the rose between his teeth and bowed low enough to brush the cobblestones. His friends had to pull him away to keep the flow of the parade, and the bard was left behind. Others took his place however, gawking, staring, cheering, and everything in between.

"It's a little unnerving." Evren said to Sol, but when she glanced over, the dwarf was having the time of her life. Somewhere along the way she'd gotten a flower crown and a hand pie, and when she looked up at Evren, her blue eyes had never been brighter.

"This is amazing!" she squealed, loud enough that the magicians in front of her whooped and shouted along with her.

Evren let her hand go the minute Sol's eyes sparked towards them and before she knew it the dwarf was a few feet ahead sharing her pie with the rose magician.

Grinning, she looked back at Sorin and Arke and wasn't surprised by what she found. Sorin could work a crowd in his sleep, and he was having a blast waving and saying hi to every little kid in the crowd. Every bard he passed he tossed coins to, and they played even louder. Men and women alike clamored to throw him presents and just to be seen by him. It was no magic, just his dazzling smile, and it was good to see it used in a situation that wasn't life or death.

Arke wasn't faring as well, but no one jeered or cursed at him. Instead they watched him in awe astride the worg, whispering and pointing to his spellbook. A dwarven teenager saw him and pointed to her mother as if to say, 'If he can do it, so can I.'

Slowly, Arke's body language shifted and he wasn't so hunched and guarded. He relaxed, he gave a tentative toothy grin, and he even waved. The moment he raised his hand the crowd cheered.

The pride welling up in her chest couldn't be contained. Evren turned back and tugged on Gyda's shoulder. "Gyda, they love him!"

She smirked over her shoulder. "He'll be insufferable the next few days. But he deserves this."

"So do you," Evren pointed out. "Look."

They passed through a cross section of the street where iron lamps covered in blooming garlands and ribbons stood at every corner. At one of them a group of children sat, being watched by a couple of stern but obviously well-meaning women. Not mothers, Evren realized. Caretakers to orphans.

At the back was a girl no older than seven. She'd climbed the lamppost to see over the crowd and was staring straight at Gyda.

Most people were. Getting past Arke's shock value and Sorin's pretty grin, it was easy to find Gyda amongst the crowd of strange adventurers. She was by far the tallest, and the only part-giant that Evren could see. Judging how people were watching her, she was probably the only one they'd ever seen.

But Gyda paid them no mind. She locked eyes with the little girl and it was as if nothing else mattered. She squeezed Evren's hand and let it go, easily snatching a tossed flag from the air. The bright blue and yellow were Terevasan colors, nothing the little girl hadn't seen before. But as Gyda approached and handed it to her, it was like it was the most precious thing in the whole world. She grabbed it, squealing with delight and smushing it against her face. Those large eyes stared up at Gyda with adoration that made their heart stutter.

Evren pressed her hand to her chest, feeling the heartbeat go back to normal. All the orphans were looking up at Gyda now, mouths open in shock and blurting out questions like,

"How many horses can you lift?"

"Have you ever strangled a dragon? I bet you could!"

"Blimey, you're so tall, miss! Have you touched the clouds before?"

Evren laughed, unable to stop herself. Gyda was so close to being overwhelmed but she answered every question. So much so that the parade was leaving them behind. Evren didn't want to pull her away though. Gyda deserved this.

There was only one orphan who wasn't watching Gyda. He looked a little older than the rest, maybe eleven, all elbows and knees with a mop of shaggy black hair that nearly covered his eyes and ears. Ears that peeked out just enough to be seen but not quite as long as a full-blooded elf.

Evren's breath caught when she realized he was staring at her, something like confusion and wonder on his face. She lifted her hand and waved, and at first it didn't seem like enough. He looked so dour and withdrawn, and she wasn't talking to him the way Gyda was talking to the others. But he perked up, brushed the hair out of his eyes, and waved ever so slightly back.

Evren wasn't sure, but she could've sworn she saw when that wonder turned to determination and hope, like the beginnings of a plan.

Gyda was making her way back to her, grinning like a fool and breathless, but Evren was turning back to the parade as something dawned on her.

The adventurers changed everything. The half-orc wearing as much gold as a King. The dwarven mages wielding magic as soft as a feather. Arke and his spells showing the world that a goblin could and would take the world by storm. There were humans and full-blooded elves, orcs and dwarves and some races she didn't recognize. But more often they were outcasts. Halfblooded races who found their place in Eith by doing great deeds. Mercenaries making a difference and living a comfortable life no army could pay for. She saw people from Gratey, Etherak, and even a handful from Vernes coexisting and walking together.

She looked back at the boy, who was watching her, and wondered what her life would've been like if she'd had someone like herself to look up to.

Gyda swept her back into the parade and they hurried to catch up to the rest of their party. All the while Evren's chest felt full to bursting. Her cheeks were aching by the time they caught up with everyone. Just in time, too, the parade had slowed down to fill a truly massive city square to the brim.

Sorin popped up through the crowd, glitter in his dreads. "There you are! Look what we did!"

The crowd of adventurers parted as he gestured to the group of bards in the center of the square. She recognized the rose bard as he put his flute to his lips and started a lively tune. Evren didn't know the song, but every other bard seemed to. They started playing together, flutes and lutes and fiddles and horns crashing sounds in the air until they all fell into a jaunty rhythm.

Evren may not know it, but her body wanted nothing more than to dance to it.

She wasn't the only one. Adventurers started pairing up, some with their own party and some with strangers. Many started dragging the people watching into it, too.

"There we go!" Sorin clapped. "Let's make this a party. Don't be shy. Anyone have an extra fiddle?"

Evren didn't get to see if he got the fiddle. Suddenly, she had a pair of hands pulling her away from Gyda and begging her to dance. She looked back and Gyda had the same problem. But these were their people. Adventurers like them. They shared a smile and a promise to find each other again, and then let go.

There seemed to be no steps to this dance, but as Evren was pulled into it by a couple of partners, her feet found a way. From stumbling and tripping, to nearly matching their steps. Her partners held her shoulders as she learned, they laughed as they twirled her about. She only remembered glimpses of their faces before they traded off. Suddenly she was in the arms of someone else. Leaner, quicker, but not as sure with their footwork. Evren led them this time, teaching without words the steps she learned that went in time perfectly to the music in her ears in heart. By the time she traded partners again, her body moved without her thinking.

She'd never been much of a dancer, but now she couldn't think of why she wasn't. The rush of air in her lungs, the music humming in her chest, the weight of the perfect partner's hand in hers, it was like flying. But her feet were skipping and dancing along the cobblestones and she couldn't have stopped even if she wanted to.

Two partners later, or maybe five, the music was still going strong and she leaned her head back as she twirled to see the bright blue sky spinning above her. There were no hands on her, her partner must've let her go, and that was just fine. She didn't mind dancing alone. She still had to find Gyda after all.

Someone bumped into her hard enough to jerk her out of her spinning. She was laughing, out of breath as she stopped and leaned on them.

"I'm sorry," she giggled. "My head is spinning, give me a moment."

Whoever it was said nothing while Evren's head centered itself again. They were short and stood still until Evren stood up straight.

She blinked in surprise. "Sol! I haven't danced with you yet."

But Sol looked far from a carefree dance partner. She was shaking uncontrollably, eyes fixed on someone on the other side of the crowd. Evren followed her gaze and caught sight of another dwarf. Dark hair cut close to his head, pale skin sunburnt on his cheeks and nose. His beard was unkept and he was missing jewelry, but she knew that man.

Mal had changed from a soft nobleman to a grizzled mercenary, and his eyes were locked on Sol.

"What the fuck?" Evren hissed and pulled Sol behind her.

Mal's eyes snapped to her, and the recognition came with an unhealthy dose of loathing. He started to walk towards them, but a line of reveling dancers cut him off. Evren snatched Sol's hand and marched in the other direction.

"He's not supposed to be here," Sol wheezed beside her. "He's supposed to be in prison. Evren, he's supposed to be *dead*."

"I know," she reassured her. "We'll figure this out, I promise. Fuck where is everybody?"

The ever-moving dancers made it difficult to walk in a straight line, much less find her party. She couldn't make out Gyda's tall form anywhere, or Sorin's manic laughter. But there was one person she knew wouldn't be dancing, she just had to find him.

Evren changed course and tried pushing to the edge of the crowd. Hands snatched at her elbows and wrists to drag her back into the dance. Sol was almost carted off by another dancer. She screamed, thinking it must've been Mal, and the reedy elf jumped away with his hands in the air.

"Sorry! No harm, eh?"

"No harm," Evren agreed impatiently and pulled Sol away.

There was no harm in the dance, but with fear instead of bliss in her veins it felt like a nightmare she had no hope of escaping from. She swallowed down the bile crawling up her throat. Sol's grip on her hand was bone crushing. It had been before, but they were running for their life from a horde of undead then, and Evren hadn't been able to hold on then.

If Mal was going to try and snatch Sol away she'd rip his damn eyeballs out before he laid a hand on her. Evren suspected the only reason Sol wasn't angry and on the same level of murder was because she was too scared.

Finally, the dancers parted. The wall of a building was in view, still shading a few people who'd rather watch than participate. It took no time to find a goblin sitting next to a worg.

The worg saw them first and jumped to his feet. He bounded over to Sol and started licking her tears. Arke looked up from his spellbook and took one second to process Sol's demeanor before he was on his feet and stalking over to them.

"Who we killin'?" he asked.

"Mal." Evren all but spat his name out of her mouth. "He's here, and he's after Sol."

"He danced with me," Sol said numbly. "I didn't know it was him until he said my name."

Arke growled. "Fuckin' how? Karas was supposed to lock his ass up or kill him. Useless fuckin' bastard."

"We'll figure that out from Mal once we get to him," Evren said. "He's got to be posing as an adventurer to get into this. Lucky guess that we would be here."

"I wouldn't count on it, kid."

Evren pursed her lips. He was right. Mal had managed to manipulate the King into stripping Sol of everything she was worth. He'd been a part of Heliodar's plans, complicit in igniting a war he had no chance of winning. He was smart enough to lie to Sol and outwit her, but malleable enough for Heliodar to bend to her will.

Evren should've shot him when she had the chance.

"We've got to round up Gyda and Sorin. Odds are Mal will try to keep us separated. Whatever his endgame is, I'm not waiting for it. Let's stick—"

"Wait." Sol crouched down on the ground, her eyes distant. "Do you feel that?"

"Feel what?"

Sol's hand pressed to the ground, and that was all it took to trigger a flood of memories. Of rocks shaking around her, of Alkimos breaking the very earth at her feet in order to get to her, of them burrowing *together*. Those memories never left.

The ground trembled beneath their feet. At first, just soft tremors, but then strong enough that the music wound to a stop and the dancers stopped spinning, staring at the ground in confusion.

Then there was a crack, as loud as thunder and as sharp as a blade. The center of the square disappeared in a cloud of dust and smoke, screaming replacing the sound of splintering rock as the ground dipped inward. The perfectly symmetrical cobblestones split like a broken egg. The stones moved like waves under their feet and she could barely keep balance.

A massive crack moved like lightning straight for Sol, and Evren lunged to push her out of the way. The crack opened like a maw of pitch-blackness. Too late, she realized she was falling. She heard Sol scream her name, heard the sizzling of a spell and the smell of crisp arcane energy in the air.

The pit swallowed Evren rock by rock until the bright blue of the Terevasan sky was consumed by debris And then she hit rock.

8

Abraxas

A braxas could breathe before he could see, so he could smell the heady scent of oil and timber without needing to see the pyre. He was stiff, skin feeling like cooled wax that cracked every time he moved. His mouth still tasted like iron, and he couldn't tell if it was from Divara's spell or the fact that he'd bitten his tongue. The skin around his wrists was chafing and hot against the iron manacles that bound him.

He shifted experimentally. Wooden post at his back. Timber at his feet. No chain around his legs, so Divara didn't think he'd be trouble. That, or she didn't care how much he tried to fight when she put flame to his flesh.

"Would you stop thrashing," a familiar voice hissed behind him, and he froze despite himself.

"Nerezza," he sighed, not sure how relieved he was that Divara hadn't just killed her on sight after dealing with him.

There was movement at his back, someone shifting on the other side of the post to get comfortable. "Who else?"

"At this point a devil would be a welcome reprieve."

His vision was coming back, albeit slowly. He could make out shapes in the shadows, the flickering of torches. He craned his head up and the fuzzy vision of the night sky greeted him. He blinked over and over until the stars came more into focus, until he could count the craters on the moon's surface.

"What happened?" Nerezza snapped behind him. "I woke up healed and then that bitch of a mage came in and turned me to stone."

"You're lucky, stone isn't nearly as uncomfortable as metal."

"*Abraxas.*"

He didn't think she would hurt him now, but he still flinched at her tone. "Divara figured out that I am not the Abraxas she knows. She thinks we're spies at best, heretics at worst."

"And this pyre?"

Abraxas looked away from the sky, taking in the neatly piled wood. It was stacked in such a way that he could almost overlook that this was from broken carts and wagons, skiffs that were already half burned from battle and Vernesian wood coffins. He rolled his shoulders back.

"This is better than I expected. She intends to burn us."

"How is that better?"

"Surely you're intelligent enough to remember how Etherak sends off their dead?"

"We're not dead," Nerezza said.

"In their eyes we are." Abraxas pointed his chin to the gathering soldiers. Most weren't paying attention to him and Nerezza, instead huddling beside friends or looking for familiar faces. Others glared at him with enough malice to make him sick and turn away. "Fire burns away corruption. It leaves the mortal shell too clean for undead spirits to inhabit or for necromancers to use. It's also a message to Vernes. Burning bodies is akin to sending a soul to the hells and make it so they are unable to return. For most, death by fire is a permanent removal from this world."

"So, by their standards this is a good sendoff, while also sending a message to Vernesian rebels."

Abraxas nodded even though she couldn't see him. "Yes."

"How many times did you light a pyre like this?"

His mouth was dry. "Too many."

There were worse ways to go, he assumed. This way his body would be burned and unusable to Nerezza, although she would also die so he supposed that was two birds with one flame. The pain would be excruciating, but he'd suffocate first. There was a little comfort in that.

"You've built these pyres," Nerezza said. "Get us out."

"I'm just as chained as you are. We're also surrounded by pissed off soldiers, so even if we were to get free, we have nowhere to go." He turned his head just enough to catch a glimpse of white hair. "Why? Magic failing you?"

"You know it is," she spat.

He did. Burning mages meant chaining them with enchanted manacles carved with runes that nullified even the most powerful of spells. Otherwise fire was simply a small obstacle for any mage with half a brain.

"I'm not dying here," Nerezza said. "I have too much to do. I have my people to save, a destiny to fulfill. I can't have survived everything else only to die at the hands of a bunch of zealots."

It was a little ironic to have outwitted death on so many occasions to die from something so simple. Abraxas had always thought he'd die in battle, sword in one hand and shield in the other. Falling into the dragon's gaping mouth was supposed to be the end. He'd wanted to die then just as he wanted to die now.

So why was fear worming its way into his heart?

That fear simmered as the crowd gathered. They were in the middle of Cuskhe, some small square he didn't recognize without blood and smoke paintings its walls. But he saw no civilians. Just tired soldiers with eyes hungry for Divine justice.

The fear spiked as the crowd parted to let Divara's red-clad form through. She wore the full War Mage robes now. Scarlet fabric mixing with metal armor in a way that made her look like a walking legend instead of a normal woman. And, in many ways, she was and would continue to be. History would remember Divara Rimel as the fiercest mage of her time, and the one who stood at Loghain's side when he turned against his brother to call off the war. She commanded respect and loyalty to the point that the men and women who followed her lead completely turned the tides against Eldritch and he had no choice but to surrender to his own people. He could see it now in the way they watched her with bright, hopeful eyes.

Abraxas knew Divara was a good woman, and that war and bad leadership had clouded her judgement. The knowledge didn't make her hateful stare hurt any less.

She stopped just shy of the pyre, her spellbook in her hands. "Give the truth freely, and I will spare you agony. Where are the shards?"

Abraxas shook his head wearily. "What shards?"

"The ones the boy was carrying," Divara snapped. "Where did you hide them?"

Behind him, Nerezza was as stiff as steel. Divara would've searched her, searched *both* of them, for these shards. If she was asking, then she hadn't found them. And even Nerezza couldn't have hidden them from her.

"I don't have them," he said. "I never saw what the boy had, and I didn't have time to grab what he had. Please, Divara . . ."

He watched her face change from cold indifference to fury. She stiffened, fingers digging into her spellbook. When she spoke, her words were final. "Give me your True Name so I might send you to the Divines with goodwill and dignity."

"You know my name," Abraxas said softly.

"I know the name of the man you pretend to be." She flipped the book open. "His name is Abraxas Kain. He is a soldier of the Divines, chosen Champion of Haphion himself. If you were truly him, no iron could hold you. No flame would hurt you. No witch would bind your soul to obedience."

He blinked at her in surprise, and she gave him a tired smile. "I know the marks of forced servitude when I see it. Strange as that magic is, it is written into your very flesh."

Nerezza was stiff behind him, but he started straining against his irons. "Then break it! Break it and I'll prove that I'm Abraxas. Please!"

Nerezza's spell had to be the reason Haphion couldn't reach him. If Divara could break it, then he'd be free. He'd have his god back and Nerezza could burn, and he wouldn't be in pain anymore.

Divara lifted her chin. "No Champion of the Divine can be taken under such a spell, their ties to their gods doesn't allow it. Either you are not Abraxas Kain, or you are. If you are, then Haphion has turned his back on you, and so shall I."

And she did. With a flick of her wrist, she tore a page from her spellbook and tossed it to the pyre. From the scattered ashes, fire sparked. Greedy, oil-soaked tinder ignited into bright flames. Abraxas drew his legs back to the post as far as he could, feet already hot.

This was how his death started, was it? He was supposed to just accept this, after all he'd done and fought for. Through the growing smoke, he caught the eyes of the soldiers watching him. The fire reflected in their eyes made them look like revenants, the spirits of the wrongfully killed who wouldn't rest until they had their justice. He didn't know these people. Didn't recognize their faces or know their names. But he knew what they'd look like soon. Dead and corrupted by necromancers, forced to fight against their own people. When the streets of Cuskhe ran red with blood and the air was black with smoke, he knew those faces would be horrors that lived in the nightmares of those that survived.

They would live in Divara's nightmares. They lived in his own.

The heat was becoming unbearable. He felt the hair on his arms burn away as the fire crept ever higher. He couldn't keep from touching it much longer.

"Divara!" he screamed over the flames. He could just make out her straight-backed form walking away. "Get your people out of Cuskhe. You'll die. You'll all die. You need to leave. Please just listen to me!"

None did. Divara didn't even slow her march. A column of flame tore through the air near his face and he pressed against the post to stay away. His cheeks blistered from the heat. The flames licked his boots. He couldn't see Divara anymore.

Nerezza was choking behind him. The flames hadn't reached her yet, but the smoke was tightening its hold on her lungs.

"Of all the fucking arguments, you went with that?" She hacked her words and sucked in large breaths that did more harm than good.

Abraxas took short sips of air. "They deserved a warning."

None would listen, he knew that. *He* wouldn't have listened to himself. That knowledge was a pain all its own, overshadowed by the flames at his feet. He was burning. The fire had reached his feet and he was dimly aware of the cries of pain coming from his mouth. He tried to close them off, to die with some dignity, but he couldn't. Every press of his lips bottled that pain up and his only release was his voice.

He arched his back against the flames, eyes searching for the stars amongst the smoke. But his Divine justice had blotted them out. The same fire he'd used to cleanse dozens before him, a weapon from Haphion himself, he'd thought, was killing him. And the irony, the symbolism, was not lost on him.

A child made a Champion. A Champion made a monster. A monster made a hero. And now? Still too monstrous for the Divines.

Abraxas's screams turned to laughter. Manic and desperate. He hadn't run out of air yet and he planned to use it.

All he could hear was the crackling of flames. Why wasn't Nerezza screaming yet? She should be burning just like him. He reached behind him with swollen, blistered fingers. She was there. She grabbed his hand with so much force the blisters burst, and her nails dug into his flesh. Oh, she was in pain. But just like Evren, she reveled in it.

Something sharp cut through the smoke and hit the post between their arms with a jarring thud. The chains went slack, the shackles heavy against his peeling wrists. Abraxas slumped dangerously forward, fire singing his long hair as it climbed ever upward. Nerezza's hand left his and he felt more than heard her say, "You don't want to die, Abraxas. Fucking fight!"

An order came with no magic pain to enforce it. Through darkening eyes, he turned back to see Nerezza slip free of her chains and push her arms out.

The orange of the fire turned a bloody red instantly and swept away from their pile as if a great gust of wind had pushed it away. He heard the soldiers screaming as the fire, now a deadly ring encircling the pyre, lashed out at them. As he fell to his hands and knees, he saw the glint of a heavy axe buried in the pole where their chains had been sliced.

The blackened wood splintered and burned his palms. His hands, oh his *hands*. Blackened and peeling and sloughing off flesh as he watched. Smoke still crawled up and into his nose.

The flames were gone but his skin screamed and his body shook with every quake of pain.

His throat was bloody from his screams. He felt the drops slide down, felt them stir when he once again screamed as hands jerked him up by his armpits. Didn't they know his skin was splitting under their touch? Didn't they know that every movement made life even more unbearable as the ghosts of flames ripped through his body?

They hauled him roughly to his feet despite his protests. Abraxas's face was dangerously close to Nerezza's flames.

"Careful with him." He heard her snap. "I need him alive."

"He's already dying." The Vernesian accent sent a thrill of fear down his spine. He struggled to get away, but those arms encircled his torso and slammed him against a burly chest. He bit back the cry, or laugh, of pain.

"You want what I have? What I took from that boy?" Nerezza questioned, and he heard only the slightest tremor of pain in her own voice. "Then you keep him alive and get us both out of here."

A snarl rumbled in the chest holding Abraxas, but they must've agreed because he heard orders being barked and feet thudding on the wood. The sound of weapons clashed through the fire as well, and snaps of cold arcane energy broke through the heat.

"We move before *khet ameksu* gets to us," Abraxas's handler said. "Quickly! Do not fight us, mage."

Whatever that meant, Abraxas never found out. Something dark was draped over his head and the fire disappeared. The whole city did. But he heard it as he was dragged down from the pyre. He heard the screams of the dying and the orders over the din of battle.

Cuskhe showed its hand early and, as Abraxas was dragged away from his death pyre, he wondered how much of history he was changing by refusing to die.

9

Abraxas

The boy Abraxas dreamt of was in pain. He was on his hands and knees, clutching his ribs and gasping for breath in the middle of a tranquil training yard. The trees were a soft shade of red, not like blood but like that of the setting sun. The breeze was cool against the boy's sweaty skin. He was older now, more a teenager than a child.

"Get up," said the man before him.

A warrior through and through, even with just a wooden sword in his hand. An aura of power radiated from him, barely controlled. He kicked the boy's fallen training sword to him.

"Up."

The boy shook his head, pushing up to sit back on his legs. He still held his ribs and winced with every move. When he looked at the warrior, he held a mixture of intense respect and fear in his eyes.

"I can't."

The warrior scowled. "I'm training you, so you can."

The boy shook his head again. "I don't want to fight."

"Not everyone has that choice. You don't."

The boy pushed himself to his feet, rounding the shoulders he was still growing into. But he didn't pick up the sword. "I can heal, master. I'm better at that."

"We have healers. We need warriors."

"But I . . ." The boy trailed off and looked at his hands. Bruised and shaking from long hours training and being hit too many times. They were soft, slender fingers normally clasped in prayer or for changing bandages. These fingers eased pain and healed wounds. They were not the hands of a fighter. He curled them into fists and it looked wrong.

"I'm not a fighter, master," the boy said carefully, head bowed to his fists. "I don't want to be. I want to heal, not hurt."

Something in the warrior's grizzled face changed. Nothing softened because there was nothing about him that could be soft, but he understood the boy's reluctance better than one might expect. He lowered his training sword and picked up the fallen one. As he strode towards him, the boy shrank back a little with his fists raised in defense.

The warrior stopped and cocked his head. Then he spoke and the timbre of his voice echoed the experience of a hundred battles.

"No one wants to hurt, boy. No one good, anyway. You do not train to hurt, you train to serve, to protect."

"A sword cuts," the boy protested.

"Just as well as a knife cuts away infection," the warrior agreed. He held the training sword out, hilt angled towards the boy. "There are infections in Eith that you can only heal by cutting out the root of the problem. You hurt, you bleed, you clean, and then you heal. Eith needs more from you than just a gentle hand to hold. Haphion chose you to carry out his will, and those powers you love so much are meant to aid you on your journeys. You don't want to fight? Good. That means you'll think before you draw your blade. But you *will* draw your blade, Abraxas. And you will learn how to use it."

The boy lowered his fists. His eyes flitted to the wooden handle of the training sword. There wasn't really a choice to be made because he couldn't walk away now any more than he could before. He'd been chosen as a baby and while there was honor in that, there was no choice. There was no family outside of the Divines and the priests that raised him. There was only ever his duty and his will to serve.

The boy grabbed the hilt of the sword.

ABRAXAS WOKE up in a state between agony and the unnerving absence of it. There were spots of him that were in so much blazing pain that he knew the skin there had sloughed off long ago, leaving behind nothing but bared flesh bubbling and black. Other parts, like his legs, he couldn't feel at all, and that worried him more.

His fingers shook with tremors he couldn't control. He was lying on a cot and couldn't move if he wanted to. The slightest twitch of his fingers made him nauseous. The smell of cooked flesh and burnt hair lingered over him like a fog. It took everything he had not to gag, knowing he was smelling himself.

He peeled his eyes open slowly and the thin skin of his eyelids cracked and swelled with the movement. He peered through narrow slits, unable to push his body further. Ruins. Part stone, part tent. The brightly colored fabric cast red and orange light across the small room. He couldn't see more without moving his head, but he heard labored breathing beside him. He wasn't alone.

He pried his lips apart, trying not to grimace. Even the slightest twitch of his cheeks made his face burn.

"Nerezza?" His voice came out as a croak. The way the

word ripped through his throat, he felt like the flames snuck down there and burned it, too.

"I'm here."

She didn't sound much better than him. Two words and he heard her whimpering just a few feet away from him.

"How bad?" he managed to ask.

"I can't tell."

"How do you feel?"

"Like every inch of my skin is being ripped apart," she sobbed. Prolonged pain was destroying her. She drew no strength from it.

"That's good," he reassured. "Means the fire didn't damage your nerves."

"Feels like the hells itself."

"Feels like being alive." But he had to agree with her. He wanted nothing more than to slip back into unconsciousness so he wouldn't have to feel this way for a little while. He didn't even remember losing consciousness if he was being honest with himself. He barely remembered anything beyond the pyre.

"And you?" Nerezza asked. "How do you feel?"

"Flame eclipses your spell if that's what you're wondering."

An awkward silence descended on them. Did Abraxas imagine the shame rolling off her in waves? Or was his mind addled by how much smoke he inhaled? After a while he couldn't stand it anymore.

"I can't feel my feet," he said. "Part of my legs too. Left one is worse."

"Healing will help?"

Healing magic would, absolutely, but he had no command of that anymore. Healing potions would as well but that would take more time and might not fix everything. And then there was the problem with their hosts . . .

"Rebels won't have much in the way of potions," he told

her, staring up at the patterns on the ceiling. "Etherak either buys up all the trade in it or lets faulty ones through enemy lines. Whatever good potions they're likely to have they won't waste on us."

"Fuck."

Fuck indeed.

"Something to keep in mind next time you ally with a rebel faction," he rasped. Then, after a thoughtful pause, "How did you do that? Divara had you watched."

Nerezza snorted but ended up hissing through her teeth at the sudden movement. "I was watched. But before we were taken, I grabbed what that boy had."

Abraxas closed his eyes. "They would've searched you."

"They did."

"Do I want to know how you hid it?"

"No."

"Carry on then."

Nerezza took a few shallow breaths. "Their army has spies, that was a given. I betted on the hope that they were watching us, flashed what I had a few times, and waited. Obviously, it's important. I don't have it anymore."

"Did you see what it was?"

"Pieces of obsidian. Parts of a larger whole. Glyphs I couldn't read."

Abraxas sighed. "They have what they want. Likely they'll leave us to die here."

A few more minutes on the pyre should've done the trick if they'd just left him. Now he considered putting up a fight to see if they'd put him out of his misery. Dying like this would be slow and pitiful. Of course, there were few good ways to die. Considering how many times he'd brushed shoulders with death at this point Abraxas was getting used to the idea of just being miserable until his body shut down.

But Nerezza was right. No matter how much he thought about it and wished for it, Abraxas didn't want to die. He wanted to see his friends again. To endure Sorin's hour long ramblings and Evren's awful cooking for just another minute in their presence. He'd spar with Gyda again and tell her how proud he was that she finally admitted her feelings to Evren. He'd sit with Arke while the goblin added more spells to his book and let the comfortable silence wash over both of them.

He wanted to say goodbye properly, but even more he longed to say hello. And that meant living.

"What's your destiny?" he asked, still watching the ceiling.

Nerezza's breathing hitched before she spoke. "What do you mean?"

"On the pyre, you said you had a destiny you wouldn't be kept from. Is it becoming a god?"

Very slowly, as if she was prying every word from her lips. "I was raised to save Serevadia. Both Mora and the cities. My mother said it was up to me where my people's futures went."

Abraxas winced at the memory of Ainthe, beautiful and terrifying, caring matron and brutal leader.

"I met your mother," he said.

"You did?" She tried to hide the hope in her voice but failed. Abraxas would've smiled if it didn't hurt so damn much.

"Yes. She saved us and then dug into our minds to see if we were responsible for taking you. She led the Mora in an attack that nearly killed us later, and she only stopped because of Alkimos."

"Alkimos," she breathed. "Oh, he's alive. I'd heard but . . . . I didn't want to hope."

"He's alive." Abraxas thought back to Evren's connection to the giant worm and shuddered. "As is your mother, the last we saw her. She had another daughter and chose to protect her rather than follow us."

"Oh."

Abraxas didn't want the pity that swelled up in his chest for her. The way her voice lost its strength and trailed off into nothing broke something inside him though. What daughter wouldn't have been upset at her mother moving on and having another daughter? Maybe Ainthe intended to replace her, maybe she didn't. Abraxas didn't care to know. But he knew which one Nerezza thought as she stewed in silence.

"Tell me of your destiny."

"Why?" She held none of her normal venom. She just sounded tired.

"I deserve to know what I'm walking into, don't I?"

She hummed in reply and for a while Abraxas thought she would ignore him just because she could. But then he heard her take a deeper breath, and while it trailed off into a whimper, it ended in a story.

"The Mora are dying because they believe in something that doesn't exist anymore. The Serevadians in their cities have grown to the point where the only way forward is up. Out. My mother believed that I could bring my people out of hiding and into the sunlight for the first time since the Shadow Dancer hid us away. We've waited long enough, after all. The surface is just as much ours as it is yours. I don't know exactly what I was supposed to be. General, politician, priestess, empress. Whatever would unite the clans and cities together. On the surface I would've been ambassador or protector, whatever my people needed to live peacefully. I was meant to lead them into the light and, growing up, I thought that meant peace and unity with the surface.

"But, after those dwarves took me and . . . ." she cleared her throat and briskly moved away from the subject. "I saw the surface was worse than below. Divided and infected with hate. Absent gods left Eith to fend for itself, and the world was tearing itself apart to survive. I thought that uniting the surface first, fixing it, would be my first step. But there's too much for one mortal to do. Too much pain and too many differing opinions. Even if I was powerful enough, no one would listen."

Abraxas stewed on that for a while, thinking about how Evren's own words had mirrored the same tone and points so many times. It was so easy to see Eith as a lost cause, this world that was so beautiful and chaotic that there was little peace for those that lived there. But somehow Evren kept fighting. So had he, and Nerezza, too, despite it all.

"Is that why you want to become a god?" Even as he said it, he hated it. It was heretical to even think that was possible. The gods were beyond them in so many ways. In power, in intelligence and wisdom. The gods were nothing like Abraxas and Nerezza, and to attempt to be one of them was like an ant pretending to be human.

"Gail gave me the idea," she said, delicately enough that the words felt like smoke in the air. "He wasn't a god, he was just a child. But the power he commanded—"

"That wasn't Divine," Abraxas snapped.

"It was enough, wasn't it? And he wasn't even trying. If I had the right power, then I could lead my people. As a goddess, I could protect them. I could help the surface, too. It needs a goddess."

"It has several."

"They're gone, Abraxas, or will be. Even now, when they're present, everything is broken."

"And you think you could do better?" The revulsion shuddering through his body awakened every pain he'd been ignoring during their conversation. He wanted to scream, both from frustration and being so gods damned hurt all the time. He was so tired of hurting, and he was tired of people thinking they could be better than the Divines.

"Maybe I could," Nerezza said. "Maybe I am a beacon for my people, and all will be well. Or maybe my destiny is to be just enough that I can get them out and then destroy myself.

You think Divinity is beyond our reach, and yet you've touched it yourself."

"That dagger was powerful but not Divine."

"It belonged to a god. It was a piece of him."

"Not my god," he said hotly. "Why did you want it anyway? What could controlling time do for you?"

"What couldn't it do? Shortsighted fool," she murmured. Then she spoke louder, as if he was a particularly dim student who couldn't grasp the lesson. "The dagger belonged to an Elder, a god of the elves. Another artifact like it was lost to my people. If I could find the sword, Serevadia would fall to my feet and follow my every word. The dagger would've shown me where it disappeared, and where to find it."

"Did you have to destroy Orenlion in order to get it?"

"Did you have to destroy Vernes to get what you wanted?"

"I didn't *want* anything! I just . . ." What little strength he had ebbed away. He just, what? Followed orders? He delighted in those orders, once. He didn't need them, they were simply a formality. So what? Why did Abraxas fight when the result was a soul inside him that was so wrecked he could barely stand himself? Why did he commit so much horror that the stain of it would never leave him, even when he passed on from this world to the next?

He didn't know. He remained silent.

After a while, Nerezza spoke again and sounded as tired as he felt. "I'm going to destroy myself going down this path, I know it. I knew it the moment I turned my back on Sahar in the White Cairn. For what it's worth, I didn't mean for Orenlion to get hurt. It was the easiest way to get the dagger without risking myself."

"People died, *died* Nerezza. You started a war—"

"That was already being fought—"

"—and you brought a dragon back from the dead!"

"All I wanted was the dagger and I couldn't get it on my own!" The shouting nearly did her in. Abraxas could hear her wheezing gasps as she tried to find her voice. "Besides, I made sure that all the ugly parts came to light. Orenlion will be better off because of what I did."

"Because of what Evren did," he corrected. "Because of what Sol, and Gyda, and Sorin, and Arke did. Not to mention the countless Khama and Hisrachi who bled because of you. They're heroes, not you."

She didn't miss a beat. "I was never a hero. Neither was Drystan or Vox or Sahar. But Eith doesn't need a hero to bandage it together again; it needs someone who's willing to break it and remold it into something better."

She believed every word she said, and it made him want to scream. Couldn't she see how that line of thinking would destroy the world instead of rebuild it? How could someone so intelligent be so blind?

"The woman who saved my life in Direwall, who killed Mortova, wouldn't think like this," he said, one last desperate plea for her to wake up. "Those souls changed you. Keres's and Gail's. It's not your fault that they poisoned your mind, but you need to be better. I know you are."

"Am I? I don't feel changed at all."

"You have changed, I can see it."

"Good," she said after a minute of contemplation. "I was weak before. I'll be strong enough now to do what needs to be done."

Abraxas wanted to fight her. He wanted to grab her by her shoulders and shake some sense into her. Burned or not, he really couldn't, but he wanted her to understand how wrong she was.

A little girl shouldn't be saddled with the legacy of her people any more than a little boy should be forced to be a god's killer.

10

Evren

It had been an achingly long time since Evren had woken up to the oppressive darkness of being under the earth, and the smell hit her first. The dampness of the rock, the cloying scent of minerals and crushed earth. When she opened her eyes and saw nothing at all, she couldn't help the sudden spike of adrenaline that washed over her.

It was as if she'd never left the Yawning Deep at all and she wasn't prepared for how much that scared her.

She jolted up, hissing as her body pulsed in pain. She tested her body with gentle fingers pressing against her flesh. No broken ribs, thankfully. She'd landed on her left side, hard. She could already feel the blood rushing up to her skin and forming bruises that would take weeks to fade. But no broken bones. Only a minor cut on her forehead that stung fiercely any time she moved her eyebrow. She'd gotten out of that fall lucky.

But how?

Her rapid breaths bounced off walls she couldn't see but felt were close. The memories of Rheinwall came flooding back. The parade, the dance in the square, Sol's horror, and Mal's face in the crowd. The ground cracking and disappearing beneath their feet . . .

"What the fuck?" Evren hissed to herself.

"Stole the words outta my mouth, kid."

Evren screamed, she couldn't help it, when Arke's voice barked right by her side. His glowing eyes squinted at her as she tried to calm her galloping heart and she heard a low scraping sound before she realized he was laughing.

"Oh, fuck you." She scooted away from him, although it was mostly for show. She couldn't be more relieved to not be alone.

"How you can hear a deer fart from a mile away and not hear me right next to you is astoundin'."

"It's been a day," she said. "We fell from . . . whatever that was. What was it?"

She heard him shrug. "Dunno. Why would I?"

"I thought it could be magic. I felt some when I fell."

"That'd be me keepin' you from dyin' when you fell." A breeze smelling of parchment and ink wafted mere inches from her face as he waved his spellbook in the air. "Got pulled in too, so I saved our asses. Still a hard fall though, didn't quite get it off like I used to."

Evren rubbed her aching hip. "No, it's fine. Is Sol here? Can you see?"

"Ain't no one here but us."

"And where is here?"

"You can't—? Oh, yeah, you can't see. Hold on."

The sound of flipping pages and tearing parchment echoed in Evren's ears. She didn't jump when it was torn from its bindings or when the sharp feeling of magic washed over her skin, but she did instinctively shy away from the ball of flame Arke summoned far too close for comfort.

Ash fell from his claws as he flicked the ball higher, illuminating the hole they'd fallen into. It was small, barely five feet from one side to another. Evren's lungs constricted at the sight. Looking up wasn't much better. The rocks that made up the ceiling had only stopped because of the pile up of larger ones that braced them, and it made Evren queasy to think how close they'd come to being flattened to pulp.

Arke peered up, his fire show catching the sheen of water and neat stones peeking through the broken earth.

"We fell below the sewers," he said.

"Shit," Evren breathed. "How bad is that?"

"Bad. Means it'll take a while for them to dig us out, and we're likely not the only ones needin' rescuin'."

"The whole square went down. Everyone in there . . ." Her mouth went dry, remembering Sorin with the bards in the middle and Gyda dancing in the crowd. Surely they'd gotten out. Surely they felt the shaking like Sol had and were fine on the surface.

"We were on the edge of the square and still got hit," Evren continued. "We have no idea how big this is."

The fact that no one might be able to rescue them went unsaid. Arke shook his head, his white whisps of hair curling when they got too close to the fire.

"Rheinwall is a big city, so it won't be all of it. And it's packed full of people like us today."

"Who were all in the square," she pressed. "At least most of them were. Do you think this was deliberate? Someone targeting a bunch of adventurers to take them all out?"

"Stupid way to do it."

"It's got to be Mal, right? I mean, what are the odds of this happening when he shows up?"

"I wanna agree with you, but I honestly don't think he's got the balls to pull somethin' like this off." Arke stood up, ears not touching the ceiling. Evren would have to crouch if she did the same. "Come on, we gotta save ourselves."

Evren blinked at him. "Um, Arke, I love the enthusiasm, but where exactly do you expect us to go?"

Arke stared at her with those unblinking yellow eyes long enough for Evren's face to start itching. She scrubbed her bitten nails along her cheeks, scowling.

"What? Why are you looking at me like I've grown horns?"

"Because I don't remember you bein' so thick. You sure Gyda didn't take half your brain in that ritual?"

"*Arke*."

He took her wrist roughly and pressed it next to the wall adjacent to her. Her fingers met a whisper of air. Warm, stale, but moving. Her eyes widened.

"Oh." She turned and looked, seeing the crack her fingers were hovering over, a few inches thick and as tall as their room. "How are you getting that open?"

"With you."

Before she knew it, her breeze-tingled fingers had a piece of spell paper shoved into their grasp. Arcane glyphs, sharp with ink as black as the shadows stared back at her expectantly and Evren's good mood curdled instantly in her stomach. She put the paper down, hating the confusion in Arke's eyes.

"Arke, I can't."

"Trollshit. I know you can. I made it for you."

Her cheeks burned and she struggled to keep eye contact and not stare down at her hands. "The problem is Gyda. When I use it, it hurts her. The last time was an accident and it brought her to her knees. That was just me getting hurt during training and unconsciously taking that power. This," she waved the paper, "is something else. We don't know what a spell like this will do to her, when before full spells exhausted me to the point of near death. I can't do this without her consent and, even then, I wouldn't want to."

Evren wasn't used to having Arke at eye level. He had an intensity to his gaze that was easily missed when she towered over him, and now she couldn't escape it. Was he angry because he spent all that time making these new spells for her only to be told she wouldn't even try? Did he want to tear his hair out because she was their way out and she was hesitating now when half a year ago she wouldn't have cared?

It was easy to risk her own life when it was just her to worry about. Back then, Blood magic was unknown and terrifying but no more than an untamed wilderness. But now Evren had Gyda in more ways than one. Not only had she promised herself and the Wandering Sols to cut back on the self-sacrificing bullshit, but her actions directly affected Gyda. Sharing a heart, both metaphorically and literally, changed everything.

"I get it," Arke finally said.

"You do?"

He nodded. "Yeah, and I'm proud of you. Really am. But we got a problem my magic can't fix, and a terrifyin' possibility waitin' for us above. We can't stay down here and hope someone finds us, we gotta go now. I swear that spell will be the last, and if anythin' bad happens, it's on me."

Evren shook her head. "Arke, no—"

He raised a claw in the air, cutting her off. "I need you to get us outta here. Gyda needs you, they all do. And the only way out is that." He turned his claw down to the paper.

Evren wrinkled the edges as she clutched it with her shaking fist. He was right, and his calm, cool tone scared her. Worse were the images in her head of Sorin dead, Sol frantically digging through the rocks to get them back, Gyda hurt and suffocating. Because she wasn't dead, Evren *knew* that in her soul. If Gyda died she would feel it, she was certain. But that didn't help her current decision.

Arke's ears twitched as she stared between him and the paper, a sign he was growing impatient but didn't want her to know. "She'll forgive you. She'd want you to."

"I know," Evren said weakly. Because she did know and that was all she could hold on to. She pressed her hand against her scarred chest, feeling the heartbeat underneath. Strong, a little faster than normal, but still beating. She tapped out the syllables of *I'm sorry* in time with the beats.

One, two, three.

Then she pulled out her dagger. The wyvern winked at her in Arke's firelight and she found she couldn't take her eyes away from it as she dug the point of it into the back of her hand.

"What does the spell do?" Evren asked through gritted teeth as her blood welled up through her skin and onto the blade.

"Moves earth. Tryin' to experiment, right? A wizard is only as good as his ability to grow. I was gonna have you test it on loose soil or gravel first since earth magic ain't my thing. But this'll have to do."

She sheathed the dagger. "It'll work, right?" The last thing she wanted was needless pain for Gyda if the spell was faulty.

Arke stared at her. "Don't trust me?"

She sighed. She trusted Arke with her life, and Gyda's. "I do. I'm sorry."

"It's on you then."

In the back of her mind Evren made a note of how much she hated that. Then she shoved it deep in the corners where she'd forget about it, picked up the paper, and let her blood seep into it.

The scarlet of her blood spread like spidery vines, clawing and not content until they hit ink. She felt her veins hum when it did, that unused and neglected magic singing in her body as blood was pulled away from the bruises and into the spell.

Evren was barely aware of the blood-soaked flakes of ash falling from her hand. All she could think, all she could feel, was that rush of strength flooding her. It had been necessary before, when she didn't have a heart and it was all she had to feel normal and survive battles. But now she had both blood and a heart.

And she felt incredible. Powerful. Untouchable.

Evren forced herself to focus on where the spell was tugging her. The glyphs and runes were seared into her eyes as if she'd stared at them for hours, and she watched them float and rest on either side of the crack in the wall.

Her fingers curled in the air, and she met resistance as if she was digging through the stone itself. Sweat trickled down her back, but for all that resistance that pure rock put up, she smiled because it was *nothing* compared to her potential.

Inch by inch, she pulled her hands apart and the crack widened. Dust and pebbles rained from above. Arke looked up as their patchwork ceiling began to shift. Evren gritted her teeth until she tasted copper, pulled until the breeze engulfed her, and then let the spell fall.

Her hands fell at her side, cut throbbing as she sucked in deep breaths. Her arms were shaking as if she'd tried to lift a boulder, and already she could feel that wonderful power fading back into her veins and waiting to be reignited. The wave of exhaustion as black as night didn't come. She'd become so used to it that she found herself holding her breath waiting for it.

When nothing happened, when the ceiling didn't come crashing down on them and Arke had wrapped her hand up, she finally spoke.

"I can see why Nerezza did what she did now, partly," she said. "It really feels like you have the world at your fingertips until it fades away."

~

THE TUNNEL EVREN had opened was barely large enough to crawl through. She found herself on her hands and knees following Arke as he tottered along with only a ducked head and his little ball of fire to keep him company. Her palms were a torn-up mess, her neck ached as if someone had tied invisible strings around her muscles and kept tightening them by the minute, and every time her knee landed on a sharp stone she had to bite down a curse.

"Not that I'm not glad we found a way out, but where is this even going?" Evren panted. "How many tunnels can we fit through before we dead end?"

"A lot."

She rolled her eyes and flicked away another stone from her path. "You're really confident of that. What secrets are you keeping?"

She laughed a little at her joke, mostly to keep herself occupied and distracted. She didn't have to worry about wasted air so long as Arke felt comfortable enough to keep his fire up. Still, she wasn't so withdrawn that she didn't notice him stiffening at her words.

Evren stopped, sitting back on her legs to give her hands some time to rest. She brushed off the pebbles and dirt embedded in her skin, and stared at his stiff back until he stopped and looked back at her.

"We've been going for hours," she said. "And you've given me nothing but two syllable answers since I opened that tunnel. What's wrong?"

"Nothin'."

"Aren't we past this?" she asked. "We've been through enough together, tell me what's wrong."

"It ain't that simple." His eyes flicked down the way they were heading, the corners wrinkling the longer he squinted. "But . . . fine. These are goblin tunnels. There's a kinship nearby. We got into their territory 'bout thirty minutes ago."

"How can you tell?"

"Remember that slimy shit you put your hand in?"

She shuddered. "Yeah?"

"It, uh, kinda marks a territory."

Evren rubbed her hand furiously on her pants and tried to

grin through the thoughts of *what* was used to mark the territory.

"Okay, so goblins! That can't be bad right?"

He scowled at her. "Don't do that."

"Do what?"

"Act like you forget what we're like."

"I don't know what you're talking about." She shrugged. "All I know about goblins is that I have the very brightest of them at my side and nothing can go wrong so long as we're together."

"Stop. You don't know that."

"Don't I?" She tried for a reassuring smile. "Arke, I've got your back. You've got nothing to worry about."

It was only then that she saw how droopy his ears were and how tired he looked. The fire at his shoulder cast long shadows that made him look sadder and more animalistic at the same time. But every slow blink was him, through and through.

"You never asked why I left," he said. "Why?"

"You never asked why I left Orenlion."

"Kinda wish I did."

"Missing a heart?" she asked, cocking her head to the side. "Got an undead army after you? Prick of an ex hunting you down?"

"No, no, and no."

"Are you in danger if we keep going?"

His face twisted into a grimace. "Not likely, but we can't really go back—"

"We can't, because we have to get to our people first. Who knows what's happening up there while we're stuck down here. Like you told me, there's only one way out. That doesn't change no matter what. I've got you."

"I ran away," he blurted out. "From a lot. My kinship . . . I ran away for a reason, and they'll hate me."

"What was the reason?" She couldn't help but ask.

He snorted a laugh. "Not so different from you. I didn't want the life they gave me, so I made my own." He turned back to her, yellow eyes serious. "Mine are down that tunnel. Knew it the moment we stepped into this city, and I know it now. But you faced Orenlion. Gyda faced Gail. Sol faced Heliodar. I can do this."

He wasn't talking to convince himself, she realized. He was convincing her. She dropped the worried hand she hadn't realized she'd been extending and tucked it under her arm. Arke wasn't scared to go back and face his kinship, he simply had no want to. Only now that there was a need, he was pushing past that for their friends.

"I know you can," she said. "Lead the way."

Without another word or hesitation, Arke continued his march and Evren followed without complaint. She bore the grit splintering in her palms quietly, remembering that she'd been through far worse, and kept her eyes on Arke.

Regardless of what he said, she was worried about him. She didn't care about what he'd run from or that he'd kept it from her, because, hells, they'd all kept their pasts secrets. None of them had planned to meet each other, let alone stick together, but when they did it was the beginning of something new. A life where they could leave behind what had hurt them the most.

As they crawled closer to Arke's old home, Evren thought that fate was a bitch to keep on dragging them back into the mud they'd left behind.

Evren counted the minutes until they gathered into an hour, mentally tied them off and then started another. She had two hours tucked away in her head and another one started when she saw light.

She'd gotten so used to the orange glow of Arke's flame that, when the tunnel turned purple, she thought there was something wrong with her eyes. But as they rounded a corner, the tunnel blissfully turning smoother, the source of the light came into view. A little wooden pyramid, stuffed to the brim with what looked like glowing purple worms, hung from its spot nailed to the wall. Arke stopped next to it, sighing deeply.

"Not far now," he said, and kept moving.

Arke was never one to exaggerate, so when 'not far now' meant the next couple of feet, another corner, and then they were mere steps from the goblin settlement, Evren shouldn't have been shocked. What did shock her was the settlement itself because it was far from the tents and campfires she expected. It was a whole damn city.

Where the tunnel ended, a generous sized cavern began. It wasn't massive, like the one that held Andovine or the many that made up Dirn-Darahl, but it was breathtaking. The same wooden pyramid lanterns hung from the ceiling in various sizes, casting a soothing lavender glow over the whole cavern. Stone buildings worn with time but still etched with painstaking detail rose from the ground. Rounded roofs, walls, and pillars swimming with so much detail that they seemed to move in the flickering light. Whole trees grew all around, white branches looking like bone and leaves so plump and green they looked fake. And they were everywhere. Growing out of the buildings, in little garden spaces, shading walkways, holding more lanterns. Where they weren't, flowers and other foliage was. There was even grass.

Evren remembered Viggo's garden of bioluminescent plants, but those had looked so foreign and strange. These plants looked like any other. Lusher, greener, and far more vibrant, but normal.

"Arke, how . . ." she trailed off, unable to keep her jaw from falling open.

"There's a lot about Goblinkin that you don't know," he said. "Ain't your fault though."

"Where is everyone?"

Evren had only seen Arke blush a couple of times, and

that was because of Neri. So seeing the green in his face deepen as he flicked away his ball of fire both surprised and intrigued Evren.

"Eh, it's that time of year again. Most are gonna be in that big building there." He pointed to the one that had the biggest roof, where flowering vines covered most of the walls. "We should be safe to go in."

"Safe?"

Arke didn't answer. He tucked his spellbook securely under his arm and set off into the city. Evren had no choice but to follow, stretching her aching back as she was finally able to stand up. Her feet had no problem taking over for her knees and keeping up with Arke's brisk pace. And no matter how fast he tried to go, nothing could've kept her from the sheer strangeness and beauty of the goblin city.

The city was built for creatures half her size, but the buildings were still large enough to make her feel like she was walking through a normal sized city. Sure, the ceilings and doorways where shorter, but the sheer number of stories the buildings had more than made up for it. Little bells hung from every doorway, tinkling as she passed them. Fallen petals still far from wilting marked the pathways instead of roads. With every few feet, she felt more in awe of the quiet city. She'd never seen architecture like it, with carvings on every available surface.

She brushed her fingers along one wall, and the smell of fresh grass hit her as she did. "What are these? Histories? Stories?"

"Our language," he said. "We can speak Core, but writin' it is hard. We got our own, and we use pictures and scents to help. That one you touched tells you what the building is for."

"What is it?" she asked.

"Fermentation buildin'."

"Oh . . ." She shook her head and hurried after him. "Doesn't smell like it."

"Our brews are different."

As they walked, Evren caught signs of other goblins. They were all inside. Some watched her through the windows, saucer sized eyes wide with curiosity. Other times she just caught a whisper of movement behind her, or a glimpse of a pointed ear around the corner. Regardless of the appearance, the city was far from empty.

"Why isn't anyone coming out?"

"You're you and I'm me." He looked at a house as the curtain acting as a door whispered to a close. "They don't wanna deal with us. And they can't technically. They're all too young or too old to be out right now."

Evren drew her face into a confused frown. "Why? What's—"

A ripple of magic rushed over the city. Soft as a breeze but as powerful as a wave, Evren was knocked back a step by the sheer potency of the magic. Her head reeled, feeling light. Everything was a little fuzzy. Pleasantly so, like she'd drank a couple glasses of wine and was able to relax for the first time in several days. She longed for Gyda's arms around her because that would just make this feeling better. The warmth of her touch against Evren's bare skin, those steely muscles holding her close, those lips on her . . .

"What the fuck was that?" Evren asked, shaking the thought of Gyda from her mind. She tried to keep her voice even, as if she hadn't been imagining something that intimate out of the blue.

But Arke eyed her knowingly. "Like I said, that time of the year."

He started walking to the vine-covered building where the wave originated, and Evren struggled to keep up.

"What does that even mean?"

They reached the steps of the building, and Evren coughed at the thick smell of woodsy smoke and sweet grass in the air. That same magic was hovering over the building, not dissipating the way it had before. Evren struggled to keep her head clear.

Arke took the steps up, not looking like the magic bothered him at all. A wide doorway with no coverings greeted them, and another set of stairs that led right into the sunken room that appeared to be the entirety of the building.

The floor was carpeted with soft grass and wildflowers. Smoke hung in the air, tinted purple by the large, wooden chandelier dangling from above. There was a dais on the far end, and an altar made entirely out of living plants that sprouted, grew, and died right before her eyes. The whole building was just one big room, but holding almost a city's worth of goblins still had it full to the bursting, especially with the compromising and undressed nature they were in.

Evren turned to face the wall quickly, cheeks burning along with her ears as Arke cackled.

"Told ya."

"You didn't tell me shit!" she hissed.

Before they could argue further, Evren caught sight of one goblin moving up next to the altar. He was as nude as they day he was born, Evren assumed so anyway, and carrying a pitcher full of liquid so sweet she could smell it across the room. His white hair was done up in many braids, all decorated with various beads and ribbons, and when he saw Arke his face split into a toothy grin. He flung his arms out, sweet liquid showering him, the altar, and the pile of naked goblins at his feet.

"Brotha!" he bellowed.

Evren turned to Arke. "Brother, huh?"

"Fuck off."

"Should we go?"

"Nah, let him have this."

Arke's brother tossed the pitcher on the altar and started wading through the bodies to him. He didn't have to fight. Soon, every goblin was getting up to look at Arke and making way for his brother. Some still held smoking pipes, others cups full of that drink which they shared with their partners. There were so many, all with brightly colored hair of reds, pinks, blues, and orange. Evren had never seen so much color and skin all in one place.

She stepped to the side as Arke's brother made it up the steps to him and swept him up in a bone-crushing hug. Evren heard the breath wheeze out of his lungs as he was rocked back and forth by his larger sibling.

When he was put back on his feet, his brother held his shoulders and couldn't stop grinning. "I knew you'd be back, yeah? Can't stay away from destiny! Don't worry, I've kept the seat warm for you."

Arke's face fell, and he tried to back away. "Tolk, it's fine. I'm not here to—"

"Nonsense!" Tolk grabbed his hand. "We've all missed you."

Tolk spun around and lifted Arke's limp arm into the air triumphantly. "Our King has returned!"

The building erupted into cheers. Glasses were clanked together, blankets thrown up in the air. A few even started dancing.

Evren spared a glance at Arke and saw nothing but misery in his eyes.

11

Evren

It was amazing how quickly the whole goblin city changed at Arke's arrival. One minute they were all naked, high, and mostly drunk and the next they were pulling off a rather large feast where everyone was, thankfully, fully clothed.

Arke's brother, Tolk, had left the two of them alone with the masses to go fetch something he called important. Evren couldn't tell how long he'd been gone but every minute that passed the crowd of goblins got rowdier.

None of them paid much attention to Evren. Despite being the tallest person in any room, all eyes were constantly on Arke, which was rather unnerving because of the sheer size of goblin eyes. Evren was squirming as she sat cross legged on the ground next to Arke, the low table in front of her filled with an assortment of foods. Some looked rather normal, like meat pies and various kinds of veggies. Other times she went for what looked like a normal roll of bread and found it stuffed to the brim with fish, scales and all. Goblin cuisine was interesting to say the least.

Evren picked the corn kernels out of her strawberry muffin as she gave Arke a sideways glance. He was sitting at what she assumed was the head of the table, although there were many tables strewn about the field they sat in, and he was the only one sitting still. The rest of the goblins were drinking and eating merrily, hopping from table to table with armloads of food and drink to share with the next goblin they saw. Arke hadn't touched his food at all. He just sat staring at it all unblinking.

"Uh, Arke," she whispered. "Do you want to talk about it?"

"Nah."

She nodded, flicking a kernel off the table. "Right, I understand. It's just we are kind of in the middle of a celebration feast in your honor and this is a far cry from what I expected."

He shot her a withering look. "What did you expect?"

"Not this!" she hissed. "You're a King?"

"It ain't as good as it sounds."

She nodded to the group of younger goblins trying to get their bright hair to stick straight up like his. "Should you tell them that?"

He scowled and turned so they weren't in his sight. "Look, this is a shock to me, too."

"Yeah? When's the fitting for the coronation robes?"

"I'm gonna throttle you."

TShe frowned. "Arke, were you embarrassed to tell us?"

"No!" He paused and started tugging at his hair. "A little. But I wasn't playin' when I said I thought they'd be angry. I really thought they'd hate me."

"Looks like the opposite," Evren said. "They couldn't be happier that you're back."

"But I ain't. I don't wanna be King."

Under different circumstances the whole situation might've been funny, with the gleeful celebration setting such a fun tone and the hilarity of ruling over people who seemed to revel in chaos. But she couldn't forget the chaos they left on the surface, and Arke's whole demeanor was not one of jokes. He was stiff and jerky in his movements, all fiddling claws and bouncing knees. Evren had an inkling of what he was feeling.

"I understand," she said so low that only his large ears could pick it up. "How do you want to do this?"

His eyes flickered back to the crowd. Was there regret in there? Evren couldn't tell. And while she desperately wanted to know what had driven Arke from his home before, when they seemed to love him so much, she couldn't bring herself to ask. She didn't need to, after all. She'd follow him regardless.

"I dunno, they're all watchin' me. I can't do a spell without them noticin'." He tore his hands through his hair. "I just wanted to check on them. Make sure Tolk wasn't hit like Rheinwall. I didn't want *this*."

Evren nodded, looking at the food at the table. *Really* looked at it for the first time. The pie might do . . .

Arke continued rambling. "I thought Tolk would take over, you know? He's my brother, makes sense. And he's better at this shit than I am."

Evren picked up the pie. "Uh huh."

"All I ever wanted was to be left alone and do my own shit and now—are you even payin' attention?"

"Kind of," Evren admitted. "Half listening, half planning."

Arke's eyes darted between her and the pie in her hands. "That's your plan?"

She shrugged, bouncing it in her palm. "Worked for Elend. Surely it'll work this time, we just have to be quick. You know another way out of the city?"

"Yeah."

"Great! On my mark then."

Evren had always been proud of two things she'd inherited from her father. Keen eyes and good aim. While killer aim she'd had to hone over years of training, she'd grown up very good at throwing things where they shouldn't have been. Skipping stones, knocking ornaments out of lady's hair, or throwing a loud distraction so she could sneak out undisturbed, it all came down to a naturally strong throwing arm and decent aim.

Of course, that had been many years before she'd learned how to throw deadlier things to kill even deadlier monsters and people, so her arm was a little stronger than she remembered it.

She launched the pie at a random goblin, one with a peach colored mohawk almost as tall as she was. It sailed through the air beautifully, flipping end over end as it soared ever closer to its fated target . . .

And hit her so hard in the face that she was thrown backwards into the ground and didn't get up.

The crowd went quiet and for the first time all those wide eyes were on Evren. She froze, arm still extended from the throw. For a few seconds no one stirred. It was like a garden of goblin statues all aimed to make her uncomfortable.

The mohawk goblin groaned on the floor, pulling the pie off her face. She sat up slowly, licking off the mixed meats, veggies, and random candies within. Those eyes zeroed in on Evren and a wild glee overtook her features.

"GET HER!"

All goblins leapt to action at the command. With the speed and efficiency of a well-trained army, they loaded their arms with food and all fired at Evren.

She yelped and tossed her table up to act as a shield. Food battered against it like a hailstorm as she ducked behind, Arke catching a roll in the face before he managed to join her.

"I thought you were supposed to make us unseen!" he growled and waved his hands around. Half a cabbage clipped his ears. "This is the opposite!"

"I miscalculated, okay? I thought they'd just start fighting each other."

"Not when you throw a pie like a fuckin' spear!"

Evren winced as another volley of food shook the table. There was a chant in the air now, and if it wasn't for the jovial tone it would've sounded like a war song. Evren snatched a pair bruised apples as they rolled away and handed one to Arke.

"Come on, lets fight our way out of here."

"Have you lost what little of your mind was left?" he exclaimed. "We're outnumbered. We'll never make it out."

"Oh, where's that fighting spirit?" She winked. "We just have to run for it, dodge, and throw back whatever we manage to catch."

"That'll end up in a chase."

"Any better ideas, Your Majesty?"

He narrowed his eyes and gripped the apple. "Fuck you. I'm gunna leave your ass here."

"Got to get out first."

That was all it took, although they both knew there was only one very messy way out, it felt natural to argue about it first. They both took a deep breath, bruised fruit in hand, and leapt from behind the table with a war cry on their lips.

The crowd of goblins around the table were only a few feet from them. Only two were hit by the apples, but the rest were so taken aback by the sudden attack that they fell backwards and tripped over themselves.

"Run!" Evren shouted to Arke, but he needed no encouragement. He darted around the table, scooping up food as he went. Evren wasn't far behind him, digging her fingers in every cake she passed to pick it up.

It took only seconds for the goblins to recover. A chorus of gleeful laughter broke out and the food came swiftly after. Evren jumped and twisted and dodged, but it wasn't nearly enough. As she ran after Arke's bobbing form, food smacked against her bruised flesh. Something soft and warm hit her head and caked her hair. It was all she could do to keep it out of her eyes.

She launched her own food as she went, hitting several giggling goblins and causing them to tumble into one another. Most of her throws were distractions, covering fire, or just plain desperate. By the time she got to the end of the tables with Arke she was blinking gravy out of her eyes and could barely see.

"This way!" Arke cried and turned a corner so fast he clawed up grass.

Evren was quick behind him, and the noise of excited goblins on the chase was hot on her heels. They bolted down pathway after pathway, mere corners from the view of their chasers.

She wiped gravy out of her eyes, flicking it on a passing wall. "You know we have to lose them, right?"

"Workin' on it!" Arke growled.

She didn't know if he actually knew where he was going or if he was just picking paths that didn't have food-spattered goblins down them. All the buildings looked the same to her. It was a blur of tall grey stone, brightly colored trees, purple lanterns, and so many carvings. Staring at a wall for too long she could've sworn she saw the pictures jumping up and running in the stone alongside her. She was relieved when Arke picked a different path seconds later.

But no matter how far they ran, the goblins where never far behind. Just out of eyesight but always within hearing range. As the buildings started to thin out and the rough wall of natural stone came into view, Evren panted, "Do they ever give up? They're going to chase us through the tunnels."

Arke barked a tired, "I know."

"We can't leave yet then."

"Know that too."

"Let's double back. Maybe hide and wait for them to get bored—"

She didn't get to finish the sentence. Arke turned down another sharp corner as she planned and then promptly stopped dead in his track. Evren barely kept herself from trampling him and had to catch herself on the wall, breathing hard.

Her legs tingled from the run. Gravy was running down her neck and she was fairly certain she had a carrot lodged somewhere in her shirt. But she shook all that off, grabbing for Arke's shoulder to usher him forward.

"Come on, we can still . . ."

The words died on her lips as she finally saw what had stopped Arke.

She was no longer the tallest among the city. The elf had a few inches on her, and was all delicate grace despite the worn traveling clothes he wore. The dirty cloak was a far cry from the robes she'd last seen him in. His white hair was tangled and pulled back with a simple leather tie, although pieces still came free to hang in his face. He was dirty, exhausted, and disheveled.

But he was every inch the Viggo she remembered.

"Fucking hells," she swore. "What are you doing here?"

He opened his mouth to respond, brows drawn into a sadder expression than she remembered him having, but Tolk swung around his legs in all his braided, beaded glory.

"Eh, this is what I was bringin' you!" He swung his arms out to present Viggo. "Handsome elf, right?"

"That's one way to describe him," Arke muttered and shook food from his hair.

If either Viggo or Tolk planned on explaining themselves, they didn't get the chance. The horde of food wielding goblins tore around the corner, saw them standing still, and threw everything they had with screams of glee.

Evren pressed herself against the wall, covering her head

and letting the food pepper her back and legs. She heard Viggo's flustered cursing and Tolk's laughs of surprise, but they were both drowned out by the sounds of splattering food and cackling.

It seemed like ages before it died down and when it finally did, her entire backside was wet and sticky. Evren grimaced as her shirt stuck coldly to her skin, wiggling for reprieve but finding none. She pushed away from the wall and faced Viggo.

He was pulling a tomato out of his hair and was only slightly less drenched in food than she was. Whatever glimmers of amusement sparked in the dark depths of his eyes faded instantly when he saw her.

"Hello again, Evren Hanali of Eith," he said softly, like he was afraid she'd run off if his voice was too loud.

There were a thousand things to say, none of which she wanted to say in this state, because it was so hard to remember what he'd done when he had fruit bits clinging to his hair. She settled on something simple and to the point.

"Explain."

THERE WERE a handful of hidden streams and ponds throughout the city that Tolk gladly let them use to wash themselves and their clothes. He showed Evren and Viggo to one, running so clearly blue that the stones at the bottom nearly looked purple at its deepest parts before it tumbled down a little dip and into another stream. It was in a secluded little courtyard, achingly quiet after the chaos they'd left still ringing in their ears, and Tolk happily proclaimed that he would make sure they weren't disturbed before dragging Arke off into the unknown.

Evren wanted to follow them. She knew Arke would hate

being alone. But maybe he needed to talk to Tolk just as much as she needed to talk to Viggo.

"Will this be awkward for you?" was the first thing he said once they were alone. She looked back at him starting to take his shirt off to wash.

"No," she said truthfully, and walked to the opposite side of the pond. "But I'm sure your small clothes are as clean as mine so keep them on."

He shrugged. "No food in them, at least."

Evren didn't know what to say to that. Small talk was always painful, and with Viggo it was worse. The way they left things, so torn and unpredictable, with no hope of seeing each other again, left tension in the air that she could taste. She ignored it, ignored him, and focused on herself.

She started taking off her own shirt and pants, ignoring how her skin prickled uncomfortably at being bare in front of him. Was this wrong? It felt wrong, but how many times had she done the same thing with the Wandering Sols? Hells, she'd seen Sorin and Sol naked more times than any lover she'd had. One of her earliest and fondest memories of Gyda was the bathhouse in Serevadia. She'd barely known her and Sol then, and all three of them had been as nude as the day they were born.

So, why did being in nothing but her small clothes and the linen and leather bandeau over her chest in front of Viggo feel bad?

She tried to ignore it while she scrubbed the gravy and celery out of her hair by dunking into the cool water and scrubbing until her scalp tingled. When the rest of her body was clean, she moved on to her clothes.

Tension-filled silence stretched between them and Evren didn't want to be the one to break it. She glanced up from rubbing a stain out of her shirt to see him frowning at her across the pool.

"What?"

He blinked. "Nothing. It's just . . . you're very different."

"It's been a while. And you're not nearly the same as I left you. What happened to the pretty robes?"

His expression soured and the water rippled aggressively as he scrubbed harder at his cloak. "I lost them."

"The robes?"

"Everything. It comes with the territory of challenging an empire by yourself."

"Empire?" Evren put her shirt to the side. "What empire?"

Viggo's shoulder's slumped and the heaviness in his eyes was second only to that of the sky itself. He looked so lost for a moment, that mask of his broken so she could see the naked grief and regret.

He shook himself out of his stupor. "After you left Andovine, everything went wrong. My plan to unseat the entire Convocation for a clean slate and keep Velcros out of power didn't stand a chance. He got there first, the Mora at his side, and swayed the rest of the Convocation with lies about how you led us into a trap with my aid and it was the Mora that saved him from certain death. No one listened to me. I had planned to lose my rank, but having it stripped from me was another matter entirely."

Evren let out a slow breath, sinking her pants into the water as she did. "I'm sorry, I didn't think it would go that bad."

He pursed his lips together. "Truthfully? Neither did I. It wasn't the first time I'd underestimated Velcros, but it certainly was the last. If I'd seen him for what he was sooner, I could've stopped him before you and I even met. But as it was, I had to watch him tear down hundreds of years' worth of carefully constructed power systems and replace it with a single ruler. Serevadia is no longer ruled by the many, but by the whims of one man."

Viggo wrung out his shirt and looked like he was envisioning Velcros's neck instead. "Words and Light had little effect, and my list of enemies grew every hour. So I left."

Their clothes were done. Evren spread hers out on a rock to dry and pulled her knees up to her chest to watch him. He certainly looked like he'd been traveling for a while. The Viggo she remembered was all smooth, soft skin. Now she could see the bruises and cuts on his shoulders, the wear and tear on his feet and hands. He'd lost weight as well. The rough look of travel didn't suit him.

"So, why are you here?' she asked. "From what I remember, Kleros is farther north from here."

"It is." He ran his fingers through his hair, combing the damp white strands he still kept long. "I thought I'd stop there and try to garner some support. Kleros lost a Herald thanks to Velcros, and I tried to prove it. They are an independent, proud people. Their distaste for Andovine is rivaled only by their rivalry with Xoria."

"Did it work?"

He rolled his neck, wincing at the series of pops. "Not as much as I'd like. Enough to sow the seeds of doubt, at the very least. I might've done more if I stayed."

Evren blinked at him, confused. "Well, why didn't you?"

His eyes flashed towards hers. "I thought that should've been obvious; I needed to find you."

"Me? Why?" There was a really nice second where Evren's mind could only compute goblin food fights and Viggo's odd presence in her life again, but then she remembered what brought her down here in the first place. The square crumbling under her feet, Mal's face in the crowd. She shuddered. "This is about Rheinwall, isn't it?"

"It's about all of Eith," he said seriously. "What happened in Rheinwall?"

Evren wanted to ask if he knew anything other than the name, but scowled when she remembered the vast, detailed map of Eith she'd burned. Of course Viggo knew Terevas's capital city, it would've been a massive point of interest.

"There was an attack, I think," she explained. "There was some sort of explosion. Then the ground caved underneath us. Arke and I managed to survive the fall, but I'm not sure about anyone else. The square that was hit was packed with adventurers like us. I also saw Mal, which I was hoping was a coincidence, but now that you're here I'm less sure."

"Mal?" he questioned and then his eyes darkened. "Malrus, the dwarf."

She nodded. "He was part of the scheme to start a war on Dirn-Darahl's end. We dealt with that in the hopes that Serevadia would remain peaceful. Judging by your expression, I take it this new empire will not."

He shook his head. "I thought you were better informed than this. A few escaped Dirn-Darahl, so I assumed the surface was prepared."

"Escaped? Stop talking like I know where this is going."

"So you'd rather me treat you as an idiot?"

"*Viggo.*"

Something like a smile curled his lips but quickly vanished. "Dirn-Darahl has fallen. Serevadia's first major strike started there. I'll admit, I expected a bigger resistance after what Solri said about her people, but what little army there was didn't stand a chance."

Evren suddenly felt very sick. She pressed her hand to her lips, trying to seal back the horror crawling up her throat. Dirn-Darahl was gone. They'd left it defenseless and floundering and hadn't thought twice. Her mind flashed to Sol's mother, alone in her wheeled chair. Karas standing against the elves that had broken his cousin and killed his men, and Temsen clutching his maps and chemicals.

She'd left them.

"Why?" she asked hoarsely. "How? How were they able to do it without the whole world noticing?"

"Whatever you did to Dirn-Darahl left it shaken. I guess no one expected to hear from a city still deciding who would lead it." Remorse flooded his features. "As for why, it was the easiest first step. And for Velcros, it was personal."

Evren wracked her brain. He said there were survivors, people who escaped the attack. The closest city would be Whitestone, but that was still a week's travel at best. Assuming they weren't being hunted.

"Do you know if anyone was sent after the survivors?" she asked. "If I was planning an attack, I'd want to keep it quiet for as long as possible."

And all the hells, the Wandering Sols had purposefully not told the world about Serevadia to keep them from attacking the subterranean civilization. No one was prepared.

"I assume Velcros tried, but we're not accustomed to the surface. From what I gathered, many of my people can't see well in your sunlight. Add to the fact that we don't know your terrain, a group of heavily armed grey-skinned elves wandering the land would raise alarms quicker than wounded refugees."

Evren winced. "He's banking on them either dying or being seen as raving lunatics. Which, if they're headed to Whitestone, is bound to happen."

"Regardless, Serevadia means to move on the surface soon. Rheinwall is a prime target."

"No army to protect it and everything to lose." Evren cursed. "What would've been an army was the adventurers caught in the attack."

Viggo paused, looking her over carefully. "And if they knew? If they survived and they knew what was happening?"

Evren hesitated. Would it help to tell the world now? Serevadia was at their door, clawing to be let into the light. At Velcros's lead there would be no peace. What fragile alliances individual adventurers made together didn't hold true for whole countries.

"I don't know," she admitted. "I can try. But . . . Viggo, you know that by doing this, the whole world will see Serevadia as the enemy."

His voice was as soft as she remembered, and she couldn't believe she'd been fooled by Nerezza's illusion of him now that he was standing in front of her. "I know. I've wrestled with that thought from the moment I decided to find you. I love my home and my people. Our history and everything we've built continues to fill me with pride. You have no idea how much it kills me to turn my back on them in favor of a surface world that will likely take one look at me and see a monster. But I don't have a choice. Serevadia is following a path it was never meant to. An empire instead of a republic, the people listening to a new god instead of waiting for the one that built us. The light is dying, Evren, and every day I fear that Serevadia's path will kill it for good."

"A new god?" A chill snaked through Evren's skin. Why was it always gods? "What do you mean?"

"There were whispers before, mainly from Xoria and the Mora. But now that they're fully integrated into our culture again, this Catarmon is all I can hear. I had hoped to go to Xoria to root out the source, but killing a false religion won't stop Velcros."

"No, it won't," she agreed. "Look, obviously I'm with you on this, but Eith is still divided. Nothing has changed since I left. I have some new connections, more people in high places, but that won't be enough. The world will have to see Serevadia as a threat before it unites, if it ever will."

"All it'll take is a couple of us on the surface." He pressed.

"Maybe, but there's been one in Eith for a while." She took a deep breath and ignored his look of confusion. "Stay sitting, this'll take a while to explain."

To explain Nerezza, Evren had to go over everything from when they first met in the Reino Terminan to their final confrontation in Orenlion. Of course, she skimmed some details, such as Nerezza's illusions of him, but the rest was genuine. Her descent into cold madness after devouring Gail and Keres's souls, her plan for the Eternity Dagger which piqued Viggo's interest, and what little of a plan she'd spat at Evren while kicking her ass.

"She'd planned to bring Serevadia to the surface, but never explained how she would do it." Evren shrugged, feeling tense just from telling the story. "We lost her, Abraxas, and the dagger just three months ago."

Viggo stared at her with wide eyes and a parted mouth for so long that she squirmed under his gaze.

"She's alive," he breathed.

"Well, she was—"

"No, no!" He cut her off and got to his feet. He started pacing the length of the pool, tugging his hair as he did. "It makes sense doesn't it? If she survived that then perhaps she's behind all of this in Serevadia."

"How, Viggo?" Evren snapped. "She's dead. Even if she wasn't, she wouldn't have had time to gather forces against Dirn-Darahl if she was attacking Orenlion."

"I know she's alive," he promised, and his eyes were bright for the first time since their reunion. "I know it because I've seen the evidence. I've seen Abraxas."

Evren felt like something had slammed into her chest. She gaped at him, hand grasping her chest as if it could dig Gyda's thundering heart out.

"That's not possible," she said, her voice quietly on the verge of hope and rage. "Don't play me for a fool again, Viggo."

"I'm not, I swear. I didn't believe it either, it hardly looked like him. He was different. But he knew me. He's the one who told me to leave Andovine for good before I would've been killed."

"He's not . . ." Evren gasped for air. "He's not working for

Serevadia. If he was alive why wouldn't he let us know? Why stay down there?"

"I don't know," Viggo admitted. He walked around the pool and knelt next to her. Evren hadn't even realized she'd been shaking until he put a steadying hand on her shoulder. "You said he fell with the dagger, yes?"

She nodded numbly.

"It's possible that it took him out of time, likely Nerezza too. Therefore saving them from the Archdruids's plans. Anything is possible with an artifact like that."

"I know," She shook off his hand and wiped away her tears, hating herself for both the hurt in his face and crying in front of him. "I've used it. So why not use it to get back?"

"He couldn't. That's the only thing I can think of. If Nerezza had it, then why not use it herself? The answer is simple. What makes a legend more than power?"

"Time."

Evren rubbed her face. She hated it, every word that he said. She hated it more because it nearly made sense. The dragon skeleton that she knew was the Storm, that unshaking feeling that he wasn't quite gone, it all made sense.

Gyda was right. Sahar was too.

She chewed her lip. "They went backwards in time, that's the only way it makes sense." Then she straightened her back and got up. Viggo watched her with unreadable eyes as she gathered up her damp clothes.

"You have a plan, I take it?" he asked. "You have that look on your face."

She tried to wipe away whatever expression was on her face. "If Abraxas was in Serevadia like you said, he's in there against his will. I don't think he would ever take your cause under his belt." She paused and spared him an apologetic shrug. "No offense."

"Only some taken," he answered with a dry smile and got up.

Evren was suddenly hit with how absurd of a scene they made talking about war and death in their underwear. She shook her head and started putting on her damp clothes with a grimace.

"Regardless, we have to stop Serevadia and warn Eith before things get out of hand," she said, lacing up her pants. "And finding Abraxas is a priority. Sahar will want Nerezza. Keres as well. Although I haven't seen them, I'm sure the corpse is lurking somewhere in her manor out of sight. We'll get out of here first, make sure my party is still alive, then work on building up a defense for Rheinwall. I can send a message to Barrion and Mei, hopefully they can send some aid to Dirn-Darahl. I'll need to give them numbers and defensive reports. Anything we can give their army will help them drive Velcros out of Dirn-Darahl."

"We?"

Evren looked back at Viggo, who was watching her rattle off the barest beginnings of plans with a look of wonder and a tinge of pride. There was also that delicate tension between them, one she'd ignored in her babbling, and he was testing like the first ice on a lake.

We? He'd asked that as if she'd talked of plucking the stars from the sky. Could there be a 'we' after the lies and manipulation? After all the nasty things said back and forth. They'd left knowing they would never have to face each other again, no matter what hopeful words they'd dropped to ease the pain of what they'd done. But now that they'd been thrust together into another world-shattering predicament, was it safe to call each other allies?

"Yes, we," Evren finally said. "I'm going to need your help convincing everyone about Serevadia's existence and power. You're also the last person to see Abraxas alive."

He stood back on his heels, a hint of a smile there. "You could say please."

"I could also drown you in this pool," she said with a

raised eyebrow, but just like that the tension was shattered. Not healed, but temporarily broken.

"All right, I'll walk the surface with you, Evren Hanali. Or is it Lady Xun?"

"Not to you. Get dressed, we have to get Arke out of here."

He bowed extravagantly, then went across the pool to get his clothes. Evren turned back to the goblin city, starting the lengthy process of extracting her friend from forced regency in her mind when she saw Arke standing there, watching them.

She took a deep breath. "How much did you hear?"

"The last bits." He flicked his gaze over to Viggo then back to her. "The important bit."

"And what do you think?"

He sighed, looking over his shoulder at the city. Evren wondered if he would ever tell her its name, or if that was another part of Goblinkin she wasn't privy to. When he turned back to her his shoulders were slumped and he wouldn't look here in the eye, but there was a strength in his voice she hadn't heard before.

"Well, if you're goin' to war the least I can do is pledge my own army." He flashed a fanged grin. "Let's get our boy back while we're at it."

12

Abraxas

lesh, when being magically knit back together, itched like a million small ants were crawling under his skin. It had been so long since he felt it that, when he woke up, he thought he was being set on fire. All he could see was darkness. He jerked in his cot, the itching turning to pain as he ripped open brand-new skin.

Cool hands gently pressed him to stillness, one on his thigh and another on his chest. Long fingers, rough and callused. A healer's hands.

"Be still, shadow," said a voice both delicate and guttural, the words laced with a thick accent and warped like the speaker had trouble pronouncing the words.

He let the healer press him back into the bed and the itching sensation returned. He was burning again, this time from the inside out. The heat in his chest gathered until it was an inferno his swelling lungs couldn't release, because short of ripping his ribcage open like a swinging door there wasn't a way to let it out. He struggled for breath, the logical part of him knowing that this was a good thing, but the raw, bleeding part of him that was tired of hurt raged against it anyway.

"Please," he gasped. "Please, I can't . . ."

But he could. He knew that. The healer knew it, and the fire didn't let up. His gasps turned to broken groans of pain. He dug his fingers around the edge of his cot, fighting to stay still as his body was meticulously pieced back together, inch by inch. Nerves flared to splintering life, spikes of pain flaring down his legs and feet. Layer after layer of flesh was regrown, until, an eternity later, he was whole again.

The hands fell away from him, and it was like oppressive chains had finally lifted. His body lurched to the side, falling on his hands and knees to the rough sandy floor. The black covering his eyes fell off his face and fluttered down to rest on his hands—just a piece of cloth. He could smell the sharp sting of herbs that had soaked it, the syrupy residue still sticking to his eyelashes.

But he paid it little attention. It was his hands that caught his eye. Whole, unmarred by burn scars. He sat up on his knees, flexing his hands and turning them over. Rolled the wrists, touched each finger to his thumbs. He had everything. The healer had not cut any corners.

"Impressive," the voice behind him purred. "Your movement is smooth."

He whirled around to face his healer, still on his knees. His neck craned up to meet their face, and just kept looking up. The wonderous thank you on his tongue dried up. Skin black as onyx, horns curling back into regal points from the top of the head. Tall, as tall as Gyda, but all willowy height instead of powerful muscle. Lines of metallic paint curved all over their black skin, tracing patterns along those clawed hands, up the arms lined with black scales at the shoulders and along the neck and chest, ending at the corner of their eyes. There was no color, no whites to see. Only pure black darkness.

"Ah, the fear is good." The Dra'Nacti grinned, baring sharp teeth. "Is there respect as well, shadow?"

Abraxas struggled to find the words. He'd seen Dra'Nacti from afar, but they were always reluctant to interact with Etherak's forces during the war. He'd never seen one so close. They were something shaped by the very desert they called home, so far from what he knew as humanoid.

They looked like a monster. They looked beautiful.

"Yes," he managed to croak out. He bowed his head. "Thank you."

The Dra'Nacti tsked, the sound strange against fangs instead of blunt teeth. "You have not examined yourself fully. Stand. Let me see."

They turned around, beads hanging from their robes and charms hanging from their horns clinking. Abraxas didn't hesitate to obey, and only then did he realize he was completely naked.

"Um . . ." His eyes darted to the cot he'd been sleeping on, damp with pus and dried blood. He wanted none of that on him now, nor the medical rag that had been over his eyes.

"You are shy, no?" The Dra'Nacti circled back, resting a clawed finger on their chin. Those pitch eyes raked over his body, cataloging through old scars and new. Their mouth quirked up into a smile when he tried to cover himself.

"I saw it before." They waved him off, then moved back to his legs. "Tell me what you think."

Abraxas looked down at his feet, finding them whole and smooth. Free of hair and dirt, it was just brand-new skin. He flexed his toes, watching how his calves responded to the movement. Muscles seemed to move fine, he could feel everything again. The only way he could tell the healer had done any work were the silvery marks along both legs where more newly healed skin met less damaged skin.

"The legs were . . . how do you say?" The Dra'Nacti grimaced and flexed their tongue before landing on the word.

"Destroyed. I had to regrow much. Very new muscle and flesh. You will need to build up your strength and endurance again."

His brought his leg up in the air, noting the shaking. Yes, he was much weaker than before, but he'd also been bedridden for Divines knew how long. Retraining his body would've been a given, but the fact still stood that the Dra'Nacti had completely regrown all he'd lost when even the best Etherakian healer would have had to cut away the worst of the burned flesh. Abraxas using Divine magic would've had a hard time, too, but he saw the process of it. He knew, if the healer was following his strategy anyway, how they had pieced him back together without sacrificing any limbs.

"Incredible," he breathed, and touched the scar where the brand-new skin met on his thigh. "I've never seen healing like this without . . ." He swallowed back the words. Dra'Nacti didn't worship the Divines any more than the rest of Vernes.

So, *how?* How had a creature without any Divine aid been able to make him whole again?

As if the Dra'Nacti could hear the question, they chuckled. A dry, raspy sound, but surprisingly soothing. "No gods here, shadow. I learn from the land."

Abraxas didn't say that, in his experience, the land in Vernes killed more than the people who lived in it. Instead, he put his leg down, swaying only a little as he got his balance back.

"Thank you," he said again, and meant every word. "This is incredible."

"So you keep saying."

"It is." He felt himself start to smile, a foreign sensation to his tired cheeks. "There're no hitches in my extremities when I move them. I feel everything. You pieced my nerves back together better than I did a few decades ago."

The healer's black eyes brightened. "You regrew your own body?"

He shrugged sheepishly. "Almost lost my arm in battle. Here." He pointed to the scar along his left forearm. It was not neat. The scar was deep, like a canyon through his skin. "When the fighting was over there was no one else to help me. I reset it myself and went from there. Not as good of a job as I would do on someone else, but it was just my shield arm, and I could learn through any of the new motion issues."

The long black fingers on his scar made him jump. The healer's feathery light touch was shiver-inducing, but he didn't pull away as they traced the scar all the way around his forearm.

"Good work done in pain is great work." The Dra'Nacti withdrew. "You did not seem like a healer."

"I'm not. Well, I am. Or was." He shook his head, noticing for the first time the lack of hair swinging along his back. It must've burned off. "I started as a healer and became a soldier later. My sword was needed more than my healing hands."

The healer tsked again and with a shake of their head sent a dozen charms tinkling. "A shame. You have kind eyes. Such hands should not be forced to kill."

Abraxas didn't know what to say. Should he be angry because of the blatant disregard for what he'd done for his kingdom? How many more lives had he saved by being a shield rather than staying in a tent to keep the dying from slipping away? This path was his now and he couldn't take it back.

No matter how much he secretly agreed with the Dra'Nacti.

"Should we greet officially naked or would you rather clothes?" The healer had moved on and left him stammering.

"Naked? You don't—I mean, I wouldn't want . . . Not that you're not, uh . . ." He wanted to say beautiful, but stopped. Would handsome be better? He couldn't tell what gender they were, or if it even mattered. *Why* was he stumbling over his words? "What should I call you?"

That same raspy chuckle filled the air and, for some reason, that put him at ease. The Dra'Nacti unwound one of the many long pieces of dark fabric from around their body, long enough to be draped over them three times, and settled it over Abraxas's shoulders.

"So, so shy, you elves. My name is Aushruk'dien, and I am more female now if it makes it easier for you to understand."

It didn't, but Abraxas nodded anyway, wrapping his body in the fabric she'd given to him and tying it off.

"Aushruk'dien," he tried carefully, tongue still tripping over the pronunciation.

She wasn't angry, she just smiled. "Aushruk is good."

He nodded again and extended his hand. "My name is Abraxas Kain."

She took his hand, long fingers unnerving as they wrapped around his palm. "Abraxas Kain," she murmured. "Strong."

He smiled a little. "You have a better grasp on Core than I do of your language."

"Well." She took back her hand to flick it in the air in a gesture he didn't recognize. "So many have been shouting it through my sands these past few years, I learn as the desert does. Come now, you are dressed and healed. Next should be food."

Aushruk turned to leave, and he went to follow her. He hadn't realized just how famished he was. How long had he laid on that cot with Nerezza before Aushruk got to him?

Nerezza.

The thought of her hit him like a ton of bricks. He turned back to his cot, finally seeing the space where she should've been at his side completely empty. Emotions warred inside him. Was she gone? Was he finally free of her?

"The woman I was with," his voice stopped Aushruk, "what happened to her? I didn't see the extent of her injuries."

Aushruk's face twisted into a frown so deep it would've

been comical under any other circumstances. "The pale one was healed before you. Her injuries were far worse, made so by her own hand."

"What do you mean?"

"She tried to get out before I came. Her magic is . . ." She bared her teeth in disgust. "Distasteful. But it damaged her more than helped her. She nearly died and was removed so I could focus on you without her breathing down my neck."

Abraxas deflated and tried to hide his disappointment. He didn't want Nerezza dead any more than he wanted to die, but it would've been a way out if she'd died from her wounds. A long, slow crawl back to his friends, but he would've been free to do as he wished.

Aushruk's eyes narrowed, catching on his shift in mood. "You are not happy she lives. Is she not your companion?"

"Somewhat," he said, unable to bring himself to tell her that Nerezza had him on a very short, very painful leash. He didn't know yet if Aushruk could be an ally, or if she was already under Nerezza's wing. He also didn't know if it was worth trusting her. He'd known her for only a few minutes, and he found her strangeness endearing, her healing reminding him of what he wanted to be. But she was likely working with the rebels, and he doubted they would be friendly towards him.

No, as much as he liked Aushruk, she wasn't his friend. He couldn't trust her with something like this in the vain hope that she could help him. Nerezza's magic was beyond the scope of any he knew, or even Arke had known. It was safe to assume that the secluded Dra'Nacti knew even less.

Aushruk was still staring at him intensely, as if she could mentally peel back the layers of his brain and snatch the root of his problems. He couldn't force a smile that would resemble anything genuine, so he turned away from Nerezza's cot and walked up next to her. Her height was a little unnerving, but not all that strange after so long at Gyda's side.

"We had a falling out. I don't wish her dead, however." Both of which were true. He couldn't lie if his life depended on it, as his run-in with Divara had shown him.

"Hmm," the Dra'Nacti hummed a little reply, rocking back on her heels to look at him more fully. He didn't flinch, he didn't back away. She'd seen him bare physically but there was only so much of his naked soul he could give her through expression alone. When at last she seemed satisfied, she snapped back to her odd grin.

"Very well. Let us go, Abraxas Kain. There are many questions to answer." She pulled back the cloth that covered the ruin and stepped out into the blinding sun. Shielding his eyes, he followed closely behind.

The sun was setting in all its orange and golden glory and seemed to be hovering at just the right angle to blind him. But, despite that, his eyes greedily drank in the details before him.

He'd been right about the ruin. They were in some sort of ancient stone town, the architecture so weathered with sand and wind that he couldn't make out any details. Just columns large enough to stand the test of time reaching out of the sand like fingers. Broken archways and crumbled buildings, stairs half hidden under the sand. Abraxas hadn't seen the likes of these ruins the whole time he'd been in Vernes. Where the stone wasn't enough, tents the same color as the sand had been erected. Large and domed, they scattered over the ruined town and blended in so well he had a hard time picking them out. Looking back, his and Nerezza's tent was the only one that stood out, both in color and the shoddy way it was built.

His feet, bound in new skin absent of calluses, burned and scraped against loose stone, but he found himself relishing in the feeling as Aushruk led him through the camp. Her shadow was a giant along the sands, cutting through the golden haze and touching every person who watched her go with darkness. There were more like her, Dra'Nacti that towered over everyone with their horns and strange half-scaled bodies. Shades of deep blue, maroon, and purple colored their skin, but none had the metallic paint along their bodies like Aushruk. They inclined their heads to her when she passed, and she smiled at them all fondly.

"My tribe is small and young." She nodded to a trio of Dra'Nacti bearing spears and shaking sand from their horns as they walked into the camp. "But we grow with each moon."

"And you help the rebels." Abraxas wanted to stare at the Dra'Nacti all day, but it was impossible not to see the smaller people around them. There were more humans, half elves, and dwarves here than their desert hosts, and they stared at him with open hostility at worst, or guarded caution at best. People with enough scars to rival Evren, some missing limbs and hobbling by with simple wooden prosthetics, others whole in body but in their eyes he could see something of their soul was missing.

People who'd been fighting for so long that there was no other way to live. It showed on their skin, the way they walked with their shoulders hunched as if expecting a surprise blow at any time, and the way they ate their food as if it could be their last. But he also saw sparks of life. Those who fought like families, eating together and sharing water. Those veterans teaching fresh-faced recruits how to properly wield their glaives and smiling when they got the stance right.

It was wrong to see this open hostility and feel warmth. He'd spent so long hating these people, for fighting and killing in the first place and then taking away the thing he loved most after that. He still wanted to hate them. But in this camp they were just people, not faceless rebels soaked in the blood of his friends. If he forgot what they were fighting for, a country with no gods where undead ran rampant and slavery was chosen at one's birth, he could completely denounce what he'd been taught back home.

The problem was, he still believed in the original goal that

Eldritch preached. To liberate Eith from darkness and evil and bring it to the light. Vernes with its strict caste system and unholy use of necromancy needed cleansing more than any other.

Didn't it? He looked down at his hands, one of the parts of him where his original scars remained because Aushruk hadn't need to regrow much skin. He could still feel the blood creasing in the lines of his palms, dripping from his fingertips.

When did a just cause become too bloody to be worth it? And what right did he have to choose for these people? When he'd first stepped on these sands, armor new and shining, he expected the common people to fight with him. He was liberating them, freeing them from their bonds. But they fought him just as hard. Every slave freed would inevitably meet his blade later on.

He loved his Divines. He knew that the common soldier in Etherak and most of the commanders had been dragged into this just like him, thinking they were doing the right thing and following their King and Divines. They weren't in the wrong for trying to do the right thing and following orders, were they?

Was he?

"The Dra'Nacti help those who need it," Aushruk's raspy voice cut through his thoughts, and he put his hands down at his sides. "These rebels are fighting to protect their home and way of life."

"But the Dra'Nacti promised Etherak to stay out of this fight," he said. "You swore an oath."

"We lied, Abraxas Kain, as one does in times of conflict." She cut him a knowing look, black as pitch and somehow still comforting. "How long would your kin wait after destroying these people before turning on mine? We are peaceful. We do not fight. Neither did the rest of these people before you came." She swept a clawed hand out to the rebel camp. "We do not share your gods. Does that make us any less than you?"

Abraxas licked his lips, looking for the right answer and finding only sand on his tongue. "There are those who would say that you are."

"I did not ask them, I asked you," she said hotly. "Do you believe only what is told to you?"

He shook his head, bewildered. "No, of course not! I know the Divines are real. I've felt them, seen their power. I was given some of that power."

"Then why did we pull you from an Etherakian pyre, hmm?"

His mouth snapped shut and he focused more on the ground and avoiding sharp rocks than on her. He'd been asked questions like these before. By Evren, who didn't approve because the Divines didn't factor in her mind at all. By Gyda after sparring when they'd both hit just a little too hard. By himself, alone at night after another prayer went unanswered.

He still wasn't sure of the answer.

"I'm a different man now," he finally said. "The one they thought they were burning has been dead for a while. But I . . . I don't know. Before, things made sense. They were simple. But now I can't grasp right or wrong any more than I can a fistful of air."

"The world is not simple," Aushruk said. "It has no desire to make sense."

He blinked up at her. She'd reached a larger tent, this one in a shaded alcove of a large ruin. Her fingers scraped the fabric, ready to tug it aside, but she paused.

"You are consumed with shadows, Abraxas Kain. Guilt and regret gnaw at you like scavengers waiting for you to fall. You must shake them loose and learn to live again."

It was so strange, to be picked clean by someone he barely knew and to have those words hit home like none had before. But it almost made sense. He was as new as the skin on his feet, tender and unprotected now without his armor.

"I don't know how," he said and gripped the edge of the

cloth she'd given him. "I've tried so hard to be better, to accept what I'd done and what was done to me with grace. I can't help this anger in me. Every prayer met with silence makes me feel like I've never done enough, and I never will. How can I be whole without my gods? How can I be whole without someone better to guide me?"

"How can you be worthy of them without being worthy of yourself?" she asked, and he stumbled like she'd dug a knife in his chest. She tilted her head enough for the charms to tinkle again, and put a hand on his shoulder. Despite himself he leaned into it. "Ask yourself this, Abraxas Kain. Do you need your gods, or do they need you?"

He frowned. "I . . . that makes no sense. The Divines need no one."

"Then why aren't they here now? Why did they not save you from that pyre if they love you so?"

"It's not that simple—"

She waved his words away. "Is it not? I do not know your gods, but I have seen their power. You want them back because you believe you are nothing without them."

He was breathless. "Yes."

She leaned down until her face was mere inches from his. Between the hand on his shoulder and her forceful gaze he couldn't back away. He was suddenly caught in the gaze of a healer he knew could destroy him if she wanted.

"That is the lie they have buried in you," she said. "Root it out, become something better, and call them back to you on *your* terms."

Aushruk let go of him and he stumbled back a step. When she straightened up she still looked at him with a gaze that reminded him so much of the grand statues of the gods in Whitestone. Hard and unyielding; she would take no excuses or diversions from the path ahead and expected the same from those that followed her.

"You have wounded Vernes with your blade. Maybe now you should take a turn at healing it?" She nodded to the tent.

He balked, a war of emotions in his chest. None of this had made the world clearer. His old masters would've died from fright at her words of the Divines needing him, that he should meet them again with his own demands. The Divine didn't work like that.

But where he was going, they weren't there. Eith survived by people like his friends, people like *him*. He had a long road to get to them, and a bigger task of surviving Nerezza and her plots. But maybe, just maybe, he could do some good along the way.

Maybe coming to Vernes didn't mean a reckoning, but a redemption.

"Will I be allowed?" he asked carefully.

She snorted. "No one is allowed to tame a dragon, they simply try. Come now." She opened the tent and stepped inside.

Abraxas, after only a moment's hesitation, followed her.

Abraxas

Abraxas blinked in the low, filtered light as the tent closed behind him. His feet found relief from the sand and stone on bare mats. Lamps flickering with naked flames lit the darkest parts of the wide tent.

Or rather, the war room.

Abraxas felt his spine stiffen at the somewhat familiar sight. He was familiar with the sight of a big table littered with maps and troop movements. Seeing the detail of Vernes on parchment, which cities were free and which were not, from the other side was like being hit with a wave of vertigo. Instead of uniform lines of troops, Vernes's rebels were scattered across the sands. But there were a lot of them. Gathered in big cities, occupied or not, dotted in small towns or huddled in hidden oases. At least ten times the force that Etherak expected, if memory served.

His view of the map was suddenly cut off as someone stood in front of it. Abraxas raised his gaze to meet the stranger and didn't flinch away. The half-elf was as tall as he was and corded with thick muscle. His dark brown skin was slick with sweat, and the beads of perspiration caught on the rows of scars along his bald head.

A slave who'd won his freedom through battle, Abraxas noted. He also noted the belt around his waist, glimmering bronze peeking through the leather. And he was awarded leadership. Impressive.

"You couldn't let this one die?" the half-elf said in Vernesian to Aushruk. "All you had to do was wait a couple hours."

Aushruk's grin was part snarl. "I am not so quick to judge, Mizan, on skin alone."

Her snarl was matched, which Abraxas had to respect. "So, he does not serve their gods?"

"More like he's had a change of heart."

Abraxas couldn't hold his tongue anymore. He let the Vernesian language snap out of his mouth with no hesitation. "He speaks your language and has a name."

Mizan's eyes found his and that was all it took to remind Abraxas why he'd hated rebels for so long. That fire in their eyes, the unquenched rage, felt like it was heating his skin. If it hadn't been for the lack of weapons and armor, it would've felt like the beginning of a very bloody duel.

"Does he now?" Mizan drawled. "And which of my countrymen did you torture to learn it?"

Abraxas leveled him with a flat glare. "None. It's not so hard to learn, unlike Core is for you apparently."

Aushruk's growl was all that kept Mizan from advancing on him. She stepped between the two, her lips curled in disgust. She tsked again, and he couldn't help but feel ashamed. He should've just kept his mouth shut.

One shared look from her proved his thoughts right.

"Mizan." She turned back to him. "He is a turncoat. Use him."

Mizan blanched. "For what purpose? He would lie!"

"You yourself picked him from that pyre. You know his own people meant for his permanent death."

"I only took him because the mage wanted him," he snapped. "We have her and the shard. What use is he?"

"He is everything," she shot back and turned with a sweeping arm toward Abraxas. "His gods have abandoned him. His people have turned their backs on him. He is lost."

Mizan folded his burly arms over his chest and leaned against the war table. "You cannot decide who deserves redemption when his kind murder our people every day. This is not just your camp, and it is not your decision."

"Neither is it yours alone."

He deflated at her words, angry expression falling slightly. Beneath all that contempt Abraxas could see respect. Mizan wanted Aushruk on his side. He wanted her words to reflect his feelings like they might've before. There were years of history between the two that Abraxas could taste in the air but not discern the details. They'd been fighting the same war for a long time.

No, not war. Rebellion.

"You won't trust me no matter what I do," Abraxas said and drew Mizan's ire once again. "You think I'm a spy. If the roles were reversed, I'd think the same."

"Do not compare us," Mizan said. "We are nothing alike."

"I can leave," Abraxas said. "You can blindfold me and toss me in the desert to die."

"I was thinking of feeding you to my hounds."

"Or," Abraxas held his hands up, "you can test me. My knowledge. For however long you want. Any piece of intelligence I give you, and you can take me with you to make sure it all goes off well. I still know Etherak's plans and movements."

As he said it he felt sick. This atonement felt like betrayal. To turn over his own people and lead them to what could be their deaths made his new skin crawl. But if this was the path he had to take to truly liberate Vernes and his soul from decades of festering guilt, he had to take it. He'd fought against Vernes for so long, he had to try fighting beside them.

He knew one thing with absolute certainty; King Eldritch was wrong. Nomien was evil and corrupting Etherak's leadership with poisonous thoughts. It would be another five decades before he was stopped, before Loghain and Divara decided that their people had suffered enough. Five decades before the Divines would be driven from the world.

Etherak's cause was founded on lies he could no longer support, and if Haphion wouldn't turn the tide, then Abraxas would have to try to do so himself.

"If I lie then you can dispose of me as you wish," he said. "But I won't. All I ask is that you burn the bodies of Etherak's soldiers and let those who surrender go free. They're following bad orders. They follow a King that lies to them. They are being misled and don't deserve to have their souls twisted into what they consider abominations. Let the dead burn. Let the surrendered go home. And you can do whatever you will with me."

Aushruk and Mizan stared at him for a long minute, a mixture of respect and disbelief mingling in their gazes. Aushruk blinked slowly at him, like a pleased mother cat would when her kitten walked on his own for the first time without tripping. Mizan didn't blink at all, which was more disconcerting the longer it went on.

"You dare make demands of us," Mizan asked slowly.

Abraxas did smile then, a wicked thing that felt both indulgent and right. "I've dared gods, Mizan. Daring you is simple."

"Oh!" He laughed without mirth. "Is it? That explains why your gods left you in our hands then. Perhaps you can find some respect while you're here."

Abraxas took a careful breath. "So you agree to my terms?"

"I agree to your test. I also agree to be the one who tears your skin from your body when you fail."

Aushruk rolled her eyes, a strange sight with no color or whites, but he recognized the movement. Somehow he thought this wasn't something she did naturally, but rather picked up from other races.

"Keep threatening to skin people and you lose your fright," she warned him.

Mizan shrugged her off and stepped aside, giving Abraxas a view of the war table and the map again.

"Aushruk is right about one thing, this is not my decision alone," he said, biting the words out as if they cut his gums to say. "There are several leaders in our rebellion that will need to be convinced you are worth the risk. However, for this trial I shall be the one to oversee you. You pass? You gain my vote to keep you here. I'm sure the other leaders will have similar trials for you."

"Where are they?"

Mizan scowled. He was very good at that. "Out. Rebellions are large, moving things, heretic. They cannot be here all the time. Now, to the map." He nodded down to the table. "Show me weakness."

Abraxas could've made the snide comment of Vernes's weakness instead of Etherak's, but he swallowed down the words and stepped up to the table. Mizan didn't move to give him space, although the way his whole body stiffened near Abraxas told him enough what the rebel thought of him. Aushruk swept aside with grace, rounding the table to watch him fully.

Reading Vernesian proved harder to remember than speaking it, but it wasn't until he saw stranger symbols scrawled next to the texts that he realized it wasn't his fault. Dra'Nacti had their own language and writing, one he'd never even tried to wrap his mind around but was clearly ingrained into the map as if everyone in camp could read it. He wasn't going to give Mizan the satisfaction of asking for help, he wouldn't. Instead, he gently laid his hands on the table and hovered over it, letting the map of his memories lay over the new one.

A century hadn't wiped away weeks and months of staring at Etherak's war table. There were times he'd found himself absentmindedly drawing it in the dirt as he traveled, or walking the roads in his mind as he slept. He knew, despite the confusion of time, which cities Etherak had truly conquered, which routes through Gratey they used and which they avoided, and what hidden caches were hidden where. His knowledge wasn't absolute—he wouldn't know as much as Divara or Loghain would, but he'd led his own troops through this war. He knew what had aided him before, and what would again if he turned the tables.

The only trick was finding something worthy of Mizan's trust, while also not leading to a full-scale battle. Abraxas was tired of fighting.

"Here." He pointed to a blank spot on the map.

Mizan snorted. "We know these sands better than you. There is nothing there that belongs to Etherak."

"But something is there," he said, tracing his finger along the coast and to Gratey's border. "You won't tell me where I am, so this is the best I've got. Etherak has paid off a number of smugglers and thieves to take your supplies and give you faulty ones. This you likely know."

"We do." Mizan shifted from foot to foot, staring intently at Abraxas's finger. "We've killed many."

"But we still need them," Aushruk said. "We haven't found the true source, only raiders hired by others. It is a very large web of lies that has been spun. Finding the spider in the middle has proven troublesome."

"I can get you the spider," Abraxas said. "They're a band of thieves out of Gratey. Nasty people, but they converted and promised to work with us. Loghain's use for them was that they would connect with your people and give you bad supplies."

"One group couldn't do this," Mizan protested. "We take supplies from many sources."

"And they've been collecting every one of them." Abraxas tapped the original point he'd had, close to the east coast but in the far north. "They have to stick close to Gratey in order to get reliable shipments to Etherak. They're doing both, so if you can take down this spider you'll free yourself from a nuisance and cripple Etherak's survival here."

Mizan glared at the map as if he could will the ink to bleed through the parchment and mark it for him instead of Abraxas. After a while, he unraveled his hand from his chest and put a small, red marker over Abraxas's finger until he moved it.

"Mizan?" Aushruk spoke and drew his gaze. "Let your thoughts free."

He rubbed his chin, still staring at the spot. "I've lost many to these faulty potions. You cannot be in battle, Aushruk. We cannot rely on your healing every time, and we have little to make these potions ourselves. Food is dwindling, even with your hunters. We need to feed our people, both here and in the cities."

"You could turn them to your advantage," Abraxas offered. "They have no loyalty to Etherak, none that goes beyond gold and survival."

Mizan's lip curled up as if the mere thought disgusted him. "Gratey thieves are no allies. Would they have supplies stocked at this camp?"

"Enough for them. They're a decent force, heavily armed. There will be Etherakian soldiers guarding them as well. But also maps to other sources. I'd bet my life on it."

"You already are." Mizan turned away from the table and leveled Abraxas with a poisonous stare. "Get ready to move. You and your mage will be coming with us, and you will not be aiding us like that." He nodded to Abraxas's bare feet and cloth covering.

"I'm not fighting," Abraxas said.

"Oh, let us hope not." Mizan grinned like a jackal. "Because if you are, you're fighting me."

~

IT HAD TAKEN them a week of hard travel to get to what Mizan called the Spider's Grave. What it actually was, what it might've been before, didn't matter. He drilled it into his soldier's heads until they believed it the same way they believed breathing air gave them life. By refusing to acknowledge the name of the thieves Abraxas tried to give, Mizan wrote them as monsters. By referring to their camp as a grave, he wrote the only possible end for them.

Abraxas was miserable the whole trip in his borrowed clothes and shoes. Even more so was Nerezza's constant, chilly presence at his shoulder. Neither of them spoke to each other the entire trip.

Aushruk's healing had made her physically whole, save for her hand. Abraxas hadn't dared ask either of them if it was intentionally left a stub or if that was something Aushruk's magic couldn't fix. Nerezza's illusion had fallen and the soldiers whispered about the deathly pallor of her skin and hair. Abraxas thought she looked like a ghost, but they looked at her with something similar to reverence and awe.

Which, he guessed, made sense.

Her long white hair had been burnt to her shoulders, fried and unevenly cut. He'd simply evened his hair out, although the short length made him feel like a child again. He fiddled with the ends near his ears often, mostly without thinking.

She barely seemed to acknowledge him at all. The most she did to even show she noticed him was take a pot of soothing cream he offered when her skin started to burn from the constant sun. Those black eyes remained fixed on the horizon as if she too believed Mizan's chants about the Spider's Grave.

The strangest part of the trip was the lone Dra'Nacti that followed them. Abraxas thought he might've been a guide, for he bore no weapons and seemed content to just wander the sands with them. He didn't respond to any of Abraxas's questions when he approached him and secluded himself from everyone at night. The rebels acted like he wasn't there. Nerezza ignored him entirely. Abraxas stopped trying to talk to him after the fourth day.

He was messing with his hair again as Mizan's people crouched in the desert around him. Gone were the dunes, as easy to hide in as it was to be swallowed by them. Now they were in the rocky flats close to the Gratey border. Shrubs and cacti were the only things that kept them hidden. Abraxas felt ridiculously exposed in the cold night air but if their trip with the rebels had taught him anything, it was that they knew how to blend in.

The moonlight seemed to shy away from them, the silvery light casting a spotlight on the encampment ahead surrounded by thick walls made of wood and packed with sand and stone. There were towers on every side, each lit with lanterns and shadowed by two to three guards in each one. There was a permitter patrol as well. Abraxas could still smell the blood even from where they'd dumped the bodies several feet away.

The night breeze cut through his thin layers, and he shivered with the brush he was crouched behind.

"I thought Etherakians liked the cold." Mizan snickered.

Abraxas ignored him. "There will be at least fifty of your spiders in there. Ten or more trained soldiers from Etherak."

"Any chances of a mage?"

"Unlikely, unless they're being escorted across the border. It won't be anyone important if that's what you're asking."

"Everyone in that grave is important enough to kill,"

Mizan said, resting his hands on the hilts of his twin sabers. He had a glaive strapped to his back as well, and Abraxas wasn't looking forward to seeing either weapon in action. "My people will even the odds, so it is a good fight."

"Ambushes are not fair fights," Abraxas couldn't help but say.

"Not fair, heretic. Not good for them, either. Good for us." His smile was blinding white in the moonlight, and that was all Abraxas saw before he was up on his feet.

In movements his war trained eyes could barely follow, Mizan rallied his small band of troops, only about thirty-five at most, and charged the front gate. It was a silent call to arms, broken only by the rush of wind and sand, and the jostle of weapons. Padding of feet, hushed breaths, *chuckling*.

Abraxas looked over the bush, hissing between his clenched teeth. This was wrong. They couldn't go straight up to the gate and expect a full-frontal assault to work. Not even the most desperate rebel he'd faced had been that stupid.

"Wait, Abraxas." Nerezza's voice hit his ears for the first time in a week and immediately he wanted nothing more than that continued silence from her. But he could do nothing other than what she said.

Wait.

The alarm went off in the Grave. A bell tolled, guards shouted. Abraxas could see the gate buckling as it was locked, even from his position. More shapes appeared along the wall, some in armor, others in leather cuirasses, and some still in their bedclothes. Arrows were drawn and Abraxas held his breath. The rebels didn't have shields. That many arrows would leave few survivors, none of which would survive the next volley thrown at them.

The arrows flew through the night air, none as precise and powerful as Evren's but they didn't need to be. The rebels were so close it was impossible to miss them. The arrows tore through flesh unhindered, and Abraxas's watched every one of them hit home. Watched them pierce bodies and shatter brittle armor . . .

. . . and land in the sand bloodless and whole.

Abraxas stood straight up, eyes wide. Mizan's people were gone as if they'd never been there. Like a mirage they'd rippled away. Murmurs of confusion rippled through the Grave's wall as arrows were notched with no real targets.

"Impressive," Nerezza said, but she wasn't looking at the spot where Mizan's troops had disappeared. She was looking off to the side where Abraxas hadn't noticed the Dra'Nacti crouching.

The Dra'Nacti huffed and shook out his hands as the spell was completed. Abraxas could taste it on his tongue now, the strange magic, like warm heat instead of the cold energy he was used to. He followed his black gaze to the far side of the Grave's wall, where the real troops were climbing up the wall unhindered.

As quiet as ghosts themselves.

It was a simple strategy, one he should've seen coming. But as the spiders caught on and dove back into the Grave with weapons drawn, he knew that it was pointless. Whatever fight happened behind those walls he didn't care to see. He heard the cries, saw the orange glow of fires burning brighter, heard the dying as they were cut down. Mizan hadn't been bluffing to give his people courage, he'd just manifested the outcome he wanted.

That wasn't magic, that was belief. One he knew deep down in his core. It was faith. Faith in his people and his skills, faith in the Dra'Nacti's strange magic to work right, and faith that they were destined to win.

Abraxas, for all his hundred years fighting Vernes, had never understood them or their drive. It was only now, watching the Spider's Grave fall at his recommendation, did he see that both Vernes and Etherak were fighting with the same purpose.

Faith.

The battle was over quickly. The gates were thrown open and cheers of Vernesian victory overtook the desert wind. Hollers and whoops were shared as crates were smashed open and potions, food, and weapons were spilled.

Nerezza stood up beside him, not willing herself towards the gates either. They both stood still and watched.

"You did well," she said suddenly.

He snapped his head towards her. "What?"

"This," she nodded to the Grave, "this is a step towards them trusting us. You did exactly what I needed you to do."

"I didn't . . ." Dread crept into his chest, sinking back into the familiar divot above his heart. "No. I didn't do this for you. You weren't even there when Mizan and I planned this."

"Oh no, I had no idea what you'd do exactly. But something along these lines was about what I expected. You're an easy read, Abraxas. So tormented by your own guilt that you'd do anything to redeem yourself. These rebels needed you, so they needed us." She turned towards him, that damned smile he'd thought had burned away still on her lips. "This is our way forward."

"Don't," he begged. *Begged.* He'd never begged a mortal soul in his life. "Whatever your plan is, leave them out of this."

"Oh, don't worry." She laid a hand on his arm, ignoring the way his skin flinched away impulsively. "You can play hero again. I'll play along. I don't want them dead, Abraxas, no more than you, but they do have something I need."

"That shard."

"More than one of them. I won't bore you with the details in case you plan to warn your new friend, that healer. But let me say this." She leaned in closer, so they were only a breath's width apart. "You want them to live? You'll help me get it. I'll let you have your pity party, but you're still mine, and we still have a mission. Understand?"

The sick feeling of her control over his blood crept back into his body, alien yet familiar and teetering on painful that he instantly nodded. It had been so long since he'd felt her presence in his body he'd almost forgotten how horrible it was.

"I understand," he said, hating himself as he did.

That, at least, was nothing new.

14

Evren

It was night when Evren and Arke, with Viggo and Tolk in tow, made it back to the surface. Tolk's exit had them crawling out of the ground and into a field of golden wheat, as if the earth itself had given birth to them. The stars were out in full force, dazzling above where the moon hung low on the horizon. The air was sweet and warm, the sounds of rustling wheat stalks filling Evren's ears with every whisper of a breeze.

This didn't look like a world on the brink of war. Evren stared out at the field, wondering how much it would change if they failed. Would the wheat burn? Would the sky be forever clouded with smoke? Would the breeze smell of carrion and steel instead of sweet grass?

Evren hadn't seen true war and she didn't plan to. But nothing in Eith ever went according to plan, especially concerning adventurers.

A low groaning behind Evren snapped her out of her thoughts. She turned back to their exit where Viggo was hunched over with his hands on his knees. Arke backed away from him, shaking his head.

"Told him not to look up," he told Evren. "Said it would fuck him up. And what did he do?"

"Look up," Evren sighed. They'd had a similar issue getting Sol acclimated to the surface. It turns out that spending your entire life with a roof over your head made the sight of no roof extremely terrifying. They'd spent most of the first day keeping Sol from falling over or puking her guts out. The rest was explaining that it was normal for wet things to fall from the sky.

"Right, I got him." She patted Arke's shoulder. "You and Tolk go ahead. You know where we are?"

Arke snorted, giving his larger brother—who was snickering and poking at Viggo's quivering calves—a long look. "He don't but I do. Won't take us long to get to Sahar's. We're just an hour northwest of her."

"Let's hope everyone else is there." She smiled thinly and walked to Viggo. Tolk scurried past her at his brother's whistle and she heard the smattering of conversation as they meandered away, taking a slow pace so she and Viggo could eventually catch up.

She stopped in front of him, hands on her hips, just content to watch him struggle for a bit. Perhaps that was cruel, but there was a twinge of satisfaction in knowing that most Serevadians would be dealing with the same vertigo and fear their first steps onto the surface.

"You're enjoying this," Viggo rasped behind his curtain of white hair.

"A little," she admitted. "Arke did tell you not to look up."

"I thought I had an advantage." He held his hand up, shuddering in the air as if it was causing him pain. She grabbed it and used it to help him stand up straight, slowly. New calluses where there'd only been soft skin rubbed awkwardly against her own. He started to lift his head, but she made a noise of warning and he kept staring at his shoes. "I've seen the sky before, through your memories."

"It's different in person," she said, still holding his hand to keep him steady. "Sol had the same issues, and dwarves live on the surface as well as underground. Goblins too, it seems. Just get used to the air for a while, then very slowly you can start to look up. And by slowly, I mean an inch at a time. And by up, I mean at the horizon, not the endless expanse of air above you."

Viggo groaned again, sweaty palm tightening around her hand. "You're wickedly cruel at times."

"I've been told."

Twenty minutes passed before Viggo was able to look ahead without falling over. His breathing was still ragged and his steps unsure, but he kept to small steps and even breaths, all the while staring either at the ground or where Evren pointed out was safe. His fingers loosened and she let go, stuffing her hand next to where her dagger laid at her hip.

They made it out of the field and onto a well-traveled road, the dirt relatively smooth despite the puddles of mud and water in some areas. Arke and Tolk were far ahead, but she could see their forms easily. Beside her, she felt Viggo's agitation as their slow march continued.

"It gets easier," she promised him. "You can't help not being born under sky."

"Daylight will be worse," he muttered. "Won't it?"

"We'll have you inside before then, but yes. Everything is brighter during the day. Sol had a hard time getting used to it, although . . . well, I have a feeling it'll be worse for you."

"Likely," he said. "I thought it would feel right."

"Centuries of living underground has you made for just that. You see better in the dark, you're built for smaller spaces." She shrugged. "You adapted."

"And how long will it take us to adapt to this?" She

watched him fight to no look at the sky. His scowl deepened, now a permanent fixture on his once smooth face.

"I don't know," she said, partly because she had no clue and partly because she couldn't see a future where Serevadians adapted to the surface while everyone else watched peacefully. All the sunlight Eith could share, the land, she knew deep down, would all be soaked with blood.

~

WELL PAST MIDNIGHT, the Al-Fasil manor burned brighter than any star. It was like the sun was pulsing through the windows, shedding golden light onto the quiet grounds. Gone were the laughing servants and singing field hands. The tunnel of trees that had seemed so warm and inviting, now twisted the light from the manor between their dark limbs.

The end of the trees marked the beginning of the manor proper in all its gilded glory. All three stories were lit up, and shadows dashed back and forth behind the lacey curtains. Hushed tones and direct words filtered through the open windows to Evren's ears. The large double doors were parted just a crack, light spilling down the steps. Standing at the doorway, in rumbled clothing and a bloodstained apron, was Sahar.

Their time apart seemed to have aged her. Her face was pinched with worry, lines that hadn't been present on her smooth skin starting to form on her forehead and around her mouth. Her hair was falling from her bun, a messy imitation of the elegant updo she'd had in the carriage. She shucked off her gloves and tucked a piece of black hair behind her ear.

"Lookouts said you were coming up the path." She started walking down the steps. "I almost didn't believe it."

The last of her words came out in a rush as she ran forward and pulled Evren into a hug. The wind was nearly squeezed out of her lungs, but she found the strength to hug her back. Sahar smelled like blood and potions, the metallic scent of healing stuck into her pores. Evren let herself be held. Sahar had been so cold after the White Cairn that she'd forgotten just how warm and sun-like the noblewoman could be.

"We're okay," Evren said as they pulled apart. She nodded to Arke. "Thanks to some quick spellcasting."

"How did you make it out?" she asked. "And how . . ." She trailed off, eyes going wide as she took in Viggo and Tolk behind Evren. "Goblin help and a painted elf? Evren, I don't understand."

"It's a long story, and you're not going to like most of it. But, Sahar." She put a hand on the woman's shoulder. "You were right about them being alive. I'm sorry."

Sahar's warm brown eyes fill up with tears, the redness around them showing she'd already cried enough. She blinked them away and took a deep breath before putting on a smile that faintly resembled the blinding mask she often wore.

"I normally am, but it's good to hear. I accept your apology. Now," she snapped her attention to Viggo and Tolk, "I require answers and I just so happen to be on my break. But dragging you through the manor will only upset a delicate atmosphere, so I'll take you to the kitchen through the servant's quarters. It should be empty by now. And I'll bring you to your friends."

Arke's eyes went wide and hopeful, sharing a likeness with the full moon. "Sorin?"

Sahar nodded. "He's alive. Everyone you know is. Not many were as lucky. I take it you have answers?"

Viggo cleared his throat and spoke for the first time. "For everything, I swear."

Sahar eyed him with unbridled distrust. "I hope so. Over two hundred souls seek rest."

Without another word, Sahar ushered them around the back of the manor, past thick and luscious gardens, and through a small wooden door. The kitchen on the other side was bigger than most taverns Evren had been in. A roaring fire and dozens of bright lanterns kept the mostly windowless room well lit. Few shadows clung the corners. Pots dangled from their hooks on the ceiling, swinging next to dried herbs and baskets of produce waiting to be used. The abandoned remnants of dinner were still splayed out on the large table in the middle; chopped veggies, jars of seasoning half opened, meat still wrapped in paper from the market.

Sahar closed the door behind them and quickly crossed the kitchen. "Stay here, I'll bring everyone we need back here."

"Sahar, what's going on?" Evren gestured to the messy kitchen. "It looks like everyone left in a hurry."

Sahar's lips pressed into a thin line. "A little difficult to focus on a big dinner when people are dying. My father opened the manor to those who needed a place to stay and heal. Not all were able to be moved, but we're helping those that did."

"How bad was it?" Evren could've kicked herself for asking that, but she still didn't know the full scale of the attack. Sahar had mentioned two hundred or more souls, but how many of those were adventurers? How many were civilians who'd been caught in the blast?

Sahar met her eyes. "It was the first blow against Terevas and the Collective in history. It was devastating."

Evren sank onto a stool as Sahar left. The boys followed her lead, although Tolk went straight for the raw food and started shoveling it in his mouth.

Viggo grimaced. "Weeks at your table, Master Tolk, has not endeared me to goblin ways like you promised."

Tolk shrugged, using his tongue to get a sliver of onion from its place between his yellowing teeth. "Can't say I didn't try." He nudged the package of meat over to Arke with his elbow. "Want some?"

"Nah."

"You're gonna get skinny. Like a little twig. Kings ain't skinny."

"Explains why your gut is twice the size it was when I left."

Tolk barked a laugh, spewing chewed food across the table. Both Evren and Viggo moved their arms from the tabletop to their laps.

"I still can't believe Viggo's delicate constitution survived your hospitality, Tolk," Evren said, grinning whenever Viggo rolled his eyes at her.

"I am not delicate," He retorted.

"Eh." Arke wobbled his hand back and forth, the way he'd picked up from Sorin. "Not when it comes to lyin' and bein' a prick. But food? Yeah."

Viggo rested his head in his hand, angling his face so he could still glare at the goblin while looking as morose as possible. "Do goblins ever let go of a grudge?"

"No," Arke and Tolk said in unison.

Tolk chuckled again and nudged the package of meat closer to him. The barest of hesitation flitted across Arke's face. He looked up at Evren, as if for advice or to ask a question, but snapped his gaze back again. He took the package, opening it gently as if it was precious.

"It ain't glass, Arke," his brother laughed. "Tear into it!"

His claws flexed, still stained black from his new inks and spells. It was like something invisible was keeping his fingers from tearing into the food, that damnable hesitation taking a physical form around his knuckles. He'd never hesitated with his food before. Time and time again Arke was a bottomless hole, no matter how bland her cooking was or over seasoned Sorin's was. The conflict inside Arke was painful to watch.

The door to the manor slamming open relieved Arke and the table of his choice. The package was shoved away, forgotten, as Sorin barreled through the door, followed quickly by

Sol and Sahar. The worg bounded after them, tongue rolling out of his mouth.

"You're alive!" Sorin slung one arm around Arke and another around Evren, pulling them close and smushing wet forehead kisses on both of them. Evren hugged him eagerly, even as his shoulder dug into her throat painfully. He pulled back just enough to look them over, checking for wounds or anything wrong.

Evren did the same, taking in his tied back dreads and stained apron identical to Sahar's. The bags under his eyes were darker than she'd seen since Dirn-Darahl, and despite his dazzling smile, he looked like he hadn't slept or eaten in days.

"Move, move, move!" Sol cried and wiggled past Sorin to embrace them. Arke fought, as he always did for someone who wasn't Sorin, but eventually gave into the dwarf's arms. "What took you so long?"

Like Sorin, she had a drawn, weary look to her. Even her eyes looked a little duller as she wiped away tears.

"We, uh, had a few stops to make," Evren offered.

"A few stops?" Sorin exclaimed. "Evvie, we thought you were dead! One minute everyone is dancing and having a fine time—"

"You fell victim to a Fey spell," Sahar said flatly.

"*Having a fine time*," Sorin repeated. "The next, the ground is gone, people are screaming, Sol was riding the *dog* and you were nowhere to be found. Do you know how hard is to dig through rubble when you're crying? Couldn't see a thing. Oh, and Mal's alive! And out. Who knew? Can't find the fucker anywhere because we've been stuck here with a quarter of those hurt. I haven't slept in two days, haven't eaten or drank anything except that weird potion of Sahar's. I feel like I'm buzzing off to another world and . . ." He trailed off, eyes finally finding Viggo and Tolk's forms at the table. He pointed a wobbly finger at Viggo, eyes unblinking. "That's a fucker I definitely shouldn't be seeing. Tell me I'm dreaming, Sol. Slipped off into blissful sleep and into this vivid nightmare where Viggo is staring at me like I've spouted two heads."

"You're not," Sol squeaked.

Viggo straightened up in his stool. "Hello again, Sorin Trinity."

Sorin recoiled as if he'd been hit. His finger still pointed at Viggo like a sword, he said, "No, fuck you! What are you doing here? Never mind that. Go fuck yourself. You!" He turned to Tolk. "Fuck you, too."

Arke grunted. "That's my brother."

"Oh, never mind. You're fine. But you!" He whirled back to Viggo, who stared at him with an increasingly bored expression.

"Let me guess? Fuck me."

"Damn straight!"

Sol had to jump to grab Sorin's raised arm and pull him back, but she glared at Viggo with just as much venom.

"What is he doing here?" she asked. "First Mal, and now him? What's next? Alkimos?"

"Unfortunately, he's dead," Viggo said nonchalantly.

Evren felt a pang in her chest. The great worm had hardly been a friend. He'd been more of a threat than anything up until the end, he just didn't seem killable to her. Strange how Mortova had been a massive challenge to put down, but she'd never believed it was impossible to best him. Even the Storm, which was the definition of unchecked power and intelligence, had died. She'd seen the aftermath of it, touched her dead bones with her own fingers. But Alkimos was different, *had* been different. She'd been connected to him and felt all that raw power, seen how large his territory was.

It didn't feel right that he'd died and she hadn't felt it. But nothing about her magic had been the same since Gyda, there was no telling how her connection to Alkimos had . . .

"Where's Gyda?" Evren asked, shutting Sorin down before he could go into another rant. His golden eyes darkened as he and Sol exchanged a look.

"She's alive . . ."

Evren stood up. "Is she hurt?"

"Not really, she's just not well enough to come down." Sol took Evren's white knuckled fist in her hands. "She knows you're here. She's ecstatic that you're alive."

"Woulda been awkward if she wasn't, eh?" Tolk snickered.

Evren looked back at the table. Viggo and his dreadful story about to unfold. Sorin and Sol who needed answers. Sahar who was waiting with bated to breath to hear news of Nerezza. She owed them her presence and her bad plans. They needed her, but so did Gyda. Gyda was hurting because of Evren and she needed to know how bad it was.

Arke met her gaze and nodded towards the door. "Go, I'll fill them in."

"Thank you." She squeezed Sol's hand and walked to Sahar. "Which way."

"Second floor, down two halls to the left. Fourth door on the right."

With that she bolted out of the kitchen, careful to close the door behind her, and into the manor. She moved too fast to appreciate the beauty and architecture. The art on the walls were just blurs. The marble floors could've been jagged stone for all she cared. She took the grand staircase up, two steps at a time, avoiding everyone in her way. Servants leaning against the rails on their breaks, hurt but walking survivors watching her go. The halls were thick with people, but none tried to talk to her or stop her. They just watched her with tired, pained expressions.

Second floor, one and two halls to the left, Evren counted under her breath and rounded each corner so fast it was a miracle she didn't run into anyone. Then came the doors. The ones on the left didn't exist at all, even if they were wide open with whole groups huddled around one bed. The right was what she needed. At the fourth door she barely paused to breathe before opening it and running inside.

It was an opulent room, fit for a noble or an important guest. Bay windows overlooked the garden and spilled in moonlight in large rectangles over the carpet and bed. The bed was the biggest she'd ever seen, with heavy curtains around the canopy to be drawn closed if the moonlight was too much.

Laying in the very middle under the blankets was Gyda.

Evren had never seen her so diminished. What little color she normally had in her grey skin was gone. Despite her corded muscles remaining she looked smaller, as if she'd fallen into herself. Her chest rose and fell with a slight wheeze, but it was moving. That, at least, Evren hadn't ruined.

Gyda's eyes opened to see her at the door. They fluttered shut as relief washed over her, strong enough to drag her oddly frail body deeper into the cushions. She took her hand out of the blankets and held it palm up to her.

"Come here."

As if she could go anywhere else.

Evren shut the door and ran to her side. The ridiculously soft mattress sank under her knees as she climbed up beside her and took her hand. Her chest was tight and hot as she leaned forward, brushing Gyda's red hair out of her face with her other hand. Her fingers paused when the red turned to white, the streak of hair brittle against the heavy, healthier strands.

"A souvenir," Gyda sighed. "Won't matter to anyone but you. Only you'll see it."

It took a moment for Evren to be able to breathe properly, her fingers stuck in those white strands as she wrapped her head around it. She'd done this. With Arke's simple spell of moving stone she'd sucked the very life out of Gyda and marked her in a way a scar never could. She untangled her hand from her hair, smoothing it down before pulling back again.

"I'm sorry," she said, pulling Gyda's hand to her chest. "I didn't want to, but we didn't have a choice. I knew it would hurt but I didn't think—"

"Shh," Gyda lifted their joined hands to brush her thumb against Evren's quivering lips. "You did what you had to do to survive. You're here now, that's all that matters."

"No." Evren shook her head. Tears were burning behind her eyes, but she refused to let them fall. "No, Gyda, this isn't right. You shouldn't be like this."

"I'm better now than I was an hour ago." Her voice was feather soft but gaining its normal strength with each word spoken. "I have been regaining strength. I'll be able to throw you over my shoulder again, I swear."

"Never again." Evren kissed her knuckles. "I won't use it again."

And then Gyda smiled the kind of smile that sent her heart stuttering. Mixed with pride and love, but also a rueful understanding.

"You will, because it isn't about us. You came back to tell us everything is so much worse than a sinkhole. The world is at stake. I can tell by the look on your face. Soon it won't be about us anymore. It won't be about gold or revenge. It will simply be survival on a much larger scale. We cannot promise the world safety and keep this from them."

"No magic is worth your life."

"No world is worth yours," Gyda said. "And I am alive now. That's all that matters."

And the day that she wasn't? The day where Evren might have to sacrifice not just her life but Gyda's to save another piece of Eith? That wasn't fair. Gyda was literally half her heart, but she'd lose her wholly if she died. Evren had lived heartless, and she never wanted to feel that empty ever again.

But saying it out loud would be pointless. Gyda knew her thoughts as well as she knew her own. Fighting with her, as with everything, came down to strength, and even at her weakest Gyda still beat Evren.

She was tired. She didn't want to argue. All she wanted was to bury her face in Gyda's hair and sleep until everything was over again. But there was work to be done.

Evren swallowed down her unease. "The sinkhole was an attack. Serevadian."

Gyda stiffened the slightest bit and nodded. "Go on."

"Viggo's plan for new leadership failed. Velcros is in total control. He marched on Dirn-Darahl, which is likely how Mal got out. Viggo said he's planning on taking the surface by force. Dirn-Darahl was personal. Rheinwall was a message."

Gyda frowned. "Viggo said."

"Yeah, he's here. In the manor. Arke's brother had been harboring him from the Serevadians until he could get to us."

Gyda grumbled under her breath, sinking into the pillows. "He's here for you, you mean."

"That ship sailed long ago, trust me." Evren squeezed her hand and earned a small smile. "Bigger news, however, is about Abraxas and Nerezza. Viggo says they're alive and in Serevadia."

Gyda sat up so fast she nearly caused Evren to tumble off the bed. Her firm grip kept her close, those eyes staring down at her as if she couldn't believe the words that came out of her mouth.

"He's alive," she breathed, her words fanning out on Evren's cheeks.

"Yes. Viggo believes that he used the dagger to move backwards in time, although we don't know how far he went or why he's still with Nerezza."

"He's playing her, he has to be," she murmured, half to Evren and half to herself. "If Viggo saw them, then . . ."

"Nerezza has to be behind this. Abraxas could be our key to stopping an invasion before it starts."

Gyda lost a little of her sudden strength and leaned on Evren, but her eyes remained bright. "I knew he wasn't gone. I knew it."

Evren smiled at her. "I shouldn't have doubted you. He's a hard man to kill. Maybe we're all just full of miracles, like you said."

Gyda didn't say anything, she just started to pull her down to the pillows. What little strength the news had brought her was fading away and Evren could feel sleep tugging at them both. But before they could fully lay down, the hairs on the back of her neck stood up and Evren stopped. Gyda did too, her muscles tensing as a gravely, raspy voice filled the air.

"Abraxas Kain is your miracle."

Evren and Gyda lurched apart, Gyda going for her sword and Evren drawing her dagger. They froze as the figure at the foot of the bed stared them down, the cloak just as tattered and the singular eye just as wickedly gold as she remembered.

Evren had forgotten about them after taking the dagger. "I thought we were done," she said slowly, laying a hand on Gyda's arm to let her know it was okay to stand down—for now.

"We're not done," the figure said. They were pointedly ignoring Gyda, their eye fixed unnervingly on Evren.

"I take it you have thoughts on this quest."

"It is the genesis of a new era," they said, as if that explained everything. "I am here to guide."

"So more vague messages?" Evren raised her eyebrows. "Great."

After the last time with the figure, she expected something more from them. They'd felt more human then, going from 'it' to 'they' in her mind without even realizing. They were bound to the dagger, that she knew, but little else. And yet they seemed so achingly familiar . . .

"What did you mean about Abraxas and miracles?" Gyda asked.

The figure didn't so much as twitch her direction. The answer was aimed at Evren. "Abraxas Kain is the reason Sorin lives. He is the reason Sol still breathes and why you lasted as long as you did."

"Sorin's resurrection," Evren said. "You know what caused that?"

"Abraxas did."

Evren shook her head. "No. He said he tried before, and he couldn't. No one can do that magic without the Divines."

"No, they can't."

"So, they're back?"

"If they were, Eith would feel their footsteps on the ground as if the mountains themselves were moving. No. The gods are not your answer. They are an afterthought, a distraction. Abraxas Kain is both miracle and key. Only he can keep Serevadia at bay."

This was the most direct they'd ever spoken to her, and yet Evren could barely wrap her mind around the words. How could one man, no matter how determined and powerful, stop an entire empire?

But that wasn't a question the figure would answer.

"Will you tell us how to get to him? Serevadia is massive. He could be anywhere."

The figure paused, as if weighting how cryptic and vague they could answer without being throttled by the two women. Eventually they sighed heavily, something Evren had never heard them do.

"You'll need the sword first, bound with the same soul as the dagger before it. Find it and you will find him."

A sword. There were so many in Eith. Many were powerful like Gyda's. But only one could compare to the Eternity Dagger. Her mind flashed back to Viggo's memory of the

Elder temple, of every depiction of the Shadow Dancer in Andovine.

Always with a sword, no matter the artist.

"It always comes back to them, doesn't it?" she asked.

But the figure was already gone. The shadows in the room had swallowed it completely and left Evren and Gyda utterly alone.

Evren was heavy. She was exhausted. A part of her believed that they were done after Nerezza had been dealt with, but now they'd been thrown back into the game. Because where there were adventurers, there were always high stakes that they had to fight around. That was an unspoken truth in Eith.

Gyda laid back down, exhaling heavily as she hit the pillows. Evren followed her, curling up beside her and basking in her warmth, in the steadiness of her embrace. Gyda was her mountain, her rock and shelter against the storm. In her shadow, she was safe.

"We'll tell the others in the morning," Gyda said, pressing her lips to her forehead.

Evren closed her eyes, relishing the kiss, the smell of her skin, the thrum of her heart. The things she'd longed for and denied herself for so long. Would she have to savor each stolen, still moment like this? What awaited them in Serevadia, at the Shadow Dancer's sword, could be the end of them, if the figure's appearance was any indication.

"In the morning," Evren agreed and took this night as her last reprieve.

15

Evren

The rainy gloom of the next morning did little to remove Terevas's color. The green shone brighter for the dark grey sky, the warm stone of the manor almost gold in the storm-filtered light. The rain battered the wide windows, shadows of drops dancing across the smooth marble floor. In the far west wing of the manor, the air smelled of decay and a door stood locked before Evren.

She stifled the urge to cover her nose standing in front of the door. "New body, same smell."

Keres grinned beside her. "Coming from someone who was a walking corpse herself, that's a low blow."

Evren wasn't surprised to find Keres lurking in Sahar's manor, although she had forgotten about them. She was less surprised to find that they'd shed Vox's body for a different one. This one was a human boy, the body so gaunt he looked little more than a skeleton still wearing skin.

"How did you get the new face?" she asked, eyes still fixed on the door.

"Servant boy was sick. Had been his whole life. Something wrong with his lungs, Lady Al-Fasil had said." They shrugged their boney shoulder. "It matters not now."

"It doesn't bother you that you're possessing a boy's body?"

They blinked owlishly at her. "Why would it?"

Evren shifted uncomfortably, adding a couple inches between the two of them. No matter how much she pitied Keres and understood their plight, they were so drastically different that it made her skin crawl. Of course they wouldn't have an issue with taking over a servant's corpse; they hadn't a shred of remorse for using Vox's before. To them it was a means to an end and nothing more.

"I asked permission, if that makes you feel better," they said.

Evren's stomach twisted. She wasn't sure it did. Had the dying boy even known what he was agreeing to? She was hard pressed to think of anyone who would give their body up to an ancient Vernesian death spirit. Then again, if he wasn't using it, Keres could be seen as an alternate form of burial. And it was better than Keres digging up a grave since Terevasans didn't burn their dead.

Evren shook her head. Everything with Keres was complicated. Maybe her perpetual headaches in the Reino Terminan had less to do with her condition and more with them twisting her brain into painful knots.

"How did you get him?" she asked instead, changing the subject to the man behind the door.

Keres scoffed. "It was child's play. If the sinkhole had caught him that would've been a challenge. Instead, the little bastard slipped away just in time and led me on a boring chase along the countryside. He has an uncanny knack for survival, I'll give him that. Even if it's only because he blunders blindly from one crisis to the next. I had half a mind to rip his throat out and take his body, just for fun."

Evren turned from the door and scowled at him. "We would've noticed."

"Would you though? It would've been a fun game."

"Well, unfortunately for both of us, killing him isn't an option."

"Yet."

Evren stared at Keres long enough for them to make an unholy giggling sound. "We need him alive, Keres."

"For now. That's why I said *yet*."

She used her disgust to hide the fact that she really did want the man behind the door dead, and she knew Keres would come up with a truly horrific way for him to die. But that wasn't up to ether of them. For fun or for revenge, they wouldn't be the one to land the killing blow when it came.

"You're a menace," she said, because anything else could be taken as permission to go killing.

"I know we're on the same page." They grinned, tapping their temple with a skinny finger. "No need to be coy."

It wasn't that Evren had forgotten that Keres could hear the thoughts of those around them, she'd just chosen to ignore that fact. She then thought a lot of curses very loudly and marched towards the door. Keres giggled behind her as she pulled the key Sahar had given her from her pocket.

"If you need a scary nudge, call me in," they said. "He pissed his pants when he saw me. I can make him do it again."

"Noted," Evren said as she unlocked the door, opened it, and stepped inside.

It shut with a satisfying thud behind her. The room was small and dark, windowless and little more than a storage closet for cleaning supplies. Now it was empty save for a lone dwarf sitting on a chair.

"You know, for a sleezy, backstabbing politician, you have a knack for not dying, Mal," she said, slipping the key in her pocket and leaning against the door.

Mal's eyes watched the key, flickering with indecision. He

wasn't tied to the chair. He could try to wrestle it from her and spring free. As the thoughts unfolded on his face, she smiled.

"You can try." She patted the pocket. "It would give me the excuse to break your fingers and try out that luck of yours."

He bristled, tearing his glare from the key to her face. "You won't kill me."

"Won't I?"

A bit of his bluster fell. "You . . . you need me. I have information you want. That's why I'm here."

"Maybe you're here because I decided to do something I should've done back when we first met." He shrunk back in his seat, throat wobbling with every hard swallow of fear. "Don't presume to know what I've got planned."

Something shifted in him. The fear was still there, and Evren could at least take solace in the fact that he was scared of her. But that anger never left. That hatred she'd caught glimpses of in Rheinwall bubbled through the fear like hot oil in water.

"I know what you are," he said. "You think blindly stumbling from one crisis to another makes you a hero? You left Dirn-Darahl in shambles. You broke it—"

"No, you did that," she snapped. "You and Heliodar's coup decimated your army, killed your King, and destroyed you people's trust."

"Sol killed the King, not me."

"Don't you dare say her name," Evren said lowly, taking a step forward and truly relishing in the way he tried to back away from her. "You sacrificed her for your own gain, you do *not* get to speak of her like she's still yours to hold and manipulate. The truth of the matter is that yes, I want to kill you. Everyone I know here does. But not because of your plots and your weak will that couldn't stand up to Heliodar. That is something we can ignore. No, you hurt Sol, used her, and tormented her. You do not get to sit her and act like you were wronged when she finally stood up for herself and her people. That dagger she threw to take down a King should've been aimed at you, and if she was a worse shot I would say it was. But the truth is, in that moment you didn't matter. You were inconsequential, someone to be dealt with after the threat was put down, if you even survived. All your scheming to save your hide and boost your status amounted to nothing in the end."

She stopped close enough that she could smell that Keres hadn't lied about Mal wetting himself. "You are still inconsequential, it's your knowledge that we need. And either you tell us willingly, or I can get the corpse that dragged you here inside so they can have some fun."

Despite his pallor and sweating, Mal managed a weak wheeze of a laugh. "I didn't take you for torturer, Hanali."

"You don't know me," she said. "Keep that in mind."

"But I do." He smiled, the sunburned skin on his cheeks cracking. "I know that you're only a hero when it suits you, that Dirn-Darahl's war wouldn't have bothered you in the slightest if you hadn't found something pretty down there to be attached to. You saved Serevadia for gold and doomed my people because we didn't fit your ideals of how the world should work. I've heard the stories of your other adventures. If it hadn't been for Gyda, you would've turned your back on the Ikedree. If you hadn't been dying, you would've let Prince Barrion kill himself trying to find Orenlion. You are selfish, arrogant, and a bully. You don't deserve the title of hero. And the only reason you're in here now is because you know that letting Serevadia survive has come back to bite you in the arse. You're not better than me, you're just the next piece of trash Solri clung to as her life fell apart."

Mal's leg jammed into Evren's knee, the bone cracking painfully as she went down. His hands fumbled for the key in her pocket, elbowing her in the face when she tried to stop him. Her teeth knocked together, her vision blacking out for only a second. She was on her feet before it came back. She lunged at him, the key clattering against the lock as he fumbled with her.

Blood coated her tongue. She refused to taste it. The screaming pain in her knee slowed every step. Evren grabbed a fist full of his shirt and he swung wildly to get her off. The blow missed and she didn't even have to dodge.

The latch clicked. Just as he pulled the door open, Evren pout her weight on her good leg and kicked with her bad one. White-hot spikes of pain bloomed, but her boot had struck true, slamming him to the ground face first just as the door swung wide open.

The airy hallway beyond was a beacon of fresh, damp air filtered through the drenched windows. Mal tried to crawl forward, his hand stopping just as it brushed a set of boots waiting for him.

He looked up, following the boots to legs, then to a leather clad torso, and then finally to Sol's face.

The fight seemed to drain out of him. He shrunk back and Evren let go of his shirt, which had partially ripped in the fight. Sol didn't give her a second glance. She just stared down at him with a cold indifference that made even Evren's skin crawl.

Sol was dressed and ready for this meeting. Her leather armor was on, shined enough to make all the wear and tear stand out just a little bit more; signs that she'd been through many hells and came back to sing about it. Her hair was down, free of braids and ties. She hadn't shaved her face either, a couple days' worth of stubble on her jaw.

"Hello, Malrus," she said calmly.

"Sol . . ." he rasped. "I—"

"It's Solri. You're not my friend." She looked up at Evren. "But you have been bloodying one."

Evren winced and wiped away the blood on her face. "I

won't lie, I forgot every dwarf goes through combat training. And he pissed me off."

"He's good at that. Are you okay?"

Evren nodded. She swung her leg back and forth at the knee. It hurt like a bitch, but it wasn't broken. She'd just have to be careful until a potion could be spared.

Sol nodded then lifted her finger towards the ceiling. "Get up."

Mal took his time, only speeding up when she started to tap her foot on the marble. Then he scrambled to his feet like an embarrassed schoolboy caught playing in the mud. He stood up straight in front of her, shoulders tense and fingers trembling at his side.

"Get inside." She nodded to the room. "And sit down."

He blanched. "Sol, we don't have to do this—"

"I said *sit*."

Evren could only blink in surprise as Mal immediately obeyed, skirting around her and back to the chair he fought so hard to leave. She snorted a laugh and turned back to Sol who was still watching him with narrowed eyes.

"It's like you've got him trained," Evren said.

Sol's gaze warmed when she looked at Evren. "I used to. In the bedroom at least. We'll see if any of it stuck." She wrinkled her nose at Evren's favored knee. "Go get that checked out, I'll take care of this."

Evren hesitated. She could still picture the look of terror in Sol's face in Rheinwall, the revulsion that shook her limbs. That was a far cry from the woman who stood in front of her now, but Evren knew Sol could wear masks to cover her true feelings like none other. She'd taken Orenlion by storm that way.

"Are you sure?" she asked. "I can stay. I've had much worse."

"I know," Sol's smile was gentle and thankful. "I'm fine

now, Evren. He surprised me in Rheinwall." She flitted her icy gaze to Mal. "It won't happen again."

Evren nodded and limped past the doorway. Putting a hand on her friend's shoulder, she squeezed reassuringly. "He wants us to suffer for ruining his and Heliodar's plans, that's likely the only reason he's not talking. We need numbers Sol. We need to know everything he saw and how he escaped."

She nodded. "I can hear this. I can weather this storm."

"It's not your fault, no matter what he says," she whispered.

Sol took a shaky breath and held her head high. Evren couldn't be sure if a real tear or a shadow of rain from the window slid down her cheek. "I know."

She pulled away and Evren let her go. The door shut behind her, the lock clicked in place, and Evren knew it wouldn't open again until Sol had her answers.

Mal wouldn't last long. He was keeping his information out of spite and fear that they'd get rid of him as soon as he talked. With the way the rest of the Wandering Sols offered to deal with him, his fear wasn't unfounded. But personal grudges would have to wait. Mal was the only one besides Viggo who'd seen Serevadia's army, and it was easier to believe two known liars if their stories matched somewhat.

Hobbling down the hallway, Evren nodded to Keres who stood by a window watching everything. They wouldn't move, just in case Mal did pull something else and get past Sol. Keres would make sure that he didn't get past them with his heart still beating. She could trust Keres in that at least.

"Don't want to go in there and read his thoughts?" she asked as she passed.

Keres made a disgusted face. "I heard what he was thinking the whole trip here. Useless, fear-soaked nonsense. Besides, it's more satisfying to let the King slayer deal with him, isn't it?"

It was.

"Watch the door. Let me know if there's any changes," she tossed over her shoulder.

"You won't be the first to know, but word will reach you eventually."

Evren rolled her eyes but kept marching forward. Her knee burned with more shame than pain. She'd let Mal's words get under her skin; she'd let her anger blind her. It hadn't been the first time she'd let her emotions guide her into doing stupid shit and it likely wouldn't be the last, but she couldn't afford any more mistakes like that. Small ones like letting an interrogation go so south that someone nearly escapes could turn into much bigger ones later on.

And Evren didn't have the best track record of great decisions or plans.

Out of the west wing, Evren found herself in the chaotic flurry of activity only found in the grand hall. She'd barely seen it when she first ran through to get to Gyda, but now it was hard not to gape at the soaring ceilings, breathtaking art, and striking staircase. It was easy to recognize Terevasan architecture and it's touches in the manor. But she could also see some she didn't recognize. Sculptures of glass that twisted in organic waves around the candlesticks of the chandelier, rugs so brightly colored in reds and golds it looked like the sunset had been dyed into the fabric itself, and pieces of old armor and weapons hung on the walls. If the carpet and sculptures hadn't been clue enough, the glaives and unique armor was.

The Al-Fasil family hadn't forgotten their heritage and kept Vernes with them even an ocean away.

Evren kept out of the way of servants and nurses. None of the injured remaining in the manor were serious anymore but the staff took their job of making everyone comfortable very seriously. Up the stairs she could faintly hear an adventurer arguing about how they didn't need their sheets changed when they'd only used the bed twice. The little maid wouldn't give up though, there was no use stopping her.

"Ah, Lady Evren, you look to be in pain. Might I help?"

Evren whirled around faster than she should've, grabbing her knee and hissing in pain as it flared up.

The owner of the voice, a silvering human with a round belly and warm brown skin helped her up again, his hands just barely hovering over her arms as guides.

"Easy there." He smiled, his Vernesian accent light, whereas Sahar's was completely Terevasan. "You look less well than when you woke up. Is there something I should know?"

She shook her head. "No, Lord Al-Fasil, but thank you."

Evren had seen Sahar's father flitting around the manor during her stay but had missed meeting him until now. There was simply too much to do between Mal, keeping Viggo hidden, and working on a half-baked plan of action against Serevadia where the only guaranteed army were goblins. Now that she was in front of him, she found it hard to believe that he was one of the heads of the Collective. He seemed so . . . soft. Even Sahar had an edge to her that made her dangerous as well as lovely and approachable. She expected her father to be similar.

"Please, call me Rayan. So many titles to keep track of. My name is a long one without adding Lord in front of it. It takes less time to simply call me Rayan."

"Rayan," she repeated. "All right. Just Evren then for me. I'm not really a fan of titles."

He nodded as if he understood her like he knew her whole story, and then held his arm out to her. "Might I? It's not a long walk to my office but I plan on helping."

"Sure." She took his arm and let herself lean on him as they walked out of the hall. "I've been meaning to talk to you."

"Sahar told me."

"Did she tell you anything else?" Evren didn't relish the idea of spilling the story all over again. Too much to say and every word was like lead on her tongue.

But to her relief, he nodded. "Yes. Troubling news, but I find I'm not surprised."

Evren didn't say anything else until they'd passed through to the east wing, away from the crowds of adventurers and servants. They didn't need to hear any of this yet, something she had to keep reminding herself any time it threatened to overwhelm her and fly out of her mouth.

They reached Rayan's office, which was a quaint word for the large room. Evren's father had had an office, but this room was as big as the kitchen Sahar had smuggled her into. The large desk in the corner took up very little space. There was room enough for a full sitting area, complete with a chaise lounge and a table set with the morning's tea gone cold. Along the far wall there was an old piano, the worn red wood showing its age more than the yellowed keys. In the wall to their right were many tall windows overlooking the dripping grounds, on the other were floor to ceiling bookshelves crammed with leather tomes and carefully filed scrolls.

Rayan guided her to the lounge and sat her down. He lifted her bad leg with a feathery touch and she immediately obeyed and stretched it out along the curve of green velvet.

"Now," he said as he stepped back. "Let's fix the leg and your nose before we talk."

"I don't want to waste a potion." She resisted, but he was waving her off and walking back to his desk. It was covered not with ledgers and scrolls but a whole network of glass tubes and bottles. She recognized it from Sahar's smaller traveling kit as the way potions were made.

"Nonsense," he said, taking a vial of knucklebones and shaking them to see how many were left. "Our people are healing. More than anything they need rest, not more magic stuffed down their throats. But you need to walk unhindered, and you make a sour face when you're in pain."

"I do?" Evren tried to smooth her face. "Sorry."

He chuckled. "Sahar would scrunch her face up into the most ridiculous expression whenever she skinned her knee or fell from her horse. She still does if she think's no one is watching."

The sound of bubbles and stirring filled the room. Evren settled back against the arm of the lounge. "Your daughter is one of the best people I've had the privilege of knowing. You raised her well."

"Yes, well, that is all a father can ask for. Sometimes I wonder though . . ."

"About what?"

Rayan stirred the pot, sniffing the steam before reaching over and adding a few dashes of an herb Evren didn't recognize.

"Her mother is an adventurer. Did she tell you?"

Evren shook her head. "No."

Rayan smiled fondly. "Fiery woman. She got me into this business with the Collective. Sahar grew up with tales of great quests and heroic deeds. She used to hide in my carriage on my way to work, just to catch a glimpse of what I did to keep people like her mother safe."

Evren's mouth was so dry she could barely form the words. "Sahar's mother, is she . . .?"

"Dead?" Rayan guffawed. "Oh dear, that is a funny joke! No, no, Evren. My fire-hearted wife is on another adventure in Gratey. I receive letters every week, on the dot. I'll admit, it is lonely in the house when both my ladies are gone, but I wouldn't stop them from following their passion for anything."

Rayan stirred the pot, some of his jolly attitude seeping from his lips. When he spoke again she couldn't see his face, she could just hear the shift in tone in his voice.

"When my Sahar came home alone the last time, I wept for her for days. Her tears had been spent by the time she came back to me with two bodies behind her. She didn't speak for so long, and I didn't push. I know better than anyone what can happen to people like you on those quests. I read the reports every day. I write letters to the families of the fallen tied to bags of coin, as if it would make their passing better. Do you know what the worst part is?"

He turned around, swirling red liquid in a glass bottle. "The worst part, Evren, is how many times I don't write those letters. Because, for so many adventurers, their party is all the family they've got. Vox was the exception. I hosted the man and his family for dinner once. Orcish cuisine is difficult to cook but rewarding. It is much harder to write those letters when you know who they're going to, and who they're about."

He cast his eyes to the rain on the window, brows furrowed. "Losing them nearly broke my little girl. For the first time in my life, I wondered if I'd been a bad father to let her get involved in this life. She should be at parties, dancing with suitors and eating tiny cakes. Not covered in blood, tearstained and wondering which disaster will hit her next."

Evren licked her lips, unsure what to say. There wasn't a day that went by that she didn't think of Drystan and Vox, and she hadn't known them nearly as well as Sahar and Rayan did. It was likely guilt that kept them so fresh in her mind. No matter how at peace either one of them had been when they died, it still felt wrong.

"This isn't a life I planned on having," Evren said. "In many ways, it was the best thing that happened to me. Despite the horror and pain, I've met my family. They saved my life, brought my father's murderer to light, and helped me admit that I was in love with a woman I couldn't have met in my wildest dreams." She sat up now, catching his eyes from the rain. "I've thought about leaving after losing one of my own.

We all have. But where else would we go? What would we do? Your daughter does this because she knows there's more than pain to it. She sees you helping us, she sees her mother being a hero. If Sahar was meant for fancy parties and little cakes, no one could keep her from that life. You know that."

"I know," he said hoarsely. "I don't know how to keep her safe, is all."

"She did more than survive the White Cairn, Rayan," she said. "She's the only reason we got as far as we did. She was our driving force when we lost hope. She kept us alive long after the fight was done, and she was grieving for Drystan. I know that, when she gets the chance, Sahar will follow in your footsteps and change the world. You can't protect her and expect her to fly at the same time."

"It is like you speak from experience." He walked over and handed her the vial. "Sip it, it's very hot."

Evren did as she was told, feeling like a child taking herbs again as the hot liquid stung her lips and tongue. She cupped the vial in both hands as he sat down in the chair across from her.

"I do. I didn't have my father around as much as Sahar has you. I mean every word when I say you two are lucky to have each other."

Rayan sat back in the chair, steepling his fingers to his chin. "And do you think that we'll still have each other after this threat is done? Serevadia sounds like a beast we are ill equipped to slay."

Evren winced. "I know I should've told the Collective about it sooner."

"You should have," he agreed. "But what's done is done. The future waits for no one and the past is pointless to cling to. Sahar told me of the elf that's staying here. Is his information accurate?"

"We're cross referencing his information with that of a Dirn-Darahl survivor now. Keres is overseeing it."

Rayan's mouth twisted into a smirk. "Devilish creature, that one, but fun. They have a stake in this as well. All seems to come back to Nerezza, poor girl."

"You knew her better than me. Did you ever see something like this coming from her?"

"No. She was introverted, yes, but many mages are. She clung to Sahar like the moon does the sun. Sahar was never afraid of being eclipsed, she simply took Nerezza under her wing and gave her confidence. Now she's leading an army to our lands with the same strength she was taught. Is there hope for her?"

Evren bit her lip. "Maybe. I want to believe there is. Keres's soul with Gail's would've been enough to change her. If we can get those souls from her then maybe she'll come to her senses."

Neither one of them wanted to admit that Nerezza had planned this from the beginning. They hoped, and it clouded their judgment.

"Can someone take the souls from her?"

"Gyda can, although she swore she wouldn't. I know she'd try if it meant ending this." Evren took a few more sips of the potion. Already the ache in her knee was fading with every heartbeat. "But that's not a problem we can solve yet. We need to find her first. And then there's the issue of the army she'll be commanding through Velcros. Where are they going to strike next? It's been nearly three days since the attack on Rheinwall. Where's the follow up?"

"Similar questions have been passed from all mouths of leadership, save the ones about Serevadia." Rayan rubbed his chin with his fingers. "I'll head to the capital soon to inform them, but we'll need to spread the word without spreading mass panic."

"Panic is unavoidable. We need people to be aware. I already had Arke warn the Hisrachi and Orenlion. Through them, Etherak should be warned as well. I'm hoping they can send aid to Dirn-Darahl."

"But how?" Rayan flopped his hands on the arms of his chair, looking agitated. "They'll be needed in Terevas too. We have no defenses, we'll be taken down easily. It seems clear that we're the first target."

"Or they've hit everyone at once to keep the element of surprise," she countered. "We won't know where they plan to go until they show their faces."

Rayan started to object, a no doubt better argument at the tip of his tongue, but stopped as the door to his study was thrown open. One of the maids bustled in, damp from the rain and wringing her hands.

"I apologize, my lord, but she wouldn't wait. She said it was an emergency."

Rayan stood up. "It's all right Lily."

Lily stepped aside, revealing a tall figure covered in a crimson cloak soaked with rain. Evren stood up too, standing beside Rayan as the maid scurried out and shut the doors behind her.

"Are you here for one of the parties?" Rayan asked. "Or do you have news from Rheinwall?"

"I bring news from King Loghain," a deep female voice said from the cloak. Her hands were scared in intricate patterns like runes and arcane glyphs as they moved the hood back.

She was an older elf, her knotted black hair streaked with more white than Abraxas's had. Her face was weathered and lined with stress and grief more than age. Despite that, she held an aura of power than made Evren shiver. She didn't need to see her spellbook to know what kind of mage she was.

"My name is Divara Rimel, council and general to Loghain Rhys." She introduced herself. "I've come from Vanguard."

"I've heard of you," Rayan said, his voice noticeably

colder than before. Sparing a look, Evren caught his hands tightening to fists before he loosened them. "What news from Etherak?"

"War," she rasped, as if the word itself was a wound she'd just ripped open again. "Vanguard was attacked when I was there. The invaders are unlike any I've crossed paths with before. They come from the ground."

Evren cursed, drawing Divara's hawklike eyes to her, but Evren ignored them to turn to Rayan. "They're cutting Terevas off. It doesn't matter if Etherak could send forces, they won't get through Vanguard if Serevadia holds it."

"Classic warfare." Rayan rubbed his hands over his face. "I should've seen it."

Divara cut in again. "You have more information than I, so let me be brief. You must be Evran Hanali. Barrion says you can be trusted.I don't know the boy as a liar, so for now I will place my trust in your hands."

"Thanks," Evren said drily. "Will it help us out of this current situation?"

Divara shed her waterlogged cloak and sat on the chair dressed in armor Evren had never seen before. Red and faded fabric, metal that was dented and repaired over and over again. Chilling. That armor had seen more battles than Evren had.

"I'm here to help you," Divara said seriously. "Eith can't survive another war, and I have no wish to be a soldier again. We end this here and now, before it can get any worse."

Evren sucked in a breath. "You want to take Vanguard back."

Divara didn't smile, but there was something in her posture that implied it. "Oh darling, I want to obliterate it. I'll need your help to do so."

16

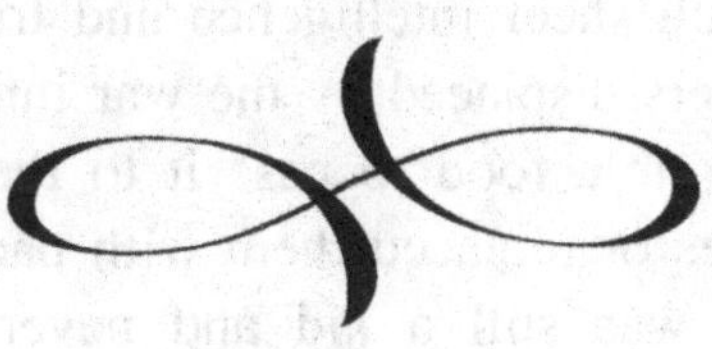

Abraxas

After the Spider's Grave, life found an unerring normalcy amidst the chaos and suffering of war. Mizan's trust wasn't easily won. Abraxas didn't think he'd ever truly get it because the rebel was never satisfied. But the other leaders he came across were different, and with each one he met he learned a little more.

Etherak had always presumed that Vernes's forces kept themselves hidden by constantly moving. This was, in part, true. The rebels inhabited the most dangerous parts of the country to keep Etherak out. Why would anyone live where there was no water? Why would anyone set up camp in the middle of the territorial giant scorpion's nests?

The Dra'Nacti were the answer. They could draw water from deep under the ground. They could convince the scorpions that they were part of the nest and should not only be tolerated but protected. It was not an easy life, but it was survival, and Abraxas could respect that.

As their camp moved, different rebel groups came and went. Abraxas worked with all of them. Nunwei, a shadow assassin who had an undead hound as her companion set him on edge until she told embarrassing stories of Mizan. Her laugh was so infectious he often forgot how deep her knife could cut with little pressure. His intelligence helped her free prisoners of war and left the prison a smoldering shell.

Jado was a dwarven teenage rebel who hadn't yet filled out his shoulders and chest. But what he lacked in age he made up for with sheer intelligence and trickery. He and a group of teenagers displaced by the war infiltrated Etherak's occupied cities, stole food to pass it to the hungry, burned letters from spies or replaced them with bad information. In many ways he was still a kid and never failed to make Abraxas feel old, especially as he sat around the fire with the teens, taller and more exhausted than the rest. He stuck with Jado longer than he should've, worry knotting in his stomach with each dangerous heist and prank. But Etherak's soldiers didn't see a rebel in the kid, and he was as slippery as an eel whenever they did catch on.

It was Oshaya that surprised him the most. Abraxas spent months preparing to meet him. All Mizan, Nunwei, and Jado would talk about was how the spy's influence and intelligence had tipped the scales in their favor more times than they could count. That he was the kind of spy who never got caught, despite being so ingrained in enemy territory. Apparently no one believed he was capable of being a rebel, despite the people he was around being generals and commanders. He mingled with Etherak's best, stole information, and planted bad seeds of his own. For the longest time, Abraxas couldn't imagine any spy being that good and not getting caught for decades, but it made sense when he finally met him in Mere.

Mere was the first city in Vernes to be taken by Etherak. For many of the rebels it was a sore spot because despite their best efforts it wasn't easily liberated. Etherak's generals and commanders lived there, close enough to the ocean that there was always salt in the air, and they could keep control of supply routes. It was a beautiful port city, filled with green palms and bubbling fountains. But a haven for Etherak was no longer a haven for Abraxas, and by the time he slipped through Oshaya's window, he was a sweating mess wrapped in dark linen.

"Show your face in my room, shadow. I don't deal with customers who cover themselves."

Abraxas blinked in the dim room. The only light was the sun that filtered through the latticed windows, his entrance and exit ajar while the rest were shut tight. Incense clouded the room, lit up by the rays of light. As his eyes adjusted, he took in the lush furnishings. Rugs and glittering trinkets, a silver jewelry box spilling with jewels, colorful glass perfume bottles, a bed almost as large as the room itself draped in deep red fabric.

But Oshaya was yet to be seen.

Abraxas pulled back the cowl and mask, letting them sit around his neck. "But you'll deal with customers who come through the window?"

A sensual chuckle came from the corner. "Most of my clients come through the window."

Oshaya unfolded himself from the bed, and Abraxas couldn't believe he'd missed him. The man was beautiful, stunning in a way that only art could capture. Golden tanned skin clear of blemishes and scars, thick arched eyebrows that matched the pitch-black of his braided hair. He wore a robe made of sheer peach material that glittered as he moved, and he was covered in tinkling bracelets and rings.

"Well, aren't you a pretty thing." Oshaya grinned. "When Aushruk sent word that I'd have a fledgling rebel in my room, I didn't expect someone so handsome."

Oshaya moved like water, fluid and graceful. Every time he moved, the scent of jasmine perfume wrapped around Abraxas, who stood stock still as the spy stood uncomfortably close to him.

Abraxas cleared his suddenly tight throat. "Thank you," he managed. "You must be Oshaya."

"I'm whoever I'm needed to be." He flicked his thin wrist, rings catching in the sunlight streaming past Abraxas's shoulders. "But for Aushruk's new project, I am who you say. Come, sit." He twirled away, gesturing to the bed. "We can talk."

Abraxas stared at the bed, unable to move. "Just talk? I'm not . . . I'm here for an assignment."

Divines, he hoped Aushruk and Nunwei hadn't sent him here for some elaborate prank. Sharing a bed with a stranger, no matter how beautiful, was the opposite of what he needed.

Oshaya peered over his shoulder. "Darling we can do whatever you like so long as you can pay. But for free, just to talk. I need only to ask a few questions. Coffee?"

Abraxas was sweating again. Between those eyes and the stillness in the air, he was a mess. Coffee wouldn't help.

"Yes, thank you." He smiled and gingerly sat on the very edge of the bed. The cushions were so plush he felt like he was sinking into a vat of quicksand, pulling him under.

Oshaya took to the coffee on the other side of the room, the ornate set of cups and the tray coated in silver so bright it seemed to glow. Steam and the heady scent of grounds overtook the incense and jasmine, though it did nothing to relax Abraxas.

It made perfect sense now why Oshaya was so good at getting information and staying in the good graces of Etherak's generals. Men and women in charge sought release and relaxation no matter where they were stationed, and a good prostitute, one that could be discreet and trusted, was hard to come by. Abraxas himself had never dabbled, but he knew many who had.

"This is how you do it?" Abraxas asked. "You get your information like this?"

"Relaxed lips are looser, if you catch my meaning."

Oshaya winked. "So yes, I do. I only take one or two clients, but at this point of the rebellion I know everyone of import here in Mere, and many who are not in Mere." He paused, turned back with two silver cups of steaming coffee. "Do you think less of me?"

"Of course not," Abraxas said, a little too quickly. "One must do whatever it takes to survive."

"Yes, one must."

Oshaya settled down beside him, slipping him his cup with soft, slender fingers. He sipped his own and simply seemed to be taking Abraxas in for a long while. He tried not to shift under the spy's gaze, although it felt like he was being stripped bare.

"What guides you?" Oshaya suddenly asked.

Abraxas stilled, fingers hot around his cup. "I'm sorry?"

"What guides you?" he repeated. "I want to know the man I'll be working with. Give me a reason to trust you."

"I don't . . ." He faltered. He'd expected a test of loyalty, of his skills or the quality of his information. He had a list in his mind of what would possibly benefit Oshaya, but this was different. "You know what I've done for your rebellion so far."

"Ah, there it is." He pointed at him. "My rebellion. Is it not yours?"

Abraxas slowly shook his head. "Vernes is not my home. This is my atonement for the wrongs I've done."

"So, you say guilt guides you?"

He paused. "Yes."

Oshaya didn't seem disappointed. He didn't seem relieved or angry or anything else Abraxas expected. There was nothing but a layer of calm over the man. And maybe, just maybe, a hint of understanding.

"Guilt will burn out," Oshaya said. "I would know. What happened to your passion? To your love?"

"It brought me here and I did terrible things with it."

"Well," he shrugged a bejeweled shoulder, "in that case, it might be time for a new passion. You will not last long on guilt alone."

"Is it passion for you?" Abraxas asked before he lost the nerve. "Everyone I've worked with is different. Mizan is driven by anger, Nunwei by loyalty, and Jado by chaos. But you're different."

"Of course I am, darling, look at me." He gestured to his body, but his smile was slipping. "But yes, passion drives me. Or it did. This job made me someone important. The danger was like a knife against my throat, but I've never been opposed to a little knife play. By now that danger is a part of life. Do you know what happens when you live each day with a blade at your neck? You sympathize with it. You grow to understand it. Something that Aushruk mentioned about you is that you believe that your kingdom's conquest is wrong and they're all being misled. Is that true?"

"Yes." He finally took a sip of the coffee, bitter and scalding as it passed over his tongue. "One of our gods has pushed this war too far. Eldridge is not of sound mind. He has our people believing that this is a holy cause, despite all evidence to the contrary."

It was easy for Abraxas to speak as if the past was his present again. It was like it hadn't let go of him to begin with. Saying 'has' instead of 'had' for example became a little too easy. He tried to ignore how much it unnerved him.

"And how does one stop a god?"

"You don't." He sighed. "People will doubt just as I do. Eventually they'll tire of the suffering. They'll want this to end."

"All of them?" Oshaya raised an eyebrow. "You think very highly of your people."

Abraxas couldn't tell him that the last straw was the banishment of the Divines. He couldn't give him that information so early when he still hoped that maybe his presence in

Vernes was enough to change the course of history. But he had to give him something.

"There are those in power who will see this as wrong. They'll have enough loyalty from their armies to make the right choice, I know it."

"Ah, this is the infamous Etherakian faith, yes?"

"No, it's a hope. I know the difference now."

"Very well. One more thing." Oshaya drained his coffee and leaned forward. His fingers reached for Abraxas's neck, lingering on the draped scarf that had once covered his face. "May I?"

Abraxas stammered. "I-I, uh, I don't think—"

"This isn't where I have my way with you, don't worry. Consent is gold, darling, whether it is for intimate relations or getting a better look at your tattoo."

Abraxas's cheeks burned and he reached up to tug his scarf down. He always forgot about the ink circling his neck, although as a child he couldn't remember a more painful experience. It had faded to nothing in his mind over time. Now, with Oshaya's fingers tracing along the skin, he remembered it vividly.

"What is it for?" Oshaya asked. "I see so many of your people with these, or something similar. Never at such a suggestive site."

"It's to show a bond," Abraxas breathed, excruciatingly aware of how close Oshaya was now. "Normally between married couples. Rings, especially for soldiers, aren't practical."

"Ah, so you're married?"

He laughed a little, a strand of silky midnight hair fluttering over Oshaya's shoulder. "No. This is a bond to my god."

"Oh." Oshaya leaned back, a little frown on his face. Abraxas suddenly felt chilled. "So you're married to a deity?"

"Not in that sense. It means my life is devoted to him.

That I will take no earthly possessions beyond what he gifts me, and a life completely devoted to him."

"So . . . celibacy?"

Abraxas was quite sure he was completely red now. "I've never had a need for anything else."

Oshaya grinned wickedly. "I can respect that. You and I are very different, but I feel a like-minded connection between us. I look forward to our working relationship in the future."

Oshaya stood up and gathered their cups. Abraxas hadn't finished his, but he was glad to see it go. Vernesian coffee always made him shaky and too unfocused, although he'd be lying if he said he hadn't missed the flavor.

He stood up as well, watching Oshaya put the tray back together with his flourishes and sways. It wasn't teasing, it was simply the way he was. Only a few minutes alone with him and Abraxas could tell. When he flicked his long braid between his shoulder blades, something dark through the gossamer fabric caught his eyes before disappearing behind the braid.

A tattoo, unmistakably Etherakian style knotwork, hidden at the base of his neck. One he recognized.

Abraxas's breath caught in his chest. He didn't say anything, but Oshaya seemed to notice the shift in the room. He turned back, slyly playing with his braid.

"It's in a terrible place, I know. I can't even look at it."

"You're . . . ." Abraxas cleared his throat. "Your clients don't see that?"

"No. I only have one client now, and he loves it."

Oshaya didn't need to say who it was, for Abraxas already knew. He could vividly recall after the last battle in Vernes, when the Divines had been banished and he was a wreck, who had picked him up from the battlefield. He remembered how devoid of armor his savior had been, screaming for a retreat as he lugged Abraxas back.

He remembered the same tattoo on Loghain Rhys's bare wrist.

That made sense now. For decades, Abraxas had thought back to that tattoo and who Loghain had bound himself to. A lifetime later, he was face to face with the answer.

"Is this what you meant by understanding the blade?" he asked after the silence had gone on for too long.

"One can learn to love a blade," Oshaya replied, his voice lost to longing and rueful acceptance.

"Loghain is a good man," Abraxas managed.

Oshaya folded his arms across his chest, guarded for the first time since Abraxas had slipped in. "Is he good enough?"

Oh, how he longed to tell Oshaya that Loghain was already doubting his brother's sanity. Maybe it had even started with him, the spy who learned to love him. If there was one thing Abraxas was certain of, it was that Loghain was a better man than he was a King, and a man who'd never stopped looking across the sea once they'd left.

How could he say that without sounding like a madman, or revealing Nerezza's secret?

"I believe he is," Abraxas said. "And I believe you are the best to make him into someone better."

Oshaya cocked his head at that, eyes undressing Abraxas again, but to bare his soul instead of his skin. What did those intense eyes see? Did they stare at Loghain like this? Or was Abraxas about to get an actual knife in the throat for saying the wrong thing?

Finally, Oshaya relaxed. He let his arms fall to his hips and had that entrancing smile again. "I think I like you, Abraxas Kain. Send me something that will help me put the magistrate of this city on a leash. Deliver it to the little Etherakian temple beside the docks, under the dragon statue, and I will come to you with good news in a week's time."

Abraxas frowned. "I can't just tell you now?"

"I'm on a schedule, darling. Another dashing elf will be crawling through my window soon, and I like him more."

Abraxas couldn't argue with that, and the idea of getting caught in the same room as Loghain terrified him. Good man or not, he would trust Divara before he trusted Abraxas.

He pulled his cowl and scarf back over his face, and slipped back into the bustling city of Mere, somehow more hopeful than when he'd first arrived.

~

THE WEEKS TURNED TO MONTHS, and before he knew it, those months were gathering up into a year. It became second nature to move with the rebels across land dangerous enough to obliterate them. He scraped the bottom of his memory for any information that would help, until it came to a point that even Mizan had accepted his intelligence would only last so long if Abraxas wasn't behind enemy lines. Soon, the only times he was called into the war tent were to provide insight.

How did an Etherakian general plan their battles?

How would an Etherakian soldier react to this show of force?

Where would a War Mage be utilized in a battle with these strategies?

How do we effectively deal with a Divine Knight?

That one was the hardest for Abraxas. Not only did it feel like painting a target on his own back, but it had been so long since he'd wielded more than a sword that he'd forgotten what it was like to fight with the power of a god thrumming inside him. But they needed this information more than any other. There were few Divine Knights compared to the army as a whole, but just one could tip the scales of a battle.

"Every knight is different," Abraxas started, trying to relax his white-knuckle grip on the table. "From their preferred weapons to their abilities, they are as varied as the

Divines they serve. A devotee of Nuris, for example, will have the ability to turn your undead against you before she puts them to rest. A Knight of Roania could manipulate the terrain to their advantage for a short period of time, and one of Nutvian's children has a measure of control of frost magic. We were always taught to never rely on our gifts to win a battle, so most will only allow weapons unless it's necessary." He paused. "Or, unless they're beyond caring about the rules."

Mizan snorted. "Speaking from experience?"

"Yes."

Aushruk bared her teeth at Mizan before he could say something no doubt demeaning. "What god did you serve, Abraxas Kain?"

"Haphion." He leaned back from the table. "God of Light, the Guiding King."

Mizan muttered a string of words so crude that it would've made Arke blush. When he was done, he looked at Abraxas with disgust. "Of course, that would be yours."

Abraxas held his arms out, too tired to fight. "Do you see him now?"

"I see no gods," Mizan spat. "Only armored fools with magic no different than a mage."

"But it *is* different, Mizan," Aushruk pressed. "It is unlike ours, which comes from the land. It tastes different than the paper mages and their ink."

The rebel rounded on her. "They're a problem to be solved, nothing more."

Abraxas shook his head. "They're more than that. You must understand that these knights have known no other magic or way of life. They are extensions of their Divine's wills, their magic comes from the heavens themselves. We were raised by priests, not mothers. Our homes were temples, not houses. Our lives are not our own, they belong to the Divines, and that is why we fight the way we do. We don't . . ."

He trailed off, wishing he could suck the words and the air they expelled back into his mouth. But it was too late. Aushruk and Mizan stared at him with pity and disgust, and he hated them both for it. Mizan, for his close-minded hatred that mirrored the man Abraxas was trying so hard not to be. Aushruk, for her pity because he didn't want it, nor did he need it.

Abraxas wasn't worthy of pity, and neither was the life he'd been chosen for at birth.

Aushruk rounded the table, long dark hands reaching out for him. The gold lines flashed in the lamp lights, and he shrank back. She stopped and let her hands fall to shadow, the gold no longer gleaming.

"Abraxas Kain, you are no longer that man," she said.

He nodded stiffly. "I know."

"You do not have to do this today. This was too much to ask of you."

Across the table, Mizan looked like he was about to explode. "He's not a child to be coddled, Aushruk. We need to know these knights. We've lost whole battles to them, cities as well. If he can fight against his own army, he can tell us how to kill a god's chosen."

The scales on Aushruk's shoulder heaved with a heavy sigh. "It is not as easy as that. He has turned against his people for us already—"

"It's about the first minute of battle," Abraxas blurted. He ignored Aushruk's snapped gaze and faced Mizan squarely. The words burned his tongue as he said them, as if Haphion himself had finally come out of his seclusion to tell him to keep his mouth shut. But the burning was just Abraxas. It hurt to bleed the truth, but what choice did he have?

"Survive the first minute, and you'll likely see the extent of most knight's tricks. They're not used to long fights. Foes that put up more of a fight are normally monsters, not men. If your people are smart enough to survive and keep track of their moves, then that's your best strategy."

Mizan's brow furrowed, but more like he was looking at a problem rather than being angry. "You said each knight is different. How do we prepare for that?"

"You'll need to memorize the Divines and their symbols. Each knight will wear it on them. From there you can expect power that relates to that god. I can . . ." He struggled to breathe. "I can give you a list. Names, domains, powers. There's normally only one knight for each god."

"Normally?" Mizan asked.

"There's another for Haphion. He won't go down easily."

"Well, your experience can help us take him down, yes?" His grin was wicked.

Mizan couldn't know that Abraxas was speaking about himself. His past self was still out there, reeling with Divara's tale of a heretic wearing his face. His past self still had light and flame at his beck and call. He still had Haphion's voice to guide him. His past self didn't stay awake at night, torn at his soul because he couldn't decide what was right and wrong. Abraxas missed his life when it had been that simple.

"Yes," he said weakly. "I can."

"Later," Aushruk snapped abruptly, her voice pulling them away from each other. "You have your answer, Mizan. He will get you your list by moonrise."

Before either man could object, she was herding Abraxas out of the tent. Hot sun hit his cheeks and he still couldn't breathe properly. His hands shook like he was a child refusing to pick up his sword again. He clenched them into fists.

"I can't do this anymore, Aushruk," he said. He sounded so weak. When had he gotten this way? "I can't . . . I'm killing my people."

"You are saving lives, Abraxas Kain."

He shook his head, backing away from her. "No. I'm fighting again. Only now I don't wield the sword. I just watch for the aftermath. Is this really redemption if I'm killing for the opposite side? Have I not fought enough?"

Sand slipped into his sandals as he paced. Around them the camp went on as usual. He'd come to like it. He knew the people. He was learning the Dra'Nacti's strange, hissing language. So why? Why couldn't he find peace on this path?

"This was supposed to help!" he cried at her. "You told me I wouldn't be a killer anymore."

"I did," she said solemnly. She was still again, like a statue. "War is death, Abraxas Kain."

He rounded on her, finger digging into his own chest as the words hissed out of his teeth. "I am *tired* of causing death. I never wanted it. All I ever wanted was to mend things. Instead, I was forced to break, to bleed, to hate. Now that I know better, all I do is put that on myself. I *hate* what I've become, but I can't see a way out. Every path feels wrong. I'm stuck in this cycle of thinking I'm doing good and being overwhelmed with the opposite. I can't do this anymore, Aushruk. I can't keep feeding Mizan information. Or Jado. Or Nunwei. Any of them. My words are no better than a sword, for all they do is cause more suffering."

Aushruk held her arms out, her void-like eyes filled with pity and understanding he despised and didn't want. "Abraxas Kain, you are not a killer."

He shied away from her. "Am I not? How long before these talks around the war table turn to me being the only one who can effectively pull off a mission? How long before you put a sword in my hand like everyone else and tell me I'm spilling blood for a good cause?"

"Never." She gripped his shoulders and leaned down so her cool shadow enveloped him. "This is done. You won't go in there anymore."

Why were his eyes stinging? Why couldn't he see properly? "I have no place if I'm not useful."

"You are more than a blade. Do you not remember how

we met? The man I revived had light in his eyes when he talked about my process. Be by my side. This army always had need for healers.”

“I don’t have magic,” he protested.

“Healing is not about magic. You know bodies and what breaks them. You know how to mend them as well.” She squeezed his shoulders. “I pushed you in the wrong direction, and I am so sorry. Let me try to help you once more.”

He was still struggling to breathe past the lump in his throat. One by one, his fingers loosened from fists. It seemed like a childish hope, a dream he’d locked away to be more mature and a better knight, but . . .

Abraxas thought back to the little boy he used to be. With his black hair always in his face, his ears never pointed in the right direction, and his smile too wide. Didn’t that boy deserve another chance, even if he himself didn’t?

“I would be just a healer?” he asked. “Nothing else? No more tests? No missions to Mere?”

“No more,” Aushruk agreed.

He closed his eyes. This wasn’t quite redemption, but it would do. “All right.” He opened his eyes. “I’m with you.”

THE NEXT FEW months were bloody. Abraxas felt very much like he was a bone that had healed wrong and needed to be broken before it was reset so it could heal properly. He stuck by Aushruk’s side whenever she wasn’t with Mizan, learning new techniques and relearning old ones. They hadn’t left him, he used them plenty of times to help the Wandering Sols, but there was still a mindset that he needed to get back into.

Potions were great, but not a cure-all. They didn’t always work properly, and some were too strongly diluted for the body to handle. Wounds had to be properly cleaned and dressed before letting the magic take over. Bones, if not shattered, had to be shifted. Checks for internal bleeding or head trauma were always the most difficult to catch, and always the deadliest to get wrong.

There was a rhythm to being a healer during war that didn't come easily. Abraxas hadn't dabbled outside of one or two injuries on the field since he was a child, and back in Whitestone healing was a sacred act that took peace and patience. More often than not, Abraxas's patients were screaming as he helped them. He had more blood on his hands helping victims of war than he ever had killing.

But this blood was different.

The man begging for mercy wasn't fighting him as he stitched a wound, he just needed to say something to distract from the pain. The woman he couldn't save didn't have hate in her eyes as she passed holding his hand. The rebels he met saw him as hope, not something to fear.

Abraxas helped people. And it hurt him. He still laid awake at night, but always thinking of what he could've done better, not about what he needed to do next. His bones were heavy with exhaustion, but he pushed on because people needed him. He was even able to avoid Nerezza because Aushruk refused to have her magic anywhere near the sick and hurt. He learned later that she'd taken up his job as informant.

It made him uncomfortable, but she knew far less than he did, no matter how smart she thought she was. Still, the idea of her working with Mizan, Nunwei, and Jado set him on edge. She wouldn't hurt them. She needed them. And somehow that was worse.

Through his time with Aushruk he learned more about her and the Dra'Nacti. They truly were the first people to live in Vernes, and their legends told that they were created from the sand when a dragon spilled his blood in one spot too many times. They were born of the desert with no desire to leave. Their magic came from the land itself; the mirages and dust storms, the beating heat of the sun and the savage sweep of the wind. They were one with the land, and it showed in how each Dra'Nacti developed.

Some never got the scales Aushruk had. Instead, they developed a sense for tremors through the ground and could tell when a snake was hunting miles away. Some took the Dra'Nacti's unique way of going without food or water to the extreme, adapting only to drink a drop of morning dew once a month. Others, normally the hunters, found themselves more like the animals they hunted. Able to spit venom or grow claws that let them climb up sheer surfaces.

The Dra'Nacti were always changing, and it was something he found fascinating. They could even change sexes if they wanted to, although it was a long process.

"It started as a way to survive with few numbers," Aushruk said, handing him a fresh set of linens to prepare the beds. "Now, it is rarely that."

"You can be whatever you want to be?" he asked.

"Whatever I feel more like, yes." She grinned. "It is so strange to me that you are trapped like you are. Do you not feel like you need a change?"

He shook his head, unfolding the linens as he talked. "I've never thought about it." He frowned and tried to stop thinking about it. "I'd rather not think of another thing to change about myself, Aushruk."

She hissed a laugh. "Very well. Not all Dra'Nacti do so like me. You needn't worry. Now, remind me how you would ask for water in my language."

He smiled at the trick question. "I wouldn't. I would have to find it myself like a true Dra'Nacti."

"Very good, Abraxas Kain."

It shouldn't have been easy to find peace in a time of war, but Abraxas felt something like it doing the hard work of stitching others back together. He thought that maybe, just maybe, he could start to do it for himself. His wounds were to the soul and mind, something he didn't know if even Aushruk could heal, but what he was doing was a start.

He sunk so deep into his work that he forgot about Nerezza unless her name was brought up. He removed her strange obsession with the shards from his mind to make room for better things. The dagger that dropped him here in the first place was locked away, because if he remembered it, he remembered his friends, and that was a pain that took the breath out of his lungs.

It was strange to exist without them after never being from their sides for so long. Abraxas found the silence of the desert nights too much because Sorin and Sol's stories weren't there to fill the air. He tossed and turned because Gyda's steady breaths weren't there to lull him to sleep. The only discarded papers and charcoal he found littered about were his own, not Arke's. He found himself picking at his nails, a habit that he'd learned from Evren and had taken with him through time.

Did they miss him? Abraxas thought for sure Gyda would, but maybe she wouldn't. After all, she still had Evren. What could sparring sessions and battles compare to love? Arke he could never read. The only time he'd seen the goblin truly upset was over Sorin's death, and he wasn't nearly as close to Arke as the Vasa was. Sol was sweet and kind, with a hidden layer of steel underneath her sunshine. He could see her mourning him, but moving on. Evren . . . well, Evren's distraught had been real when he fell. He'd never forget the look in her eyes.

But Sorin? He and Sorin had been at odds since Dirn-Darahl, and that was Abraxas's fault. He'd pushed too much to get him to see the miracle when all Sorin remembered was the pain. The Vasa was a good partner to have in an adventure. He was creative with his solutions and as quick with his blade as he was with his wit.

But Abraxas didn't believe Sorin would miss him, and that hurt him far more than he cared to admit.

Abraxas was alone in the healing tent for once while he stewed in these thoughts, with half-baked promises to do better by the Vasa when he saw him again. There was no one to see his grim face as he boiled linens over a small fire of Aushruk's making. It was good to not have anyone hurt, but his mind wandered when he was alone and tore at his heart as much as he tore at his fingers.

The flap of the tent was pushed open aggressively, a gust of dry wind following the footsteps.

Abraxas cleaned off his hands and turned around. "Are you looking for . . ." He trailed off as his eyes landed on Nerezza, clad in leather armor and a black cowl to cover her bone-colored hair. "I'm not in the mood. Don't you have Mizan's ass to kiss?"

She rolled her eyes. "I've been away for two weeks on an assassination and that's the first thing you say to me?"

He shuddered, not willing to ask who she killed. "You mistake what we have for friendship."

"Dramatic, as usual." She sat down on one of the beds.

"So says the woman who destroyed a city with a reanimated dragon. What do you want?"

She crossed her legs in a very ladylike manner he was sure she never learned in Serevadia. "Less attitude for one, but I won't hold my breath. Mizan sent me."

Abraxas turned his back to her, stirring the pot of linens again. "I don't work for him. I'm not doing any more for him. Unless he wants to do something about that growth on his foot, he's got nothing to say to me."

"It's not just him. It's Nunwei."

Abraxas stilled, steam gathering in his sleeves.

"And Jado."

He closed his eyes, praying for an end.

"And Oshaya."

The steam was hot enough to burn now. He slowly withdrew from the pot but couldn't find the strength to turn around.

"What is it?"

He heard her smile, felt it in the back of his mind. "We're marching on Cuskhe, and we need a healer for the battle."

He whirled around, and hated how her smile grew at his obvious pain.

"No," he rasped. "Cuskhe was taken when we were burned. The rebels fought to save us, that ended the battle."

She cocked her head to the side. "Who told you that?"

He froze, and that was all the answer she needed. Nerezza unfolded her legs and stood up gracefully.

"Look, Abraxas, this was bound to happen eventually." She shrugged. "Our presence here hasn't changed much at all, judging by the history records I read before. We need to keep playing along."

"Why?" he snapped. "Why do you do this? These people mean nothing to you."

Her smile slid off her face. "Do you really think I don't sympathize with them? My people will be facing a similar battle eventually."

"Don't compare this," he gestured outside, to Vernes and the war turning the sands red, "to your plans. You don't care about these people. You're letting this happen because you can't kill them all to get your way, because you need them just like you needed Evren to find the dagger for you."

He took a step forward, forgetting about how a snap of her fingers could end him. All he saw was red, both from fear and anger.

"You are no hero," Abraxas said. "Stop acting like one."

"Oh, a hero? Like you?" She stepped forward to mirror him, now only inches apart. "Abraxas, you were only special because of a god. Now you're a shell of a man, dissatisfied with anything but blood on your hands."

Nerezza laid a cold hand on his cheek, fingernails scraping

along his cheekbone. "And now you're mine. We are not heroes. We are weapons, nothing more."

She stepped back, and the cold imprint of her hand lingered on his cheek. "Get ready for Cuskhe, Abraxas. War waits for no one."

17

Abraxas

Cuskhe bled like a cut artery.

Abraxas didn't know why he expected any different. Watching the battle from the other side was worse. He could feel the panic in his bones when the black night turned into an orange haze of fire that dragged confused soldiers out of their beds. His throat was raw, as if he was the one howling those pained screams and battle cries. Fear curled the air, overpowered by the stench of blood.

It always came down to blood.

The battle started exactly how he'd remembered. Stealth first, and then the fighting. Weapons were snuck in days before, hidden caches marked secretly for civilians or rebels who lost theirs in chaos. Next, an attack from the inside by a small group that'd been masquerading as civilians, who started a fire in the barracks. Soldiers burned alive or cut down as they tried to escape. The alarm bells tolled, deep and ominous, as guards from the wall were pulled away to deal with the fire.

They thought it was a small riot, maybe a little show of

force from the rebels to be put down. They didn't see the gathered army in the sands, hidden by Dra'Nacti magic. They didn't feel the desert hold its breath like Abraxas did when the guards left on the wall turned their attention back to the city, firing into the streets. They moved their aim, whoever they were targeting running toward the city gate. Some of those arrows had to hit, but with every reload the stances shifted, ever closer to the entrance they guarded.

Shouts of alarm, of cursing and swearing and *Just kill it already, you fools!* ballooned out into the star strewn sky. The gate creaked. The arrows fired faster, a hollow scream of victory and pain sounding over the cracking of wood.

The gate swung open like the maw of a waiting dragon. It had been one rebel who'd done it. Arrows littered her back. She swayed, lurching a step as another shaft hit her. Blood gurgled from her lips, pouring down her chin. Her smile was red as she raised a single first in the air, and with her dying voice she let out a single cry.

"*Vu dalaz!*"

The army shed the sand and the magic, hundreds of bristling glaives and spears catching the moonlight. Their cry echoed hers as she fell, a hundred times stronger, a hundred times louder.

"*Vu dalaz!*"

For death.

How do you fight an enemy with no fear of death? While Mizan and Aushruk asked questions about defeating people whose faith blinded them, Abraxas couldn't help but remember the problem that had plagued him when he was on the opposite side of this rebellion. There was no end for them. Etherak fought for their lives, but Vernes fought to seek out death and welcomed it with open arms.

They didn't believe in gods, because there was only one sure thing in the universe for them; that death would take them, and it wouldn't be the end. And Etherak threatened to burn that belief to cinders. No wonder they fought so hard.

It was faith. Bloody, broken, monstrous faith that mirrored his own.

Abraxas was in the thick of the battle by the time the sun came up, not with a sword in his hands or armor on his body, but with a clinking bag of potions and a single knife to defend himself. He didn't need it. His body and mind reacted to the sounds of battle accordingly. He kept to the shadowed alleyways, reeking of fear and piss. He avoided all fights unless they were finished. With everyone either making final stands or screaming for death, his shadow slinking from one wounded to the next was overlooked.

He pulled his cowl and mask tighter around his face, as if it could block out all the horror he witnessed. The closer the sun got to its peak, the more his skin crawled. Etherak would be getting reinforcements soon, a small battalion who were scheduled to rest in Cuskhe before pushing towards Tatesai.

He knew because his younger self would be among them, and he didn't know what he would do if they crossed paths.

Abraxas pushed the thought from his mind. Mizan could deal with his younger self, or maybe Nerezza. Her magic had become a boon to the rebels once they learned of her necromancy. She was in the battle too, slinging spells and raising the dead. Maybe younger Abraxas could kill her and do what he couldn't do before. He wasn't a soldier now; he was a healer and people needed him.

Abraxas darted across a street, blocking the din of swords and crackling flames. He cut a corner, and then another. Bodies from either side grew more numerous at his feet. He forced himself not to look at them. Would he recognize these faces if he did? If he saw Divara he might break. If Nunwei's body appeared at his feet he'd be blinded. He prayed that Jado had stayed out of the fight like he promised. He prayed for a better outcome than mutual destruction.

He stumbled onto his knees and on a body, still fresh enough to be warm. He pushed himself up, eyes to the blue, blue sky. He just had to keep moving. Don't look at the face and risk finding someone you know, just move.

But when he pressed against the chest, a low groan hummed from the body. He froze, his fingers immediately going to their neck. A pulse met his touch.

"You're alive?" he asked in Vernesian and was answered with a sob.

He forced himself to look, to assess and take in the damage. Vernesian clothes. He was young, his helmet had been torn off. His face was caked in blood, and the whites of his eyes stood out in stark contrast. Abraxas looked at the rest of his body. Dislocated shoulder, a heavy blow to the chest that had sundered his patchwork armor and left a slowly bleeding wound. The armor had been all that kept the blow from being fatal.

"You're all right," Abraxas said, forcing his voice into the calm, cool tone he knew healers were supposed to have. "You'll live. Let me help you."

The boy's chest rose and fell with gasping breaths. "I thought I was dead."

"Not quite. I'll need to put your shoulder back in place."

Tears cut through the blood on his cheeks. Abraxas didn't deserve the look of gratitude in his eyes.

"I wanted them to think I was dead," he rasped. "I got separated from my people. I couldn't take them on my own."

"You don't have to explain to me," Abraxas said and set his bag on the ground next to him. "You survived this part. Now, I can't give you a potion until we fix your shoulder."

"It's broken!" the boy cried.

"No, I just need to pop it back into place. It'll hurt, but I need you to stay still. Back flat against the ground. Don't fight me."

The boy nodded, still breathing too fast but at least he was breathing. Abraxas placed his hands over the shoulder, one on top of the other. Knitting his fingers together he took a breath, and then another. Soon the boy was breathing with him. Slow, deep breaths that relaxed him. Abraxas breathed in again, letting their breaths pitch to the top. Just as he was about to loosen the breath, he slammed all his weight against the shoulder.

Bone crunched under his palms, the boy's scream rang in his ear. But when it ebbed away he was crying, tenderly moving his shoulder as Abraxas took his hands away.

"It still hurts," the boy said.

"It will. Give me a moment." He reached for his satchel, digging through the various vials for one that didn't slip through his sweaty hands. He held the bottle up to his eyes, watching the swirl of liquid to make sure it was still good. Even after taking out the Spider's Grave, bad potions had been a problem and he always found himself double checking.

Light caught on the glass, a strange, bloated mirror of the buildings around him reflected to his eyes. A shadow from the buildings behind him got bigger, a sword flashing in the light. He felt the boy beneath him stiffen, he heard the alarm slipping from his lips far too late. The sword crested through the air, angled to go through him.

Abraxas dropped the bottle and spun on his knees. The blade whizzed inches from his face, parallel with his twisted body and still moving. Without thinking he caught the hilt and jerked it back. The sword suddenly swung back from its deadly arc, meeting with the boy's chest. Abraxas tightened his grip, bare hands meeting steel gauntlets, and slammed it up into the wielder's face.

With a loud clang the helmet they were wearing kept the blow from breaking their nose or jaw. They stumbled backwards, still reeling and grasping for a better grip on the sword. But Abraxas didn't let go. He stood up smoothly and ripped the sword from their clumsy fingers. He kept the momentum up, swinging the sword around him before driving it forward, one hand on the pummel and through the neck of its original owner.

The armored foe gurgled. Blood coated the blade, the silver armor, the crest of a dragon holding a ball of flame. Abraxas froze, all at once the fight draining out of him.

A sword in his hands again. A potion shattered on the ground. A body slipping off his blade.

He jerked the sword out and the body collapsed at his feet. He knelt. Hands shaking, he tore the helmet off. Glassy blue eyes stared up at him. Freckled lips. Auburn hair tied in a braid too intricate for battle.

Vesper Norvern. A noble lady who wanted adventure. Bad singing voice, worse taste in men. Had a betrothed waiting for her in Gratey. Abraxas had visited the man himself to deliver the news of her death. He could still remember the man falling to his knees, his wailing heard across the town.

Vesper had been his friend. He'd grieved her.

He'd killed her.

Abraxas stumbled away from her corpse, his lungs too tight. He'd killed. He'd killed a *friend*. More than that, he'd killed a member of his old battalion.

Abraxas looked to the sky, knowing even before the familiar sound of a war horn pierced his ears that reinforcements had come.

Abraxas Kain, Champion of Haphion, was here to paint the walls of Cuskhe red.

Abraxas didn't know if his panic showed. He felt like a taut bow string, pulled so far, and held for so long, that he was about to snap. The boy he'd been healing pushed himself up into a sitting position. "How bad is it?" he asked, and then flinched as the horns sounded a second time, closer.

Abraxas didn't answer for a while. Vesper had been a scout of sorts, sent ahead of the battalion to see how many survivors there were and tell them that help was on the way.

He and the boy had been in her way. It made sense to eliminate threats before they could hurt those she loved. He held no malice towards her for that, even though he trained her better than to attack a healer, enemy or not.

He had been her enemy. He'd be their enemy, too, once they came through the gate. Zeli, with her flail and her penchant for overkill. Cael, who never spoke more than to pray over dead bodies. Florentus, old and seasoned and likely cracking jokes as they marched into battle. Urias, hiding his fear of an early pyre by flashing his daggers for all to see. Marion, pounding a war drum to their steps, a song of courage on her lips and their ears.

He never thought he'd see them again. He didn't want to. For the first time in his life, he cursed the cruelty of the Divines.

"Very bad," he told the boy.

Blood slick fingers gripped Vesper's sword. He turned to the broken potion bottle, the sagging bag at the boy's curled legs. Had this life ever been for him? Had his wish to be something soft and gentle been nothing more than that? What was a wish under the cruel weight of fate and destiny?

The war horn sounded again. He could visualize Cael's face as he tucked the horn away for the last time, his warning for the innocent to flee falling on deaf ears. There were no innocents in Cuskhe.

The boy flinched when Abraxas turned to him, and a part of Abraxas shriveled up and died. He pushed that feeling aside and pointed with the sword to the bag.

"Take one. Drink the first half and then wait before sipping the rest. When you're ready, hand those out to the people who need it."

The boy took the bag with shaking hands. Divines, he was so young. How had he not seen the roundness of the rebel's faces when he'd first fought them?

"What will you do?" the boy asked.

Abraxas closed his eyes. He let the faces of those who'd be fighting swim up to meet him. Mizan and Nunwei, Nerezza and Divara, Aushruk and her band of hidden Dra'Nacti, his old battalion.

He opened them again and saw a sky black with smoke. He said nothing to the boy. He simply took his dead friend's sword and marched into battle.

Abraxas didn't trip over the bodies on the ground. He didn't stick to the shadows and peek around each corner to make sure it was safe. He didn't want it to be safe. There was only one thing he was worthy of doing—fighting. There was only one person who could stand up to the Divine Knight marching through the gates with a god's power at his fingers, a god's voice in his ears. One person who knew him better than any other; his hatreds and insecurities, his vulnerabilities and his very soul.

How had Abraxas not seen this outcome? As if everything he'd suffered had been leading to this point, this fight.

History remembered Cuskhe's bloody battle being a victory for Vernes so costly that it could hardly be called that. Abraxas intended to do his part to keep it that way.

He rounded a corner into a street thick with fear. Buildings burned, the crackling of fire and burning of flesh reminding him too much of his pyre. The fighting was so thick he could barely distinguish the opposing sides. All armor looked beaten, blackened, and patched. Faces were a blur, streaked with blood and soot, some still hidden behind helmets and masks. Ash-covered civilians were picking up fallen weapons and joining the fray, their clothes torn and bloodied around their mangled bodies in seconds.

Battle was chaos, the only kind Abraxas ever let himself indulge in. He stilled himself, breathed it in. Blood, ash, fear—sweat—all of it, let it pool in his lungs, sink into his corrupted marrow, dig its claws into his muscles. He'd ask for forgiveness later.

He let out a breath and took a calm step into the fight.

The first person to notice him was Etherakian. They charged, screaming a battle cry full of rage. It made them fast, but sloppy. Abraxas easily stepped to the side, bringing up Vesper's blade as they stumbled past him and slicing through the weak point in their armor. They crumbled; their leg useless from where he cut behind the knee. Without so much as a second glance, he stabbed downward at their exposed throat and kept going.

More foes lined up. None Vernesian; they recognized his black-clad form. All the Etherakians saw was a threat.

An enemy came, he sliced their throat and moved forward. Another leapt at him with little more than his sleeping tunic. Abraxas was impressed he'd lasted this long but found the lack of armor easy to cut through. He didn't need to find weak points, he just stabbed through the chest and stepped over the body to meet another. One after the other, body after body fell at his feet. A block, a disarm, a killing blow. Using the hilt to knock off an enemy's helmet before driving the blade through his face. Cripple knees, elbows, groins in heavily armored foes. A block, a stab, a kill. A slash, a parry, a kill.

A kill.

A kill.

Another kill.

Abraxas didn't love the fight the way Gyda did. He didn't relish the burn of his muscles and the weight of his weapon against the hot air his enemies breathed. The adrenaline curdled in his stomach rather than fuel him. But he fought anyway, the way he always did. Because he had to. Because destiny demanded him be a monster.

As a monster he tore through street after street, refusing to look at the faces of the people he killed. Only two from Etherak needed to survive. Everyone else was dead in his memory. If they died by his sword, at least he'd make it quick. He'd pray for redemption later.

Redemption.

He sliced a man's artery, hot blood spraying on his clothes and making them stick to his skin.

Redemption.

He cut off a woman's sword arm, and then her head before she could scream in pain.

Redemption.

He parried a soldier's thrown dagger, picking it up and jamming it directly into his throat before pushing his bleeding form into a house fire.

No. He took another lungful of metallic air. He was past redemption. Abraxas hadn't been worthy of that since he lived through Cuskhe the first time. By now, all he could pray for was salvation; not to be redeemed from his sins and mistakes, but to be saved from them.

He'd fallen so far. Borrowed sword in blood-soaked hands. A trail of bodies in his wake. He'd never felt so far from Divine.

The Divines could give redemption with only the need that the one who asked for it was worthy and willing. For salvation, the cost was greater.

Salvation requires martyrdom.

As the trail of bodies grew, he chanted that in his head. The words never lost meaning, burned into his mind through Divine fire that would never go out. Every inch of his soul was black as pitch, black as the clothes he wore and the armor he left behind. Everything but those words like a beacon, burning bright and terrible.

Martyrdom requires sacrifice.

The battle lulled. Abraxas had cut through so much that he'd run out of enemies. The street was wide and bare. The sky was black, streaks of blue sky slipping through before it was swallowed up by smoke yet again. The sand was red. The walls were red. The bodies would've been painful to look at if he'd pushed himself to study them, but he let his eyes skip away. He let them follow the trail through the street, up near the end were the sunlight managed to break through the smoke. A single ray of golden light haloed a knight in glittering armor nearly blinding in its light. Only his shield and sword were bloody, and yet still bright even as he stepped on the back of a fleeing rebel and skewered him with the sword.

Abraxas had found himself. Bright, filled with holy light and purpose. He intended to beat it out of him.

Look at you, he thought, gazing at his younger self as he kicked the body off his sword. *Do you even see what you're doing? Are you so blinded by Divine light that you follow any voice that calls your name? The shadows won't be kind to you once His light is snuffed from you. The dark will eat you alive, and you'll want it to. Because no matter how much your friends and mentors tell you that you are worthy of life, you are not. You are worthy of nothing but the rotting battlefield at your feet.*

I hate you. Abraxas's sword arm trembled as he stepped forward, as he faced the light of Haphion's Champion as a broken, shadowed husk of what he used to be. *I hate you because you are me, and there's nothing more that I hate than myself.*

"Leave." Abraxas didn't bother to disguise his voice. He let it carry across the sand and corpses to catch the Champion's attention.

The Champion turned to face him. There was no helmet to hide his face. Pale skin, unmarred by time. Eyes full of hate. Black hair pulled away from his face, ink-dark locks spilling down his back.

It was him, and it was not. Abraxas didn't know whether to be jealous or hate him even more. Instead, he distanced himself. This was *not* who he was, for better or for worse. This man was an enemy, an obstacle. And he loathed him.

Abraxas leveled his sword, the tip of it pointing across the street towards the Champion's chest. If he recognized

Vesper's sword, his face didn't show it. Their eyes met, and Abraxas wondered if he noticed that they were the same.

"You're all the same," the Champion sneered. "I'd offer you mercy, but you don't deserve it."

"We don't," Abraxas agreed. "I'd hoped you'd take mercy and run, for both of us. But I know you won't."

"So, you know your death will be here."

Abraxas smiled, still hidden under his cowl and mask. "My death started here long ago, as will yours."

In the back of his mind, Abraxas was aware that he should be scared. The man in front of him was fully armored, save for his face. He had his own shield and his sword—made for his arms and reach, unlike Vesper's sword, which was smaller than he was used to. He also had Haphion's power at his side, power Abraxas hadn't felt in a century.

Abraxas wasn't afraid. He didn't pray for salvation. One did not pray for salvation, one earned it. And he would, one way or another.

He put both hands on the hilt, slipping into a fighting stance he knew well. A flicker of recognition came across the Champion's eyes, but it lasted only a second before he lunged.

The clanging of steel rang in his ears. The burning of muscles against another blade. The scraping of metal as they jerked apart. Loud, jarring, chaos. Abraxas didn't shy away from it. He put everything into his next swing.

He feinted right, angling his sword for the straps of the shield. Something he'd blocked opponents from doing before. Something he knew how the Champion would react to.

The Champion swung his blade, catching Abraxas's and trying to wrench it from his grasp by twisting his wrists around. Abraxas let it happen. He dropped his blade, letting the satisfaction in his opponent's eyes spark as it was flung away. Vesper's sword clattered to the ground a few feet away. The Champion swung his sword around, blade angled for Abraxas's neck.

Abraxas dropped to his knees, legs sparking with dull pain as the blade whooshed over his head, so close that it shifted the cowl. He grabbed a handful of blood-damp sand and tossed it into his opponent's unprotected face. He reared back, trying to blink the sand from his eyes, but Abraxas was on him in a second.

The edges of the shield were hot and slick with blood. He grabbed them with one hand, tearing open the Champion's guard. He smashed the fingers gripping the handle of the shield with his fist, enough to bruise both of their fingers. He didn't scream. His opponent did. He swiped at him with the blade, but Abraxas was too close in his guard, the angle too awkward. The blade passed through sand next to Abraxas's boot.

The halo of light was eclipsed as the sword was raised again, this time pointing straight down. It didn't shake or hesitate as it fell downward.

This time, when Abraxas tugged at the shield, the Champion's bruised fingers gave way. He rolled back with the shield as the sword missed him by inches. Sand flew as he hurried to his feet, and he flung the shield to the wall.

The Champion stared at him with narrowed, sandy eyes. He jerked his sword from the ground it had impaled.

"I can kill you without my shield, heretic," the Champion hissed.

Abraxas edged sideways as the Champion did. He didn't take his eyes off his opponent as he kicked Vesper's sword up and into his hands. Gritty, bloody, but a blade regardless. The playing field was much more even now.

"You can't kill me," Abraxas said and charged.

It was easier to be on the offensive when he could see all of his opponent. The bend of his legs, the grasps of his fingers, the angle of his shoulders. He knew every move before it happened, watching for the tells in his body that he knew so well. He knew what swing would carry through to a secondary attack. He knew when a block could be twisted to disarm, like before. He knew which side he favored, the left now that it was without a shield, and how to punish him for it.

But knowing was all that kept Abraxas on top. The Champion fought with a rage that his own hate couldn't overshadow. Every blow felt like it would crack Vesper's sword. Every feint was followed with an attack so quick and deadly Abraxas had to dart away or lose a limb. They were as evenly matched as they could be, trading blow for blow, block for block. Passion and strength versus experience and determination. Light and shadow dancing amongst the corpses.

Abraxas didn't stick to his training. He fought dirty. He kicked at knees like Evren did to bring larger foes down. The Champion only ever fell to one knee, his sword arching out to keep Abraxas away until he got back up.

Abraxas was relentlessly aggressive with his attacks until he backed away, baiting his opponent to make an angry, desperate swing that he could exploit, like Sorin did. But the Champion didn't lunge after him, he let Abraxas make the room to breathe and waited for him to attack.

He fought messy and bold like Gyda, putting all his strength behind a sword that wasn't meant for it. With no shield, the Champion had to retreat step by step, narrowly avoiding the swinging steel and the earth swept up by the sword.

It wasn't enough. Every blow was caught or avoided. Every attack had him slipping away untouched. Abraxas's body burned. He couldn't keep this up for much longer.

Another strong, heavy swing that would've crumpled his armor, and the Champion swung around and slashed at Abraxas's back. He pulled away last minute, the blade catching his thigh instead of his back. The pain that bloomed was as hot as the shimmering air around them. After Nerezza, he barely felt it.

But the shame he felt. His opponent had drawn first blood.

Abraxas was losing, and he hadn't even seen him draw Haphion's power yet.

This time, when he withdrew to catch his breath, the Champion knew the signs of exhaustion. He'd tasted his blood and wanted more. He dove forward, barely a second after Abraxas had stepped away. Abraxas brought his sword up just in time to catch the blade, steel screaming with his arms as he locked them in place.

"You fight well for a godless heathen," the Champion hissed between his teeth. Sweat was dampening his hair, running down his temples and sand encrusted eyes. "But you are no match for the Divines themselves."

Divines, had he always sounded so pretentious?

"I see no gods, just a murderer in gilded armor," Abraxas said, and then rolled to the side. The Champion fell forward, carried by the force of his own push and barely keeping his footing.

Abraxas stood up swiftly and swung at him.

Any other foe would've been beheaded. But the Champion felt the blow coming and dodged. Not enough, however. The blade cut his cheek, scarlet blood welling up against porcelain skin.

The Champion backed away, touching the wound and pulling away to see the blood on his fingers. He stared a moment, and Abraxas held his breath. He knew what was coming.

Bring Him, he thought. *End me in His light.*

The Champion let his fingers fall to his side. His eyes were furious as he closed them, a prayer on his lips. Abraxas had the notion to dart forward and take the opening that was so obviously there, but he knew better. He'd killed dozens himself that way.

The Champion's bloody fingers met his sword. Blood smeared along the blade, and where it touched, Divine fire ignited. Blue and white, hot enough for Abraxas to feel on his skin even from there. Heavy with the taste of magic so beyond his tethered soul he could barely imagine the source.

He wanted to cry. It had been so long since he'd called those flames. The sheer, intense longing that hit him nearly drove him to his knees. But then the blade moved, and he reacted on instinct.

The Champion let out a cry and swung the blade. Normally too far away to be hit by the sword, Abraxas wouldn't have cared if he didn't know better. But where the blade cut, an arc of searing holy light cascaded. He dodged to the side, clothes singed as the wave crashed through corpses and houses, leaving nothing but black ash in its wake. The bodies burned too, leaving nothing behind. The only metal that could withstand that magic was the kind already blessed by Haphion. The kind that the Champion wore and wielded.

The kind Abraxas didn't have anymore.

Another arc of light was flung at him, and he dodged again. The next one was so quick that he had to roll back the way he'd come to avoid it. One after another, he was forced to roll and slide until he was confined to only a few feet of space, the street around him blackened and charred. The only thing that remained was the shield he'd tossed aside.

The Champion's sword came up again, a wicked smile on his face. He saw the shield the same time Abraxas did.

"Go on." The flames crackled along the length of the blade. "If you can make it, you can have it."

The shield was across the street, half buried in ash, far from the space he'd been forced to survive in. There was no way he'd survive that, and yet . . .

Salvation requires martyrdom. Martyrdom requires sacrifice.

Abraxas ran and, as he did, he heard his younger self laugh. He heard his friends in his head, laughing too. Evren shaking her head and telling him that impossible, suicidal feats were her job. Arke's manic cackling, driving him forward. Sorin betting that he was too old and slow to do it, just to get him to run faster. Sol's sunshine cheers of encouragement. Gyda's bellowing laugh, completely confident that he could.

And for a moment he thought he did.

The light hit him like a mountain of white-hot flame. The blood on his thigh started to boil away. His skin peeled, all of Aushruk's hard work burned away. He was melting, layer by layer. Skin and muscle, nerves and bones, until his soul was exposed. Haphion's flames scorched him, pain so intense he couldn't even comprehend it. He was stuck somewhere between anguish and elation.

Abraxas *felt* him. For the first time in a century, he was one with Haphion as he was torn apart.

A tear slipped past his eyes, landing on his cheek before boiling away and leaving salt on his skin.

Cheek.

Skin.

Through the flames, Abraxas touched his face. His skin was hot, but there. His clothes were gone, as was Vesper's sword, burned away by holy fire, but the rest of him remained.

He was alive.

Abraxas reached out, the torrent of flames still not letting go of him. What had been a wave before seemed to be an unending shower of Divine energy pouring from the Champion. His mind was reeling with the pain and revelation.

He was *alive*.

The shield was cool in his palms. He fit his arm through the leather straps, fitting perfectly just like he remembered. He turned against the torrent of flame, shield raised high, and they parted for him. He gasped as the pain ebbed away. All around him the fire raged, consuming the street.

But not him.

The battle cry was on his lips and in the air before he knew it. He broke into a run, gaining speed as the flames grew hotter. The air was thick and swallowed by them, but the shield was cool against his skin. He ran towards the source like he was being pulled there by an unknown force and threw himself at the Champion.

The Champion fell with Abraxas on top of him. The sword clanged to the ground, just out of reach, and the flames died instantly. The air was cooler, not sweeter. Ash and burning bodies were all he could smell. And past the shield, the Champion was frozen with shock.

Abraxas didn't let it last. He brought the shield down on his face once, twice, three times. Bones crunched, blood spurted, but he struggled to stop.

He hated him. Everything he was, everything he did that led Abraxas to where he was now filled him with the type of loathing that threatened to choke him if he didn't continue to hurt the source.

Most of all, Abraxas hated him because he was still everything he longed to be.

Abraxas tossed the shield away. His younger self was barely alive, his face a bloody mess. Those eyes were fixed on him, so confused as he stared at the face that should've been in a mirror.

Abraxas grabbed his broken jaw and leaned in until their noses touched.

"Look at me," he hissed. "Look at what you'll become and remember this. You are going to lose everything. You are going to deserve it. No matter what rational explanation you have, or what Divara tells you, I am your future. And I hope you despise me just as much as I do you."

He let go, let the fallen Champion's head lull to the side as he slipped into unconsciousness. Abraxas found the war horn strapped to his waist and took it when he stood up. He brought it to his lips, blew three times in rapid succession to the war-torn sky.

Retreat from a knight's own horn would be listened to.

Abraxas pulled the Champion to a wall that hadn't been destroyed and sat him up against it. He put the horn in his limp hands. He put the sword and the shield back beside him and then stood back.

They weren't his anymore.

More horns of retreat sounded, from inside and outside the walls. Someone would come looking for the knight, Abraxas knew that. And he didn't have the strength to drag him to the city gates.

So he gave the fallen form of his past another long look of pity and loathing, then turned his back and walked away.

18

Evren

"Mal's story lines up with Viggo's as much as they could, being on opposite sides of this conflict." Sol slumped in her chair. She was drained, as if the continuing rainstorm had leeched the color out of her.

The storm raged steadily, thrumming against the stained-glass windows of the Al-Fasil's extravagant dining room. The table was long enough to seat twenty comfortably and made of wood polished to a sheen so bright it could've been a mirror. Evren smudged her finger across the reflection of her scarred face, trying not to fidget in the overly cushioned chair.

Sahar and her father sat with the comfort of home on their side. Across the length of table, Divara Rimel was as stiff as a petrified tree. Viggo and the Wandering Sols sat between them. Sol had thankfully left Keres to keep an eye on Mal. Evren hoped the death spirit had the self-preservation to stay away, or else things between them and King Loghain's right hand would get ugly.

"So." Sorin tapped the table in time with his words. "Serevadia just made the first move. Fantastic."

"That we know of," Sahar reminded him. "Just because we haven't heard from Gratey, Vernes, or Melkarth means nothing. It's not like Dirn-Darahl could get a message of warning out."

Sol flinched as if she'd been hit, but she tried to smooth it out by turning to Arke. "Anything from Neri?"

Arke thumbed the piece of the Fey mirror, its glass catching grey light from the storm and shining it over the room.

"Yeah." He nodded. "They ain't got anythin' from Serevadia. They're tryin' to decide what to do next. Orenlion and most of the nests haven't been completely rebuilt. Sendin' the rest of Etherak's soldiers away could leave them open to attack."

Evren frowned. "They haven't gotten the city's defenses back up?"

"Nah. Hasn't been an issue with the new alliance. No need."

"Besides," Sorin leaned on his elbows, "no matter how good everyone in that forest is right now, pack them all inside one ruined city to wait out an attack that might not come? They'd kill each other."

Evren couldn't even find the energy to disagree with him. She glanced over at Viggo, who'd been sitting very still trying not to look outside the windows. As if he could feel the weight of her gaze, his eyes met hers.

"When I destroyed your map, it said that you had no idea where Orenlion was," she said. "Is that still true?"

Hesitantly, he nodded. "As far as I'm aware. Orenlion, until very recently, had little to do with the rest of the surface. I doubt the knowledge that its changed alliances will have reached Velcros yet."

"Let's hope it stays that way," she murmured and turned to Rayan, who had yet to relax around Divara. Evren could hardly blame him. According to Sahar's family history, Rayan and her mother had been young when they left Vernes, fleeing the occupation. Even still, they must remember it vividly. Divara stood for everything they'd run from.

"Rayan." Evren drew his attention to her. "Anything from Rheinwall?"

He sighed and shook his head. "No. Key members of the Collective are hurt or missing. There's still a lot of rubble to go through. But the monarchy and heads of state remain. They've been informed of the issue, as General Rimel requested. But with no army and our border's cut off, we have little choice other than fleeing to the port cities like Noxcairn and preparing boats."

"The other cities didn't have a similar attack?"

"No. Noxcairn and all the others, small and large, remain untouched for now."

For now. Yet. Those words were always tacked onto a hopeful sentence. Evren was rather sick of it already.

"Divara," Evren started.

"General—" She cut her correction short, blinked away her confusion and then waved her on. "Divara is fine. Go ahead."

"Right. Divara," Evren began again. "You said Barrion sent you?"

"I said Barrion trusted you. Loghain sent me."

Rayan scoffed. "For what reason?"

Divara was a statue, cold and unmoving. But whether it was the weight of everyone's questioning gazes, or the answer trapped on her tongue, she shifted uncomfortably. A rumble of thunder shuddered through the sky, shaking the windows, and making Viggo jump. Divara looked at the storm with a strange fondness.

"There was something that happened to me in Vernes that I wrote off as coincidence or trickery," she said, eyes fixed on the rain and voice low. "Something that no one knew but myself, not even Loghain. When Barrion came back from

Orenlion with a wife, an alliance with two separate people and a story bigger than any I could comprehend, it reminded me of something I saw during the occupation." She turned back to the table. "Barrion brought news of Abraxas Kain's death. I knew him. I grieved for him."

Sahar sat up in her chair. "He's not—"

Divara put her hand up to silence her. "I'm aware. And while I cannot explain it, I feel rather strongly that I met him —your Abraxas—during the occupation. I don't know how, short of Divine guidance, but he knew things that he shouldn't have. He was different than I knew him to be. And he was . . ." She trailed off, pursing her lips together. "He tried to warn me of a disaster, and I ignored him. And I paid the heavy price for it. This is something I never even told Loghain, until mentions of a dagger that could bend time was brought up. Loghain thought it best if I brought my story to you."

Evren could barely breathe. Abraxas had been in Vernes? *Again*? She knew the darkness in his eyes when he'd talked to her about it. To relive that again . . . could it have broken him? Were they too late?

Gyda's hand was on hers, an anchor when the storm of her emotions threatened to blow her eyes. All at once she was aware of her breaths and how fast they'd become, of the way their heart kept the same steady rhythm regardless of that. She looked at the reflection of Gyda in the table, laden with the same guilt she felt in her.

Evren squeezed her hand. Gyda had made herself get up for this meeting. She'd tied her hair back, hiding the white streak. She kept her back straight and strong, as always. But her fingers trembled around Evren's.

How long had Abraxas been alone, at Nerezza's mercy? How much had he endured, crawling his way through the past to get back to them? More than ever, Evren hated that she'd let him fall with the dagger alone. If she'd gone with him, maybe . . .

No. She shook herself of that thought. She knew better than anyone that there were some things in the tapestry of time that were knotted into place. No matter what attacked Orenlion, Mei was still hurt and still married Barrion. No matter the events leading up to it, the Matriarch's death still rioted Anep and the Hisrachi to war. Saros still lost his ability to fly, either from one battle or another.

The blood-red moon over a decaying city filled with monsters was guaranteed. The massive canyon-like a scar in the ground that led to nothing but darkness was written to happen. Fate had a plan, and while it made her sick to think that Abraxas's suffering was a part of that, it was the only way she could stomach the guilt.

Evren stood up, keeping her hand in Gyda's and leaning on the table. "We get to Abraxas through Serevadia. We get to Serevadia through Vanguard by learning how they got there in the first place. That fortress was made to repel enemy forces. How did they take it?"

Divara scowled. "For one, there were no soldiers to fight them. The skeleton crew that did work there were little more than clerks and glorified bodyguards. Though it wouldn't have mattered if there was a whole army. They appeared inside the fortress, not beyond the walls."

Viggo brightened a little. "There must've been a way for them to get into Vanguard from the caverns below. The network below the mountains is enormous."

"Could we use it to get in ourselves?" Evren asked.

"Maybe." Viggo shrugged. "I'd bet Tolk has an idea of how to get to it. His people know those tunnels better than most, second only to Serevadian's themselves. They've likely dismissed the goblins, believing they're not a threat."

Arke growled. "Big mistake."

Viggo raised an eyebrow at him. "I was under the assumption you didn't care for your fellow goblins."

"I left. Don't mean I take kindly to assholes thinkin' we're some savages." Arke turned away from Viggo and to Evren. "I promised you an army. We could take Vanguard that way."

Divara cleared her throat. "Perhaps, but I would not place my bets on that. And no, not simply because they are goblins. Serevadia's entrance will be watched. At the very least, it'll be in the middle of Vanguard, surrounded by the small army that took the fort. A much bigger challenge than those they disposed of to take it."

Divara radiated experience. All those years leading an occupation and commanding a war must've amounted to something. Evren looked to Rayan and Sahar, a silent question between them. They nodded.

"Divara." Evren looked back at the older elf. "You have far more experience in these matters than we do. I know you don't want another war, but you also seemed to have a plan for this. Could you give us some insight?"

Divara slowly stood up, her chair sliding smoothly on the polished marble. "We don't have the forces to take Vanguard. Not easily, anyway. From the numbers I saw before I fled, the Serevadians have a few hundred in those walls. That is not a number Terevas can match, even with goblin help."

Arke grunted. "We don't force our kind to fight wars. We'll get volunteers. Maybe a hundred."

Sorin grimaced. "That doesn't exactly even the odds. Especially not with Serevadia's shiny armor and magic."

"No doubt they've made themselves at home in Vanguard." Viggo agreed solemnly. "The defenses in place won't be like what you're used to. Weapons made of our Light heed no armor."

Divara's face was grim. "I saw enough to get that impression."

Evren shuddered. She remembered seeing the weapons and armor of Serevadia through Viggo's memories. Metal crossbows that shot beams of light. Armor light enough to move unhindered but laced with Light to keep back deadly blows. She'd fought the Mora more, with their chitinous armor and regular weapons of stone and bone. Even then, they'd been deadly.

"Maybe we could sneak inside," Sol offered. "Sabotage their defenses?"

"In my experience, those missions are often suicide," Divara said. "It would be one matter to sneak around the blockade for help, something we could do with the help of the goblins and your . . . informant," she nodded to Viggo, "helping us get past the army no doubt lurking under the fort. But we need to take Vanguard back so Etherak's forces won't be hindered in the next attack, be it on Terevasan soil or Etherak's."

"They're counting on you being divided," Viggo said. "Eith is easier to conquer if taken in smaller chunks rather than all at once. By taking Vanguard, we'd rob them of that fantasy and buy time for the rest of the surface. Present a united front, and Velcros will pull back to reconsider."

"But how?" Sol pressed. "Etherak can't get to us. Orenlion either. All we have is us. Wounded adventurers that Velcros tried to wipe out at Rheinwall. What army Terevas might've had in us is gone."

"She's right," Evren said. "It's just the people in this room. We should let the people here know what's going on so they can send word to their contacts and family. Fan the flames before they're snuffed out. But we can't rely on anyone else but the ones that are here now."

"And just how do you intend to take a fortress that has closed its walls to you?" Divara crossed her arms. "If we used the adventurers here to fight, we stand a better chance of breaking through. Those walls won't be breached by arrows or simple magic."

"Then why should they if we have more bodies to throw at them?" Evren argued. "It seems to me that no matter our numbers, getting through Vanguard's walls is the biggest problem."

Sahar suddenly spoke up. "We can get through."

All eyes turned on her and she didn't flinch. Her eyes sparkled dangerously, the flames of a new idea overtaking their dark brown depths.

"Sahar, dear." Her father gently touched her arm. "Whatever do you mean?"

"We stop looking at this like a big battle. It's not, not yet." She turned to her father. "Papa, could you retrieve the designs for Vanguard from the archives?"

"I . . . Yes, I could. But what would you need it for?"

"A map of the layout could be helpful," Divara tentatively agreed.

"Oh, I'm sure, but not for us. Sol." She reached across the table to grab the dwarf's arm. "Architecture and it's weak points are a hobby of yours, if I remember."

Sol nodded. "Yes."

"Looking at the designs, do you think you could find out which would be the best place to destroy a portion of the walls?"

The fire in Sahar's eyes leapt to Sol's. Suddenly her whole drained, weary demeanor switched to one of an inspired woman seeing a plan unfold.

"Yes!" she cried. "I mean, theoretically. Things will be different once we get there, but a little scouting around could go a long way."

"Something we should do regardless," Gyda rumbled, surprising everyone. If she cared, she didn't let it on. "Sahar, how do you plan on destroying a wall, even with a weak point?"

"I can make something," she said. "Technically, it's already created. I'll just need to fine-tune key things like detonation and such. This isn't like my normal concoctions either, so we'll need to be careful. But it should work."

"Should?" Divara asked.

"It *will* work," Sahar corrected. "Sol and I will make sure of it."

"I remember what you made on the fly in Direwall," Evren said with a smile. "Having time to prepare will make you deadly."

"That's the goal." She winked.

Sorin was tapping on the table again, his leg jiggling up and down. "All right, we have shit for numbers. We need surprise. We need to make them think there's more of us. Scatter them, make it easier to deal with. Bit by bit, right Viggo?"

"Precisely."

"So," Sorin splayed his hands out, "we work in teams. We won't be the main force at play anyway. That's on Arke's army. We need to get in, cause destruction, take out as many as we can, so the goblins can do the rest. Arke, are you going with Tolk to raise an army?"

Arke bared his teeth. "Ain't a leader like that. Tolk will get this done. I'm with you."

"Okay." Sorin nodded. "Two points of entry. From below and from the wall. That's not enough. What about the draw-bridges? Natural weak spots."

Evren shook her head. "They have the portcullises behind them. We'd need to get inside to make sure they weren't used."

"Great, you can do that, right?"

Evren struggle with words for a moment before finally getting out. "You want me to disable the portcullises from the inside? How?"

"Climb the walls," Sorin said plainly. "You've done crazier shit. I'll bet my left leg that you were going to volunteer for the scouting party anyway, likely with Viggo. Gyda should go with you both. Between the three of you, you can take the main entrance they'd expect an invader to blast through, giving Sahar and Sol leeway to blow the wall open."

"Why do we need both?" Gyda asked. "We destroy a wall, we don't need the gate."

"Because I want them scared," Sorin said. "I want them to think they got it wrong, that an entire army is coming for them that they can't see. Fear is fucked to deal with when you're the one who's scared, but if we can use it against them then we have a chance to look a lot bigger than we are."

Silence settled over the table, only interrupted by the sounds of rumbling thunder and pattering rain. The plan was stewing in all their heads, but Evren could taste the desperation of it. Act big to buy them some time to wreak havoc. Make enough noise to sound like a full army. Take a fortress held by three hundred highly armored and armed elves that already had every advantage. It was suicide. Nothing they hadn't risked before, but this was somehow different. At the other end of this impossible fight was Abraxas, and a way to stop the invasion before it truly began.

The unspoken truth bled in the air. That they might not make it out, that this was all just a fruitless gesture that would amount for nothing. But to not even try felt like a failure, and it wasn't a choice Evren could consider.

Facing Heliodar's army had seemed impossible at the time, a gamble that hinged on Sol's pull and Sorin's words. Direwall had felt like the end, facing an endless hoard of undead and a sea serpent in the bay. Even fighting for Orenlion against Nerezza and the Storm had an air of hopelessness to it. The only difference between Vanguard and all of those battles was the simple fact that they were acting instead of reacting.

"Sorin's right," Evren finally said. "I'll take Gyda and Viggo to scout ahead. We'll send back what we find and take the wall. Sahar and Sol will break the wall. Arke and Sorin—"

"We'll be coming through the front door you open,

Evvie," Sorin said. "Lighting things up, causing mayhem, the things we do best."

"That leaves Sahar rather vulnerable, doesn't it?" Rayan asked.

"Fear not, Lord Al-Fasil." Divara inclined her head to him. "I will accompany her. While I'm not as able as I was fifty years ago, I assume you won't turn away an experienced mage."

Sahar hesitated until Sol nudged her, and then she shook her head. "No, we wouldn't. We'll be glad for your help."

"Three different entrances to a fort that is supposed to withstand an army." Sol shook her head, smiling. "Seems a little funny, right?"

Evren thought Divara might bristle at that, but she just smiled back at the dwarf. "You're not wrong. Etherakian architecture isn't as well rounded as far as dwarven standards go. The fort was built for strength, to be immovable. But things unwilling to bend tend to snap in half. I wouldn't mind seeing it fall. It is rather ugly."

Three separate entrances, three separate chances, all in the hope to reach each other in the end. They've faced monsters and armies before, surely they could do so again.

"How much time do you need to make your explosive?" Evren asked.

Sahar shrugged. "Give me a day and I'll make more than enough for us to take care of the wall and then some."

"Lord Rayan, those designs for Sol?"

"Will take a few hours at most," he promised. "You have my word."

"All right then." Evren sighed. "Let's start getting ready for this. It's quite a trip to Vanguard, and we'll need to be careful. Gyda, Viggo, and I will leave in the next couple hours. I don't want Serevadia getting too comfortable in there. Remember, our goal is to take Vanguard and then continue into Serevadia. If we find Abraxas, then we can put a stop to this, so pack for what you'll need for a longer trip and give most of it to Tolk before he sets off."

"He'll leave as soon as you give the word," Arke said.

"How do we give him the signal to attack from below?" Sahar asked.

"I'm assumin' your explosion will be a big boom we can hear?"

Rayan laughed nervously. "Most definitely."

"Then he'll use that."

"Good. Tolk will leave with us and we'll get him back to the hole we left, and continue to Vanguard. We'll pass information on through Gyda's mirror shard that you can use, and then wait for you to meet us. Let's get started on this." Evren rapped her knuckles on the table, trying to hide her nerves as everyone stood up. "War waits for no one, and we have people depending on us."

They left the dining room in the same groups they'd been paired off in, a strange foreshadowing of the days to come. Pushing open the doors and marching into the halls, Gyda put her hand on Evren's shoulder.

"You're getting very good at this," she said.

"Leading?" Evren eyed Sol, Sahar, and Divara as they branched off into a different hallway. "Then why do I feel like I'm going to be sick?"

"Because this will likely go poorly," Viggo said on her other side. "Yet, there is no other outcome we can accept but success, so we have to keep that in mind."

"Optimism?" Evren asked.

"No." He shook his head. "Realism. There is no room for failure, so I will not allow myself to indulge in the thought of it. There is no other path for Eith if you do not take Vanguard from Velcros."

Evren let that sit on her bones like oil on water. There was no other option, no way to take failure and use it as momentum to win again. Abraxas needed them to win this, and if they couldn't, then he could be lost for good.

There might be death, but there would be no failure.

~

"THESE WILL HELP you scale any wall," Rayan said, handing Evren a pair of supple leather gloves. They were fingerless, letting her grip her bowstring and arrows the way she needed. But along the knuckles were strange metal plates. Rayan nodded to her to put them on, and when she did she instinctively flexed and curled her fingers into a fist.

From the plates came long metal spikes, curving through the gaps of her fingers. Like a wyvern's claw, curved and smooth, but strong. She flexed again, and they retreated into their plates.

"They make excellent knuckles for breaking noses as well," Rayan said with a thin smile.

"Thank you." She shook her head in amazement. "I've never seen their likeness anywhere. What enchantment did you use?"

"Oh, I didn't make them. An inventor in Rheinwall did, mixing Fey magic with metal architecture. More things like this will come, I'm sure. Hopefully before we're all wiped off the map."

His warm attitude drained immediately, replaced with a dour hopelessness that left Evren speechless. He'd been so calm during the meeting. Although she supposed that was for Sahar's sake more than his own.

"You don't need to give me these," Evren said. "I have tools enough to climb—"

"If you are to save my home and my daughter then you will have the very best. I know you're attached to your bow and what remains of your armor. Could I interest you in some replacements to further protect yourself? New gauntlets perhaps? Better arrows? Your partner has agreed to better armor, although I have nothing to top her sword."

"Rayan, you're very generous—"

"My daughter's survival depends on yours, Lady Hanali," he interrupted. "Allow me to make sure she has the best chance possible of coming back to her mother and I. Do you understand?"

Evren breathed, fixing the gloves more snugly to her palms. "I do."

"I know it is a fool thing to ask," he said. "But with my wife an ocean away and a war on my doorstep, I will ask anyway. No, I will simply say." He stepped forward and laid his hands on her shoulders. "Bring Sahar back to me, alive. Do not leave me in a world where I outlive my little girl."

Suddenly she was back in a blue-lit cave, dripping healing water and chest full of a heart she hadn't had before. She was in the arms of her father for the first time in years and he was whispering in her ear something achingly similar.

Yuhan would outlive her regardless now. He likely would've before, since her human blood wouldn't allow her to live as long as a full elf. But that didn't matter then, and it didn't now. With one father pleading for his daughter's safe return, and her own in the back of her mind, she found herself choking back tears.

"I will bring her back; I swear on my soul," Evren said. An oath she couldn't possibly keep, but one that was inevitable in its making.

"Then that is all I need," Rayan whispered and whisked her away.

Evren's old armor had been through the hells and back. She'd lost most of it in Orenlion. Still, it was difficult to put away the worn leather with its colorful stitches and put on something new. As with all new armor, it was stiff. She'd have to break it in as much as she could on the ride to Vanguard. Beautifully oiled dark brown leather, layered with studs for extra protection. Her pauldrons and gauntlets were covered with thin, overlapping pieces of metal for added protection. Her thighs had something similar. While easily more protective than her old gear, it was surprisingly easy to move in it. She lunged, stretched, rolled, and practiced drawing her bow to get the movements down in the new armor until she weas satisfied she could climb in it and fight even better.

She drew her cloak around her next, the deep green of the fabric almost black as it fluttered to rest on her shoulders and around her frame. Her dagger was at her hips, wyvern gleaming the same color as the metal studs and plates of her armor. Her quiver was buckled over her cloak, bristling with new arrows.

The oldest piece was her bow, and was nearly as jaggedly scarred as she was. She ran her fingers along the limbs, tracing every mark and remembering how it got there. She'd restring it on the road, just to be safe. But otherwise, it was comforting to have something that had seen her through every trial so far.

She looped it over her shoulder and head, picked up her pack laden with potions, rations, and everything else she thought of, and left the room she and Gyda had shared. She didn't look back at the gilded walls, the plush bed, or the large tub in the corner. She promised herself she'd visit again when it was all over.

At the top of the stairs Gyda waited for her. If she hadn't seen her so weak in bed a few days before, then Evren couldn't have pictured her as anything less than strong. Her new armor was more metal than before, covering her chest and torso but leaving her arms bare. New ink swirled on her skin, runes and symbols of the Ikedree Evren was slowly starting to understand. They invoked power from her ancestors, strength she needed for the battles ahead and a promise to accept the death that was right for her, but none other. They were little more than prayers, but they gave her strength enough to feel worthy of her sword.

It gleamed strapped to her back, the runes unlit and waiting to be used.

"You look ravishing," Evren said, stopping just in front of her. "I love a woman in armor."

Gyda smirked. "I know. You look . . ." she cleared her throat. "Well protected."

Evren laughed. "You can literally give me your heart and tease me relentlessly about not seeing that you loved me, but you can't utter a compliment?"

"We all have our strengths," she muttered, rubbing the back of her neck. She started down the steps, and Evren giggled behind her.

"Well, I find you so impossibly beautiful that I would compare you to the Divines themselves."

"They're not here, stop."

"Ah, you're right. You are more like the midnight sky. So fiercely beautiful and awe inspiring that everyone that looks at you can't help but stare."

Her neck was red. "If you don't stop I'll put you over my shoulder again."

"Promise?" Evren asked with a grin.

Gyda groaned but didn't get a chance to make good on her threat. At the foot of the stairs was a crowd of people that stopped them in their tracks. Most looked like they had just gotten out of bed, sheets and robes slung messily over their shoulders. Others looked like they hadn't slept at all, letting the injured lean on them as they waited. A mix of people so colorful and capable, all staring at her and Gyda. Evren recognized the half-orc even without his golden mantle supporting the spindly elf on his arms as she teetered back and forth on one leg. The dwarven mages were a mess, eyes red and beards askew as if they'd been tugging at them as they cried.

"Is it true?" one of them asked, taking the first step

towards them. "That we're at war? They've taken Vanguard, the grey elves. You're going to stop them."

Evren looked out at the crowd. These were people like her. In any other circumstance, she could've been in their place, hurt and distraught, desperate for answers. What had Rayan told them?

"Yes," she said carefully. "The people that caused the sinkhole in Rheinwall are the same that are in Vanguard, and there's a lot more of them."

"Why are they doing this?" the elf asked. Her blonde hair hung limply in her pleading eyes. "What did we do?"

"It's not as simple as that." Gyda spoke for Evren. "You did nothing. You were a threat they sought to take out."

"They didn't succeed." The half-orc brought the elf back to his chest before she could fall. Then he looked up at Evren and Gyda. "They didn't succeed. We should be going with you."

Murmurs of agreement rose to Evren's ears. Heads of all shapes and colors and heights nodding. Evren's stomach lurched. She couldn't bring these people, wounded and recovering, into battle, even if it would even the odds.

"If this were a normal enemy, then I would agree." Evren stepped down a step. "But Serevadia is unpredictable. The threat isn't just to Terevas, but to all of Eith. I know you're angry. I was there. I'm still there, still seething over this whole problem. But we're not just adventurers of Terevas, are we?"

Slower than before, but still there, heads started to shake. The anger in the room ebbed.

"I know we are all different. We all came from separate corners of the world. We all got into this life for different reasons. The one thing that binds us together is each other. Our loyalty to our fellows and our world. Serevadia is massive. They've hit Rheinwall, Vanguard, and Dirn-Darahl in short succession. There's no reason to believe they won't do so somewhere else. We need Vanguard for Etherak's army, which is why we're going. But the rest of the world needs to know what's at stake, and that's not something I can do. Use your contacts to spread the word. Speak with Lord Rayan about specifics. Let your allies and friends know that the ground beneath our feet from now on must be watched. And if we fail to take back Vanguard . . ."

Evren let out a breath. The weight of the armor and the cloak on her shoulders dragged her down.

"If we fail to take back Vanguard, the rest of Terevas needs protection," she finished. "My party and I are doing this because its personal. They have one of ours and we intend to get him back. I know you've lost people. I know you're hurt. But however much we need you in this battle, Eith needs you more."

The most skilled warriors, mages, rogues, and mercenaries settled down. Her words were sinking on them like rocks in a lake. Slow and heavy, with a final destination they all understood. She knew she hadn't reached all of them. Adventurers were as stubborn and brave as they were varied, but no one spoke against her.

"We'll handle Vanguard because it's our fault it got this far," Evren told them. "It's our responsibility to make sure they don't make it any farther."

No one spoke in agreement, but slowly, like the tides on a beach, they retreated. A small path through them opened up. The half-orc looked her in the eyes, completely opposite to the joyous, golden hero she'd seen before.

"Send them to the hells," he said. "And if you fail, then we will do it for you."

Gyda's hand on her back was all that moved her forward. Down the last few steps and through the crowd of broken heroes. Past the entry hall, the doors were open, the sky still pouring grey rain onto an emerald field. Three horses and a pony waited for them, Viggo completely covered in his cloak and shivering against the rain. Tolk's pony was going in circles, trying to lick something off the goblin's feet. Gyda's horse was a large beast with hooves as big as Evren's torso. The warrior patted the horse fondly before climbing on.

Evren's own horse was a gentle looking black mare. She shook the rain from her mane, eyes on the road, as Evren swung into the saddle and took the reins.

"Never thought I'd say this," she said, pulling her hood up against the rain. "But I prefer wyverns."

"I think Viggo prefers anything but rain." Gyda chuckled.

He glowered at her through his hood. "It isn't natural for water to fall from the sky."

"Maybe not for you." Evren shrugged. "But storms are how we survive."

"That makes sense. Something so uncomfortable and chaotic had to be your source of life."

"One of." Evren grinned. "You haven't seen the sun on a clear day. Endless blue and giant ball of fire and light in the sky looking down at you . . ."

Viggo groaned. "By the Light, please be quiet. Don't we have your surface to save?"

"We do." Tolk cackled. "Makin' fun of you is just gonna pass the time!"

He kicked his pony and suddenly the little creature was off down the muddy road. Evren and Gyda spurred their horses after him, Viggo not far behind. Hooves ate up lengths of mud and grass, the sky thundered and poured, and Vanguard waited.

19

Evren

"How much damage could they do?" Evren asked from her alcove wedged between rocks. Vanguard stood imposing above them, their little shelter from the unrelenting storm providing enough cover so they weren't seen. The ramparts were alight despite the weather, bright green and blue lights bouncing from one Serevadian to the other as they paced the walls. Some lights stood still, hovering in clusters around groups of soldiers as they worked around massive heavy crossbows to secure them to the ramparts. It was hard to get any accurate measurements from their distance, but a crossbow that size would have bolts as big around as Evren's arm.

Beside her, Viggo stood huddled as far away from the rain as he could. Water leaked in rivulets, dripping down the walls and worming past their cloaks. He shook some from his hair, eyes fixed on the crossbows.

"They were prototypes before I left Andovine," he said. "But they use metal bolts laced with Light. The damage can be severe enough to churn the ground and make it difficult to get through. I won't describe what it does to a body."

"There are only four."

"You say that as if it's a good thing. They only need four."

Evren winced. "They'll tear us apart if they spot us. We won't last long as distractions for Sol and Sahar to blast the wall. No blast, no Tolk and his army."

"Assuming he can get to us," Viggo said.

"Right." Evren rubbed her face, flicking water off as she did. They'd been watching the fortress for nearly two days now, and the crossbows were new. They darkened an already shadowy plan to near pitch darkness. Divara's numbers were correct from what they could see. Heavily armed, seemingly well-fortified. Nothing new to worry about until now.

She turned back to the deep recess of the cave where Gyda sat with her mirror shard lighting up her face.

"Did you tell them?"

Gyda nodded. "None of them have any clever ideas. It's a lot of, 'oh, that's bad.'" She stowed her mirror. "They're close. Should be here within the hour."

"Which means we need to deal with those first." Evren hissed. "Fuck. Any bright ideas?"

Viggo shook his head. "I'd have to get closer to do any damage. Even then, I'll be noticeable. Taking out one will bring the rest."

Gyda grunted. "No magical remedy to fix all our problems?"

He glared at her over his shoulder. "I have a select list of talents, much like yourself. I cannot change reality with a piece of paper. I can shield. I can illuminate. I can kill if necessary. But if you want me to make those disappear, we will be here a very long time."

"Aren't you supposed to be helpful?" Gyda asked.

"I am try—"

Evren cut them both off. "I can get them."

Gyda blinked at her, then over her shoulder at Vanguard's looming form as she gauged the distance. Evren had to, so she knew what Gyda was going to say before the words left her mouth.

"Your bow doesn't have that reach, Evren."

"I know. The plan remains the same. Except I'll have to disable the crossbows first."

Viggo hissed. "Have you lost your mind? That'll take circling the entirety of the fort. It was risky enough to sneak into the gatehouse and lift their defenses, but this is something else entirely."

"You'll be seen," Gyda said flatly."

"I know, but what other choice do we have?"

Viggo started pacing in their small cave, wringing out his damp white hair as he did. He'd been agitated since they'd settled down to watch Vanguard, but she'd never seen him so worried. Even in Serevadia he'd been collected.

"If you are seen, they will simply raise the defenses, making this whole attack pointless," he argued. "You don't even know how to destroy those things! They're made out of metal and Light."

"If you hit anything hard enough, it'll break." Evren shrugged.

"And they're still surrounded by guards! Not to mention those on the ground level that we can't see."

"Most of the ramparts are blind spots from the ground," Evren said. "Gyda saw it too. All I need to do is make sure to kill those in my path quietly."

"That won't last for long. There are too many eyes in that fort for you to go unnoticed for so long."

Gyda stood up and grabbed her sword. The dribbling rainwater that pooled in the runes slid off as she strapped it to her back.

"Then we'll give them something more noticeable," the warrior said. "You and I."

Viggo's pacing froze as if the ground had enveloped his feet. "Now you're mad as well?"

"What is more distracting than a disgraced Serevadian and me?" Gyda asked.

"They'll kill us on sight!"

"Better come up with a story that keeps them talking then." She turned to Evren. "This is what you need to get those crossbows out of the way before the others come, right?"

Evren's stomach churned. Viggo was right. He and Gyda would be out in the open before the gates. Even if they said something to convince the soldiers not to kill them immediately, they'd last only a matter of minutes like that.

"You'd be exposed until I could get the gates open," she warned. "And I still don't know how much time I'll need to disable the crossbows."

"You'll have whatever we can give you," Gyda said. "It'll have to be enough."

Evren felt her chest tighten painfully. Her anxiety or Gyda's? She could never tell. Death had always been an outcome they'd courted with this plan, but now it lingered too close. She could feel it weighing on her like the storm-heavy sky above. She could lose her for good today, and while that had always been a risk, it didn't make it easier to accept.

"Okay." Evren rolled her shoulders and ignored the initial problem. "The gate will have to be open before Sorin and Arke arrive, which means that you'll be heading inside alone. I'll give you covering fire as much as I can. After that, we hold out until Sol and Sahar's signal."

Viggo closed his eyes, his face lined with worry. A part of Evren hated that she was throwing him into a battle when he had very little experience, especially one so unbalanced against them. But Viggo had every opportunity to leave before, and he hadn't. Staying to fight was his only option.

He opened his eyes, set his jaw, and nodded. "Fine. I'll

buy you some time, Evren. Try to keep us alive long enough to get past the gates."

"That's the plan." Evren looked at the dark sky. She'd hoped for sunlight to blind the Serevadians, but rain would have to do. "We need to move now to get this done on time."

Minutes later, they were out of the alcove they'd made their home for the past two days. The rain fell in sheets, icy and invigorating. It quelled the rising fire of fear climbing in Evren's chest. She kept low, following the long, marked path they'd used to remain unseen from the fort's walls. It took them awhile. They went slow, and the path took many twists and turns that weren't a direct route but kept them hidden. Mountainous rocks, slick with rain, hid them, but Evren knew it took only one slip up and a keen-eyed soldier to sound the alarm. She didn't want to see what those crossbows would do to rocks.

As they neared the bottom, Gyda pulled her back into the shelter of a tall, jagged rock.

"What is it?" Evren flattened herself against the rock. "Were we seen?"

"No." Gyda leaned over her and cupped her face. The rain stopped pattering against her cheeks as she leaned down and pressed her lips against Evren's. Gentle and slow, she kissed her under the thundering sky. Vanguard and Serevadia faded from Evren's mind. All that mattered was Gyda's embrace, her lips lingering until raindrops slipped between them and their breaths pushed them apart.

"Do whatever it takes," Gyda murmured. "I'll see you when it's done."

"However it ends," Evren finished. She kept the memory of Gyda like this in her mind. Rain falling around her like a halo. Her eyes dark and wholly for Evren. Her wet hair slipping from her scarf and sticking to her forehead.

They broke away then, because if they didn't Evren knew she wouldn't want to leave and turn to Vanguard's dark walls.

But they did leave each other, shared heart aching and a heavy promise still on their lips. Gyda walked away, brushing past Viggo, who was watching Evren with an unreadable expression.

It felt stupid to care about what he thought at a time like this. Whatever Evren and Viggo might've been had been destroyed long ago at both their hands. But she hadn't mentioned her and Gyda's closeness. She didn't know what he would think, if he'd even care or if he'd be hurt.

But Viggo gave her a rueful smile and turned to follow Gyda.

Evren took her path alongside the wall. While they would head to the front gate, she'd slip through the rain-slick shadow past the first corner. The length of ramparts were mostly open walkways at the top of the walls, broken by enclosed towers and the crossbows in between. Evren chose the space between the gatehouse and the first tower. The first crossbow would be there, along with the group of Serevadians working on it, but she needed to be quick more than careful. If Gyda and Viggo's distraction worked, she wouldn't have to worry about too many of them anyway.

Evren got to the wall unnoticed. Her fingers met rough wet stone, the rain pouring down in sheets like a gentle waterfall. She flexed her fingers and the claws from her gloves sprung out. They clicked against the stone as she put her fingers around the first handhold, barely big enough for her fingertips, and pulled her weight up. Her fingers slipped, just as she expected, but the claws caught on the stone and held firm.

Evren let out a shaky breath and put her other hand up. It was a slow climb. Her boot clad toes found little purchase to support her, and her fingers were raw from grasping at the stone and falling off. The claws did most, if not all, of the work. Rain wormed its way into the gloves, the leather slipping on her palms as she climbed foot by foot. She gritted her teeth, adjusting her grip as much as she could. She wouldn't look down. The wind tugging at her cloak was enough to let her know she was high enough to die if she fell. And all she had to hold her up were metal claws.

Every tink of metal against stone made her flinch. The closer the top of the ramparts loomed the more she swore the soldiers at the top could hear her claws and labored breathing. Her armor creaked; her muscles screamed. She tried to keep herself quiet and found herself panting harder.

She was a foot from the top when she stopped. Her arms burned keeping her in place, but she forced herself still and silent. She listened, hearing the grumbling Serevadian language between soldiers. Still the same five she saw before. Something metal thudded against the stone, shaking her fingers, and earning a colorful swear from one of the soldiers above. Another laugh, his joke drowned out by a rumble of thunder and then a flash of lighting.

Evren blinked the rain out of her eyes. Lightning came first, not thunder. She craned her neck towards the gatehouse and saw a flash of light, brighter and tinged green. She couldn't see past the corner of the gatehouse, but she smiled anyway.

It had begun.

Armor clanked and footsteps pattered as the soldiers next to the crossbow ran towards the gates. Evren couldn't hear anything over the sound of wind and rain, thunder and labored breathing, save for the distant notes of Viggo's voice. She didn't linger on his words because they weren't for her. She pulled herself up to the edge of the ramparts and peeked over.

Two of the five soldiers remained, one on either side of the crossbow. It was large enough to dwarf them, silvery metal gleaming when real lightning struck.

Evren waited until the thunder rumbled and then hauled herself over the edge. Her shoulders rejoiced as her feet hit solid ground behind one of the soldiers. Like the other one, his gaze was fixed in the direction of the gate. Viggo was still talking, so Evren took that as a good sign. She flexed her hands, and the claws retreated.

Lurching up, she wrapped her arm around the soldier's throat. Before he could so much as gasp, she snapped his neck and tossed him over the edge. His armor scraped against the stone as he plummeted and his partner wheeled around, grasping for his sword.

Evren's dagger was in her hands and flying through the air to land between the other soldier's eyes before he could draw his sword. His hand fell limp, and then the rest of his body followed. Evren circled around the crossbow to him, taking back her dagger and sheathing it. It would take too long to shove his body over the side, so she left him there, blood pooling around his head, and turned to the crossbow.

It was beautiful, all sleek, elegant lines, just like she remembered from Serevadian work. Its limbs were nearly as long as she was tall. She thumbed the string, and it thrummed lowly. Metal, thick and braided strong. She couldn't cut through it.

To the side, thick metal bolts were piled neatly. They looked heavy enough that two people would be needed to lift them. Beside them was a covered basket. Evren pulled back the cover. Inside were glass orbs, swirling with a familiar green light.

"Someone was in a rush," she muttered to herself. "Bolts aren't laced with Light yet."

It didn't mean they wouldn't be deadly, or that the other three crossbows were in the same unfinished state. But it was a small stroke of luck.

Raised voices from the gate rose over the chorus of the storm. Whatever Viggo had done was getting heated. Evren couldn't hear Gyda and forced her out of her mind. She needed to take this crossbow out, but every inch of it seemed pristine. The way it was anchored to the ramparts, the mechanism it used to swivel completely in a circle so it could fire at all angles. Evren tried to use her claws to cut through the wire string but didn't so much as bend it.

All or nothing. Evren didn't have time doubt. Gyda didn't have time.

Evren plunged her hands into the basket of Light orbs and pulled three out, each the size of her palm. They glowed like green stars and the moment they left the basket they were like a beacon. Seconds passed before sounds of alarm went up from the rest of the ramparts. She'd been spotted.

Evren hugged the orbs to her chest and backed towards the gatehouse. She was only a few feet from the door, and several away from the crossbow. She didn't know what they would do, but there had to be a process to infusing metal with Light, and she doubted it was smashing the orbs into each other, and being too close sounded like a death wish.

From the tower opposite her, soldiers poured out, silvery armor glistening and swords drawn. They stopped when they saw her, and their eyes went wide as they saw the orbs in her arms.

"Well, that's a good sign," Evren said to herself and hurled one of her orbs into the basket of others.

The smashing of glass heralded the chaos to come like a trinkle of rain before a hurricane. The basket shook, light pouring out of it as one by one the glass orbs shattered. The soldiers scrambled back, crying in alarm, just as the basket exploded in a ball of searing green light.

Evren was slammed back into the wall of the gatehouse, breath knocked out of her and vision swimming. The soldiers who'd been closer hadn't been so lucky. The Light ate them, tendrils of green sizzling in the rain and lashing out at living flesh. They were consumed, screaming, leaving ghostly specters made of light and bearing their form before they faded away.

The light ebbed, leaving nothing but scorched stone in its

wake. No soldiers, no crossbow, just Evren and a ringing alarm.

Evren turned and kicked the door to the gatehouse open. Warm and blissfully dry, but filled with five Serevadians.

The closest one rushed her. Evren ducked under the sword, tucking one of the orbs into his belt as she did. Rearing back, she gave him a solid kick, glass crunching under her boot as she sent him careening into his allies.

Two were consumed by the Light, much smaller this time but no less potent. One managed to back away but his arm was burnt off, leaving nothing but a bloody stump at the shoulder.

Quick as she could, Evren set the last orb down, drew her dagger, and rushed in. She slid on her knees under the wounded soldier, slicing at an artery as she passed. She stopped in front of the next one as he raised his sword. Swinging her leg out, she hooked the back of his knee and sent him tumbling to the ground next to her. A quick slice to the throat ended him.

Evren barely dodged the next blade. It skimmed so close to her face she could see her reflection. She rolled back, landing on her feet just as the soldier lunged again.

A dagger was useless against a sword. Evren gritted her teeth as she backed away, holding her dagger in front of her. The sword had more reach. She just needed to get closer.

Evren feinted left and the sword twitched so quickly in that direction that she would've been impaled if she hadn't spun away. Too late the soldier caught onto her plan and tried to bring the sword around for a vicious follow up. Evren was inside her guard, dagger in her throat even as the sword bit into the back of her own calf. The soldier gurgled, her black eyes refusing to close even when Evren pushed her away.

Her calf throbbed enough for Evren to limp, but she ignored it and barred both doors quickly. The floor had an iron trellis covering a hole in the floor; she could see straight down to where Gyda and Viggo would be walking through. The pully systems for both portcullises were made of thick rope and took up walls on either side of the large room.

Evren frowned at them. They were designed to be lowered and lifted by a team, but if the voices outside were any indication, she didn't have time to struggle against them.

She pulled out her bow, nocking an arrow into the taut new bowstring. Already her shoulders burned with a familiar ache, made worse by the added tension in the string. Evren savored the burn, arrow tip following her eyes as she picked apart the system. Which ropes did what, which sandbags held the thing aloft and which needed to be lowered for it to rise.

Seconds later she found them and fired. The rope snapped, the heavy sandbags fell and the grating rattle of the first portcullis rising shook the gatehouse. Evren nocked another arrow and did the same, the sound like thunderous music to her ears as the final portcullis rose.

Not long after, the gatehouse shuddered as the heavy wooden doors were pushed open. Evren watched through the floor as bodies of Serevadians were thrown on the ground, Gyda marching past with her sword bloody and Viggo at her heels. They passed out of her sight, and Evren's heart began to sing Gyda's battle song as swords clashed.

Behind her, the door that she'd entered through began to splinter as bodies slammed into it. Opposite, the other door was muffling shouted orders.

Evren snatched the last orb from the ground. The thought to save it until she got to the next crossbow struck her, but she couldn't stand her ground against attacks from two sides. She tucked it carefully into her belt.

She chose the unsplintered door, tossing aside the wood she'd used to bar the door, and threw it open.

The storm met her skin, as alive and brimming with destruction as she was. Her fingers latched onto an arrow and nocked it as she strode onto the battlements. The crowd of

Serevadians before her were confused and scattered. Rain and spit flew from their commander's mouth as she shouted orders at them to fall in line, then blood and brain matter joined them, as Evren's arrow pierced her skull.

In the seconds it took for the body to fall and the shock to wear off, Evren had already fired another arrow. By the time her third was nocked, the soldiers sprang into action.

Evren fired arrow after arrow as she walked. To the throats, the faces, anything that would kill them quickly and get them out of her way. It was a continuous line of moving targets, few getting past her initial range.

Where one body fell, another Serevadian was there to replace them. One charged at her, narrowly deflecting an arrow, and swung wildly at her. Evren spun out of the way, grabbing an arrow from her quiver, and ramming it into his neck. She pulled the blood-soaked arrow out and fired at the next screaming solider. Her cries cut short as the arrow hit her square in the eye.

The remaining soldiers started to retreat. The gift of language she'd stolen from Ainthe made the shouted orders clear.

"Range!" they bellowed over the storm. "Bring the archers!"

Evren didn't have time for that. She shot the one shouting orders and ran. Before they even fell, she was past them, cutting soldier's exposed ankles, inner thighs, and necks with her dagger as she passed. She left a trail of wounded and slowly dying behind her.

The battlements took a turn, curving her to the next side of the fort. The crossbow gleamed like a beacon, a gauntlet of soldiers in front of her. Surprise and momentum was all that kept her ahead. Evren kept that up, tossing her dagger into the chest of the closest and firing two arrows at the next two. She retrieved her dagger as she passed the body, sheathing it and reaching for the orb next.

The line of soldiers in front of her formed a wall, swords drawn and shields of pure energy blocking her path.

Quick decisions were the worst, but Evren took it anyway. She slung her bow over her shoulder and veered to the left, leaping up to the wall that kept the battlements separate from the open air over the fort. Cries of alarm came from the line of soldiers as she hopped from one toothlike stone to the next. Stone slick under her boots, she leapt before she could slip, getting nearer to the line that turned its focus to blocking her wall path. A foot away from the first soldier, his shield raised high as he backed away from her, she paid him little attention. Her eyes were on her goal—the crossbow that would be clear once she got past them.

The crossbow that was manned and aimed directly at her.

Too late, she tried to turn, to correct her course. The gleam of silver and green lightning arched from the crossbow directly towards her as she tried to jump away. Evren's feet had barely touched the next stone when it erupted underneath her. Her momentum plummeted. Her feet churned against open air and shattered stone. Fragments of rock, white-hot with burning Light stung her face and sizzled against her armor. She fell with the rocks, with the rain. A chorus of disaster carried to the rocky ground of the fort below.

Evren didn't fall long. She swung her body around, carrying her momentum enough to grasp the wall and engage her claws. The metal hooks stuck to the stone, and she slammed into it hard enough to see stars. She hung there until the rocks settled and her breathing caught up with her.

She was dangling above the courtyard with just one arm. Below her was a frenzy of blood, steel, and magic. Gyda and Viggo were fighting side by side. Her sword was glowing a deep, vibrant red Evren had only seen once, cutting through the armor and carving up arcs of blood to join the rain. Viggo's spells were arcs of grand Light—shields that turned the toughest of blades, bubbles that encircled them both only to expand and burn all those foolish enough to surround them. Rain sizzled and hissed, turning to clouds of steam wherever it touched his Light.

Viggo turned to look where she'd fallen, his eyes missing her and catching the lightning of another bolt instead. His mouth went wide to scream something at Gyda behind him, arms going up and pulling a shield of Light above them.

Light hit Light, and stormy night turned bright daylight. Evren shut her eyes, gasping as steam and heat flooded her nose and mouth. She buried her face into the crook of her arm until the Light suddenly vanished, and the intense heat went with it.

Evren looked up the wall, blinking away rain. She wouldn't look back to see the aftermath. She couldn't bear to look upon what would remain if the bolt had beaten the shield. Their heart still beat. That had to count for something.

She heaved her dangling arm up, biting back any screams of pain or frustration that threatened to bubble up. One clink of claws against stone at a time, she hauled herself over the edge.

Evren stumbled behind the line of shocked soldiers, gasping and holding her ribs. They swung around, leveling their swords at her. Behind them, she could see the ones she'd left breaking into the gatehouse charging to join them. To her other side, the crossbow was being loaded again.

She brought out the final orb of Light, and the shields shrank back an inch. Through the translucent light she could see their worried faces.

"You really should find a better way of storing this," she said, then turned around and tossed it at the crossbow.

Glass shattered at its base, hungry green tendrils eating up metal with startling speed. The metal creaked and groaned as the heavy crossbow swayed precariously, once, twice, then fell to the side with a stone shuddering boom. One of the Serevadians couldn't get away in time and screamed as his spine was crushed under the heavy metal limbs.

The shields took no time to push towards her, a swath of angry Serevadians close behind them. Out of the corner of her eye, Evren could see more coming from the opposite direction to pin her down. The dim, glittering star of the next crossbow was so far away but she could see it swiveling towards the courtyard below.

Distantly she wondered if that meant Gyda and Viggo had survived the first shot. Why else would it be aiming there now? But her back was to the courtyard, to the answer to a question that wouldn't matter in the next few seconds.

Rain dazzled under the flash of true lightning arching through the low, heavy clouds. Evren allowed herself to taste it on her tongue, to feel it pattering on her cut, burned skin as she nocked another arrow. How many did she have before she ran out? How long would she last with just a dagger against an army?

There was no room for failure, she reminded herself as she drew back the arrow and aimed it between the shields.

No room for failure because Abraxas needed them. Because a world without Gyda was too colorless to imagine. Because Serevadia and Eith would tear each other apart and it was her fault that she let it get this far.

Evren Hanali, wounded, surrounded, at the mercy of an army she had no hopes of beating by herself, could not fail.

She let the arrow loose, and the whole fort shook as if it was tearing apart at the seams.

Evren grasped the side of the battlements to steady herself as the walls seemed to convulse and wave. The soldiers who'd been charging at her, mere feet away, stumbled back. The bright orange of fire lit up their horrified faces as they stared behind her.

Evren whirled around, still gripping the stone. Where the next crossbow had been was a gaping hole of fire and crumbling rock. Plumes of noxious black smoke filled the night air, but it wasn't enough to disguise the pillar of fire it it's depths.

Natural fire spread outward, forever looking for fuel. Even unnatural fire like Sahar's ghostly white flames ate and grew until it was forced to wither and die. These flames didn't. Their plumes of orange and yellow shot out, grasping for wood to survive the downpour like any normal flame. But then they were sucked back, swirling around each other in a deadly cyclone that rose higher than the wall itself.

Soldiers screamed as the fire shot up from its hole in the wall and spread to the battlements in either direction with cruel, focused, precision. Evren threw herself back over the edge of the battlements just as the wave of flames tore through the soldiers surrounding her. Her fingers burned as her ears tried to block the screams. But as suddenly as it started, it ended. The fire left the night air cool, and the rain continued to fall.

Evren hauled herself back over the edge, arms and legs shaking. There was nothing but blackened stone and burnt corpses left. Standing amidst it all was Divara, a vision in blood-red and black.

The War Mage pulled her sleeves down, but not before Evren caught the sight of burning flesh spiraling on her forearms where ink had once been. The remnants of many scars like that colored her deep skin a sickly white in arcane swirls and runes.

"I take it that was you?" Evren panted as she nodded to the broken wall.

Divara's lips quirked. "No. I took Sahar's fire and used it to clear this side of the battlements, but I did not destroy the wall. A smart mage knows when to use what is already available rather than create on their own."

Evren nodded, waving her lecture off to take in the battlefield.

Through the massive gap in the wall, Sol and Sahar cut

through the recovering soldiers with flashes of alchemy and daggers. They were both covered in soot, their faces grim. Farther back in the courtyard, Gyda stood between an advancing army and a very dazed, but alive, Viggo. Lines of bodies fell to Gyda's blade, but she couldn't hold them all off. Evren's fingers twitched for another arrow just as a thin blade sliced through the Serevadian attacking Gyda. He fell and Sorin laughed, darting away from the rest of the small army's attacks as if the wind itself was guiding his feet. And maybe it was. The way he moved, as quick and fluid as water versus Gyda's hard, ground-shaking attacks, was mesmerizing to watch.

"Where's Arke?" she asked.

Divara nodded across the fort, to the opposite side of the battlements. "He decided to 'experiment,' as he called it. I believe your distraction over here was enough for him to do so unnoticed."

Another question was working its way up Evren's throat when the final crossbow shot it's glowing bolt into the court-yard, missing Sorin and Gyda and taking out a massive chunk of Serevadians. A few minutes later, Sahar and Sol were cornered between the armory and the barracks, and the next bolt skimmed over them and carved a path through their enemies so they could run out.

Evren grinned so wide it hurt. "Arke's got the final one."

"So it seems." Divara regarded the chaos with an amused quirk of her brow, as if she could hear the goblin's cackling over the storm and the battle.

Serevadia's greater numbers were dwindling, but the Wandering Sols fought like devils. Turning fire and Light against the soldiers, breaking defenses, and just refusing to die. Evren felt warm hope swell in her chest. Tolk's army would be coming soon. They might actually win this.

She and Divara took up positions along the wall. Divara swept her hands over each of Evren's arrows, infusing them with smoldering fire, crackling lightning, or hissing ice. The smell of burnt flesh wafting from Divara after every arrow was ignored. She enchanted, Evren fired, Serevadians burned. They were encased in ice, statues that shattered under Gyda's heavy blows. They shuddered and screamed as lightning coursed through their body, still enough for Sol's or Sorin's quick slashes to take them down.

But for every Serevadian cut down, three more seemed to take their place. Evren's quiver was growing lighter. Arke's crossbow fired less frequently and then stopped all together. Sorin, Gyda, and Viggo had made it near the center of Vanguard with Sol and Sahar where they all stood clustered together as Serevadians pooled around them.

And Tolk was nowhere to be seen.

"He didn't make it." Evren's throat felt tight. Had he not heard Sahar's explosion? Or had he not gotten close enough to the tunnel entrance near the fort at all? They knew there was a possibility of the entrance being guarded, but enough to take down a hundred goblins? That would need a sizable force. But the only other option was that Tolk had simply decided not to come, and she knew he wouldn't do that to Arke.

The brothers were many things, distant and different being among them, but they wouldn't betray each other.

The minutes that passed without the sound of goblins joining the battle only solidified her fear. They needed a new plan.

Divara was watching her, not an ounce of worry on her face. It was all calculation, breaking the battle below into numbers instead of people and names.

"We need a way out," Evren said. "Some way to pull our people out and circle back. Maybe grab volunteers from the adventurers we left behind and come back with a larger force."

"The only reason we've gotten this far is because of

surprise," Divara said. "If we leave, that will give them time to prepare for us. No amount of numbers can change that."

"We can't stay! We'll be overwhelmed."

"And if we leave, we fail," Divara snapped.

There was no room for failure. But they'd lose the battle if they died or not. Evren wracked her brain as her friends fought below. She could see flashes of Arke's magic along the battlements as he fought to get down to join the fight. Even he wouldn't be enough. Sahar's blazing white fire lit up the night. Viggo sent short bursts of searing Light to all those in his path, each burst getting weaker. Sorin was still smiling but his laugh was gone. Sol had lost one of her daggers. Gyda was limping. They were backing themselves up the stairs that would lead to the fort's main hall, fighting off attackers from above and below.

Divara removed an arrow from Evren's quiver. She held it tightly, her face and voice devoid of pain and emotion as magic seeped through her fingers and into the arrow.

"Get your people out," she said. "The tunnel the Serevadians used will be in the building next to the main hall, just up against the wall. Take that path, and use this to get through the army." She held out the arrow.

Evren took it in between her fingers. It felt heavier, as if it had the weight of fifty arrows instead of one.

"If Tolk didn't come through, then that tunnel could be a death trap," Evren argued.

"Then you'll deal with that, and I will deal with this."

"What are you going to do?" Evren asked.

Divara's eyes moved to the tower in the middle of the fort, and a look of intense mourning passed over her tranquil features.

"Vanguard was built by a friend of mine," she said. "A mentor. He used the fire underneath the mountains as a weapon." She nodded to the tower. "He would call it through that."

"This is a volcano?"

"The whole range is, somewhat dormant thanks to this use of the energy. I can use it to destroy what's left of Serevadia's occupation here, but you won't be able to come back this way."

"You'll be safe though, at the top of the tower?" Evren pressed. She knew her friends were running out of time. She knew it was only a matter of minutes before they were overrun. But Divara's quiet resolve echoed Abraxas. She felt like she was on Saros watching him fall all over again, and when Divara didn't answer, it was like a punch in the gut.

"Divara, you can't," she argued. "Loghain needs you! Abraxas will, too."

"You are in no position to tell me what I can and cannot do," the War Mage said, and shed her cloak. Almost every inch of her skin that Evren could see was covered in white burns. There were only a few black tattoos. "I am already burnt out, a shell of my potential. I can sustain the mountain's fire enough to clear this place and make way for Etherak's army. That is *all* I care about. That is *all* that matters."

Divara leveled a flat look at Evren. "This is not a sacrifice for you, it is for Eith. Your deaths are meaningless here. If you are to die, do it somewhere that'll make a difference. Now go, or I'll burn us all."

Evren knew Divara didn't care about her enough to lie to her. A woman whose whole life had been war saw only outcomes. Etherak and Terevas needed Vanguard, and Divara would give it to them. All those that got caught in the blast were necessary casualties.

Evren stowed her bow over her shoulder, tucked the arrow in her teeth and hopped over the wall. She didn't question Divara about how she would get in the tower. She didn't ask if there was any family she needed to talk to, or something for Loghain that she wanted to pass on. Evren climbed down the wall and ran the moment her feet hit the ground.

Mud and water splashed along her ankles as she weaved between fallen bodies in a race towards her friends. They were at the top of the stairs now, stuck between two forces. Evren couldn't see Viggo's light, or Sahar's white fire. Before her was a crowd of enemies blocking her path to and up the stairs.

Evren took the arrow and nocked as she ran. She ignored the bubbling fear that she had no idea what Divara had enchanted it with or if it would hurt her friends. Just as she was about to draw it back, a swirling ball of fiery glyphs burst to life opposite her and raced towards the Serevadians. Between the glyphs she caught a glimpse of the worg running at full speed, carrying Arke on his back as ash fell from his ink-stained hands. He had a manic look in his eyes, and no smile. He caught Evren's eye and nodded towards the army.

He'd clear the way; she'd pick off the stragglers.

She raced to follow him, stumbling when she saw another figure following him. Lanky and small, moving impossibly fast.

"Keres?" she cried over the storm.

They grinned. "Didn't think I'd let you leave to get my soul back without me, did you?"

Evren had never been so happy to see the ancient corpse-possessing spirit before. Their paths converged into one deadly line behind Arke as the flame-encircled goblin surged at the Serevadians from behind.

Too late they saw their doom. Glyphs of fire exploded as Arke sent them out to all in his path. Glyph by glyph, explosion by explosion, they carved a burning path to their trapped friends. By the time the army was catching on to Arke's plan, Evren and Keres were there to keep them back. Evren's dagger was slick with blood, her boots tripped over all the bodies she made. Keres threw limp corpses at those running at them, taking them down in dead weight and heavy armor. Enemies dove off the stairs by the dozens to avoid the three of them, Divara's arrow itched to be used, but Evren kept it back. With each step they grew closer, until Evren could hear Sorin's laughter again. His taunts filled the air with Gyda's battle cries and Sol's voice counting number by number.

They reached the top and Arke sent his last glyph of fire out to clear the closest enemies. He went to burn another page, but Evren shook her head and put away her dagger.

"I have this," she said and pulled the arrow back.

She wanted to see her friends, to look over all their injuries and see what had happened. But she saw them moving out of the corner of her eye. She heard Sorin's breathless words of praise to the worg, and Sahar's cry of relief at seeing Keres. She knew Gyda was alive. She felt her heart beating, and how it calmed at the sight of Evren.

She turned to the army in front of them, the only ones keeping them from their escape. Behind them she heard all those who hadn't been caught in the blast regrouping. The ones in front held their glowing shields and swords high. Her eyes spotted the building next to the great hall that Divara mentioned, so unassuming she would've ignored it if she hadn't known. She saw her path, perfected her aim, and fired.

The arrow hit a soldier near the middle of the pack and cleaved straight through his armor into his chest. It held there for a moment, like a regular arrow. But then the air changed. It chilled significantly, rain turned to sleet. Frost webbed across the soldier's armor. All the air in the area seemed to be sucked towards the soldier, who let out a wordless scream and then blew apart.

Pieces of him went flying as all the air gathered pulsed outward again. Serevadians were thrown back against walls, through doors and into each other. Evren lost her footing and started to fall back down the stairs, but Keres's cold arm snaked out and snatched her up.

"So clumsy," they tsked.

The door was in sight. Evren shoved Keres and Arke forward. "Get in there! Go!"

No one argued. Their thundering feet tore up the open path, passing by crushed, broken bodies. Evren darted to Gyda, who was half carrying Viggo. His white hair was red with blood from a wound on his temple, but his feet were moving sluggishly as Gyda dragged him along. She circled around and took his other arm, and the three of them took up the rear.

"New plan?" Gyda asked.

Evren choked out something like a laugh or a sob. "Of course! When do our plans ever go well?"

Gyda did laugh and beheaded a crawling Serevadian just before they got through the door.

The building looked like it was for food storage and might've connected to the main hall's kitchen. But Evren's concern was the massive hole in the floor, which looked more like a grave than an escape route. There was only one Serevadian guarding it, and before she could bring up her sword, Sahar rushed forward and slammed a familiar hand axe in her chest. She kicked the body off, wiped the blade clean, and sheathed it at her hip.

"I take it there's a change in plan?" she asked.

Evren kicked the door shut. "Sorin, Keres, bar this please."

Sorin went to work immediately. Keres waited for Sahar's approval and jumped in once she nodded. They found the wood to lock the door from the inside and got it in place just as the shouting outside got worse. The door rattled as someone shoved against it, but it held.

Sorin backed away. "I love being trapped. Such fun."

Sol wheezed off to the side, shaking her head. "No. Not trapped. Hole."

He frowned. "I see the hole, Sol, but the plan was to kill most of the Serevadians so Vanguard wouldn't be overrun.

I'm all about saving my ass, but they'll just send people after us like this."

Evren put her bow across her shoulders. "Divara said she's taking care of the rest, but we can't be here when she does. They won't follow us."

The door shook again, more weight being put on it. Keres leaned against it casually.

"Goodie for her, I suppose." They sniffed. "Die a hero to make up for being someone's villain."

Gyda scowled at them. "We are all someone's villain."

"Oh, did love give you a brain? How fortunate."

"Enough, Keres," Sahar snapped. "We don't have a choice. If Tolk didn't . . ." she trailed off, softening when she looked at Arke. "I'm sorry."

Arke, stiff and quiet, peered over the edge of the hole. The worg nudged his side, whining when Arke didn't respond.

"Let's go," the goblin barked. "I ain't gonna die here."

Without hesitation, he jumped into the hole. After a few moments of tying off rope and lowering everyone down one by one, Evren and Sahar were the last ones at the surface. The ground was rumbling, the door had splintered, but the attempts to get in had stopped.

"Do you think she knew she was going to die when she walked inside my house?" Sahar asked, staring at the door as if she could picture the scene outside—of Divara at the top of the tower, calling forth molten rock with her will. How it would glow, lighting up the fort like a beacon. The last of her tattoos burning away. Would she close her eyes? Would she think of something better, or would she relish in the cries of horror from below as the mountain's destruction obliterated everything in its path?

"I don't know." Evren grabbed Sahar's wrist and forced her to look at her. "Her story is ending, ours is not. And we still have people to save."

Something exploded outside, but neither woman broke

eye contact. Sahar's fingers brushed the metal of Drystan's axe, and she took a deep breath.

"Let's bring them home," she said. "Both of them."

"Both of them," Evren agreed.

The screaming started as they turned towards the hole. Below, the remaining Luminstones were brought out and Arke had lit a ball of fire for light. Evren let Sahar go down first, and she followed.

The tunnel ahead was empty and dark. Their breathing echoed the sounds of dying above. The black shadows pressed against them, and Evren picked up Viggo's other arm again.

"Sol and Arke, lead the way." She nodded. "We'll rest once we're far enough."

Into the dark depths they plunged, shards of fire and light in their hands, death at their backs, and the unknown in front of them.

20

Abraxas

Finding clothes off a dead man to replace the ones he'd lost had been easy. Finding the corpses left over from the battle had not been.

Mizan's death had been quicker than Nunwei's, but that was the only mercy Abraxas found kneeling beside his body. The rebel's throat had been cut, bleeding scarlet into the sands outside of Cuskhe where he'd been found. There'd been a fight. Scuffling along the sand, Mizan's glaive tossed aside.

"What were you doing?" Abraxas mused.

Mizan, even in death, would not give him an answer.

Surely he hadn't been running away. Mizan was many things, but a coward he wasn't. He'd wanted Cuskhe badly. Why leave?

Abraxas looked back at Cuskhe, or rather, what remained of it. There'd be no living in that city. It reeked of death. The sand might've soaked up the blood, but it couldn't swallow the bodies of the fallen, many of whom had been civilians. Vernes had won, but the battle left him just as hollow as it had when he'd lost with Etherak. The more bodies he recognized, the worse he felt. As if that pit in his chest was growing to consume him.

Nunwei hadn't been a close friend, but she hadn't deserved to be pinned to the city wall with five spears and burned alive. Her undead hound had burned himself to get to her, his body no more than a shriveled husk with skin as brittle as dried parchment. Abraxas had found the boy he'd left with his potions bag a few streets over, dead, the bag picked clean even as it had been clutched to his chest. Jado hadn't been found yet, but there were many bodies to go through, most of them burned. Abraxas wasn't confident they'd find the laughing youth at all.

And then there was Mizan.

Abraxas looked back at the man. How had he died while Abraxas lived? It seemed like some cruel twist of fate to have a man with so much life and purpose fall, and for him to keep living. Oh, Abraxas still despised Mizan even in death. But there had been respect there. It took a strength Abraxas didn't have to rise so far above what the world deemed you to be, to come from nothing and lead an army of loyal rebels against an army with gods at their side. Mizan had strength. That, at least, Abraxas could admit.

He could also admit that he was no longer an honorable man, or perhaps never had been. Maybe that is why, when the instinct to search Mizan's pockets sparked, he didn't cringe away at the idea. In the past, looting the dead would've disgusted him.

Oh, how far he'd fallen.

Abraxas gently rolled Mizan over on his back. His cut throat was caked with sand, his black eyes staring sightlessly at the sky above—and mercifully not at Abraxas. He carefully searched his armor for pockets or hidden objects. Mizan was a fighter, yes, but always a rebel. And if there was one thing Abraxas had learned from his time in the rebellion, it was that every single one of the leaders had secret missions on top of the ones they were carrying out. What else would've driven a man like Mizan to abandon the field of battle?

Abraxas's fingers brushed against fabric amidst the leather armor. A bag, or a pouch, of soft velvet. He frowned and tugged it free. It was crusted with blood, but of fine make. The scarlet color of the velvet, the gold thread embroidering the circular brand of the Greyreach Conclave; it had clearly belonged to an Etherakian mage. A War Mage, specifically.

Abraxas opened the bag and poured the contents into his hand. Five glistening shards of onyx stared up at him, each looking like they were parts of a greater whole. Etched onto their surface were cut-off symbols, too broken now to make any sense. His fingers tingled, starting to push them together. Would they all fit? If he could just read what they said . . .

Abraxas shoved the shards back into the bag and shook the fuzzy feeling from his head. He couldn't read magical symbols. What had he been thinking? These stones were like the one Nerezza described, the one she'd taken from the boy and had hidden when Divara found them.

What had happened to that stone? He'd never cared to ask. She'd said she used it to bargain for the rebel's help and that it had been taken from her, but then why would *they* want it? Why did Divara need it badly enough to slaughter a whole village and a young boy to get it?

And why did Mizan have them, obviously stolen from a War Mage?

Abraxas tucked the pouch away, ignoring the way the stones itched at the back of his mind to be brought out again. He didn't know magic. He wasn't Arke. Staring at them would do no good.

He stood up, sand falling from the spots it had been pooling in his clothes. Not so far in the distance, Etherak's retreating forces were waiting in the sand. They'd wait until nightfall to make sure there were no stragglers or prisoners of war that needed to be traded for. He knew his younger self was amongst the banners and tarnished armor now. Divara would . . .

He froze.

Abraxas hadn't seen Divara in Cuskhe during the battle at all, nor afterward. He'd seen remnants of her spells, but not the mage herself.

His fingers went to the bag again, tracing the circular stitching of the Conclave. Abraxas had been in a daze for months after being burned. He'd ignored everything that didn't pertain to himself and had avoided Nerezza at all costs. But there were a few things he was absolutely sure of.

One, Divara had wanted the stones and would not have easily burned them if she thought she could get answers from them.

Two, Nerezza also wanted the stones, and hadn't spoken about them since their rescue.

Three, he could always expect Nerezza to lie, or exaggerate the truth, in order to get what she wanted. She was all about long, patient plans where all the small moving pieces suddenly came together in the end to form a larger picture.

Four, he was just a pawn in her game, one she expected to be too wrapped up in his misery and self-pity to fight her. One she needed to get closer to the rebels.

Abraxas turned on his heel and raced back to Cuskhe.

The broken gate, the red-stained walls, the piles of bodies, they were all blurs. After so long of the constant clash of metal against metal, of the snaps of magic, the roar of fire and the cries of the dying, Cuskhe was dizzyingly quiet. The survivors spoke in whispers. Many wept. But the rest was a buzzing emptiness in his ears that he couldn't ignore.

He needed Aushruk. She was alive, of that he was certain. He needed her. He needed to find Divara. And eventually he would have to face Nerezza. The pouch in his pocket weighed heavily as he took each corner with more purpose than he'd had in months.

"Abraxas! You live!"

A small voice stopped him in his tracks. He turned just in time to see Jado limping up to meet him. He had a nasty cut above his right eye, causing it to swell closed, and he hugged the arm on the same side to his chest. His limp didn't look too bad. While the arm was bloody, the leg looked fine. Probably a sprain or pulled muscle. He could check . . .

No. He shook his head, and waited for Jado to catch up.

"You survived." Abraxas's smile, while small, was genuine.

The young dwarf laughed. "Of course I did! Look at you, old man. You aren't even hurt. It seems the rumors are true."

"What rumors?"

Jado leaned in, waggling his bushy eyebrows. "That you fought like the avatar of Death. That no soldier could touch you and you stood against a Divine Knight with nothing but a sword. How did you do it? You must teach me! I'm a good student, I swear."

Abraxas's throat felt tight. People were talking about him? He doubted it was all good things. Most of the rebels distrusted him on principle. Their tales were likely not as glowing as Jado promised. And he didn't like the idea of being an 'avatar of Death.'

"Maybe later," he said, and pointedly ignored the way Jado's face fell. "Have you seen Aushruk? Or maybe a War Mage that hasn't been traded for yet? Please, this is very important."

Jado frowned. "No War Mage. I would've remembered seeing them. But we haven't cleared the whole city, yeah? Could be anywhere."

"And Aushruk?"

"Thought you'd know, being her apprentice." The boy shrugged. "I'd like to see her. My arm is on fire."

So young, so brave. In pain, and yet standing there with a

glittering in his eyes and life still in his lungs. Abraxas envied him and his youthful optimism.

Abraxas held his arm out to corral Jado. "Come. Let us find her together."

Jado brightened and limped forward. Abraxas followed him, still with purposeful steps but at a slower pace to match the injured boy's limping march. He listened while Jado talked about his side of the battle. How he'd lost a couple of his people before they stopped outright fighting and went to their tried-and-true practice of laying traps and ambushes. Half of the fires on the east side of the city were their fault, but it had been enough to push Etherak into harsher forces like Mizan's army. Most of Jado's young crew were hurt, but they were alive. If the boy was bothered by the bodies in the streets, he didn't show it.

"You still want us to burn these people?" Jado wrinkled his nose as they passed an alleyway where an Etherakian soldier had made a final stand against a dozen rebels. All were dead. "It feels wrong."

"You have your ways of putting people to rest, they have theirs," Abraxas said. "It's the honorable thing to do."

"They don't honor us by being here, so why should we show them any kindness?"

Abraxas sighed. "Because they are wrong and you know it. Why hurt the dead further when it is the living that need to acknowledge their faults?"

Jado's mouth twisted into a frown. "They'd burn us if it was the other way around, old man."

"But you claim to be better. You won't prove it?"

"It won't matter." Jado kicked a pebble that hit a cracked breastplate with a dull ping. "Etherakians see death and that's all they care about. At least for us, this death is not the end. There are those of us that will come back once we find the right necromancer. Nunwei would." He looked up at Abraxas. "Wouldn't she? She had so many more stories to tell me."

Abraxas couldn't answer. The idea of the undead still made his skin crawl. He hadn't even liked being in the same room as Nunwei's hound, and the dog didn't even talk. Unlike Keres, back in Direwall, who hadn't shut up.

Abraxas scowled, thinking about Keres and its smug glee at getting Evren's trust. Jado shifted away from him, thinking the scowl was for Nunwei or her stories. Abraxas didn't correct him.

Jado stopped suddenly, and grabbed Abraxas's wrist. "Look! Nerezza can raise the dead. Do you think she can bring Nunwei back?"

Abraxas followed Jado's finger to a scorched-black alleyway. He could just make out Nerezza's hunched form. She was bending down over something. Or someone.

Abraxas gripped Jado's shoulder. "Go get Aushruk and bring her here. Tell her it's about Nerezza and the black shards."

Jado blinked, bewildered. "The shards? But she doesn't have them. The mage took—"

"I know," Abraxas said, Jado's words just confirming his fears. "But we've got them back. Tell her to get here, and quickly."

Jado's eyes flickered towards Nerezza uncertainly, and then back to Abraxas. He nodded stiffly, slipping out of Abraxas's grip on his shoulder, and limping down the street as fast as he could.

Abraxas touched the pouch in his pocket again. His fingers hummed when he touched the stones again, the same way they'd felt wrapping around the Eternity Dagger's hilt. As if there were parts of him that recognized the strange artifacts and longed to be nearer to them. He shook off the feeling, as he had before with the dagger, and took his hand away.

One step towards Nerezza, fear and hatred rising in equal measure, before he forced one step and then another to follow. His feet followed every painful order of the brain, obeying like they would if Nerezza had ordered it herself. His body revolted at the idea of being so close to her, remembering what she could do to him.

Aushruk was coming. But he needed answers first.

Before he knew it, he was in the cool shadow of the alley, a few feet behind Nerezza. She was bent over a fallen body, her hands slick with blood, scarlet as the robes she'd torn. Divara lay beneath her, dark skin ashen and eyes rolled to the back of her skull. She was breathing, barely. Nerezza was carving into her torso, digging through her flesh with thin fingers.

"Where are they?" Nerezza hissed.

Divara whimpered in response, and Nerezza's cutting grew frenzied.

"What did you do with them?" she screeched. "What did you do—"

"Nerezza!" Abraxas wrapped an arm around her chest and pulled her back. "Stop this."

He'd acted on instinct, without thought. All he saw was Divara's lifeforce leeching out into the sand at Nerezza's careless hands. All he could think of was their shared childhoods. Her secluded in the Conclave except for the rare moments she came to Whitestone to visit the gods, and him. How they used to run around the garden Roania's priests kept, snatching their favorite flowers and trying to catch birds before they were found. He saw her elation at being accepted to train as a War Mage, at getting her crimson robe for the first time and twirling in it like it was the most beautiful ballgown made of the finest silk. Their shared drinks after Vernes, staring at the walls unable to express the horror and grief in their hearts, but unwilling to leave either.

Of course, he saw her face through the flames of his pyre. Her cold voice as she sentenced him to death and turned her back on him, and that betrayal hurt more than any flame. But Divara couldn't die. Loghain needed her to turn against

Eldritch. Her troops needed her if they were to survive the grueling march from Cuskhe to safety. Etherak needed Divara Rimel alive far more than Nerezza needed her dead.

Nerezza's magic swallowed him. His vision went black, his lungs constricted. His muscles seized to the point of uselessness and Nerezza easily slipped out of his grasp. He couldn't breathe. His eyes were bulging out of their sockets as she whirled around to face him, seething and bloody.

"How dare you!" she snapped. "I let you play the hero and you can't let me have this?" She gestured to Divara. Abraxas couldn't tell if she was breathing or not.

He gasped. "She . . . needs . . . life."

Nerezza scoffed. "She tied us to a stake and tried to burn us, Abraxas. This is a mercy."

"Etherak—"

"Oh for fuck's sake, you've killed more Etherakians today than you ever have, and you balk at her death?"

Tears streamed down his face. Out of emotion or the lack of air, he couldn't tell. His knees were buckling, but he refused to kneel. Not to her.

"Please . . ." he begged again. "Don't."

Nerezza tsked, looking back at Divara's dying form. "I can't kill her yet. I need the rest of the shards she has. You promised, Abraxas, that you would help me once you were done redeeming yourself. Well, time for redemption is over. Our part in this war can end just as soon as she gives up the shards."

She knelt beside Divara again, and Abraxas was choking, clawing at his throat. He'd never wanted something as simple as air so badly in his life. Nerezza was the only thing that could give it to him, but her back was to him, her fingers tracing bloody swirls on Divara's cheeks.

"I thought you were like me," Nerezza crooned. "I thought you hid them inside yourself. Then in your robes. Maybe in your boots. But nothing. Did you foolishly send them away before I found you? Did you know that you couldn't stand against me without manacles that left me powerless, so you made sure I couldn't find the stones even if I ripped you apart bone by bone? Well, Divara Rimel, Iron Witch, you are many things, but a fool above all else if you think I won't scatter your remains to every corner of Eith to find those shards. And if you have sent them away, I'll find whoever you gave them to and kill them just like this. So, last chance for a merciful death and a pyre to your Divines. Where are my shards?"

Divara's eyes focused on Nerezza. Her fingers stretched for Abraxas. And then she stopped breathing.

Abraxas broke, the shattered pieces of himself only held together by the needles of red pain from Nerezza's spell. Nerezza, who screamed and dug her nails into Divara's still chest with animalistic frenzy. Faintly, Abraxas wondered how he ever thought the capable, intelligent woman he'd fought with in Direwall had ever been inside the monster she was now. Nerezza of the Ashen Bond was fierce and terrifying, but never insane. Never this . . .

Abraxas's vision blurred. His lungs burned, his head screamed. But if he couldn't see Divara's corpse, he didn't see the last hope for Etherak being torn apart like an animal. He didn't have to see another friend's corpse. He didn't have to hate himself for not saving her or keeping Nerezza from her.

Or speaking about the shards still humming in his pocket.

Life rushed into his lungs, and Abraxas gasped. He fell onto his knees, still grasping the wall. Out of the haze of his blackening vision, he saw Aushruk's lithe form step beside him.

Aushruk was a healer, but above all she was a leader. Abraxas knew her as gentle and kind, but he wasn't fool enough to think that was all she was. Aushruk was the desert, beautiful and welcoming only to those she deemed worthy enough to survive in her presence. To all others she was unpredictable, deadly, perhaps even monstrous. Did Nerezza see a monster when she turned to face her? Abraxas thought he'd never seen anyone as beautiful as the Dra'Nacti in that moment.

"Looking for something, pale one?" Aushruk asked. Her black eyes flitted to Divara's body, narrowing when she looked back at Nerezza.

Nerezza flicked a chunk of flesh off her fingers, her lip curled into a sneer as she did. Abraxas wanted to scream as he looked at her, covered in Divara's blood. How had he ever seen a woman worth sympathizing with in her? After all the monstrous things she'd done and forced him to do, all under the pretense that she was simply following her destiny, he was just now seeing her for what she was. Oh yes, he'd hated her since she'd dug her magic into his veins and enslaved him, but this was different. This reminded him that she'd manipulated Evren and exploited two cultures to get what she wanted. This reminded him that she would've killed Arke if Saros hadn't grabbed her, and that her undead came so close to tearing Sol and Sorin apart during that battle.

Nerezza Quill, if she'd ever truly existed, was gone. The woman who'd taken her place was a bloodstained creature grasping for the Divine. She was clinging to an ideal, a hope, that would destroy the surface, and she showed no signs of stopping to recognize the horror she committed.

Sahar was wrong. Nerezza was past redemption just as much Abraxas was. Divines damn both their tainted, shredded souls.

"I respect you, Aushruk, although I know you do not extend that feeling towards me," Nerezza said. "Because of that respect, I will ask you to leave. This is not your business."

"Abraxas Kain—"

"Is not your pet," Nerezza spat. "I let you keep him for a time, but he's mine. You tried to make him into a healer, someone with soft hands and a gentle voice. But he is a killer, one that served you well today, just as I have."

"A man is not something you can own," Aushruk said.

Nerezza snorted. "Cheap words coming from a Vernesian."

Aushruk scowled. "We are not Vernesian. We are Dra'Nacti."

The elf shrugged. "Doesn't matter. You all bleed the same."

Nerezza's hand snapped in the air, palm facing Aushruk. Abraxas wasn't even the recipient of the spell, and he could feel his own veins smarting as she pushed against the flow of blood to try and tear Aushruk off her feet.

But the Dra'Nacti stood still, eyes level and unblinking. Nerezza's palm lowered, something close to fear flickering across her face as Aushruk took a step closer.

"What makes you think we are so primitive that we *bleed*, pale one?"

The sand beneath Nerezza's feet surged to envelope her. Abraxas stumbled back as he sank too, the ground under him sucked away into a whirlpool to surround Nerezza. She screamed and fought, magic of shadow and blood arching through the air towards Aushruk, who stood as calm and still as if she was watching a sunset.

"I saved your life," Aushruk said with a barbed voice over Nerezza's cries of outrage. "I let you stay in my home. I let you fight, eat, and sleep with my people knowing what you are. We, the Dra'Nacti, are life. We are the air, the earth, and everything in between. But you," Aushruk bared her teeth, "you are stagnation. You are rot. Your magic pulses like an infected wound, and the power you harbor is not your own. You are poisoning yourself, and Abraxas Kain. I will not let your infection spread to any others."

The swirling sand had reached Nerezza's chest now. She

writhed, eyes wide and bulging. She turned to Abraxas with round, pleading eyes.

"Abraxas! Don't let her." She tried to arch away from the sand crawling up her neck. Her arms wiggled uselessly against her side. "I can get you back to your friends. Only I can!"

Abraxas's mouth was dry. *Monster!* his mind screamed at him, but in his heart he heard an echo of those screams. The rage and consuming grief when she thought she was alone after Direwall. The way she clung to Sahar as if she was afraid she'd slip through her arms like smoke. That chilling yet comforting look of determination in her eyes to find and destroy Gail, a feeling he had shared.

Were they really so different?

He hesitated, and with a consuming wave of pain that feeling was gone, reminding him that his body was not his own and his leash belonged to a woman he didn't recognize anymore. He didn't scream, although his jaw ached, and his mouth was dry and full of desert air. He didn't remember getting to his feet, but he was. He was walking towards Aushruk with stumbling, jolting steps.

Aushruk looked over her shoulder at him, and there was the pity he hated to see. Worry too. Worry for him? Or what he would do?

"Oh, Abraxas Kain, you do not have to do this," she said, rooted to the spot. The sand around Nerezza faltered at her neck as the Dra'Nacti split her focus.

I'm sorry, he wanted to scream. *I am more a monster than she is, but I am sorry.*

His hands were reaching out, his fingers spasming towards her neck. She wouldn't move. Why wouldn't she move?

A small but strong figure rammed into him and slammed him to the ground. Jado sat on his chest, pinning his arms to the ground with his knees. He was still hurt, arm bent awkwardly and leg still bleeding. Abraxas didn't fight, but Nerezza did. She howled and his body responded as he tried to throw Jado off of him. But the young rebel wasn't so easily overpowered. He put all his weight on Abraxas's arms and then rammed his good elbow into his face. Pain, like a drop of water in a rainstorm compared to the magic coursing through his veins, sparked. His nose crunched. He tasted blood. But he wouldn't stop fighting.

"Abraxas, stop!" Jado begged. Through the haze of blood, Jado was turning towards Aushruk. "Do something! Help him!"

"I cannot," she said solemnly. If Nerezza's howls of rage were any indication, she'd resumed her focus on her spell. "Short of killing the pale one, Abraxas must break this on his own."

Jado was distracted by her words. Abraxas bucked and tossed the dwarf off him. He hit the wall with a yelp, landing on his bad arm and cradling it.

Abraxas was back on his feet. There was a chant in his blood, in his mind, all in Nerezza's voice.

Kill her.

Save me.

He took another step towards Aushruk, body convulsing with each word laced with agony. He hadn't fought this hard against her since Noxcairn. He was practically blind. There were no tears in his eyes, just rivers of blood. His gasps for air were shallow and pathetic.

Kill her.

Another step, toe dragging the ground. Aushruk was good to him. She was kind, everything he dreamed to be. Killing her would take the rest of his shattered heart and grind it to dust.

Save me.

Divines, he was torn. Nerezza was the key. Nerezza was the monster. She was everything and nothing to him all at once. He wanted her dead the same way he wanted himself dead, but who else would walk through time with him? Who else could understand the blistering loneliness he would endure if he survived this without her?

Save me!

Another step. And then a voice, strained and sweet.

"Abraxas Kain, you are bound to your own suffering," Aushruk said. She was close enough now that her voice was a whisper. "You need not this devil anymore. Forgive yourself."

"I . . . can't," he gasped.

His fingers brushed her skin, strangely cool and rough with the scales on her shoulders. She didn't throw him off.

Kill her!

Aushruk's voice was tight, as if she was holding back tears. "You were chosen by a Divine. You have touched the heavens themselves and returned unbroken. Your weakness, her strength, is that you believe you are not strong enough without their help."

KILL HER!

His fingers were around her neck. Her skin hummed under his fingers with every word.

"Your Divine chose you for a reason," Aushruk whispered to him. "Ask yourself why. Why you above all others? Why a boy who wanted nothing more than a family and to nurture those around them? You know the answer. You know it in your heart."

Her hand laid on his chest, above his frantically beating heart.

Beyond the pain, beyond his fingers tightening around her neck and Nerezza's dying screams in his head, Abraxas was somewhere else.

He was kneeling over Sorin's body, shutting out Sol's wails of grief and Arke's spitting words. His hands were over the Vasa's chest, cupping the gaping wound where the dagger had been. He'd prayed, as he did every night, as he did over Evren's dying body before. He reached blindly into the darkness where Haphion's power had once been and begged for a drop to save his friend. But the power he'd been rewarded with was not Haphion's. It was not a burning flame of Divine light coming from above. It was something else, and it came from within.

He was in Direwall, ash and snow falling in equal measure. Rot and death in his nose, battle sounds in his ears. He was praying again. Nerezza was behind him, running low on spells and desperate. He didn't know what he prayed for. He didn't know what he needed. He simply felt that same rush of power from within flow through him and to her. The blinding wall of light that destroyed the undead and protected them was his, shaped by Nerezza's will and quickly forgotten by both of them in the heat of battle.

He was everywhere, the Eternity Dagger clutched in his hands and familiar in its power. He felt it like he felt the shards. The tapestry of time was not a mystery to him, but a puzzle that Evren couldn't solve and had passed on. When he'd caught it, somewhere in the depths of the maze, the world made sense. He knew he needed to pass it to Gyda so she could bring the Storm and unite the Wood. He knew that through those actions Arke would stand alone against Nerezza, and Sol and Sorin would split up to handle the rest. Had he known then that he would forever be shorn from their side? Had he known, as the dagger had been passed back to him in the heat of battle, that he would be the reason for his own suffering by going back in time?

Abraxas Kain didn't know what he was, only that he'd survived when he shouldn't have. Against Divine fire and hellish magic both, he'd come out breathing. The artifacts of an ancient group of gods sang to him. His miracles were not a mystery, they were his own.

There is power in knowing one's strength, in knowing that the things that happened were not left to chance but in the hands of oneself. And Abraxas had power.

That strange force came to his call like an icy wave to douse the fire of his pain. The needles of Nerezza's magic shriveled away, washed from his bones and sinew. Her voice echoed a scream in his mind, but that too was washed away.

He was alone. He was in control.

Gasping, Abraxas sprang away from Aushruk, tearing his hands from her neck. The Dra'Nacti sucked in a grateful breath, one clawed hand going to her neck. With the other, she grabbed his shoulder.

"There you are." She smiled, although he could see fear lingering in her eyes. "I can see you now."

Abraxas blinked the blood from his eyes. He could stop shaking. A thousand things to say but the only one that came out was, "I'm sorry." He choked out. "I never . . . I thought—"

"I know." She squeezed his shoulder and pushed him behind her. "I know."

Jado was staring at him, both hurt and amazed. Before he could utter an apology to the boy, Nerezza's muffled sobs pulled him away. He turned to see her sinking into the sand, eyes squeezed shut as her mouth filled. She wasn't fighting anymore, she just . . . accepted this.

Nerezza had never given up. The sight made him instantly wary. But then, how long had she fought? Since her birth. Since she was stolen and forced onto the surface. Since she became a part of the Ashen Bond and then lost them. Since the White Cairn, and Orenlion, and everywhere in between. She'd never stopped—until now.

"Don't kill her," he rasped, surprising even himself.

Aushruk gave him a curious look out of the corner of her eye. "Oh? The object of your suffering is on the brink, and you won't let her go?"

"She isn't the object of all my suffering," he said. "And she wasn't always like this. She isn't all mad. I . . . I need her. I need to help her."

Aushruk's face softened. "You cannot fix everyone."

"I know," he said softly. "But I'd be betraying myself and others if I didn't try."

The words tasted like ash on his tongue. To let her die would be easy. Why should she live when so many had suffered at her hand? Sure, he knew her madness came from the souls she took, but without Gyda he didn't know how to separate them. And what of the plans for Serevadia? Surely those wouldn't just go away if she died. It started with Ainthe, and likely far before her.

And again, the hardest truth—he'd be alone without her. That he despised her was no question, but she was out of her place in time, just like him. With no Eternity Dagger in reach, for he still couldn't remember where he'd let go of it, he'd be stuck trudging through the darkest years of his life again, alone.

Mercy didn't stay his need for blood, but neither did practicality. He wasn't sure what drove his next words.

"Please, Aushruk, let her live. Contain her, isolate her, but for the love of whatever you deem holy, keep her breathing."

The sand stopped, freezing as if it would solidify there, then fell away as if it had never been called from the ground in the first place. Nerezza tumbled out of the pillar once it reached her knees, head lolled to the side and eyes closed as the sand was pulled from her mouth and nose. She breathed, her body still.

Aushruk straightened. "Jado, find those manacles the Etherakians are so fond of. We will need them."

Jado nodded and pushed himself to his feet, while Abraxas shook his head.

"He's hurt, he can't—"

"I can," Jado said firmly. Then he smiled. "I'm okay, Abraxas, I promise."

Whether the words were for his injuries or to soothe Abraxas's worry over hurting him, they helped. Aushruk wouldn't refuse healing unless she thought Jado could manage until bigger things were taken care of, and Jado was far stronger than most gave him credit for, Abraxas included.

The boy limped off, leaving Abraxas and Aushruk alone with two limp bodies, one breathing and one not.

The weight of Divara's death hit him all over again, and suddenly he was racing towards her side. Her chest and stomach were a mangled mess. Organs were torn, her rib cage was cracked open. It looked like a wild animal had been at her, not an elven mage.

Abraxas looked up at Aushruk. "You can heal her, right?"

Aushruk shook her head sadly. "If she still breathed, perhaps. But Death has claimed her, Abraxas Kain. She is beyond even my reach."

That made sense, even if he hated it. Healers could do extraordinary things with their magic, so long as their patient lived. It was the only reason he'd recovered from his burns. To bring back the dead veered into necromancy. No one mortal had successfully brought a soul back into a living, breathing body before.

No one, except him.

Abraxas gathered Divara's body in his arms, careful not to damage her body any further. Her blood, colder now, seeped into his tunic as he stood up and looked Aushruk in the eye.

"There's a temple here dedicated to the Divines built by Etherakians. Tell me your people haven't destroyed it yet."

"They haven't."

"Bring me there."

21

Abraxas

Cuskhe's temple was small and pitiful compared to the ones Abraxas had been raised in. Its stone was rough and yellow, the fourteen altars to the various Divines far emptier than they should've been. Instead of incense, it smelled like rotting offerings and stale, smokey air. The skylight at the top of the domed ceiling shed little light as the sun set, casting shadows in the temple where the many candles should've been lit. The floor was older, perhaps even the foundation of the original building before the temple had been built. Faded, colorless tiles tiny enough to be mosaics blurred under his feet.

Abraxas didn't pay attention to any of it. He hardly felt the prickling sensation on his skin that always came with entering a temple that was being watched by Divine eyes. Who watched him? Was it Nomien, seething over his loss? Vuhione, raging at the injustice of the battle he'd fought? Or was it Haphion? Was he watching the child he'd taken walk back into his temple after fighting against his will, bloodstained and broken, but not so much so that he couldn't bow in reverence to his carved symbol on the wall?

He laid Divara on his altar, keenly aware of Aushruk watching behind him.

"You know what I am?" he asked as he wiped the blood off his hands.

"No," Aushruk said. Her feet whispered across the floor, her voice echoed in the wide room. So empty and cold. "I know you are not entirely elven. I know your magic is Innate, and not a gift like you were led to believe."

"What I used with Haphion at my side was Gifted magic," he said.

"Yet it is gone, and this remains. It is not something you learned."

He pressed his lips together. "No."

"And it is not Haphion's gift, for that was snatched away. So, it is within you. Like my magic is, or that of the seafaring Vasa."

It would be easier to accept if his power was as tangible as manipulating the earth and storms, but it wasn't. He wasn't even sure what it was. But it had healed Sorin, surely it could heal Divara.

He closed his eyes, laying one hand on her cooling forehead and another on her chest. Raw, jagged flesh didn't make him flinch, only the knowledge that it was hers did. He took a deep breath, and then he prayed.

"I know I am different from when you left me," he whispered. "I don't even know if you're aware of why I am like this, or what I've become in your absence. But I know you're there. Unlike before, I know you're watching, and you could heal her. She is a believer, and always will be. She is faithful, and good, and loyal. Etherak will need her when you're gone. I need her back. Please."

He kept his eyes shut as the seconds ticked by. Nothing happened. Aushruk sighed behind him.

"You know you can do it yourself. Why do you ask?"

Abraxas swallowed the lump in his throat. A part of him thought that being untouched by Haphion's fire during the fight meant he was showing favor to him again. But more silence met his ears. The weighty sound of a Divine's voice in the back of his mind didn't ring. Haphion still refused him.

He pushed down the bitterness rising in him. He refused to acknowledge the deep-seated hurt that had been building with every quiet day since he'd been thrust back into a time where he *knew* Haphion could see him. All that hurt would do nothing for him, so he bottled it up and breathed deep.

Abraxas grasped for the power from before. In the shards in his pocket, in the dull ache where Nerezza had been wiped from his bones. Unfamiliar to being called by name, it seemed to shrink away from him. This power that had been dormant and unused, except when he hadn't even realized he had reached for it, was unknown to him. And yet, it had been with him his whole life. What could he do with it, beyond healing people? He'd broken a spell. He'd funneled that power through Nerezza to take the form of the spell she wanted. What else could he do, given the time?

What else did he want?

He drew back a little, afraid of his own ambition. He only needed one thing now.

"Bring her back," he muttered to himself. Not a prayer, but an order.

That power surged within him. It poured out of his hands, the light making his squeezed eyelids burn red. Behind him he heard Aushruk gasp, but he couldn't think of her. He focused on Divara, on healing her and dragging her soul back to her body. The organs knitted back together. Bones popped back into place. Under his palm he could feel the blood retreating, the shredded and missing skin starting to regrow. As the body made itself whole, he reached out for Divara.

She was there, lingering around her body. There was so

much she'd planned to do that Nerezza had cut short. She wasn't sure where to go now.

Abraxas coaxed her back into her body, and felt her chest rise with her first breath.

His eyes snapped open. She was whole before him. Armor and robes shredded, but her body was healed. Even the dark swirls of ink across her stomach and chest remained intact. She heaved lungfuls of air, staring up at the carving of Haphion above her. Then she rolled her head over to Abraxas.

He held his breath. Their last words had been so cold and desperate. It was true that he wasn't the man she knew, but he longed to see the warmth in her eyes again.

"Abraxas," she said weakly, her lips barely moving. "You came for me."

He smiled, feeling hollow. Did she realize that he wasn't the younger self she wanted? Did she see the lines on his face or the shorter hair? It didn't matter in the end. She was in shock, so she saw what she needed to see.

"I did." He took her hand. "You're going to be all right."

She smiled, eyes fluttering closed. "I knew you'd win this for us. The man on the pyre . . . he was wrong. We won."

Her breathing deepened as she fell asleep. Abraxas placed her hands on her stomach and stepped away.

"You'll need to send her out before she awakens," he said without looking at Aushruk. "Trade her for another prisoner of war. Oshaya has a list, I'm sure."

Aushruk stepped beside him. "Our people will want her head."

"If you want Etherak out of Vernes, you need her alive and on the other side. She'll talk sense into Loghain."

Aushruk looked at him sharply. "How do you know?"

He squirmed under her gaze but kept his head high. "I haven't been honest with you."

"That much I gathered."

He winced. "It's difficult to explain. I've done this before. This war has already ended for me. I've seen it."

Aushruk took a shocked breath, blinking rapidly. "We win?"

Abraxas wanted to suck the words back into his mouth, but she deserved the truth. After everything she'd done for him, it was the least he could do.

"Vernes wins." He nodded. "It isn't an easy victory, and it doesn't come quickly after this. In truth, I know very little about the process. Only that what you will do will change Eith forever. Etherak will retreat into its borders and won't leave them again. Vernes changes everything."

"You say that with a bitter tongue," Aushruk noted.

He tried to wipe the scowl off his face. "Because of your victory, I lost Haphion. I lost a lot. In hindsight, I deserved it. I'm trying to be a better man, but I keep failing."

Aushruk nodded, as if this suddenly explained every previously unexplained detail about him in the past several months. The mere idea of him having already lived this time didn't seem to faze her at all. In fact, in all the time he'd known her, very little of what he'd done had surprised her. Or maybe he wasn't as good at reading Dra'Nacti facial expressions.

Aushruk looked around the temple, pitch-black eyes absorbing every detail of the room. Every carving, every altar, every sad, rotten offering. She seemed to breathe it all in.

"I feel them," she said suddenly. "Your Divines. They do not appreciate my presence." She grinned wryly. "They'll appreciate what I have to show you less. Come."

The thought of displeasing the Divines in their own temple didn't soothe Abraxas. He looked back at Divara, worried about what she'd do if she woke up alone to her lost city. But with the trauma she'd endured, she'd sleep for a while yet.

He turned and followed Aushruk.

She didn't head outside the temple. Instead, she went behind the ring of altars and started scuffing at the floors.

"What are you doing?" he asked.

"Your priests know sites of power well. This was a ruin before it was a temple. They tore down the old bits, but the floor remains." She nodded to the obviously aged stone. "Worry not, what I will show you is still here."

He wasn't worried. A little curious, maybe even afraid, but not worried. He followed her around the whole temple before she let out a hiss of excitement and crouched down.

Abraxas peered over her shoulder, watching as she pried a strangely glowing tile from its spot behind Mituna's altar. The moment she pried it from the ground, a wave of energy rushed out. All the tiny tiles on the floor rippled and turned over one by one. From bare, dull yellow to faded, but rich colors, the mosaic came to life beneath their feet.

Abraxas stepped back into the middle of the temple, eyes so wide he felt like they might fall out. The mosaic was old, not even the art style he was used to of Vernes. It reminded him of Serevadia, of the ruins Evren had described from Viggo's memory. It felt like the maze where he'd found the dagger, that same strange energy that hummed in his pocket. Touchable, but nearly unfathomable.

"I know this story," he murmured. "This is Zelmis." He pointed to the feminine figure wrapped in black. Her face wasn't shown. None of the Divines were. To do so was to risk madness for even attempting to comprehend their true forms. "This is her death at Nomien's and Haphion's hands. The end of her war against the Divines."

Nomien was represented by a vaguely humanoid form of fire and dark armor. By his side was Haphion, stylized as a great dragon. There were other gods in the background. Mituna's seafoam form behind her father. Vuhione a faceless figure in armor. Roania as a great tree with burning branches. They all watched as Zelmis, Goddess of Darkness and Chaos, was destroyed.

He backed up as the mosaic continued. From the five pieces of her Divine body, things grew. One, a pale figure in white, hunched around an amulet that radiated darkness. Another in gold, he recognized by the dagger in his hands. A figure draped in blue, wearing a crown of stars. And one in black, bearing a sword of shadow.

The last piece fell to Eith, to the waiting throngs of mortals. Abraxas tamped down his discomfort. Chaos had been a Divine trait until Zelmis's death had caused it to run rampant in Eith. At least there the goddess had won after all.

But his eyes found the four figures. The Elders Serevadia and Orenlion worshipped as gods. He looked up at Aushruk.

"The Elders were Divine?" he whispered, as if uttering those words would earn the ire of those still watching him.

Aushruk cocked her head at the mosaic. "I follow not your religion, nor these Elders, but the land remembers the time they walked among us. Powerful, immortal, the sand says, but not Divine. I would think a soul ripped in five pieces would lose its luster. To kill a god is no easy thing, even for other gods."

Abraxas couldn't stop staring. His teachings hadn't even mentioned the Elders. He didn't know of them until Serevadia, where the Shadow Dancer was everywhere. By now he knew they were real, but never had he thought they were from the heavens themselves.

His stomach roiled. Zelmis had been a being of pure, unadulterated evil. How good could the beings that came from her have been?

Why, then, did he feel a connection to their artifacts? What did the shards have to do with anything? What *was* he?

Without thinking, he brought out the bag of shards and handed them to her. "I found them on Mizan's body. I think he took them from Divara, but didn't want Nerezza to get them."

Aushruk took the bag and poured them into her hand. The black stones blended in with her skin nearly perfectly.

"He never trusted her," she said. "Or you."

"I know."

"At least that he was wrong about," she said with a smile and started to walk out.

"Wait." He turned to her as she paused at the door. "Those shards, why did you want them? Why does everyone want them so badly?"

Aushruk hummed thoughtfully, nudging them in her palm. "I heard they were the key to something powerful. Something that would help us win this war." She bared a feral grin. "Now that might be true."

He sank back on his heels, disappointed. The stones felt Elder. Could they be what banished the Divines? How could things so small cause such a destruction?

"May I stay for a while?" ne asked.

Aushruk blinked at him. "You have free will. You may do as you wish."

She left him with the mosaic and his sleeping friend. He sat on the ground, careful to tuck his legs up between the Shadow Dancer and the Horizon Walker, as if they would be offended if his blood-crusted sandals touched them.

Abraxas sat until the sunset, and someone had come to retrieve Divara. She wasn't awake, so he didn't bother with goodbyes. He stayed on the floor, lit only by the single brass lamp the rebels had given him. The colorful tiles jumped and spun with the flame. He could almost imagine seeing Zelmis writhing in pain, hands reaching for Nomien's throat as Haphion delivered the killing blow.

All the while, he begged the silent question—*What am I?*

The Divines had no answer. Neither did the tiles. He stared at them, remembering how the dagger felt in his hands. Nerezza told Evren that the dagger was an extension of the Eternity Keeper's soul. Evren had initially thought Nerezza planned to gain power from that, but she'd laughed him off when he suggested that as her plan. Of course, that could've been a lie. But he heard the fervor in her voice when she talked about the Shadow Dancer's sword. That was not a lie. She needed that sword like he needed Haphion. It was an ache that never left, a longing he couldn't describe but felt incessantly.

"Did you take me because I'm different?" he asked the mosaic of Haphion. "Am I something closer to Divine than mortal, and that's why you kept me?"

Tears pricked his eyes, still tender from Nerezza's spell causing them to bleed. He sucked in a breath that rattled in the empty room.

"Why not take me now?" he whispered. "I am here. I am willing. I've changed, but I swore myself to you even when I didn't understand. I would swear again, knowing what I am now. Knowing that what I did was wrong. You . . ." He faltered. "You never stopped me. You never cautioned against the atrocities I committed. I felt like I was doing your will."

He wiped his tears away, feeling like a foolish boy all over again.

"If I am not worthy of you now because of what I've done, then I should never have been worthy of you to begin with. What do you want from me?"

The dragon didn't answer. The tiles twinkled. Nomien seemed to wink at him, and Abraxas recoiled.

He'd never stooped to vengeance, even when Gail had taken Gyda and Sol. Even after everything Nerezza had done, he wouldn't kill her or hurt her out of vengeance. He'd worked with the rebels to prove that he could rise above that hatred and become something more. Surely Haphion would be proud that . . .

He stilled. "You hate the rebels, even if their cause is just. Why?"

Abraxas didn't expect an answer, so he kept talking, an awful fear growing with each word.

"You condoned this war," he said. "You all did. I always thought this was Nomien, and you had to sit back and watch for some reason. But you wanted Vernes, too."

How could he have not seen it? After all this time, stewing in his regrets and sins, he'd forgotten that he wasn't alone in them. That Nomien wasn't the only god who'd let this war happen. Hadn't he told Evren that the Divines were just as varied and unique as the mortals they protected?

Haphion had wanted Vernes. And when Abraxas fought with the rebels, he'd fought against his old god.

Abraxas felt sick. His skin was hot, like a fever was flashing through him. What had he done? *What had he done?*

He'd killed his friends. He'd aided heretics. He'd gone against everything his Divine had wanted, and then raged when he was met only with silence. Of course Haphion ignored him, he was going against his will.

And now . . .

Abraxas went to his knees. Haphion was just. Haphion was forgiving. Haphion *needed* him.

"I'm sorry," he whispered to the dragon. "I was lost without your guidance. I thought you'd want me to be better. *I* wanted to be better." He pressed his forehead to the floor. "All I ever wanted was to make you proud. Please. Please. Can you hear me?"

There was no answer. Abraxas felt frustration welling up inside him so strong that his palms, flat against the ground, turned to fists. He was so close. So. Close.

He'd felt Haphion during the fight. He could feel his gaze now. But why wouldn't he answer? What did he need to do to make up for his sins?

He sat back on his heels, head dizzy from the sudden change. He put his fists on his knees. Did Haphion want him to kill Aushruk? Jado? Oshaya? Did he want him to take back

Cuskhe with his bare hands and turn the tide of Etherak's holy war?

Something glittered on the floor, near the Shadow Dancer. He leaned forward, squinting in the low light. He saw nothing but the inky black tiles in the shape of a man and a sword. He pressed his fingers along the sword, and his breath caught when his fingers hummed.

A stone along the hilt was singing to him. Abraxas methodically pried it up with his fingertips, never cursing when the stone fell back into place. When he finally got it free and held it to the light, his breath caught.

Another shard, etched with a strange glyph. In his mind's eye, he could see it being the final piece.

He stood up, blood rushing with excitement. The shards *were* Elder. And if they were, then they were connected to the Divine.

His chest hummed with a passionate fire he hadn't felt in a while. He tucked the stone into his palm, pressing it against his chest. He bowed to Haphion again, staying low as he spoke.

"I know what to do," he said. "I can't change history, of that much I'm certain. But I know how to shape the future."

~

"THEY ARE IN THE POUCH, Abraxas Kain. Take them."

Abraxas stood in Aushruk's tent, holding his breath. She had her stiff back turned to him. The pouch was indeed on the table next to her.

The many wounded were lined up to be healed. He felt that same itch to go help. To wash his hands and pick up bandages and needles while she did the worst work. But he couldn't. He wasn't a healer.

"You knew I'd come," he said softly.

She tsked, not looking at him. "Your air changed. You have a new direction."

"You won't fight me?"

"I saw the way you looked when I took the shards. You want them, perhaps you even need them. No matter. I will win this war without them, as you said."

Abraxas flinched. Despite his new goal, he didn't want to leave Aushruk. Her tone was far colder towards him than it had ever been.

He took a hesitant step forward. "Aushruk, I—"

She whirled around, and he forced himself to stand his ground. Those teeth were bared, the eyes black and bottomless. She was still beautiful, but with those horns she looked every inch a monster.

"You apologize?" she asked coldly. "You do that a lot. I wonder if you truly mean it."

He shook away his fear. She wouldn't hurt him. "Don't say that. You of all people know I mean it."

"Do I?" She regarded him with a snarl. "I leave you alone with your gods for a few hours and you come back reeking of a purpose that opposes mine."

"I will not interfere with this war. You'll win, just as I said, but not with me."

"Did they speak to you?" she asked. "Your lovely Divines? Is that why you do this?"

He darkened. The shard in his palm cut into his skin as he clenched his fist. "No."

"Then why do you run back to them?" she hissed. "You can live without them. You can do good without them. You have power—"

"I want them!" He shouted over her, startling her and the few wounded awake. "I've always wanted them, Aushruk. It's all I ever wanted. Good or ill, I love them. They are my family."

"They abandoned you." she spat.

"They're teaching me a lesson."

"That is not what family does," she snapped. "Family does not hurt to teach. It does not break to mold into something better. You have a choice now to do whatever you wish, and yet you chain yourself to them again? Why?"

"Because where I'm going there is a threat only they can fix," he said. "In my time, Eith is crumbling without them. I'm going to bring them back, and it starts now, with those shards."

It made sense in his head. Alone, he couldn't stop Serevadia. Without Nerezza he couldn't understand the shards or what he was. But combined, they could save the world from Serevadia. Like pieces to an enormous puzzle, the Elders made a Divine being, their artifacts were their souls, and he felt himself being called to them. It had to mean something.

"I want you to win," he said, stepping forward.

Aushruk took a step back, curling her lip at him the way she did at Nerezza. "No. You want to walk away without feeling guilty. Cut the strings that tie us, Abraxas Kain. Abandon all that you've done here. Run back to your gods and live with the consequences."

He recoiled. She was talking to him like a child who didn't know better than to poke a coiled snake.

"I'm only doing what you told me," he said. "Face them on my terms, bring them to me."

"That would be more convincing if it didn't feel like you were chasing after their approval like a scavenger chases a dragon." She shook her head and turned away. "I saw potential in you. Such a bright man. You will drain yourself for Divines who will not remember your name."

"They will. Aushruk—"

"Goodbye, Abraxas Kain. Our ties are cut. Our time together is done. Our souls will not meet again after this moment, and I do not wish to see a dead man in my tent."

He closed his mouth, swallowing back any of his arguments. What had she expected? That he would keep fighting as a rebel? That he would take Mizan's place and lead the rebellion against his own people? No, Abraxas had done his time as a rebel. He'd been a soldier, an adventurer, and a murderer. Now he'd become something else entirely, not because he wanted to, but because Eith demanded it.

And if he had to sacrifice a friendship to save the world he loved, so be it.

"Fair winds, Aushruk," he muttered, before snatching the pouch of shards and walking away.

~

PILES OF DEAD were lined up, waiting to be buried, outside the city gates. They wouldn't be until the wounded were cared for, so the night air stunk of rot and blood. Nerezza was chained to a wooden pole not far from the first pile of bodies. Divines knew how long Aushruk planned to keep her there.

"I suppose you're very proud of yourself," she spat as he walked up. "Have big plans of being the hero Vernes needs now? Going to spend the next fifty years fighting the same war on another side?"

He walked past her towards the bodies. Her manacles rattled as she shifted to face him.

"Abraxas! Don't fucking ignore me. Look at me!"

He didn't. He rummaged through the bodies. The people who were supposed to take armor, boots, and weapons that were still in good condition hadn't been through. Maybe they hadn't survived. He picked through until he found a suitable sword and strapped it to his waist. It wasn't much, just a simple short sword, but it would do.

Nerezza was still ranting behind him.

"—and I should've left you to rot in that dragon but—"

"Enough, Nerezza," he said, turning to face her.

Surprisingly, she shut up. He walked up to her, regarding

her coldly. It felt different to look at her without the red chains of her magic under his skin. She didn't look nearly as threatening.

"I am going to let you go," he said slowly. "And then we are going to Serevadia."

She blinked in surprise. "What?"

"Do I need to repeat myself?"

"What game are you playing?" She laughed. "You don't care about my people."

"No. I don't. But I need that sword as much as you do, and you know how to get to it."

"Not without the shards," she spat.

"Lucky for you," he dangled the pouch in the air, "I have them. You know, you really must be lucky for these to show up in your path time and time again. To think, that boy we found was an accident." He shook his head and put them in his pocket. "Then again, maybe I'm the lucky one who keeps drawing these types of things to you. Divine-touched things. Things you need."

She stared at him, somewhere between petrified and intrigued. Her lips kept curling into a smile and then falling, only to twitch up once more.

"Oh." She shuddered in the night air. "You've gone mad."

He shrugged. Maybe he had.

"Are you going to behave if I cut you down?" he asked "Because I will not drag you around if you plan on stabbing me in the back. If we do this, we do this as equals."

Nerezza raised her chin. "And why would you help Serevadia by letting me get the sword? That's not like you."

Abraxas raised an eyebrow at her. "Oh, you can try to make yourself a god. Fill yourself to the brim with power until it breaks you, I don't care. But, when you're done, I get the sword."

"Why do you want it?" she snapped. "It's not yours."

"My reasons are my own, but this way we both get what we want."

She studied him for a second, then grinned terribly. "You want godhood too, don't you? You're tired of reaching for the heavens and getting nothing. Isn't it better to just break down the door instead of knocking politely?"

Oh, let her think he'd fallen that far. He almost laughed. Instead, Abraxas made a big show of looking uncomfortable. Downcast eyes, grinding his jaw. Sol was a better actress, but Nerezza's giggles told him he'd passed.

"Let's make a game out of it." She cackled. "Whoever gets to the sword first, wins it, and all its power. Second one has to follow the other around until they're dead or done."

Abraxas snorted. Just like her to make this a competition. It didn't matter when he got the sword, so long as he eventually got it. And if she got it first, all the better. She was on the edge of complete mental destruction, all it would take was a sneeze of power to send her careening over into true madness.

"As equals to the sword, then whoever gets it first?"

"As equals." She nodded. "I swear on my . . . well, what do we swear on?"

He rounded the post, drew his sword, and cut the manacles off. Whatever fear he might've felt at her being free and turning on him was tamped down. He knew what he was capable of now, and so did she.

"Nothing." He sheathed his sword. "Potential gods swear to nothing at all."

22

Evren

There was a timelessness to being underground that Evren hadn't missed. No sky to remind her of how long she'd been walking. No sun or stars to light the way. She could count the seconds as they turned to minutes, and then hours, but her mind was needed elsewhere. Her people needed her.

More injuries popped up the farther from Vanguard they went. Gyda had taken a lot of hits she'd stubbornly covered up. Sahar and Sol had been caught in their blast and had cracked a few ribs, and Sahar had taken a nasty cut to her shoulder outrunning a soldier. Arke was mostly unharmed, but his exhaustion shone brighter even than his worry for his brother. Sorin was limping and trying to play it off, although he grimaced with every other step.

Even then, Evren knew they were lucky. Viggo and Gyda had taken the worst of the damage, but Viggo couldn't stand up to the same beatings and had exhausted himself with his Light. He still hadn't woken up. They were slow, sluggish, and scared. Any longer in Vanguard and they would've started dropping like flies.

The only one who wasn't affected was Keres, who decided mere minutes after Sahar had left for Vanguard to follow her.

"Did you really think I wouldn't follow you to get my soul back?" they asked, taking over for Gyda to lift Viggo. They weren't gentle, slinging the unconscious elf over their shoulder so his hair was dragging along the ground.

"We needed to keep you away from Divara, just in case she wasn't as open minded as Abraxas." Evren wiped away the sweat on her brow.

Keres snorted.

"And you were supposed to be watching Mal," she said louder.

Keres shrugged, Viggo's limp form rising and falling. "There's a whole house of capable people to watch him. Trying to keep me away was rather stupid of you. I thought you'd grown out of that."

Evren bit back a retort, instead watching the way Keres clenched their jaw and refused to look at her. It was strange to recognize the spirit's mannerisms in a different body, like the way they tended to lean to the left when they stood still, or furrowed their brow when they were debating something. Stranger still was how she saw less of the body of a sick boy and more of just Keres. Had that happened when they possessed Vox? Was there a moment that she'd started to see Keres instead of the soft-spoken orc who'd died right in front of her?

Regardless, Keres was becoming easier to read. It was so easy to dismiss them as an outside variable, one that could help or hinder on a whim. But they'd fought for a reason, and it wasn't loyalty.

"I tend to forget this is personal for you as well," she said. "I'm sorry."

"Why wouldn't it be personal?" they asked. "Nerezza took my soul, and I didn't see it coming."

"None of us did."

"Can the rest of you hear thoughts?"

Stunned, Evren shook her head.

Keres went on, stepping down an incline and nearly knocking Viggo's head against the ground. "I heard everyone's thoughts. Abraxas's loathing for me and himself. Arke's constant memorization of spells. You thinking only of Gyda and still so blind about why." They shook their head. "But her I tuned out. Just another mage, I thought. Ambitious and cunning, but driven by nothing more interesting than the rest of you. I purposefully ignored her, like I did with most of everyone's thoughts because it is easier for me that way. If I'd paid attention . . ."

"Keres, you couldn't have stopped her," Evren said.

"Couldn't I have?" Then a shadow passed over their face. "In the past, it would've been easy. A mere snap of my fingers. Now I am subject to taking one husk after another as my form. The fact that I have my will and personality is a miracle; she and Gail stole so much of me than any lesser spirit would've been reduced to the very basest of their emotions."

Evren smirked. "Keep fanning that ego."

"It is the burning fire that keeps me going," they said flatly.

Ahead, Sorin was talking animatedly to Sahar, earning a few pained chuckles from her. Sol was stuck by Arke's side, whispering with their heads bent together. Gyda kept the hound at her side, her stride never showing how hurt she was.

"Keres," Evren said, lowering her voice so it wouldn't bounce off the narrow walls up to Sahar. "What do you plan to do with Nerezza?"

They sighed. "If it was up to me, I'd destroy her. But it is not. Sahar wants her alive, and I think Nerezza's death would be the final push over to darkness for her. I cannot, in good morality, do that."

Evren's chest warmed. "You care for her."

Keres finally looked at her. "She is the blood of my home, my people's future. She deserves to be cared for."

Evren didn't argue with that as they plunged deeper into the abyss.

~

THE YAWNING DEEP beneath the Vanguard Mountains felt different than it had underneath Dirn-Darahl. The endless darkness remained the same, but the stone was different. Blacker, porous in some areas and mirrorlike in others. Sol made note of the rock, relaxing everybody when she said that they were out of any danger Divara might've brought them by tapping into the range's fiery power.

Once they felt relatively safe, they picked a spot to rest. Potions were handed out, tougher wounds like bones and the beginning of infections were tended to. Gyda fell asleep while Evren bandaged her wounds, and she found herself smiling despite the serious situation they were in.

The Luminstones and Arke's fire were pooled in the middle, and everyone laid out in a ring around the light. The only reason any of them were able to sleep was due to exhaustion. Evren fought hers off to take watch. Keres didn't sleep, but sat with Sahar until she started snoring, and then they spent the rest of their time frowning at the ceiling. Arke, Sorin, and Sol were curled up around the worg, physical wounds healed but mental ones only bandaged.

Evren checked everyone, rubbing her tired eyes. The dark made her incredibly exhausted. Despite all the horrors she'd witnessed in the Yawning Deep and during the Long Night, all she wanted to do was curl up beside Gyda and slip away.

She'd wait for Sorin's shift, though. Or maybe she'd just let him sleep.

She settled down beside Viggo. His head wound had been healed, though blood still caked his hair. The rest of his injuries weren't nearly as bad, and the potion they'd gotten down his throat had worked wonders. Even still, she found herself checking for cuts and blood they might've missed.

"Didn't anyone tell you that doing that while a man sleeps is entirely improper?" Viggo murmured, his eyes still closed.

Evren rolled her eyes, but pulled back. "You're right, checking for signs of internal bleeding is improper while someone is unconscious."

He cracked open an eye. "I am conscious now."

"Well then, you can check yourself."

He groaned as he sat up. He started to comb through his hair but stopped when his fingers caught on the blood-caked knots, scowling.

"What happened?" he asked finally.

"Tolk didn't make it," Evren explained. "We're fairly sure he ran into the bulk of the army on the way to help us. Divara improvised and gave us time to escape. She didn't make it."

Viggo's shoulders slumped. "Two very different tones of 'didn't make it.'" Do you think Tolk still lives?"

"I think that any other option isn't worth considering," she said. She massaged her scalp, willing the dull thrumming of her headache to go away. It didn't, and wouldn't, until she slept. "We haven't run into any Serevadians since we've been down here. I'd be worried we're going in the wrong direction, but I haven't seen another path."

Viggo reached over and touched the wall beside him. "We're close to Kleros. I doubt that will work in our favor if they've reached Vanguard."

Evren frowned. "You think Kleros has lost its resistance."

"What little it had." He let his hand drop into his lap. "It didn't stand a chance, even if I'd stayed. Velcros needs complete control over his empire, and Kleros was the biggest opponent. And then there's the vulnerability of the surface. This was a victory practically given to him."

"But it wasn't," she pressed. "We took Vanguard away."

"At what cost?" he asked her, eyes sorrowful. "Would you deem it worthwhile if Arke lost his people in the process?"

Slowly, Evren shook her head. "No."

"That is what Velcros will do. Victories at a price too high to pay. That is how he'll break you."

"Not if we break him first."

Viggo looked at her, truly looked at her, as if he was seeing her for the first time. She let him, no longer worried about what he saw in her. What she was, what she stood for, was no longer a mystery, so she had no fear of him seeing it before she did.

"I've said it before," he mused. "You've changed."

"I cut my hair."

"Beyond that." He shifted closer, lowering his voice as if they were sharing a secret. "I did not see your taste being in women like Gyda."

Evren stifled a laugh. "Did you even see my taste in women?"

"I'll admit that I didn't." He pulled back, smiling. "Regardless, you seem happy with her."

Happy wasn't accurate. The word itself wasn't enough to describe how she felt around Gyda. Content, invigorated, whole? It didn't matter.

Evren looked over at Gyda, still sleeping soundly. "She's everything to me. Always was, I think. I was a fool to have not seen it."

Viggo didn't move but somehow drew her gaze back to him. "There was a time you might've looked at me like that."

"Well, we both fucked that up, didn't we?"

He chuckled. "That we did." Then he grew serious again, the still light of the Luminstones making him look like he was carved from weathered stone and perpetually creased with worry. "Do you have a plan to deal with Velcros?"

"No," she admitted. "I doubt it'll be as easy as getting Abraxas and Nerezza back, and then ending this all before it begins, but I hadn't thought that far ahead. Abraxas knows war better, he'll know what to do. And as someone on the inside with Serevadia all this time, he's going to be the difference between winning and losing this war."

"All our hopes rest on a knight who's relived the worst hundred years of his people's history." Viggo sighed. "Do you think he might not be able to help?"

Evren didn't want to think like that. She wanted to keep the way she'd known Abraxas in her mind. Thoughtful, serious, but never too grim to smile. He'd cared for them, both on the battlefield and off of it. There was so much he hid from her, she knew that. Old hurts and regrets, all those desperate prayers to a silent sky. She couldn't fathom the war he endured in his mind daily, but she didn't need to.

Abraxas was her friend, her partner in battle and the calm to her chaotic plans. She owed him her life ten times over, and so much more.

"Whatever he is, he's still a good man," she said. "He's done what it takes to survive. I know he's come all this way for us. There's no other reason he'd be in Serevadia."

Viggo nodded. "By the Light, I hope your faith in him is true. For all our sakes."

Viggo didn't know Abraxas, not really. He saw the cold, withdrawn warrior, not what truly made Abraxas who he was. But the same could be said for the rest of the Wandering Sols. Viggo hadn't taken the time to get to know any of them besides Evren.

The light on his features flickered, like a candle in a strong breeze. Evren frowned, turning to the circle of light. Arke's ball of fire was fading, shrinking. As Evren pushed to her feet in alarm, the flames started hissing. Their dying light exposed flickers of tendrils smothering the fire, inky shadows that swallowed the orange glow until it snuffed out entirely.

"Viggo," she couldn't get her voice above a whisper. The Luminstones were fading too. There was no hissing, no primal fight between light and dark. The constant glow of almost sunlight she'd never seen falter was simply vanishing. Leaking away, consumed by the dark.

"Viggo!" she screamed, just as the last of the light went out.

There was only a split-second of absolute darkness, but Evren felt it stretch on for eternity. The inky tendrils pried open her mouth, caressed her shoulder, wrapped around her ankles. She was frozen as the unseen hands grasped her. Feeling, searching, gnawing for something.

Then the light came like a bursting sunrise. The tendrils snapped away, screaming. Or was she screaming? She grasped her neck, choking on the feeling of cold slithering out of her throat. She was so cold, like she was stuck back in the White Cairn entombed in ice.

Viggo sent his Light out, catching everyone in a shield-like bubble of light green. Beyond that shield, the shadows pooled thick and opaque. He was shaking, staring at her with wide eyes.

"What happened?" Gyda was on her feet first, sword already in her hand. The others were awake too, jolted out of their exhaustion by Viggo's light and Evren's alarm.

Evren opened her mouth, but the words wouldn't come out. They were right there, she knew she could speak them. But her throat closed up. She was so afraid, and so, so cold.

Gyda rushed over to her, using her free hand to pull her close. Evren still shivered in her embrace, but her touch felt like a bonfire against the ice in her skin.

"Evren, what happened?" Gyda asked again, softer this time.

Evren shook her head, closing her mouth. The words were simple—the shadows came to life and destroyed the light. But it was more than that. It *felt* bigger, more sinister. All her life she'd been the hunter, rarely the prey, but even the times she knew she was outmatched she hadn't felt fear like the kind that clung to her.

The feeling of being trapped, of being eaten by something she couldn't even see, made her want to bolt. It made her feel weak.

Behind Gyda, Sorin was grasping at the dead Lumin-stones. Without their glow, they looked like dull, yellow quartz.

"What happened to my stone?" he asked. "It doesn't do this. Sol, they don't do this!"

Sol shook her head, staring at the stones. "Never."

Keres stood up as well, cartilage creaking. "The goblin's fire went out as well."

"It ain't supposed to do that."

"That is why I mentioned it." Keres turned to Viggo and crossed their arms. "Well?"

Viggo grimaced, holding the Light with one splayed palm in the air. "The shadows came to life. They seemed to be eating the light."

"But not yours," Keres pointed out.

"Not for a lack of trying," Viggo gritted out. "I can feel the strain. Whatever it is, it wants in."

"It's looking for something," Evren said, drawing herself out of Gyda's hold. The warrior's hand never left her shoulder, but she stepped back to give Evren room to breathe. No air seemed to be enough. "I felt it searching me. Inside me."

She shuddered. Gyda's grip on her tightened.

Sorin cursed. "Searching for what?"

She shook her head. "I don't know. But I don't feel . . ." She swallowed. "It was only for a second, but I feel different. I don't think we'll be okay if it touches us again."

"Viggo, my friend." Sorin flashed a smile. "How long can you keep this up?" He waved to the bubble of Light.

Viggo shot him an irritated look. "I'm stronger than I was, but the battle still drained me. And this *thing* is straining me."

"That really isn't an answer . . ."

"As long as I can," he snapped.

Keres groaned. "I feel so safe knowing that."

Sahar rose slowly, shaking her head. "Don't, Keres."

"How are we supposed to defeat an army, save goblins, and find our two elves in this?"

"We'll figure it out."

"That, Lady Al-Fasil, is no comfort at all."

Arke snapped his fingers at them and, even from his spot a few feet shorter than them, got their attention. He glared at them, and then Viggo and Sorin.

"Shut. Up," he hissed.

And they did. He bent down for his spellbook, flipping through the pages to count them, and then tucked it under his arm. He poked the worg, still fast asleep, and the dog got up with no objections.

"Arke, buddy." Sorin was the first to break the silence, as usual. "You look like you've got a plan."

"Nope." He climbed on top of the worg.

"Then, what are you doing?"

Arke glowered at him. "I ain't gonna just sit here and wait for somethin' to happen. Tolk's out there."

'We know," Sorin said gently. "But what we don't know is what's out there besides Tolk. We can't just charge in blindly."

Sol stepped up to the wall of light, eyebrows twitching into a worried expression as she peered outside of it. Evren watched her, trying to quiet the churning panic in her stomach. After a few blinks of her eyes, the dwarf turned around.

"We didn't fall asleep in a city," Sol said.

Arke and Sorin broke off their conversation long enough for them to both say, "No."

"Then why do I see buildings outside?"

Evren, against her better judgement, turned to look where Sol did. She saw nothing but darkness. But both Arke and Viggo acted as if they saw the same. Arke let out a string of curses that made Sol blush, and Viggo visibly paled.

"I know those buildings," he said.

Sahar crossed her arms. "A city? That's not possible?"

"And yet, Solri Amet can prove that I don't lie."

"About the buildings being there," Sol said. "I don't know if you're lying about recognizing them."

"It's Kleros. I'd know those towers anywhere."

That brought Evren out of her stupor. She still couldn't see beyond the shell of Light, but that wasn't surprising. Sol, Viggo, and Arke had grown up underground and would see far better in the dark than she did. She patted Gyda's arm to let her know she was all right, and stepped up to Viggo.

"We weren't anywhere near towers," she said. "Kleros wasn't in sight."

He looked at her, her own buried fear mirrored in his eyes. "I can't explain it, but I know I'm right, and that's worrying in more ways than one."

"The shadows," Gyda said, circling around to Sol. "They're alive. And where is this army? Why haven't we seen them?"

"My guess?" Sahar smoothed her hair. "The army suffered a similar fate."

Arke growled. "Don't say that! What about Tolk?"

Her face softened. "I know your people to be resourceful and clever. He could've survived this."

There wasn't much hope in Sahar's voice, and Arke turned his back on her. Evren picked up her bow. She needed the comforting weight in her palm. Although, what good would arrows do against living shadows?

Viggo's light was fading, and Evren panicked. She whirled on him. Was he hurt? Had the shadows become too much. But he shook his head, lowering his hand until the bubble of Light collapsed into a star in his palm. Evren shuddered, feeling exposed without it, and gripping her bow tighter.

"What in the hells?" Sorin rounded on him. "Did we not have the same conversation about living fucking shadows?"

"They've retreated," Viggo said. "I felt them go. I'll be ready when they come back."

When, not if.

Viggo's Light casted an eerie glow on their surroundings. Evren's heart was in her throat as she took them in. No more cavern walls or rough rock. They were surrounded by buildings. Smooth, elegantly carved, with wide arches and columns that stood several stories high. They stood in the middle of the street, dwarfed by the rise of towers around them.

But that was as close to Andovine as it got. Where Andovine had been filled with light and laughter, Kleros was dark and silent. She felt like her breaths could be heard across the city and struggled to calm them.

There was only one other place that had felt like this. Dead, reeking of horrors waiting just under the rotting skin to be pulled back and revealed. The city in the Eternity Maze, where the monster with too many eyes had chased her as a blood-red moon watched.

But that city had been on the surface, and its architecture was vastly different. It didn't stop her from readying an arrow.

Gyda's runes began to glow. "I take it you did not leave this city like this."

"No." Viggo let out a shuddering breath. "By the Light, what happened to everyone? Kleros had twice the population of Andovine. They couldn't have just disappeared."

"Maybe the shadows got them," Sol whispered.

"Or this Velcros fellow put down a rebellion before it

could start," Sahar said. She looked pointedly at Viggo. "You said you tried to rally the city against Velcros. Maybe you did a better job than you thought. Maybe he dealt with it like this."

"The Mora have control over shadows." Evren suddenly remembered. She cursed herself. How could she forget? Ainthe had nearly killed her with magic like that. Nerezza shared it too. "Could they have done something like this?"

"If this is Mora work, then they've grown in power," Viggo said. "I have never seen anything like this."

Evren remembered the figure over the dagger, whispering about how great change comes with great disaster. Was this the aftermath of one of those? Or simply just the beginning of one?

"Eith is changing, and so are we," she said, stepping out onto the street. Her footfall whispered a soft echo across the stone. "It's natural that our enemies will as well."

Enemies, because if she thought about what lurked in the shadows as anything else she wouldn't be able to draw her bow. She'd tried so hard to keep Serevadia safe from the surface, and now she was paying for it. True, not all Serevadians were like Velcros and Ainthe, but enough followed them to make a difference.

For the first time since she'd left Dirn-Darahl, she found herself doubting. Should they have left Heliodar to her plots? A promise to keep quiet could've kept her from killing them. A dwarven army might've been enough to hold back the beginnings of an empire. How many lives would that have spared on the surface? How much more would her honesty have saved?

Evren dug her fingers into the wood of her bow. She'd promised her friends no more secrets, and she'd been truthful in that. But standing in the dark corpse of Kleros reminded her that they all had kept one massive secret from the world, and Eith was going to pay for it.

"Evren?"

Gyda's voice made her turn back. She and the rest of her friends stood in the halo of Viggo's Light. Even Keres instinctually stayed closer to him, though they were quick to keep themselves acting nonchalant. They were all staring at her with a mixture of apprehension, fear, and resolve.

There would be no failure.

"We've got a lot of people counting on us," Evren said, wincing inwardly as her voice bounced from building to building. "But Tolk, Abraxas, and Nerezza are our priorities. They're in there." She gestured behind her to the waiting city. "But even if they're not, we're not the type to back away from a challenge."

"As a rule," Keres cut in. "I do tend to stay away from obvious traps."

Sorin snorted. "Really? You marched right into the White Cairn."

"Days cramped with you buzzing nonstop in my ear had me feeling suicidal."

"Ass."

Keres sniffed. "Quite."

Sol was the first to step forward, hands resting on the hilts of her daggers. All the color was draining out of her face as fear took hold, but she stood tall anyway and forced a shivering smile onto her face.

"Look at it this way." She forced her cheery optimism out. "No army to fight makes things easier for us."

Gyda returned the smile. "I was looking forward to it, actually."

Sorin groaned. "Of course you were. You and Evvie really were made for each other."

Sahar said nothing. She was gripping Drystan's axe like it was a lifeline, her wide eyes taking in Kleros. But she wouldn't back down. She had the same drive as the Wandering Sols, but worse. She'd lost everyone in her party before this. Evren was lucky to have a handful of close calls.

Finally, Arke spurred the worg forward. He rode up until he was beside Evren, his face grim as he stared ahead.

"Get us to them," he said. "Then get us home."

She nodded. "I will."

She and Arke led the way, Viggo not far behind for his illumination, and the rest sticking close to him. Gyda ended up in the rear with Keres, some silent agreement passing between the two of them that they would be the best to hold the line if they were ambushed. Evren didn't like it. She hated it in fact, but knew it was the best choice.

At the front, she saw a city in the very beginnings of decay. There were no signs of fighting. No crumbling buildings, scorches of magic or looted buildings. There was just a gaping silence that couldn't be filled. A sucking void where many lives used to be. Kleros had a lot of the same things she remembered from Andovine. A coliseum, grand and well loved by the looks of its stonework. But nothing stirred in the seats when they peeked in. There was no breeze to whistle lonely tunes across the soft sand in the arena, and no dust to settle where crowds once gathered.

Shops and open-air stalls were bare and still. Jewelry hung in glittering waves from a jeweler's booth, the stones winking in Viggo's Light. Vats of dye held heaps of silk now so colored they were black. Food rotted and wasted, but the stink wasn't noticeable until she got close.

There was no sound, no movement, no breath of life in Kleros other than Evren and the people that followed her.

Sorin swore, causing everyone to jump. When the shadows didn't rush for them, they all turned to him.

He had the good grace to wince. "Sorry."

Arke glared at him. "What was that for?"

They'd been silent except for a few murmured comments every now and then. Sorin's sudden voice grated her ears.

"It's getting colder," he said. "It never did that in Andovine. It certainly shouldn't be here, close to fucking volcanoes."

Sahar hissed at him to keep his voice down and he mouthed an apology. Then she turned back nodding.

"I feel it too," her voice was just a whisper.

Evren thought it had been just her. The chill the shadows had embedded hadn't left and she had been struggling not to shiver. But everyone started murmuring in agreement, save for Keres who just shrugged.

"We're nearing the city center," Viggo said, as if that explained everything. "Our answers should hopefully be there."

He was hopeful, but Evren could see Kleros dragging him down. Not just the expense of keeping the Light up, but the sheer, quiet horror of what happened. The mystery was nagging at him, but the knowledge that the answer would be worse than whatever he could imagine made his steps hesitant. It didn't help that they'd passed through large swaths of the city, nearly half by Viggo's remarks, and still hadn't found a single sign of life or evidence of a struggle.

They pressed on, finding more of the same. The markets became grander and felt even more desolate. Homes were shells that were once full of life. The roads started sloping down, gently but notably. Libraries were nothing more than empty maws too dark to step into. Government buildings, not nearly as grand as in Andovine but much wealthier than the rest of the city, eyed them as they passed.

And all the while, the chill grew. Evren felt it now, creeping along the back of her spine, dancing from bone to bone with every shiver. Her exposed fingertips ached from how tight she was holding her bow. There was no cold quite like the Reino Terminan, but this, like the shadows, seemed to have a life of its own. In the stagnant air, it danced. When her breath fogged in front of her, it took sharp shapes of teeth and daggers.

By the time they got to the city center, it started to smell.

Viggo gagged first, his Light flickering as he struggled to maintain his concentration. Sahar held her hand to her nose. Sorin looked like he was trying not to breathe at all.

Death had a familiar smell. Sweet and cloying at the surface but beneath was a putrefaction that soured all it touched. It hung heavy in the air, strengthened by the chill. It didn't leave Evren's nose when she exhaled. The stench stuck like a parasite along her throat and lungs.

The road finally leveled out when it deposited them into a massive city center. The circle of paved stone, lined with imposing buildings, made Evren think they'd stepped into another coliseum. Whatever it had been used for in the past—citywide meetings, gatherings for holidays, or a training yard for future soldiers—it was the home of horror now.

The smell was overpowering, and Evren coughed to dislodge it, but it wouldn't let her go. The only thing worse than the smell was the sight of what it came from.

The walls of the surrounding buildings were covered in corpses. They were hung by their feet, hands and hair nearly brushing the ground. Their throats were slit, the stains on the ground sticky and black with blood. Fluid still seeped out of their bloated necks, gathering in a large black pool at the center of the round city center.

Evren squinted. No, not fluid. Shadows.

She took a step back, herding everyone behind her. Shadows leaked like heavy fog from every dead body. Their slit throats poured like a cut waterskin, the vaporous black falling to rest in the wide pool. There were easily a hundred bodies, all Serevadian. Not a single one bore the armor of a soldier. All were commonfolk. Loose dresses and tunics, some had expensive robes. All wore the same terrified expression on their face.

Viggo's cry of despair shook the air. His Light flickered as he fell to his knees. He couldn't take his eyes off the bodies. Pain, not grief, threatened to overwhelm his features, as if the sight sent daggers through his chest. His fingers curled around the ball of Light as if to crush it.

"Why?" he wailed. "What is this for? This senseless violence, this needless death. What has been done?"

No one answered as his voice tumbled through the silent city. The only other sound was his own echo.

Sahar took a hesitant step forward, gently brushing his quivering shoulder. "There aren't enough people here to be the whole city. There's still hope."

He shook his head. "These people . . . I talked to them. They weren't the only ones, but they were the ones I found first, the ones who believed me when Velcros's lies didn't add up. I know their names. I know their families. They fed me, housed me, hid me. And I left them for this fate."

"You couldn't have known," Sahar said. "This isn't something you've seen Velcros do before, is it?"

Viggo shook his head. "This isn't like anything I've seen before. This is madness. This is destruction and vengeance on a level I can't comprehend. Why?" He turned to Sahar, and then to Evren. "What is the point of this?"

To send a message. To cut a rebellion off before it even began, like Sahar said. To cause pain. For a man like Velcros, and all those like him, there didn't need to be another reason. All he needed was to induce pain.

The shadows moved, and in an instant Evren's bowstring was taut and Viggo's Light was as bright as the sun. It flooded the scene with horrible detail, the sharp contrast of light and dark making all the bodies look even more monstrous. Metal hissed as more weapons were drawn. Arke was already burning a piece of paper as their eyes went to the pool in the middle.

From the black, a creature that looked more bone than

elven emerged. Pale, skinny, with arms and legs that were too long for his body. His face was gaunt, his mouth open. He was Serevadian, or the remnant of one.

He didn't notice them at first. He crawled out of the shadows, sometimes on all fours, sometimes bouncing from leg to leg. He held a single stained dagger loosely in one hand. He flipped it around, not even flinching when he cut himself. Blood leaked out, with trails of shadowy mist that joined the pool.

And he sang.

"Catarmon speaks, Catarmon sings," the elf hummed idly, picking through the bodies and poking more holes for the shadows to leak from. "Catarmon stirs with gifts to bring. Out of the blood and out of the blight, Catarmon gifts the end of shadow's light!"

He continued to circle around the corpses, cutting and slicing with merry glee. He was dancing to his tune, the same sick lines over and over. *Catarmon, Catarmon, Catarmon.* Evren wished she hadn't forgotten about the Mora's new god. At the same time, the very name made her want to run. It was one thing to dismiss Catarmon when there was no evidence. It was another when she heard his name being sang.

The elf paused his cutting and singing, throwing his hands in the air as if he'd forgotten something. Then he trudged back to the pool, jammed his hand in and yanked something out.

A goblin. Lifeless, pale, still bleeding.

Arke snapped. A wave of fire rippled from his hands, directly towards the elf. He finally noticed them, screamed, and tossed the body straight at Arke. The flames dissipated, Arke's face balking as the body thumped to the ground next to him.

It wasn't Tolk. It was disfigured, tortured, and horrible but none of the signature braids appeared on this goblin's head. Whoever they were before, Evren didn't recognize them.

The elf was scrambling away, shoving bodies aside to hide. Arke was just staring at the body, mortified and frozen.

Evren shot two arrows in quick succession. One at each boney shoulders as they shot through the elf's flesh and pinned him to the wall. A curtain of bodies threatened to close over him, but he thrashed and fought hard enough to kick them away. His bare feet caved in skulls, sunk into bloated flesh and came out covered in congealed blood.

"Let's get closer," Evren said. "But keep an eye on the pool and don't go near it."

Everyone murmured in agreement, except for Arke, who was still staring at the disfigured goblin. It was Sorin who got to him first. The Vasa put his arms around Arke's shoulders and whispered low in his ear. Arke listened, blinking back tears before shaking his head firmly. With every word from Sorin, he kept shaking his head, anger building up in his tiny body.

"No," he whispered, then shouted, "NO!"

He shoved Sorin away and scrambled off the worg. The worg tried to grab his cloak with his teeth to yank him back, but the goblin was too fast. He bolted, and left Sorin looking stunned and hurt as he marched towards the thrashing elf.

"Where is he?" Arke snarled. He tore another fistful of paper and his palm went up in flame. The elf struggled even more. "Where's my brother?"

Evren ran after Arke. She skimmed close to the pool, yanking her boots away before they touched the shadows.

"Arke, wait!"

Too late. He rammed his burning fist into the elf's side, and his screams of anguish shattered the still silence encasing Kleros. Arke let his hand sit there, the smell of cooking flesh overtaking the smell of death, and bared his teeth in a vicious snarl.

"Where's Tolk?" he yelled over the elf's screams.

Evren skidded to a halt behind him. She knew that anger

well. She wouldn't pull him away. But her stomach churned at the sight. She'd only ever seen Arke this angry once before—when Sorin died after she'd promised to protect him. He'd been so blinded by anger he'd turned into someone she didn't recognize. Here, she could see it again.

The rest of her friends gathered around him, conflicted and angry as well. Sorin went up to pull Arke away, likely the only one safe enough to do so, but stopped when the screaming changed to something stranger.

Laughter.

The elf was laughing. Still burning, but consumed by hysterics, he wiggled under Arke's fist gleefully.

"Arke, stop," Sorin said.

He didn't. The burning continued.

"Arke!" Sorin pulled his shoulder this time and jumped away as the flaming fist arched back towards him. It was inches away when he stopped, breathing heavily. The laughter continued as if he was still being burned. The flames went out, but the anger didn't. Arke didn't look at Sorin.

He glared at Evren. "Get him to talk." And then he walked to the back of the party.

Sorin looked like he'd been stabbed. The hurt and confusion on his face was just like when Heliodar had plunged a dagger in his chest. Evren watched him blink tears out of his eyes, silently asking him if he was okay. He shook his head once, and turned back to the cackling elf.

"You heard him." Sorin's voice shook. "Where are the goblins? Where is his brother?"

The elf continued to laugh, shaking his head.

"He won't speak Core," Evren reminded Sorin gently. "Viggo was the only one—"

"Oh, I learned your language, sky-touched," the elf said, hiccupping between his words. His voice was reedy and sharp, almost piercing to the ears. "I know what you say. I know it all."

Evren froze. He'd been singing in Serevadian, she was sure of it. But now he spoke in Core nearly as good as Viggo's, only slightly accented.

"You understand us," Sorin said.

"Your words, not your heads." The elf grinned. "I don't understand sky-touched. I don't understand you at all! Living with so much light, it is never truly dark on your surface. And yet, so much shadows! So much rich darkness hiding in your hearts! Makes my job much, much easier. Thank you!"

Evren started to speak, but Sorin moved in front of her so he was facing the elf fully, his focus narrowed down to the spindly man.

"Tell me what happened," Sorin said calmly.

The elf blinked, his glibness fading away a bit as he stared into Sorin's eyes. "Tell you . . . ?"

"Yes." Sorin's smile was as sharp as a blade. "We're friends, you and I. Tell me what happened to the goblins, please."

Before her eyes, the elf started nodding. "Army brought them through. I was very excited. Was running low, you see." He jerked his head to the bodies. "No more screaming. No more fun. Thought the goblins were for me. But they *took* them. Took them and left me only with three already dead ones. Not fair. City's so quiet now that no one screams for me."

Sorin didn't flinch. "Where did they take the goblins?"

The elf nodded to the pool of shadows, as if it was obvious.

Evren felt like she was going to be sick. The cold memory of darkness was embedded in her flesh now.

Viggo stepped next to Sorin. "Ask him about what he was doing here, please."

Before Sorin could, the elf let out a gleeful yell at the sight of Viggo.

"Herald of Light!" He kicked his legs against the wall like

a child. "Oh, I'm so glad you're back! You missed all the fun. I wanted to cut you so bad."

Viggo took a step back. "You did this?"

The elf nodded. His heels cracked against the wall.

"Why?"

The elf squealed. "Why not? It's fun! Killing Light, making shadows. Catarmon doesn't like it, all this death, but mistress gets what mistress wants." He hummed, trying to shrug his shoulders but just making the wounds in his shoulders wider.

There was that name again, Catarmon.

Sorin remembered. His face soured and he leaned in closer to the elf. "You work for Catarmon. Who is he?"

"Shadows and Divinity." The elf's eyes shone wildly in Viggo's Light. "We were nothing. We were lost. He brings us back, gives us purpose."

"He's causing you to kill your own people," Viggo said.

The elf blinked quizzically. "So? Not my people anymore. Why should I care?"

Sorin's voice seemed to ripple as he spoke, sugar sweet but burning with hate. "Catarmon is not a god. You realize this. He and his mistress serve Velcros to give him power."

The elf stopped laughing. His smile slipped and was replaced with a sneer. Evren grabbed Sorin's shoulder to pull him back, but he wouldn't budge. He stared the elf down as the Serevadian cocked his head to the side, his neck cracking audibly.

"Velcros serves *us*," the elf said. "We are pain. We are shadows. We are sacrifice. And we do not tolerate heretics."

The word was strange on the elf's mouth. It was not a Serevadian word. Even Viggo looked confused. That was a surfacer word, a nasty one used with hate and ignorance to another people's way of life.

Evren hated that word so much, she didn't realize the elf

was digging the shafts of her arrows deeper into his skin before it was too late.

"Sorin!" She ripped him away just as the elf tore free of the arrows. The wounds were jagged and raw, ripping through muscles and tendons that would've left a normal person unable to move. Blood gushed from the wound in a river, pattering against the stone and coating his broken feet. The elf grinned at her.

"Mistress said you would recognize what I am," he said, finally turning his attention solely on her. "She said you'd hate me for it."

Sahar was choking back a sob. The elf was stepping closer, and Evren was shielding Sorin. Another blood mage, like Nerezza. Like *her*. Except she couldn't use her magic without hurting Gyda.

The elf had no such restrictions.

The spasming pain of someone taking a fistful of her veins and dragging her with it made her eyes spark with stars. She wasn't the only one.

Her boots slid uselessly on the ground as she was dragged backwards, towards the pool. Her friends were with her, doubled over in pain or fighting back and getting nowhere. Panic surged in Evren's chest as the pool got closer.

The elf watched from the side, still gushing blood. "Tell mistress hello for me. I do miss her so."

He waved, a chilling grin on his gaunt face, and then Evren's world was engulfed by shadows.

A blackness so infinite she couldn't breathe. A cold so deep it cut through her skin. She gasped for air, and something crawled into her mouth, slithered down her throat. Her blood felt like icy sludge, veins still sore from the Blood magic, but she couldn't even think about that.

There was nothing but black. Above her, below her, crawling inside of her and making a home. She couldn't choke it out. She couldn't pull away.

There was nothing but black, except for her. She was becoming one with it, with every second that passed. She felt herself becoming undone, shadows tearing her apart, crushing what good she harbored in her soul and nurturing the veil in her.

Had she had so much before? Her hate, her ruthlessness, her apathy she'd thought she'd buried deep enough to forget. But it was all rising to the surface to overwhelm her. To consume her and—

Light shattered the dark and left her gasping. She collapsed, choking for air on her hands and knees. There was a floor. She couldn't see it. There was nothing but complete black under her.

All around her, her friends were in the same position. Gyda was holding her throat. The terror on her face made Evren want to cry. Sahar was crying. Sol was hyperventilating, trying to grab Sorin's hand to keep him from yanking his own hair out. Arke stared blankly at the black, his spellbook at his feet. Even Keres looked shaken and angry, massaging their chest as if they could still feel the tendrils inside them.

Viggo was the only one standing, both arms out and his shield of Light encasing all of them. Tears and sweat rolled down his cheeks. His chest heaved. What had the shadows seen? What had they done?

Evren stood up on shaky legs. Her bow made her sick. What was she capable of with it when she didn't have her morals to aim right? What about her blood when she didn't care about Gyda? She desperately hated what the shadows had shown her to be.

She went to Gyda's side and grabbed her hand, ignoring how the normally strong grip felt weak as Gyda laced their fingers together. Evren looked up at Viggo.

She could barely choke out the words, "How long?"

He gritted his teeth. "Not much. They're pressing me. They won't leave this time."

Evren shuddered. She couldn't go back to the darkness. She wouldn't survive.

Viggo's eyes met hers and he felt the same. "I can't keep this up much longer," he said. "You need a plan."

"What plan?" she asked. "Nothing keeps them back except for you."

He let out a pained laugh. "Flattering, but not helpful."

"Viggo, please, we need you."

"Always with the right words and the wrong time, Evren Hanali of Eith."

"Don't do this," she begged.

"I am expending everything I have for these next few seconds," he said. "I don't know what else to give you. My Light isn't—"

Three sharpened points of shadow pierced through the Light, zipping through Viggo's back and out his chest with a wet slice of flesh.

Viggo's face went slack with shock. He looked down at the daggers of shadow and the blood leaking from his wounds. His chest heaved with a strangled laugh. The Light flickered and held as he looked up at Evren.

She couldn't speak. All she saw were the shards of black and his eyes. He was in so much pain but there was something else. Relief. Cool and comforting, as if he was finally resting after so long of burning himself out. A candle reaching the end of its life, the wax drowning the wick.

"What a poetic end," he murmured.

The Light went out. The darkness was absolute. Viggo's body barely made a sound as it hit the ground.

23

Abraxas

Abraxas dreamed once more of the boy. This time, he was barely old enough to walk. His hair was a mass of black curls that would turn straight as he aged. His ears didn't quite hold their point yet.

It was all so fuzzy, this dream. This memory. In it, the world was so bright. Whitestone gleamed like it was glowing from the inside out. The air was warm and sweet, despite the snow gentle hands brushed off his shoulders. He'd liked snow, but never the cold. His trousers were soaked from playing in it, and he scowled, earning a little laugh from the owner of the hands.

He smiled. He liked that laugh. But it trailed off too quickly. Before he knew it, his hand was in hers and she was leading him through the streets.

There was a sorrow about her that he couldn't understand as a boy. The way her fingers held his tightly, as if she was afraid the wind would snatch him away. It was the same way she held him when he talked about the voice in his head. He never understood why. The voice was kind and gentle. It never scared him, but it did scare her.

That was why they were there. He remembered now. It wasn't to play in the snow and explore the city like she promised, it was because of him. As they climbed the seemingly endless stairs carved into the mountain, he pulled back. He was afraid for the first time in his life. She never taught him to fear anything, so the sensation was new.

He dug his sodden heels against the white marble, and she stopped. With a soft sigh she picked him up and set him on her hip to continue her walk.

He sniffled, burying his head into her shoulder. He felt her breathing get heavier with every flight, but she never set him down. She clung to him, silent and fearful. He found himself growing even more scared, but made himself stay still. Squirming would make her climb harder, and he'd already made it worse by having her carry him.

It seemed like forever yet no time at all when she stopped climbing, winded and tired. She set him down and there just a few more shallow stairs. They led up to a great archway, so blinding in its white stone against the sunlight that he had to squint. Two figures stood there as well, each cloaked in silver and light grey. Kind faces, soft smiles. Priests. He knew what they were and knew they could be trusted. Every child in Etherak knew.

He relaxed. Her hand found his again, tight and sweaty as she led him up the stairs. The priests nodded to her, and the oldest started talking to her. Good words, melodious, the way all priests talked. Her words were curt and cold. He squirmed. She never talked to Brother Gavril back home like that. She *liked* Brother Gavril. She brought him honey that Abraxas harvested from their beehouses.

The other priestess was younger. She knelt down to his level, all warm smiles and auburn curls.

"Abraxas," she said. "Your mother gave you a strong name."

He gripped her hand tighter.

"No, no." The priestess shook her head. "It's all right, little one. You're safe."

He was always safe with his mother. Honey-stained fingers and stories before bedtime. She made shadows on the wall to animate the stories, her fingers turning into dragons and monsters, Kings and heroes. All of a sudden, he wished desperately to go back home. He missed his bees. He missed Brother Gavril's laughter echoing in their small temple. Whitestone's temples were beautiful, but they didn't smell like the incense Gavril used, or the cookies the kindly baker left as offerings.

Abraxas buried his face in his mother's cloak, also damp from the snow. He foolishly thought that she'd pick him back up again, and that when he opened his eyes they'd be back home after a short journey and a long nap.

"Abraxas." Her voice was too tight, too forcefully sweet. But she melted into her hug all the same. He didn't mind that she was holding him too hard. He just let her hug him because he was scared and didn't know why she was sad.

"Mother . . ." he started.

But she shushed him, the familiar sound soothing as she pulled away and held his face in both hands. The sun was in his eyes. He couldn't see her, but he knew she was crying.

"You said you didn't like to cry," he said softly. He knew it happened. She always told him it was okay for him to be upset and let his emotions out. But he'd rarely seen her do the same.

She pressed a kiss to his forehead, her hair falling in his face like a curtain and smelling of honey.

"I love you so much, angel," she murmured against his skin. "So, so, much. Never forget that."

It sounded like goodbye. He started to panic, tears welling

up in his eyes. What was happening? They were fine earlier today. Had he done something to upset her? How could he make things better?

Be calm, child, the voice in his head said. *She is bringing you to me.*

His panic did subside, but his tears did not. He didn't know who he was talking to, his mother or the voice, when he asked, "Why?"

Because I need you. Because I can protect you. Because she loves you and knows that no harm will ever come to you while I am here.

His mother heaved a sob, oblivious to the voice in his head. "Because, angel, you are very, very special. And to keep you to myself is selfish." She brushed his curls out of his face. "The Divines have marked you, but I have known since I held you for the first time. Remember, Abraxas, I did this because I love you and for no other reason."

"Mother, you're scaring me," he whispered.

"I've taught you never to bow to fear. Never forget that, either." She pulled him into a fierce hug, her lips on his ear as she whispered, "You have the heavens in your heart, angel. Do not let the world take them away."

She pulled away and stood up. Before he could move to follow her, two gentle hands pulled him back by the shoulders. He didn't fight; it was rude to fight against priests, but he did cry freely as he watched her turn and walk away. She looked back once, the sun haloed behind her. He couldn't make out her face. Out of all that he remembered, he'd forgotten what she looked like.

She disappeared down the steps, and he was without her for the first time.

You are never alone, child, the voice said. *I will never leave you. Since the beginning, I have been here, and so long as your heart is pure and your intentions are true, I will remain.*

He nodded and let the priests usher him inside. The temple didn't smell like home, but he tried to dry his tears. He felt more of the voice here, comforting and warm. His clothes dried, the damp the snow had left completely gone. One of the priests pulled a pink candy from his robe and offered it to him.

The boy took it, but didn't eat it. He squirmed out of their hold and marched up the massive tree in the middle of the temple. Trunk like white marble, leaves like flickering flames. He was not afraid.

He placed the candy in a spot between the roots and knelt.

"Hello," he muttered self-consciously. He didn't like talking to the voice when others were around. He knew the two priests were watching curiously.

Hello, child. Welcome home.

~

Abraxas was so very, very far from home.

He'd never felt at ease under miles of rock. Dirn-Darahl was one thing, but the rest of the Yawning Deep set him on edge. The very air felt like it was being pressed down, sacred as it sheared its way into his lungs. The dampness, the knowledge that he wasn't built for the world away from the sun and stars, grated him.

No, he never got used to being underground, even after being there so long with the Wandering Sols. They hadn't seen how uncomfortable he was, nor how relieved he felt when he finally stepped out into open sky. They really didn't know him at all.

Whose fault was that? He pondered that as the rocks became slicker under his boots, ones he'd traded his sandals for at the Gratey border. That was months ago, a barely tangible memory eaten up by dark caves and darker thoughts.

Gyda knew him best. He had, after all, spent the most time

with her. Evren as well. The conversation between just the two of them in the giant ruins, where he'd explained Etherak's war with Vernes to her, always stuck with him. But he worked very hard to be the one that cared for his friends, not the other way around. They didn't need to see the rank depths of his soul. They could ignore it like he did. But in so doing, he'd only shown a sliver of who he really was.

Maybe Evren saw more in *Mortova's Maw* when she stood against him to protect that thing, Keres. Maybe Sol's keen eyes and intelligence had picked up more of him than he thought; she was always very good at reading body language and facial expressions.

But did she see his pathetic desperation? How much he would claw at to get his Divines back? Did Evren see what he was capable of? That the kind defender he pretended to be, the gentle mentor trying to outrun his past, was simply another suit of armor? The man underneath was capable of terrible things. Vernes had only been the beginning.

Abraxas still hated him. But that man was who Haphion wanted. No, who he needed. Abraxas's heart hadn't been pure for a long time, but at least, in this, he could say his intentions were true.

This was beyond a simple want or need now. What Abraxas wanted didn't matter, and perhaps it never did. It was what the world needed.

He couldn't blame Aushruk for banishing the Divines. But he needed them back now for Eith's sake.

"We're getting closer," Nerezza said from just ahead of him. Her skin and hair almost glowed a ghostly white in contrast to the darkening walls. Between them they had only a small globular of light, barely enough to expose the ground below their feet. Another bit of teamwork between them had created it, although it required Nerezza to start using a spell-book again.

The amount of magic in her body was enormous. Souls,

blood, and shadows, on top of the magic she wielded when she used her spellbook. All three types of magic intertwined in one. Written, Gifted, and Inherited. Although he wondered if the Gifted part should be corrected to Stolen, since Keres's necromancy wasn't freely given, nor Gail's Vasa powers.

He slid his hands along the walls. Slick with moisture. The air was heavy with salt and brine.

"How long?"

She didn't turn around to look at him. "I'd know more if you handed me the atlas."

That made him laugh. "You've already had it today."

It seemed childish at first glance to horde the bag of black shards they'd come to call the atlas, but Abraxas would never trust Nerezza fully. He knew now that she had the ability to manipulate her flesh in a way to open it, stuff something inside, then seal it up. It wasn't pretty, and it wasn't comfortable, but she *could* do it. So he limited her time with the stones like a parent keeping track of how long a child could play with their toys.

Like a child, she almost pouted. He could see it in the way her shoulders hung. But she caught herself just in time and straightened her spine.

"Fine," she said curtly. "We'll wait for the water, then."

"I guess we will."

But secretly he pulled the pouch out. There wasn't a time where the shards weren't calling to him, and the moments where they all fit together made that call even stronger. He discretely poured them into his palm, the obsidian chunks not even making a sound as they fell on top of each other.

They shivered in his palm. A quick glance ensured Nerezza wasn't watching, then he went to sorting them. By now it had become second nature, but there was something oddly satisfying about lining the glyphs together one by one. Once together, they formed a bigger stone, oval-like that took up most of his palm. The shards fused together as if the cracks had never existed, and the glyph was complete.

As always, the atlas formed in his mind rather than in his hand. It was an odd feeling to see something without it physically manifesting in front of him. The entirety of Serevadia was laid out in front of his mind's eye in a way simple maps couldn't compare. He *felt* the land. The wet of the underground rivers and lakes, the heat of the thermal vents, the thrumming melodies of the mushroom forests. But the biggest draw was always what was ahead, what the atlas had been built to show him. Deep black Divinity, hidden in the depths of the Boreal Sea.

Waiting for them.

More and more, Abraxas knew his fate was not his own, not really. He'd been called back to Cuskhe time after time for that last shard. He'd cut the path through the desert that found the boy carrying the rest of them. He'd found his way through the Eternity Keeper's maze faster than the rest of the Wandering Sols, although something had kept him from the dagger entirely. He should've beaten Evren to it, he knew that clear as day now.

Abraxas closed his fist, and the stone broke apart, the atlas flickering out of his mind as he shoved the stones back in the bag. Whatever had kept him from the dagger wasn't around anymore. It wouldn't keep him from the sword.

The next step he took squished under his boot. He looked down and saw fine sand.

"I told you we were close." Nerezza turned back to him. Beyond her, he couldn't see anything other than darkness. But it was colder, the air caressing his skin with chilled fingers. The smell of salt was thicker.

Nerezza's eyes flashed to the pouch in his hand. "Finally loosening up?" She held her hand out.

He tossed the pouch to her, only a little disappointed she snatched it up easily without fumbling for it. "No."

Abraxas stepped beside her as she started putting the atlas together. Smugness radiated from her. Nerezza still believed that only she could use the atlas, and Abraxas was content to allow her to believe that. Her Serevadian blood seemed to be enough to make it work, and she assumed that was the *only* way it could be used.

He almost wished she was sane again, so she'd be smart enough to catch on.

Rocks turned to sand at his feet, damp and littered with shells and algae-slick formations like columns. But there were no walls. The black around him moved and undulated. Bits of it flashed as the light from their orb caught the water around them.

He shivered. Stone above him was one thing, but water so deep he couldn't see the sun? He'd be glad to be rid of this place.

"We're on the right path," Nerezza said. Her eyes were glazed over. Whenever she used the atlas she focused on it completely, never moving or seeing anything else. It was likely another reason she never noticed him use it because he always pulled it out while they were walking.

"The Boreal Sea is massive," Abraxas said. "You expect it to be right in front of us? Along one of your people's bridges?"

Nerezza's eyes focused again and the shards broke apart. She glared at him. "This bridge hasn't been used since it was built. Everyone that's tried to use it to cross has never returned. Likely it accidentally cut into where the sword was hidden, and therefore has been subjected to whatever trials were put in place to protect it. You should trust me, Abraxas. We want the same thing."

He scowled, but it was mostly for show. Fighting with Nerezza was natural. She expected him to question her each time she used the atlas, so he had to keep up the appearance of being suspicious.

Although, her knowledge of Serevadia had been welcome. If it wasn't for her, he would've had to resort to finding a lone Serevadian and torturing them for the bridge's location, which would've been messy and near pointless violence. This way there was only one person hurt.

"Keep the atlas up," he said. "Just in case. I'll guide you."

Her eyes brightened. "That's more like it. Straight ahead now. Be watchful for anything that falls through the waters. It can happen."

Abraxas lodged that into his mental list of terrifying things he didn't want to think about and stepped further into the deep.

In a way, traversing the bottom of the sea wasn't all that different from the depths of Eith. The ground gave way to dips and climbed up hills. The walls were black and impossible to see past. And it was achingly lonely with just Nerezza.

The difference was it wasn't nearly as quiet. The water murmured with currents that ran alongside the magical bridge. Occasionally the walls would shiver with ripples as something bellowed a low tone.

Despite Nerezza's warning, nothing came through the water and into the tunnel. It seemed like everything living avoided it. Few shadows in the waters dared to get close enough to investigate their light, everything immediately shied away before getting closer than a couple feet away.

"I can't believe I'm so close," Nerezza murmured behind him.

He didn't spare her a glance, even as he grabbed her arm to help her step down from a rock.

"My whole life has been building up to this." She clasped the atlas reverently, eyes unseeing and steps unsteady. "From the moment I could speak I knew I was meant to be here. Do you think . . ." she paused, blinking her eyes clear of the map to find Abraxas beside her. "What do you think it'll look like?"

He shrugged. "I'm more worried about how to get to it. The dagger had a maze that sent us through time before we could find it."

"But that's the Eternity Keeper," she said. "He's chaos, even when time demands him not to be. The Shadow Dancer was another entity entirely, so his trials for the sword will be different."

Abraxas bit his tongue before he could point out that the Elders were not different people. They were pieces of the same soul; to Zelmis the way the shards were to the atlas. Their powers might differ, but their souls remained the same.

"My mother should be here," Nerezza said suddenly.

Abraxas cut her an odd look and she shrugged sheepishly.

"She always dreamed about bringing the Shadow Dancer's sword back to Serevadia. She'd use it to unite the different Mora clans and then the rest of Serevadia's cities. The sword is more than power, it's a symbol to our people. She taught me that." Nerezza bit her lip. "She would've loved to see this place."

Abraxas doubted Ainthe would love anything about their quest, but he forced himself to nod along with her. Which was a mistake because then she turned to him.

"What about your mother?"

Fingers sticky with honey. Shadow monsters on the wall slain by shadow knights. His favorite bowl, chipped along the rim but never fixed or thrown away, filled with a warm stew to beat back the winter chill. Snow in his hair from handfuls being tossed back and forth, cheeks rosy red and sore.

"I don't have one," he said and walked past her.

"Eith has been cruel to us," Nerezza called after him. "It's not fair."

"Nothing is fair," he spat over his shoulder.

"We could make it fair."

Her words stopped him in his tracks. He couldn't help but turn around to face her, the little orb of light casting cold shadows on her face.

"We can make things better, Abraxas," she said, her eyes wide and pleading.

"You mean for Serevadia," he said. He wouldn't let her try to twist her words to suit his whim. Better to lay down the facts now.

Nerezza stepped closer. "I mean all of it. Eith doesn't just mean the surface anymore. It includes Serevadia now. What we could do with the power we're about to hold could change everything! No more monsters. No more corrupt kings and nobles exploiting lesser people for power. A land of harmony where everyone can live together."

"It's not that simple, Nerezza. People don't work like that."

"But we could make them." She breathed excitedly. "Imagine it—no war or fighting. Just complete peace. We just have to make them see what we do."

"And what do you see?"

She paused, glancing down at the atlas in her hands and then back up at him. "Hope for a world where I don't have to hide and apologize for who I am. Where *we* don't."

She reached out and squeezed his arm and he didn't pull away. For a moment he let himself see her utopia. The surface filled with people of all races and colors. The land growing without the destruction of war. Bustling cities free of plagues and corruption. It was beautiful.

It was also a child's dream.

Abraxas put his hand over the one she had around his arm. "You would do that? Work with the surface and the people already there?"

She nodded. "We'd have to cull the bad ones first, obviously. But after everything we've done to get here, that'll be nothing. I wouldn't want a world without Sahar in it. I don't want her angry with me."

Abraxas started to tell her the truth; that Sahar wasn't angry, she was simply grieving. That the human noble who'd left the comforts of her life behind to travel and save people was alone and abandoned and wanted nothing more than her last remaining friend back. It would be the first truth he'd spoken in a while.

But he stopped himself when he felt something like ice touch his ankle. He jerked away, swinging around to see the way ahead completely black. Not the empty darkness of the ocean and the bridge, but true darkness that took up space and stared through him.

The tendril that had touched his foot had retreated like a snake rearing back but, faster than he could blink, it lashed out and took his whole leg.

Abraxas couldn't even yell as he was yanked off his feet, his whole leg going numb. Nerezza still had a grip on him, but the shadows were darting out for her too. She stubbornly clung to his arm. Did she actually care about him now?

It didn't matter. He was yanked back hard enough that he felt his bones pop and Nerezza was thrown off her feet. Together they tumbled into the abyss, screams trapped behind their lips.

Future gods don't scream.

The black was heavy and consuming. Abraxas knew he was being dragged somewhere but he barely felt a whisper of wind to ruffle his hair. There was nothing around him, which was strangely comforting. Even as a cold chill crept over his entire body, he didn't panic. Here, alone, there was no one to hurt or be hurt by.

All good things for Abraxas ended though, and this nothingness ended quickly. Before he knew it, he could see again and was tossed down into a foot of saltwater with an unceremonious splash. Nerezza landed beside him, floundering to stand up against the sudden buoyancy.

Abraxas looked up from the water, hand already going for his sword.

The space they found themselves in was cavernous but beautiful. Low lights from twinkling sconces bathed everything in a soothing green light. Smooth planes and columns of obsidian made up the surfaces he could see. His fingers dug through a thick layer of algae and corals to find the same of the floors. The ceiling dripped water in musical rhythm from the corners and sporadically down the length of the room. A massive window took up the far wall, showing nothing but black and the occasional burst of bubbles rising to the surface.

At the far end, under the window and a stream of salt water, laid a black blade embedded in the floor.

Nerezza gasped, seeing it a moment later than him. She let the shards of the atlas fall to the floor, plopping in the water as she stood up.

Abraxas cursed, fishing the shards out and putting them in his pocket. "Nerezza, wait."

"It's here, Abraxas. We can really do this." She sounded like she was in a dream. "I didn't think it would be quite so big."

Abraxas didn't have time to comment. Picking up the last shard, his eyes followed a ripple in the water. One traveling towards him, and not coming from Nerezza. He darted out of the way, not as fast in the water as he could've been, and narrowly avoided a spike of shadow aimed in his direction.

"Nerezza!" he snapped and drew his sword.

He slashed through it, and the spike fell like water. He could've sworn he heard it scream.

Nerezza was mere inches from him now, back to him and palms filled with nasty red energy. Another two spikes leapt from the water and she hurled the magic at them. But it passed though, completely unphased. She froze and he swung around her and cut the shadows down.

"No blood," he barked at her, and she nodded. Whatever they were fighting wasn't natural.

Nerezza grasped for her spellbook, damp from its dunk in the water, as Abraxas cut down spike after shadowy spike. They jumped from the water like snakes but were as rigid as thrown daggers. Wherever they nearly cut him he could feel ice form on his skin.

Seconds later, the smell of burning parchment hit his nose and it was like they never left Direwall. They stood back-to-back, slinging spells of fire that boiled the water and swinging steel that slashed again and again. They shouted when the other's guard was open, or when something was coming in their blind spot. Together, the shadowy knives couldn't touch them.

As if they knew they couldn't win, the shadows retreated with nothing more than ripples to announce their trail. They all turned to the same place and Abraxas watched with growing unease as they churned under the water in the middle of the room, growing bigger and bigger.

"Give me your sword." Nerezza held out her hand, dusted in ash.

Abraxas obliged and she ran the ash over the blade. It wasn't anything more than a simple short sword, not suited for his normal fighting style and not weighted to his preference. But under her fingers it grew. Longer, weight all in the right places. Where water once dripped from the blade, orange flames spouted and lit up the air.

Something was growing in the middle of the room, the shadows hard at work. But for the moment it was just the two of them. The light of the flames flickered in the black depths of her eyes, stern and determined, probably the most sane she'd been since the White Cairn.

"The magic won't last long when I start casting other spells," she said. "Make it count."

The blade hissed through the water as he swung it into a familiar stance. "I always do."

Together they turned to the middle of the room. The shadows were finishing their creation, and out of the water came a giant, monstrous hound made of roiling saltwater and clashing shadows. Its fangs were made of the same spikes as before, but larger. It was nearly as large as the whole room. It would take only a step for it to reach the two of them.

Eyes like black whirlpools found them and Abraxas charged.

Water flew from his wild run. Salt was all he could taste. He saw the black jaws snapping down at him and he dashed backwards. The snout hit nothing but water, collapsing and reforming as it brought its head back up. But Abraxas was already attacking.

His blade cut into shadow and where once it felt like he was slicing water, now he *felt* something. The fire burned bright along the cut, illuminating it even as the hound pulled away howling so low the building shook.

Water trembled at his feet and Abraxas moved under the beast. He slashed at the closest ankle, spinning just out of the way as the same foot clawed at the water he'd just been standing in. The hound tried to jump from Abraxas's reach and expose him again, but Abraxas hung close. Every sidestep or jump, he rolled right into it and followed the hound.

Water and shadow against fire and steel. He was soaking wet, slower than he liked, but there was a thrill in his bones that he couldn't shake. He felt like he was on the walls of his childhood home, playing out a scene his mother made up.

The terrible hound spun around, jaws gnashing at the hero.

He ducked out of the way, going forward instead of backwards and away.

The spray of water and foul breath coated him as he lunged forward, blade digging into the neck of the beast.

Another great howl tore through the arena and more water fell from the cracked ceiling.

The hero tried to take his sword back for another attack, but found it stuck. Shadows had taken hold of it, extinguishing the flames and trapping him.

He pulled with all his might as the beast reared back and pulled him off his feet. With a great heave, the hound sent the hero sailing across the room and colliding with column.

Abraxas fell to the water, gasping for air. From the corner of his eye he could see the hound circling back to him, snarling and pissed, but very much alive even with Abraxas's sword in its neck. The fire was gone, although it still smoldered.

Across the room, under the legs of the beast, Abraxas met Nerezza's eyes. A silent agreement, a curt nod, and he was back on his feet and running towards the hound.

He sloshed through the water, a cry of rage and desperation that had been built up inside him since he was left finally coming loose. He was not a hero from his mother's old stories. He wasn't a tragic adventurer trying to redeem himself by saving pieces of Eith.

The water at his legs withdrew as Nerezza commanded it to make a clear pathway to the hound. The hound stood ready, teeth bared in a savage grin too human to belong to a dog.

Abraxas didn't belong in anyone's stories. He was not a knight in shining armor fighting for good. He was not a Champion of a god, pure and righteous. Eith had broken him, tainted him, left him for dead.

Abraxas was mere feet from the hound when the water swirled up in front of him and froze into jagged, icy steps. Nerezza's path made it easier now. He took them two at a time, boots slipping on the slick sea ice. He leaned over as he reached the top, snatching his blade from the beast's throat and jumping onto its back.

Abraxas was not a holy man, not a healer, not a hero.

He landed on the hound's back and raised his sword. The beast bucked underneath him but he kept his hold, grabbing at that well of power deep inside him. The blade began to glow in his hands, not with fire but with a holy light. Not from a god, but from himself. The air shimmered as he slashed at the hound's back, cutting deep and terrible.

The beast screamed and the window cracked. It bucked more violently, reaching heights that made Abraxas nearly touch the ceiling. He lost control then, flying off. The hound fell down first, his feet leaving its back as he started his own plummet straight down.

He grabbed his hilt in both hands, point facing down towards the waiting beast.

Abraxas Kain was the culmination of every great and terrible thing that had happened to him, and it made him powerful.

He slammed down on the head of the beast, the glowing blade sinking up to the hilt. The hound screamed again and threw its head back and forth, but Abraxas clung to his hilt. He twisted it, causing more pain.

"Die," he hissed.

In its death throes it worked hard to throw him off but he held resolute. Slowly the shaking stopped. The beast let out one last mournful howl before collapsing on the ground.

The only thing that kept Abraxas from falling was his grip on his sword. The hound's head came to rest awkwardly, angled to the side so that Abraxas had to slide off. He willed his strange magic away and pulled the now normal blade from the beast.

He landed feet first in the water. He was barely breathing hard. Water rained from new fissures in the ceiling, but he didn't care. Nerezza walked up to him, eyes wide.

He turned just in time to see the hound dissolve into shadows. He readied his sword again, but the black smoke merely zipped away as if sucked by a massive inhale of breath. The sword consumed it all, every last shadow. The room even seemed brighter as the sword waited for them.

It was pitch-black, from pommel to the blade. From what he could see, it was beautifully wrought. The etched filigree on the blade had a life of its own, catching the rivers of saltwater that ran down it.

He and Nerezza stood side by side, staring at it.

"This is it," she said hollowly. "The moment everything changes.

"Yes." More than she knew.

Nerezza turned to him. "Share it with me. I wasn't lying, Abraxas, we can do this together. Partners that hold each other in check. Eith could finally be a place where we find ourselves belonging."

He tore his eyes away from the sword and he tried not to look too eager. "Are you sure? This was your dream, your destiny."

She smiled. Genuinely. It made him sick. "It is both of ours now."

Abraxas turned back to the sword, it seemed to bulge and writhe with the shadows within.

"I don't think we can take it at the same time," he said. "The dagger had one wielder at a time, so I would assume this would work the same." He looked back at her. "This is a relic of your people. Take it first."

She took in a sharp breath. "You trust me to give it to you?"

"This is your plan, and I helped you get here. Remove the sword, test it, and then we'll draw out this new world of ours." He smiled, but it felt cold. "I have ideas."

Nerezza smiled back. "As do I."

She turned to the sword and walked towards it. Water

didn't give way for her. Her robes hung heavy around her legs and her white braid was limp and flat along her back. She dripped sea water as she took the two steps up towards the sword. It was big, a greatsword then, but he had a feeling she could lift it easily.

Nerezza closed her eyes, and he watched her murmur, "When we see our friends again, the world will be better."

Then she wrapped her hand around the hilt and pulled.

There was no resistance. It slid out of the stone like a knife through butter. She stumbled back into the water to get it out fully and held it before her. The sword dwarfed her, but she held it with little problem.

And then she started convulsing.

Nerezza fell to her knees, sword glued to her hand as the shadows kept inside it rushed into her skin. Her veins turned black against her alabaster complexion. They dug in with a ragged ferocity. He wasn't surprised to hear her scream in pain.

Abraxas calmly circled around her. Her back was arched almost into the letter C, her mouth gaping. Shadows filled that too and cut off her screams. She shook so hard he was sure she'd fall apart. But she didn't, and she didn't drop the sword.

Abraxas waited in front of her, watching until all the shadows left the blade and filled her. She collapsed on all fours, sobbing. Somewhere in the sobs he heard her gasping. She did so three times before he could make out the words.

"Help me," Nerezza begged.

"No," Abraxas answered.

She shuddered. Something was moving under her skin. He could see it dancing between her shoulder blades.

"Abraxas, please . . ." She sounded like a little girl, broken and alone. He knew what that felt like. She could take marinating in the feeling a while longer.

He knelt to her level. She didn't even have the strength to

look up from the floor, but he noticed her fingers inching towards his boot as if to cling to life. He scooted it away.

"Now, Nerezza, don't you like how power feels?" he asked softly. It should've unnerved him that he used the same voice that he used for his patients, but it didn't.

She shook her head. "I can't . . . breathe."

"Look at me."

Nerezza refused. He gritted his teeth.

"Look at me, Nerezza."

Slowly she did. The green light of the lanterns caught her face, and he barely contained his surprise.

Little of Nerezza remained. Her eyes were black as the void, swirling like the whirlpools of the hound's eyes. And she had three extra sets of them dotting her face in neat rows. Her full lips that might've been pretty once looked like they'd been torn away, raw and bleeding. That was the only bright color left in her. The veins in her skin pulsed a steady black. Ink-dark tears fell from each of eight eyes.

There was a reason no one could depict what a god looked like. Nerezza was only a sliver of an example.

He took her chin between his fingers, gentle and soft. Healers hands could be useful.

"Don't cry now, you got what you wanted."

"You . . . knew?" she gasped.

He hummed in agreement, looking her over. Divinity didn't suit her well. At least not in his mortal eyes.

"Nerezza, this is what happens when you start shoveling power inside you that you barely understand." He tucked her hair behind her ear. It had blackened, blood falling from it as well and leaking into the water at their feet. "The Divines are much more than we can comprehend. I knew that there would be trials and tests, and there were. I also knew that something as vaguely powerful as shadows would not be as simple as taking a sword. We had no idea what it could do and you just took it. All the time in the world to sit and study, but you got greedy." He frowned disapprovingly. "You were supposed to be smart."

"What are you going to do?"

"Nothing." He shrugged. "I will sit back and watch you try to bring Serevadia together. I say we start in Xoria. I remember that being a particular thorn in my side in the future. We give them you, a new terrible god bearing the powers of the one they lost. They'll follow."

He stood up and she collapsed at his feet, hugging the sword as if it were a lifeline.

"W-why?" she sobbed. "Why do this? We were supposed to change the world!"

"Oh, we will," Abraxas promised. He looked down at her and felt a twinge of pity, then buried it. She was a monster. "The world will be different by the time we reach our friends, that much is true. But it'll be worse. Far, far worse."

Nerezza wailed. He didn't need to understand her to know what she was asking.

"Because I need the world broken and dark enough that the Divines are seen as a blessing. Because when you're done playing god, I will use that sword to bring them back, and you will see what true Divinity does."

Abraxas stepped over her prone form, water licking his calves. He took a deep breath, loving and hating the freedom that came from the first part of his plan falling into place.

"You'll need a new name," he said. "I'm thinking Catarmon."

24

Evren

Evren had never been afraid of the dark. As a child, Yuhan taught her to be wary of things that could hurt her. Hisrachi, wild wyverns, witches and the like. But never the dark. The only thing scary about darkness was not being able to see. Did tarrying monsters use that to their advantage? Absolutely. Evren herself had used the cover of night to her advantage.

In Serevadia, the dark had been a challenge to overcome. In the Reino Terminan, the Long Night had its dangers but the dark itself was never truly one, just the undead Gail collected during that time. No matter her experiences with either of those, she never feared going into a room with no light, or wandering into the woods on an overcast night.

Here, however, darkness had a will of its own and Evren was terrified.

Deafeningly quiet. Still and cold. Black so deep there was no end in sight. Was this what it was like to lose all her senses? No sight or sound, nothing to taste or smell. She couldn't feel anything other than the cold.

Inside her, the shadows searched for something again. Coils of black caressed her bones, prodding tissue and slithering around her spine. They shied away from her heart, from her veins, actively avoiding them at all costs.

Devoid of all other feeling, Evren was keenly aware of this. Of every pump of Gyda's shared heart, the shadows shivered and moved quickly away. Was it possible for the dark to be terrified of her?

No, it didn't care about her. Who she was, her thoughts and dreams, what remained of her ambitions and hopes, those didn't matter. There was no color or brightness in them where they once were. Where the dark touched, color leeched. Where it moved, bravery drained.

But her blood? That it feared, or at least respected enough to stay away. It was as if it inherently knew that her blood could hurt it, if given the chance.

Evren felt a tiny spark of hope, a flicker of light in the dark, and she grasped it before it could be snuffed out. That spark held back the cold just enough. She still couldn't feel anything, but her power had never come from pain, that was just a side effect. She felt her fingers twitch, though she didn't feel anything when she grasped for her dagger. No press of her hand on her thigh, no brush of leather against her fingertips. She was moving, she *knew* she was, but she could've been hit with a boulder with as much as her sense of touch was working.

The gloves!

Her mind rejoiced even as the shadows coiled inside her jumped at the thought. She could cut herself with the climbing gloves. Surely that would be enough to awaken something inside her. How much blood would she have to spill to get the shadows out? It didn't matter. Any was worth it if she could just *feel* again. She'd spent so long emotionally numb in Orenlion, she couldn't go back to anything like that after—

Gyda.

Evren paused. The shadows did not; they dug deeper. But she was frozen again, hands twitching into a fist but not quite committing. Would this hurt Gyda? If she was stuck in the same situation, how much worse would it be?

Could Evren live with herself if the price for freedom, for feeling again, was losing the woman who made it worthwhile?

She never got a chance to find out. The shadows retreated with sickening speed, zipping out of Evren's body as if yanked out by another hand. Evren collapsed on the ground, heaving for breath.

Cool stone beneath her hands. Air in her lungs. Ragged breathing, her own, in her ears and the sound of something murmuring but muffled by thick stone. Evren opened her eyes and nearly sobbed.

She could see.

Black stone, smooth and without imperfection. Bare walls. Small room, but a wide window showing a deep blue color outside, almost too dark to see through. Evren pushed herself to her feet, inhaling deeply. Salt. Damp that stuck to her skin.

Puzzled, she moved towards the window. She'd almost reached it, still seeing nothing but a blue abyss, when she heard gasping behind her.

Evren whirled around. Shadows retreated from the small room, sliding under the crack in the door and leaving Sahar's crumbled figure on the floor.

She raced over to her and knelt beside her. The human looked awful. Her tan skin was pallid and ashy, cheeks streaked with tears. She kept opening her mouth as if to scream but no sound came out. When Evren touched her arm, she was shaking so badly that she nearly collapsed.

Evren drew back. Maybe touch was the last thing she needed right now.

"Sahar, are you—"

The woman's hand lashed out and gripped Evren's in a

fierce hold. Evren could feel her own blood fighting to pump through her fingers and past Sahar's death grip. But she didn't pry her off. She sat and waited. She put her other hand over Sahar's and watched the other woman shudder in waves.

They sat like that until Sahar stopped shaking. Her fingers never loosened around Evren's hand.

"I thought I was dead," Sahar finally croaked. "I thought that was what death would feel like. Endless, numbing, and so dark." She squeezed her eyes shut as another shudder wracked her body. Her voice was on the very edge of a sob when she spoke again. "Is that what he felt? Is that what Drystan endured with Gail?"

"No." Evren's tone was forceful. "No, Sahar, it wasn't. I was there. Drystan wasn't alone, and there wasn't darkness. It wasn't anything like that."

"And afterward?" Sahar looked at her with red rimmed eyes. "When you let him go, how was death for him."

"I don't know," Evren said truthfully. "And I . . . I'm sorry."

Words said over and over to her after the White Cairn. Words Sahar had swallowed and smiled through. If she blamed Evren for not saving Drystan, she never showed it. Evren never told her that Drystan had deemed it impossible to come back to her, and had chosen not to fight a hopeless battle. Sahar refused to say what vow Drystan had broken with his death.

Sahar took a deep breath, steeling herself. When she opened her eyes again, she'd buried her grief. Not deeply; it was a shallow grave, to get the job of surviving done before she could do real work. Evren had a feeling that her grief would always be there, just under the surface, waiting for the slightest gust of misfortune to blow away the dirt that kept it hidden.

Sahar took her hand back, and Evren's fingers tingled as blood returned to her fingers. She sat back as Sahar pulled herself up and studied the room, smoothing her hair and clothes as she did.

"We're underwater." Sahar squinted at the window. "Deep enough that glass windows shouldn't be intact."

Evren shook out her fingers, standing up. "We were a long way from water when Viggo . . ."

She trailed off. He was dead. She watched the light leave his eyes. He was really, truly gone. Not a ghost hinting at it like Nerezza, or a possibility that Evren could ignore while she was on the surface.

It was hard to breathe suddenly, like there was a hand around her lungs squeezing each time she tried to force air in. She got in just enough to speak.

"When he died," she finished.

Bury it. You didn't even love him like Sahar loved Drystan. You have no reason to be so upset.

"The same thing when the shadows first found us." Evren shook her head, trying to dislodge the thoughts. "They took us to Kleros, and we hadn't been there. Teleportation, maybe?"

Sahar frowned. "That's not possible with the magic we have."

"Serevadian magic is different. We don't have anything like it on the surface. Maybe they can do this."

Viggo would've known. He didn't know what to make of being in Kleros, but he would've given them some sort of insight.

Bury him. You have no right to grieve.

Evren eyed the water outside the window. Her mind fell back to the memory of Viggo showing her Serevadia's underwater bridges that cut through the ocean floor and connected Xoria to Andovine and Kleros. She remembered the soft way of his words, the way he smiled when she asked him questions, the passion in his voice.

Bury him and leave him like you did before. You don't deserve to mourn him.

"Evren." Sahar spoke gently, but it was enough to cut off her thoughts. "He was your friend. You can take a moment for him."

She wanted to. Evren had sobbed for hours when she'd lost Abraxas. Sol being taken by Gail had nearly destroyed her and left her an emotionless husk. There was no one else to grieve Viggo, so why shouldn't she?

Evren swallowed back her tears and shook her head. "I have friends that are still alive. I can think about him when we get out of here."

"Wherever here is." Sahar frowned.

"I think I know." Evren squared her shoulders, straightened her spine, put Viggo out of her mind. "Serevadia has a bridge that cuts through the ocean floor. We must be somewhere along it."

"I take it that's the only reason we're breathing? Aside from the shadows just tossing us aside."

"They didn't need us anymore," Evren said. "They were looking for something and didn't find it in us."

"I'd like to know what." Sahar eyed the door. "Think it'll open?"

"I think we should try."

There was no latch or doorknob on the door. Evren tried pushing it open, with no luck. Sahar pressed her fingers under the door to pull it, but nearly got them stuck for her efforts. She hissed in pain, massaging them as she drew back.

"I'm going to have to use one of my chemicals." She winced. "I'm running low as it is, I'd hate to waste it on a door."

Evren hesitated, remembering how large the blast in Vanguard was. "Maybe nothing as fiery as last time."

Sahar snorted. "Hells no. I didn't bring enough powder with me for more than one explosion. Do you have any idea how dangerous that is? Oh, what am I saying? Terevasan secret, of course you don't. Anyway, I'm not using that. A little bit of acid should do the trick. Basilisk is very good against stone. Maybe mixing it with . . . no, too volatile. I'd melt my hands before the door. Here, hold my bag."

Sahar took off her bag and dumped it into Evren's arms. Evren squirmed as the bottles inside clinked. She'd only seen pieces of what Sahar could make. Ghostly fires and minimal potions. She pretended that was all that sat in the bag as Sahar rummaged through, a little more aggressively that Evren would've liked with so much glass.

"Please tell me nothing is breakable in there," Evren murmured.

"Nothing is breakable in there," Sahar said offhandedly.

Evren frowned at the obvious lie, but took it as Sahar produced a very small vial of yellow liquid.

Evren had never seen a basilisk, since they were creatures that preferred warmer, humid climates like Terevas, but she knew enough about them to recognize a deadly amount of venom when she saw it. When a creature turned everything it saw to stone, eating prey required being creative. Evren was only mildly surprised that Sahar had some on her.

Sahar took a metal rod from her bag, as thin as a quill, and turned back to the door. She murmured to herself as she opened the vial of venom and dipped the rod into it just enough to coat the tip. Then, like an artist, she began to paint a door.

The venom sizzled the moment it touched stone. Yellow-tinged smoke rose from where Sahar painted, smelling like rotten eggs. Evren wrinkled her nose, but Sahar didn't seem to mind. She dipped her rod in and drew calm, quick lines. She never spilled a drop. Before long, she'd outlined a large enough hole for them to fit through and sat back as the venom did its work.

"Impressive." Evren watched the rock melt and pop like grease in a cooking pan.

Sahar knocked the rod against the glass vial, and the

remaining drop of venom went back with the rest. It didn't seem to like metal, or maybe it was that particular kind. Regardless, it was repulsed by it and left no residue, so Sahar was able to stopper the vial and put both back in the bag without risking anything inside it.

"You say that as if you didn't already know." The human smiled and took back her bag.

Behind her the stone gave way with an echoing thud, leaving an opening.

"Assuming there are guards that heard that, we need to move." Evren hurried to the door. She slipped though, careful to avoid the still hissing edges, and stepped out into the hallway beyond. It was empty, lit only by the weak light coming from the windows at the ends. One side, where their room had been, was solid stone. The other side was open air, like a balcony. She peered over, getting just enough light to glimpse a stairwell connecting their level and going down.

Sahar stepped up beside her. "I won't complain, but where is everyone? I expected an army."

"Maybe they're all strung up and bleeding shadows," Evren whispered. "We need a better vantage point. I can't see anything."

"Window?"

Evren frowned. This deep underwater she doubted she'd see anything at all, but the idea of walking blind made her skin crawl. She had no idea where everyone else was, enemy or friends, and the quickest way to find out was to see what kind of building they were in.

Picking the window that would lead to the landing of the stairs, Evren crept closer to it and willed her feet as quiet as possible. Sahar was close behind, her footfalls barely heard. There didn't seem to be anyone around, but the shadows clinging to the corners and walls made her nervous. Who needed guards when magic could do the work for you? She shied away from them as much as she could and grasped the windowsill.

Evren expected to see nothing but a blue abyss. Instead, she saw a black palace entrenched in the sands. The waters around it were inky black, the blue only showing through because of the bright beams of light along each of the jagged towers lighting up the water. Nothing swam between the towers, or even touched the light. It was like all marine life avoided the place.

But what made Evren's heart sink was farther out. Skimming just along the edge of the palace was a wide bridge of air stretching as far as she could see in either direction. The same lights on the towers kept the bridge lit, illuminating it for miles as it carved along the ocean floor.

Beside her, Sahar's gasp was strangled. "That's an army moving in there."

"I know," Evren said softly.

An army marched inside the bridge. Bristling with familiar armor and bright weapons, they kept in an orderly line. One on one side of the bridge, and on the other. Few came from the palace itself, but those that did bore weapons like the massive crossbows Evren had destroyed, or cages that shook as they rattled along, as if something inside was trying to get out.

This was an army of thousands, and she was only seeing a portion of them. How many were already miles in each direction? How many were past the bridge entirely?

"So, this is Serevadia," Sahar mused. She put her hand on the glass, which fogged up at the heat of her touch. "There're more bridges like this, aren't there."

"Probably." Evren shivered. "Serevadia is massive. These stretch from under Gratey to Etherak. I wouldn't be surprised if more came from Melkarth, Vernes, or Terevas."

"There's no army on the surface that can stand against this."

"No," Evren agreed. She thought of Dirn-Darahl, already fallen, and Vanguard destroyed instead of recaptured. Serevadia would push them to do the same with other parts of the world. Give them up or destroy them so nobody could use them again.

She gripped the sill with white knuckles, the army below blurring. Evren looked away. She could've stopped this. It would've been a bloodbath. It would've gone against her word to give Viggo time to calm Serevadia. But it could've saved so many.

"People in Eith are going to die because I didn't tell them about this," Evren whispered.

Sahar frowned at her, the blue glow from the window making her look even more washed out. "Was Serevadia like this before? You mentioned it was a republic before it was an empire."

"I only saw a bit of it, through the eyes of someone who loved it and gave me only the good things. If I had been more proactive, gone to the Collective immediately after leaving Dirn-Darahl, I could've—"

"Back on your self loathin' bullshit again, kid?"

Evren whirled around, a riot of emotions inside her as Arke climbed the stairs. He wasn't alone. Keres lumbered casually behind him, earning a sigh of relief from Sahar.

"Good to see you both still alive," they said with a too wide grin. "Enjoying the view?"

"Nothin' like imminent death to get you movin'." Arke glared out the window.

"You saw this?" Evren gestured to the window.

"Couple levels down, yeah. We've been out for a while. Tryin' to find everyone."

Sahar smoothed her hair back again. "We just got out. You've seen no one else?"

Keres shrugged. "None. I was planning on taking over a new body, one with more muscle and armor. Besides, Serevadian would be a new look for me. But, alas," they sighed. "No one to kill, no one to possess."

"Sorin?" Evren asked. Sol and Gyda's names were on the tip of her tongue, too, but Arke shook his head.

"Ain't none but us. Not that I've seen."

Sahar waved him away. "The shadows aren't done with them, evidently. Evren was right, they're looking for something. They must think one of us has it."

Evren worried her lip. "This puts a damper on our Abraxas and Nerezza plan."

The four of them mulled that over in silence. The army outside marched on, as if there was no end. The weight of the ocean seemed to press down on Evren's chest.

It was Keres who spoke, frowning as they did. "As much as it pains me, and it does, we need to scrap this suicide mission of yours." He looked at Evren before she could protest. "This is bigger than the two of them. We can't make it out of this without a good escape plan."

"Nerezza has always been a key factor in this," Sahar argued. "I won't leave her again. These shadows could very well be her doing."

"Then why did they cast you aside?" Keres asked, none too gently.

Sahar looked away, jaw tight, back to the window.

Evren was torn. On one hand, she knew Abraxas and Nerezza were the key to stopping all of this. On the other, she was very far from what she'd planned. Miles beneath the ocean, trapped with sentient shadows and an army they couldn't sneak past, missing members of their party and heavily outnumbered. She should cut her losses and run, shouldn't she? Tell the first person she sees about what is brewing under the surface. Adventurers were already spreading the word, but everything was so much worse now.

Eith's world leaders needed to know just how bad things

were going to get, and they were the only ones who could drive home the severity of what they were seeing.

"How would we even get out?" Evren asked, hating herself for it. Viggo had died for this. Divara had sacrificed herself for a chance to save Eith. Now both were gone in vain.

"I've been workin' on that," Arke said, unusually soft, as he moved closer. "Those shadows are teleportin' us places, only we have no control. Aside from marchin' with an army that would sniff us out in minutes, I think our only way out is to use them shadows."

"You said we have no control," Evren argued.

"Ah!" Keres raised a finger. "The brilliance of a good mage is *making* them obey us. The magic is already there, it is simply a matter of rewriting enough to take us somewhere else."

A chill ran down Evren spine. "Use what's available rather than create something on your own." She recited Divara's words, then looked at Arke. "Can you do it?"

If there was one thing Arke was confident in, it was magic, but there was doubt in his eyes. "I'm workin' on it. But we'll only get one shot, and I want to get all of us out if we can."

"What about Tolk?"

Sorrow flashed in his eyes, and he looked down at his spellbook. Evren hadn't even noticed it was open, the beginnings of a complex spell circle scribbled on the parchment.

"I'm lookin' for him still," was all Arke said, and all she knew he would say.

Keres clapped their hands, making them jump. "Now, we have places to explore, rugged friends to find, and a spell to complete. Arke, do be sure to write out the correct amount of people involved in this teleportation."

Arke gave them a quizzical look. "Everyone?"

Keres blinked and cocked their head in that way that made

them look more animalistic than humanoid. "The number we discussed."

Arke scowled, as if he suddenly remembered something he would've rather forgotten. But instead of arguing he just nodded.

Before Evren could press the matter, Keres was already pulling her and Sahar down the stairs. "Don't argue, it is very tedious. You want to find that big brute of a woman, yes? Let's find her."

Evren didn't fight. She let Keres lead her down the stairs, her heart heavy but still beating. She pressed her hand against her chest, feeling the thrum of life even through the armor. Gyda was alive so long as their heart still beat. They would deal with this together, one way or another.

If there was one thing Evren could do, it was find Gyda, and she wasn't leaving until she did.

25

Abraxas

It had been a long, lonely road back to the Wandering Sols, and Abraxas was exhausted. A little less than a century spent waiting, planning, hidden from the sun. He hadn't stepped foot on the surface since leaving Vernes, and the memory of heat and warmth had all but left him.

His constant companion was Nerezza, who swung violently between docile and out of control. Abraxas let her have her tantrums, because in the end she always came back. Those displays of power were good. They got Xoria believing in Catarmon before Nerezza had even shown her face, then worked on the Mora of Andovine next. If it bothered Nerezza to manipulate her mother's people into believing in a false god, she didn't let on. Slowly but surely, their plan for a new Eith was working.

Of course, there were doubts. Nights spent staring out the black windows, grappling with his morality. Through this line of action he was dooming so many to die. Eith, as Evren had pointed out in the beginning, was fragile and still healing.

What he was doing would essentially be taking a hammer to broken leg and shattering the bone.

But the more time went on, the less often those episodes of doubt came. He looked into the face of Serevadia and saw its true colors. A race of elves made by a piece of an evil goddess. Of course they were inclined to do evil things. Viggo had manipulated and lied, Velcros had betrayed and planned war, Nerezza had done all of that and more. Abraxas was no better than them, he knew. In every way, he was becoming the dark thing he always feared, the kind of man that he'd fought to kill in Vernes. Worse, even, since he was fully aware of the path he now walked and didn't dare backtrack.

This was what Haphion wanted. This was what Eith needed. A cleansing of darkness and holy fire to cut away the infected bits of the world and let the rest heal. Nothing about serving the Divine was good or easy; a common mistake for people who didn't know better was that those who served in temples were as holy as the gods they served. Nothing could be further from the truth. The Divines didn't dirty themselves with the deeds of mortals, but they needed those like Abraxas to do things in Eith they couldn't—or wouldn't—do.

He was both blade and fire, executioner and healer, for Haphion.

Abraxas took a deep breath. His fingers hovered in the empty air before him, wherethe Shadow Blade would materialize if he called it. He could almost feel the cool kiss of the pommel just beneath his fingertips.

"I suppose you always knew that I wasn't entirely elven," he murmured to himself, to Haphion. He rarely prayed these days, but he spoke as if the Divine could hear. "That is why you chose me and brought me on this path. I understand now why you wouldn't tell me, why I had to walk my own path back to you."

He paused, fingers humming as the blade started to shimmer into existence. "You always knew that you'd be pushed away and that you'd need someone to cut you free. I still don't know how."

Abraxas frowned, rubbing his thumb over his fingers. "I'll admit, I thought nearly a century would give me enough time to figure it out. Now, I have maybe a year? Less than that, likely. Nerezza has built a mighty army. Now that I'll be leaving it soon as an enemy, I wonder if I encourage her too much. If I . . . no. No, you were right. Great stakes mean great reward."

Serevadia had turned into an empire capable of conquering the surface, if they were smart. Velcros was greedy enough taking Dirn-Darahl before the rest of the army had been in place. They had planned for a series of devasting attacks on each of the nations simultaneously, just to get their point across. From there they would've no doubt gotten the attention of every adventurer in Eith, but one in particular would be very familiar with the threat.

As he expected, the Wandering Sols found themselves in the thick of it, but far quicker than he anticipated. He grimaced to himself. Viggo escaping had been Velcros's fault, but Abraxas had pushed the Herald away. Seeing his friends earlier would be good.

They'd know what to do. He had nearly a hundred years to plan what he was going to say to them. They might hate it all at first, but once things were explained they'd understand. Abraxas had no other choice. One way or another, Serevadia was going to be a threat. Now, a year, maybe four hundred years down the line, so why wait?

Yes, they'd turn this all around. Arke would find out how the Divines were banished for him. They'd come up with a plan to free them using the blade. Evren and Sorin would hate it, but they'd come around before. They would again.

He was missing one thing now. One thing he'd lost after diving after Nerezza and the dragon. He'd spent the years quietly searching for it. Something that powerful didn't just become lost. It landed somewhere, in the hands of someone it knew. If there was one thing he'd learned from his time with the Shadow Blade, it was that the Elder's artifacts preferred people they were familiar with. It was as if they had a mind of their own, and would seek out the ones they preferred to wield them.

The Eternity Dagger had been lost to him, so it had to have stumbled back into the hands of one of his old friends. The shadows at his command searched of their own accord, tingling the back of his skull with hums of disappointment.

Abraxas sighed and mentally scratched Evren off the list. The shadows would place her somewhere secure so she wouldn't hurt herself. He'd talk to her later. But he'd been so sure the dagger had returned to her. Frustration threatened to well up inside him, but he squashed it down. The shadows made quick work of Sahar, then left her with Evren. The human would have no connection to the dagger anyway.

Footsteps sharper and more confident than their owner echoed along the black stone of his room. The same room he'd fought the shadow beast in. Drained of water, cracks patched up, and the rest of the truly massive building uncovered, the palace deep under the Boreal Sea almost felt like home.

"What did you do?" Nerezza's shrill voice cried out.

Abraxas sighed audibly, her footsteps freezing as he did. Satisfaction twinged in his chest.

"Be more specific, Nerezza," he chided, not turning to face her. "Use your words."

"The sword! I can't . . ." She trailed off, choking on her words. She did that a lot. Her confidence had long since shattered with her mind. "I can't summon it."

"I know."

"I-I need it to retrieve Istnar from Kleros. I left him—"

"Your pet is fine waiting there," Abraxas muttered distastefully. He didn't like the broken Mora Nerezza had adopted as her servant. It kept her from her fits, sure, and gave her something to focus on that wasn't Abraxas. But the creature was mindlessly obedient and loyal only to Nerezza. It tolerated Abraxas because Nerezza told it to, something that would change soon, assuming either one of them survived his plan.

"You took it, didn't you? You took the sword, and you didn't even warn me! You said—"

He finally turned around. She'd gotten closer to him while she talked, but now that his back wasn't turned she rushed away. She wore an ashen veil to cover her mutated face, another thing she never gotten over. The blade's power had been too much for her, and even after she'd tried to gouge her extra eyes out, they always returned. Abraxas stopped caring the fourth time he found her crying in a pool of her own blood.

"Why aren't you changed?" she cried. "I-I don't understand."

"The blade and I share something in common," Abraxas said. "Something you did not."

She whimpered behind her veil, drawing back and hugging her herself. More and more she seemed like a fragile flower rather than the powerful mage he knew her to be. Her Blood magic was still there, as well as the magic she inherited from her mother. She hadn't touched her spellbook since she took the sword. Nerezza was fully capable of putting up a fight, she just didn't. She was a monster who acted like she had a chain around her neck when she had all the freedom in the world.

That fact Abraxas loved more than he should've. She'd brought him to his knees with foul magic and forced him to be her slave. It was all too satisfying for him to control her with nothing but a cold stare.

"You knew," she whispered accusingly.

"As did you, deep down." He frowned at her. "Surely you

could've understood that no mere mortal can use a weapon of the Divines."

"He was my god! Mine! You have no right to that sword."

"Ah, and did our original agreement mean nothing? You gave me permission."

"That was before." She hugged herself tighter.

"Before you threw yourself into a trap the old you would've seen coming, yes I am aware," he said flatly. "I upheld my end, Nerezza. You got to play god. You've set up your side of the chess board rather brilliantly, I must say. But your time is up. Now, it's my turn."

Her veil blew out from her face following pathetic sobs. "No no no. I'm not ready . . ."

"You had ninety-eight years to be ready."

As with every time he mentioned the years that passed, she froze rigid as if the passage of time had completely been erased from her mind and she was just realizing it again.

"That long . . ." she murmured, then hiccupped another sob. "Oh, Sahar. You're here."

"Yes." He stepped over to her and ignored the way she flinched away from him. "She's here."

The veil shook back and forth, swishing in time with her murmured objections. He drowned them out with his own voice, speaking over her easily.

"They're all right here, Nerezza," Abraxas said. "I felt them come in. They're all alive. Well," he scowled, remembering Keres, "mostly. Sahar is safe inside here, waiting for you. I made sure of it."

Using the shadows, commanding the blade was easier than he imagined. Mere hours after he'd taken it from Nerezza, he felt like he mastered it. The blade *wanted* him, so it worked with him.

He'd pulled his friends closer to him, bit by bit. Too much all at once and he risked losing them. Besides, seeing Kleros was good for Viggo. Abraxas had no doubt that Istnar made a nasty display of harvesting the shadows from the residents of the city. It pained him to put down a rebellion he could've used later, but power demanded sacrifice, and that power had been enough to bring the Wandering Sols back to him.

Viggo, of course, had to go. His magic was interfering with Abraxas's, to the point of annoyance. Evren would get over that loss easily, now that she had Gyda. He could've killed Keres, too, but that might've been too cruel, so he stayed his hand.

In the back of his mind, the shadows searched while he talked. It was refreshing how easily he was able to do both at once. They knew exactly what to do when they were done searching. If his friends had nothing, they'd be safely put in separate rooms along the palace. He'd decided to pair them up if he could. Sorin wouldn't do well with just his thoughts to keep him company. He could take—

The shadows trilled with confirmation. They found it! They wanted it as much as he did.

Abraxas's heart beat faster. He gave himself a moment to breathe, then nudged the shadows to bring his friend to him. Their first reunion since he'd left. They'd be happy to see him, right?

"It's time for you to leave, Nerezza." Abraxas stepped away from her. "Sahar is at the fifth level. I put her in a room near the staircase with Evren. Try not to kill my friend on your rush to meet your own."

Nerezza wavered as the floor beside her started to pool with shadows. She sidestepped easily, gathering her grey robes in her good hand. "What are you going to do, Abraxas?"

He ignored her, stepping around to the very front of the shadows and clasping his hands behind his back. Divines, he was nervous. It had been so long since he'd seen any of them, but for them it couldn't have been more than six months. How much would he be changed in their eyes? Would they embrace? Would they cry?

He pushed down his nerves. Out of the corner of his eye, he saw Nerezza slink to the edge of the room but didn't quite leave. One pointed word could send her away, but before he could open his mouth, the shadows molded into a figure and then withdrew, leaving them gasping on the floor.

She was on her hands and knees, shaking off the effects of the travel. As useful as they were, Abraxas knew the shadows weren't comfortable to be with. But she was alive, whole, unharmed. Just as he asked.

Abraxas held his hand out to Gyda. "Hello again, my friend."

Gyda's head snapped up. There was a piece of hair falling in her face, white as snow, but other than that, she was unchanged. There was less shock in her eyes than he expected, but the way she exhaled, as if she'd been holding her breath in the hopes of seeing him and was now finally allowing herself to breath, made him smile.

"Abraxas?" she whispered, as if she was afraid he'd disappear if she spoke normally. "Is that really you?"

"I'm afraid it is. Tell me I don't look that different?"

Slowly, she shook her head. "More grey in your hair than I remember."

"In yours as well." He smiled again. "Time is a cruel mistress."

Gyda grabbed his arm, pulling herself to her feet. She didn't let go as he stepped back to give her more room. She gripped his arm tightly, towering over him with a strange expression on her face.

"What happened to you?"

He stilled, even as she held onto his arm. If he closed his eyes he could imagine the times they'd sparred together, muscles burning and cheeks sore from smiling. Gyda never expected anything out of him, not even loyalty. He loved her for it.

But that simple question held weight. A hundred years of

pain and suffering, of waiting in the dark and doing things that made his skin crawl but his soul sing. He grappled with the right and wrong of his actions for so long, and even now, as he'd decided long ago that his path was the righteous one, he found himself hesitating before her.

Gyda caught the fall of his expression and leaned in. Her worry was sickeningly stark on her face.

"Abraxas, what is it? You can trust me."

"I know," he said. "It's just been a very long time since I've been in the company of a friend. I find myself overwhelmed."

He patted her hand and removed his arm from her grip. She reluctantly let him go, and he moved back a few paces to give himself some room to breathe.

"I used the dagger to get myself to safety," he admitted. "I didn't even know what I was doing, only that I did it and it sent me farther back in time than I would've liked. I have waited a hundred years for this reunion, for you." He looked at her with a tired smile. "As an elf, a hundred years doesn't normally mean anything to me. But this was the longest wait of my life."

Gyda took in the room with a frown. "You waited here?"

"Not all the time, but most of it, yes. My ties kept me bound to Serevadia."

Her expression darkened. "Nerezza."

"Yes."

"Where is she?"

Abraxas looked at where he last saw Nerezza, but the woman had wisely vanished. She could have Sahar for a while longer, at least until Abraxas decided to let Gyda have her fun. He was done with Nerezza, after all.

"She's here, just not in this room. Likely looking for the rest of our friends to torment."

Gyda hesitated, looking him up and down. "You do not seem concerned."

He scoffed. "A hundred years tied to that woman has taught me much. She was formidable at first, but I broke free of her magic recently. She has no power over me and is too drunk on her own power to realize it. I've been working out a plan to stop this—" he waved to the window, indicating the army outside "—from destroying Eith. It won't be easy, but working with them long enough has given me key insight. With your help, we can destroy Serevadia for good."

Gyda's wide shoulders slumped in relief. Across her back, her sword heaved with her breaths.

"That is good to hear," she said. "Evren said you could help us. I knew you would have a plan."

"I do." This time he let his eagerness slip out and started to pace. What were a few white lies sprinkled on the truth? They would never believe Nerezza over him. "It won't be easy. Velcros and Nerezza have made quite the army to deal with. However, I know of ways to stop them."

"How?" Gyda asked.

"The Elders' artifacts, like the dagger. Nerezza searched for the dagger, and then the Shadow Dancer's blade. Both are incredibly powerful for one reason. Gyda, my friend, they harbor the souls of the Elder's themselves, which are pieces of a dead Divine. Individually, these things are capable of amazing things, but together? Could you imagine what they could do?"

"No." Gyda shook her head. "I can't. But I leave the imagining up to you and Evren. This plan of yours would involve getting them all?"

"Yes."

"But we have no idea where the others are."

He winced. "That's true, but we know of two. They're all connected and can lead us to the others."

"So we take the Shadow Blade from Nerezza."

Abraxas wave her off. "I've already managed that. All we need to escape this place is the dagger."

Gyda scowled. "Easier said than done. We don't have that."

"Yes, we do."

Abraxas stopped in front of her, exhilarated. She looked puzzled, but the shadows didn't lie. They couldn't, because unlike him, they were not tainted by a mortal soul.

"Why do you look at me like that?" Gyda asked.

"How did it end up with you?" Abraxas asked instead of answering. "I thought for sure that the dagger would return to Evren, seeing as she's the one that used it the most. I dismissed Arke because he never touched it. Sahar and Keres for the same reason. But Sol and Sorin, they could've had it. Why you, Gyda?"

Gyda took a step back, and Abraxas felt a thrill shiver his bones. Did he scare her? It was one thing to break Nerezza into submission, but to make Gyda fear him? She faced a dragon head-on and dragged it through time. In a way, her plan to destroy the Deep Wood to the point where the Archdruids needed to help them had inspired him.

He took a step forward to match her. "Evren gave you the dagger in Orenlion without even realizing it."

"Trust transcends time," Gyda said, narrowing her eyes. "I don't have the dagger, Abraxas."

"Oh, you do. I can feel it. Pieces of a singular soul aching to be brought together again." He blinked up at her. "There's no need lie to me, I know you have it. You don't need to feel guilty about not using it. After all, you wouldn't be able to control it long before it overwhelmed you."

Gyda wasn't listening to him. Her eyes were darting around the room, looking for an exit. So paranoid, his friends. She looked down at the spot where the shadows had dumped her, now bare and smooth.

"You said you have the Shadow Blade." She looked back up at him. "How long?"

"Does it matter?"

"How. Long?" she gritted out.

Abraxas didn't answer. He rocked back on his heels and watched her. Her face was like an open book, he could read every emotion that crossed it. The confusion, the frustration, and, of course, the dawning horror.

"It was you," she said. "Your shadows that brought us to Kleros, and here."

He sighed heavily. "I needed you here now, is that really so bad?"

She stared at him. "You killed Viggo."

"Was that a bad thing to do?" He raised an eyebrow. "The man was a manipulative traitor."

"He was on our side."

"For now." Abraxas corrected. "How long before he decided to switch sides again? I did you a favor."

"And Kleros?" she asked, taking a step forward. "Was that you as well?"

So, she *wasn't* afraid. Even better.

Abraxas drew himself up. He didn't have an ounce of shame in him when he said, "Sacrifices are necessary. It was unfortunate, however."

"Unfortunate?" Gyda hissed through clenched teeth. "Abraxas, they were hanging from their toes, throats cut, spilling shadows. What was necessary about that?"

"Well, how else could I get you here?" he asked. "The creature did the killings, and he's Nerezza's beast. I have no control over him. We can detour to rip his arms off, if you prefer."

"Catarmon," she said, part reverently and part repulsed.

"Yes, that's what Nerezza has built for herself. She insisted. The woman has a flair for the dramatic. But that does make sense, right? All those whispers when we were in Andovine led us right here, full circle."

"No," Gyda said. "You're Catarmon. That elf made a

distinction. Catarmon was a 'he,' and the elf served a mistress. A mistress that taught him Blood magic."

Abraxas stilled and closed his eyes. Inwardly he cursed. He should've sewn the Mora's mouth shut. Where did he get these lies about Abraxas being Catarmon? It had always been Nerezza. Abraxas stayed in the shadows, unseen, pulling at her strings but that was it. He was not the monster Nerezza was.

"I am not Catarmon," he growled, opening his eyes.

"Then why lie to me?" Gyda asked softly. One last chance, her eyes seemed to say. Give me a reason to trust you.

Anger flared within him. A reason to trust him? Hadn't he done enough for her? He'd risked life and mind to drag her back from the White Cairn. He'd been her shield in battle, the one who'd nursed her wounds when there were no potions. He accepted her lies about her past with grace, even though they'd nearly cost him Sol, and she had the gall to talk to him about lies?

"I have never lied to you," he said carefully.

"You did," she said, shifting her feet subtly. A fighting stance? "Not with your words, but with your eyes. I knew this would happen. You've spent too long on your own, my friend. Your mind is not your own."

He laughed bitterly. "My mind is perfectly clear."

"You killed hundreds of innocents."

"Thousands," he snapped. "And they weren't innocent. Everyone I killed deserved it."

"Those people in Kleros were rebels," Gyda shot back. "They could've helped us. If you call their deaths justified you are a mon—"

"I am well aware of what I am, which is your only way out of here. I am the key to defeating Serevadia."

"I've been told."

"Then just trust me!" he yelled, all the pent-up anger and frustration entering his voice at once. She didn't flinch as his voiced bounced off the cavernous walls. He took a moment to collect himself, then spoke again, calmer this time. "I have changed, but I am still your friend. I still want to destroy Serevadia and save the surface."

"Then put down the sword."

Abraxas blinked and looked down at his hand. He hadn't even realized he summoned the blade, inky black and dripping shadows like water. It was ridiculously light for its size, like it was made for him.

He looked back at Gyda. "Please, Gyda, the dagger."

"Even if I did have it, I would not give it to you."

Abraxas held the sword in front of him. He had no armor, but he knew he wouldn't need it. How had it come to this? Once sparring partners, laughing between their blades, and now this? He should've convinced Evren first. Her word would've swayed Gyda.

"Does trust not transcend time?" he asked bitterly.

"Not now, my friend." She drew her blade, the runes lighting up a dazzling blue so bright it was nearly blinding and she wrapped both hands around the bone hilt.

26

Evren

Evren was tired of seeing black. The underwater prison, or building, or palace, was massive. It was a maze in its own right, rivaling the one that led to the dagger simply because the open hallways and stairs tricked her brain into thinking common sense applied to this place.

It didn't.

Hallways dead ended mere feet into their existence. Stairs led straight to windows or circled back down to the landing they were just on. There were no doors, except for the ones Sahar and Arke had to get through from the first rooms they were in. Just an endless maze of stairs, hallways, and windows.

Evren gritted her teeth as they stopped at a landing that connected another three sets of stairs, each going off into different directions. They'd been there before. She'd marked the banister the last two times with her knife.

"We can't keep walking blindly," she said, planting her feet and waiting for everyone to stop as well.

Arke turned back to her, ears drooping. "Any other suggestions, kid? It's how we found you."

"You only found us because we were already out. Sorin, Sol, and Gyda don't have magic or potions to break them out."

"So?" Sahar raised an eyebrow. "We can't just sit here."

"And running in circles doesn't help us either," Evren protested. "Keres, back me up."

Keres was quiet, staring at the spot behind Evren, still and cold. She whipped around, drawing her bow as a figure in a grey veil picked down the stairs towards them. They didn't flinch at her bow, nor did they stop.

"Stay right there," Evren called in warning. Was this a new Serevadian mage? Some security they hadn't met until now? They didn't look threatening. The way they swayed on their feet made them look like the only thing keeping them standing was the banister.

"You won't find your way through without help. The shadows won't let you see the clear paths," a familiar voice said through the veil, chilling Evren's blood to an icy sludge.

"Nezza?" Sahar croaked.

The figure in grey froze at the foot of the stairs. With the veil, Evren couldn't see their face. But she looked at their hands. One gripping the banister, the other hidden by a long sleeve.

Nerezza shuddered. "It's really you?"

Sahar pushed past Evren, knocking her bow down as she raced towards Nerezza. She meant to embrace her, arms wide and welcoming, but Nerezza shrank back.

"Don't!"

Sahar froze, face falling. "Nezza, it's me. I know what you've done, but it's not all your fault."

"I'm broken," Nerezza choked out.

Was she crying? Evren and Arke exchanged glances, each

shrugging. This was not the Nerezza they remembered, hell-bent on crushing Orenlion under her heel for the dagger.

"I know," Sahar said reassuringly. "But that's okay. We can fix you. You'll be back to normal in no time."

Nerezza's body shook. She leaned on the banister heavily, pressing her hand to her veil as if to dry the tears.

"You can't. Not like this. It's my fault, he was right, but it still hurts."

"Whatever happened, we can fix it." Sahar stepped up to her, reaching for her veil. "Just take this off."

"NO!" Nerezza shrieked and scrambled up a few stairs. She didn't have to, Sahar had jumped back, holding her hand to her chest as if she'd been burned.

Nerezza slumped on the stairs, breathing heavily. "No. Please . . . please, don't do that again. I can't bear to have you see what I've become."

Sahar nodded. "Okay, I won't. I won't, I swear."

Keres was at Evren's side, whispering quickly. "Her mind is shattered. There's nothing left to save."

Evren frowned. "By the souls?"

"By something else. Concentrated, Divine magic." They sucked in a breath, which was strange because she knew they didn't breathe. "She's terrified. Her thoughts circle around a sword. It destroyed her, but she doesn't blame it. She blames a man."

"Abraxas," Evren finished.

"Yes. Evren, I have tasted fear. This woman showed no ounce of it before. Whatever he did to her has resulted in the creature we have in front of us."

Nerezza rose, a figure made of wispy ash and frail bones. "He wants the dagger, like I did. But not for Eith. He wants something so much worse."

She trembled as she stepped down, shying away from Sahar's offered hand but not avoiding her entirely.

"I pushed him too far, I think," she went on. "I wanted the

sword to unite my people, but I lost focus on how. I thought it would be simple. It belongs to us, after all."

Arke frowned at her. "It wasn't as simple as takin' it, I'm guessin'."

She shook her head, veil swishing. "No. Abraxas knew, somehow. I don't know how, but he knew it would break me. He let me take it, told me I could try and build something that could withstand the Divines." She sobbed again, curling around her middle. Evren could see the individual vertebrae of her spine through her robes. "I tried. I tried so hard. But every time I did something he told me it was perfect, as if I was playing right into his hands! Nothing I did was right. Not Dirn-Darahl, or Rheinwall."

Sahar gasped softly. "That was you?"

Numbly, Nerezza nodded. "I pushed Velcros to attack early, to show his hand. It meant people would escape, that maybe someone would get word to the rest of you. It was all I could do, but it wasn't enough, was it?"

Evren swallowed past the lump in her throat. "It got us here, didn't it?"

"Yes." Nerezza sniffed. "But that works in his favor, too. He wants the dagger. Gyda has it."

Panic tore through Evren like a flash of lightning. She quickly quelled it. "Keres, is she telling the truth?"

"As much as she believes is truth, yes." Keres nodded.

"Abraxas wouldn't do this," Evren insisted.

They gave her a pitying look. "Are you so sure?"

"He wouldn't!"

"We were stranded a hundred years in the past," Nerezza said. "A hundred years, alone. He relived Vernes. He fought and killed again. He broke then, too, I think. He learned something there that I didn't. He *can* wield the sword, like I can't. There's something different about him. I should've seen it. I should've done something, but I-I was so blind." She shook her head vigorously. "Now I see too much!"

Nerezza dissolved into a fit of bawling, so hunched that Sahar had to catch her before she fell over. The elf didn't fight her as they sank to the final step, holding each other.

Evren was numb. Her mind was racing, trying to make sense of the ramblings. Could she trust Nerezza after she'd done so much to hurt them? Especially if she was as mentally broken as she claimed. And then there was Abraxas. Her friend, her guide, her support. The stern voice she needed to snap out of sullen moods, and the soft one to coax her into eating enough to make the day.

All she could see was his smile before he fell into the dragon, dagger to his chest.

Tell them I loved them.

She pressed her hand to her mouth, trying to keep herself in check. He wouldn't do this. Even if he was responsible for Nerezza's breaking, that could be justified. If Sahar wanted to forgive Nerezza for her crimes, she could forgive Abraxas for his retaliation. But the rest . . .

"Arke." She looked back at him, fearful of what he had to say but knowing she needed to hear it anyway. "He wouldn't. Tell me he wouldn't."

Arke pressed his lips into a long, thin line. If he believed Nerezza, then he believed that Abraxas had taken Tolk and his army. That he allowed that strange elf to hurt them, to kill them.

"I think this is opposite to what happened with Gyda," he said, finally. "When she turned, we didn't know nothin' 'bout her. But Abraxas, we do know him. We know what he's capable of because he's told us. We've seen him fight to keep his faith and his morals. And," he sighed, "we've also seen that he can lose that battle with himself."

"No." Evren shook her head. She'd doubted Abraxas before and done nothing but hurt him. He'd suffered and he was trying to be better. They all had their faults. He didn't hold hers against her, and she refused to condemn him for his.

"No, Arke, he's better than this. The Abraxas we know wouldn't do this."

"He would, and is," Nerezza said from her spot in Sahar's arms. "You don't trust me. I barely do. But it's been a hundred years; he's not the same man."

"That's not his fault," Evren snapped.

"No," she said hoarsely, "it isn't. But one thing has remained the same. I thought he'd lost it in the beginning, I even hoped he had. But something changed in him in Vernes. He found something." She shuddered. "He wants to use the blade and dagger to bring back the Divines, and he doesn't care who he hurts to do it."

It was as if the shadows never left her, and Evren was just eternally cold. Cold, cold, cold. He couldn't, but he'd try. And out of all the things Nerezza had said, that horrible reality stuck with her.

That if there was one thing Abraxas would risk everything and everyone for, it was his Divines.

Evren turned to Keres. Terror didn't suit them well. "We need to move."

"They'll destroy Vernes," Keres murmured in a daze. "They'll kill millions if they come back."

Evren hated herself. She wanted to fight, to believe he was still the man she remembered. Kind and compassionate and brave. A hundred years alone in the darkest corners of Eith would corrupt anyone, but there was always hope that a sliver of them would remain.

Evren wanted to have hope, but found herself lacking.

"Arke, finish that spell quickly. We'll need it soon. Keres, get Nerezza up. We need to find Sol and Sorin."

Keres blinked at her. "And then what?"

"Then we stop Abraxas from destroying the world."

~

"I DON'T WANT to fight you," Gyda said.

Abraxas didn't believe her. There was one thing she loved above all else, even Evren, and that as the thrill of battle. Well, he could give her that at least.

There was a sliver of him, like a drop of water in an ocean, that begged him to stand down. He shouldn't be looking at her with this much malice. He shouldn't be fighting against her. Gyda was his friend, probably the only true one he'd ever had. If he killed her—

No, he wouldn't kill her. Even he couldn't go that far. But he would make her see his side, not through kind words and reunions, but through blade and battle. That was what he was good at.

"A shame then," Abraxas said, slipping into an easy battle stance. "I rather think I'll enjoy this."

The shadows coiled at his feet, waiting and ready, and he dove into the fight.

The Shadow Blade was like an extension of himself, swinging smoother than any sword he'd ever used. He was faster too, the shadows pulling him away before his muscles could react to an attack. The blade itself seemed to move with a mind of its own, like it knew exactly where to strike and when to back away.

But even with it, fighting Gyda was no easy task. Her sword was bigger than his, her arms and reach making him dart out of the way of her wide swings. She was a halo of blue energy and fluid muscle, slower but with more power behind her swings. And that blue blade . . .

Abraxas rolled out of the way, narrowly avoiding a heavy attack from her. He knew what her sword could do better than she did. A normal glow meant more strength and stamina, simple but useful. Red channeled any injuries she sustained and dealt them back tenfold against her enemies. Green— rarely used—brought back the souls of the undead, Gail's gift to her.

But blue, the most recent, was the deadliest. The blue rune could ignore any armor and weapon to cut straight through flesh. He knew firsthand how dangerous it could be when she wasn't trying to hurt him.

It was a dance then, the two of them and their swords. Dodging and swinging, but eerily silent save for their panting and grunts of exertion. No clanging of steel, no war cries or taunts, just them.

Abraxas was quicker. He always had been. But now in the duel it seemed even more obvious. He spun away from her sweeping attack, smile wide as she left her left side open, as she usually did.

He rushed forward, blade ready and swinging. Something blue flashed out of the corner of his eye; Gyda's sword swinging back around. Her attack wasn't through like he thought.

Abraxas swore, jumping back. But he was too late. The edge of her sword cut across his cheek as he pulled away, the brightness dazzling and the metal colder than the pain it left.

He staggered away, hand to his cheek. She lowered her sword, breathing hard.

"Abraxas, enough," she said. "We don't need to fight."

Calmly, he looked down at his hand. It was coated in his blood, black instead of red. The shadows around him quivered and thickened in time with his heartbeat. He couldn't decide if he was furious at being the first to bleed, or exhilarated. It'd been such a long time since he'd fought someone that could keep up with him.

He placed his bloody hand back on the hilt. "Oh no, my friend, this isn't a sparring match that ends at first blood."

The shadows thickened until the room disappeared. It was just him and Gyda on a plane of absolute darkness, the light from her sword the only illumination.

"Things just got interesting," Abraxas said, and leapt at her.

～

SAHAR USED the last of her venom with shaking hands. "This has to be them or else we're never going to make it in time."

Evren squirmed in her boots, agreeing but not trusting herself to speak. Her heart was beating far too fast for her trips up and down the stairs, and it wasn't slowing down. She gripped her bow, trying to stay calm.

Gyda was alone with Abraxas. If anyone could talk him down or hold their own against him, it was her. So why did Evren feel this gut-wrenching worry?

Minutes later, the venom did its work and a round hole opened in the wall. Sahar stepped back, putting away the last of it, just as Sorin charged out sword-first.

"Sorin, it's us!" Evren cried and barely got out of the way.

Sorin stopped inches from driving the sword through Keres's chest. They regarded him with a practiced, bored, expression, and shoved the blade out of the way with their finger.

"A little late to be skewering me, Vasa," they said coolly.

Sorin looked around with wide eyes, doing a double take when he saw Nerezza's veiled form.

"Is this some rescue mission?" he asked.

"Nah, we're gonna break you out and put you somewhere new." Arke rolled his eyes. "Obviously we're fuckin' rescuing you."

Sorin relaxed, sheathing his sword in one smooth motion and then ducking back into the room.

"Well, if he wants to stay there . . ." Keres shrugged.

Evren frowned, peeking inside. "Sorin?"

He poked back out, carrying something in his arms and forcing her back. A small bundle of black leathers and bright blonde hair. The worg followed, whining lowly.

Evren gasped. "Is she okay?"

Sorin held her like she was made of glass, his frown darkening his normally bright face. "I don't know. She's breathing, but whatever put us here did a number on her. She just popped out of the shadows maybe a few minutes before you started making the door. She hasn't woken up."

Nerezza swayed on her feet. "Too long in the shadows. Abraxas must've forgotten about her when he found Gyda."

Sorin looked at her bewildered. "I'm sorry, *what*? Is that Nerezza? What did Abraxas do?"

Evren grabbed Sorin's shoulder and pulled him away. "It's a long story. We'll fill you in on the way. But we need to find Gyda and Abraxas before things get much worse."

~

WHEN ABRAXAS ATTACKED, it was as vicious as it was beautiful. This was not the careful, perfected attack of a Champion. This was wild, erratic, and free. The speed took Gyda off-guard, and for the first time since he'd met her, she was on the defensive.

Inky black streamed from his blade as he arched it, the shadows only caught by the glow of her sword. He jerked it away before they could clash, swinging it around to regain momentum and drive back at her left side.

She barely sidestepped. The whites of her eyes gleamed in the light she carried, fearful and torn.

Abraxas was not. As he brought his sword up for another devastating blow he felt nothing but certainty in his heart. The battle with his past self had been desperate and full of rage, but this was nothing like that. With the dark enveloping him, keeping him light and moving fast, he welcomed the chaos of battle and, this time, he didn't hate it.

He relished it.

He pulled back a little and gave Gyda room to breathe. He didn't want her dead. She took only a second before going on the offensive, bright and furious.

Abraxas was pleasantly surprised. He was smiling as he stood his ground and brought his sword up to block, the meaning of the blue rune momentarily forgotten.

The ringing of metal struck his ears like temple bells, and the force of Gyda's blow made him stagger back a step. But he held, arms quivering. And so did his sword.

Gyda's face was slack with shock. The black of his blade was locked with the blue of hers as if the rune was useless. Abraxas swallowed down a laugh. Oh, he really loved this sword.

"That about evens the odds, doesn't it?" he asked with a terrible grin.

~

SORIN WAS pale as they raced through the palace. It had all been explained to him—the army outside, the events leading up to Viggo's death, why they were all there. and why Nerezza was staggering ahead, leading them ever upward.

Evren expected something from Sorin; a comment on Abraxas's faith or how he always saw this coming. But the Vasa was unnervingly quiet and holding Sol tightly as they took the stairs two at a time. He didn't complain, didn't falter, just looked straight ahead.

They reached the top of the stairs and met a wall of shadows. The wall almost hissed at the sight of them, and dozens of the dagger like tendrils that had killed Viggo formed and launched at them.

Sahar let out a scream, but Nerezza waved her hand in the air and the shadowed tendrils froze, shuddered, and stilled.

"You obeyed me first," Nerezza bit out and twisted her hand. The shards withdrew slowly, as if fighting for every inch Nerezza was forcing them. Her fingers contorted, pain obvious in the way they twisted. Evren could hear the grinding of her teeth from under the veil. They sank into the soft wall of blackness, and then that too began to retreat.

"Kid, look at me."

Evren tore her gaze away from Nerezza to look down at Arke. He shoved a piece of paper in her hand and forced her fingers to close around it.

"That's gonna get us out of here."

Evren's eyes widened. She fought to give him back the paper but he backed away, taking the first of many steps downward.

"No! Arke, what are you doing?"

"I gotta find Tolk," he said. "I'm sorry, but I left him once. I can't do it again."

Evren looked at the paper. The spell of teleportation he'd been working on. She felt sick.

"I can't cast this!"

"You can," he said.

"I can't just leave you here!"

"It's just in case." He took another few steps down. By then, the wall of shadows had retreated a good foot. The beginnings of a grand entryway had appeared. Behind Evren, Sorin watched but didn't say a word.

"Arke, please don't do this." She couldn't cast this spell. The last one had been simple and still nearly killed Gyda. And if she had to cast it, then Arke wouldn't be there. She sure as hells didn't trust Nerezza to do it, even now.

"I can't leave you," she croaked.

"And I can't leave him." Arke blinked away what might've been a tear. "I'm sorry."

Then he disappeared down another staircase, and Evren lost sight of his tuft of white hair.

~

NOW THAT THEIR blades could touch, Abraxas was past the dance and into a flurry of death. He held nothing back, enraptured by the thrill of the fight pumping in him. He didn't even feel tired. He was still just as fast as he was when the fight began. Gyda was decidedly not.

She was tiring, heaving great breaths between her blows, and throwing all the strength she had into them, hoping for a lucky hit. Now more than ever, her lack of speed was apparent.

He feinted to the right, then swung around to slice her leg. It would've been a serious but nonlethal blow, but she managed to block it just in time. The blue light flickered but stayed true. She held him there, panting.

"Just give me the dagger, and this will be over," he said breathlessly.

She bared her teeth. "I. Don't. Have. It."

He sighed. "Must I cut off a limb before you give it up?"

"You can certainly try."

She shoved him back hard enough that he lost his footing. The shadows caught him and put him back on his feet.

"And try I will."

Gyda could afford to lose a hand. Or maybe just a finger. She wouldn't miss one of those. He fought harder now, taking her invitation to try as a challenge. With every swing, she blocked. Every parry sent his blade in the opposite direction than her skin. But he never relented. He gritted his teeth and put everything he had in the blows. Hit after hit, the clanging of steel was all he could hear. With every hit, he pushed her back. With every block he saw her blade's glow flicker, and the worry mount in her eyes.

Good.

Abraxas took a running start and leapt in the air, his sword high above him. Gyda brought her own up to block, the attack unavoidable. He felt alive as he fell towards her, streaming shadows like water, and brought his sword down on hers with a thunderous clash.

Gyda's blade shattered.

Pieces of blue-lighted steel flew everywhere, cutting into both Gyda and Abraxas. Surprise or force brought her to her knees, and he only just kept his sword from cutting into her flesh. The wisps of smoke curled from his blade and licked at the blood leaking from her cuts. The hilt of her sword rested in her hands, all runes dark.

"Well, a blade, a hand." He shrugged. "Same thing."

Gyda just stared blankly at the pieces of steel that littered the ground. She was crestfallen, grieving as if she'd lost a friend instead. She was lucky she hadn't lost a friend. Abraxas was still willing to extend her a kindness.

He removed the blade from her neck. The shadows that darkened the room started to curl back on his command. Blue, watery light bathed her features again.

"Don't look so glum, Gyda," he chided. "We can fix your sword. Come now, all I need is the dagger in exchange."

Icy eyes glared at him, barely looking up. "I do not lie, Kain. I would've given you the dagger. I would've used it if I had it. This . . . this is not what I wanted."

"No, you *didn't* lie," he corrected her. "Now that you're sharing a heart with Evren, you've got all her weaknesses. Lying being one of them, especially when she thinks it's for the greater good. Believe me, I am not an evil to keep away from. I'm trying to fix Eith."

"Is this what you call fixing?" she asked, extending her arms out. They were covered with gashes, some from the shattering of her sword and others from his own blade. He was pleasantly surprised to see that he'd landed more hits than he thought.

"Kain!" Gyda snapped his attention back to her face. "I am your friend. I love you. Do not go down this road."

"This is the only road," he said. "If you were truly my

friend, you'd be walking it with me rather than digging your heels in. You don't even know what I want to do, and yet you're opposing me. Why?"

She paused, then looked down at her hilt. "Because I looked into your eyes and saw an enemy, not the man I respected."

The lingering thrill of battle, the thrum of power in him, vanished. Abraxas's heart sank like an anchor. She didn't see what he did. She didn't understand at all. Divines damn him, she was supposed to be the easy one! He couldn't do this without them. He couldn't walk Eith alone again if it meant walking away from them.

His grip on the sword started to loosen, and then he felt a jolt. He remembered why he was doing this, why he fought so hard in the first place. He had a mission, one he couldn't abandon. He had to bring Haphion back because at least when he abandoned Abraxas, he'd been forced to. Everyone else was turning their backs on him by choice, even Gyda.

Salvation requires martyrdom, martyrdom requires sacrifice.

Abraxas never thought the sacrifice would be his own friends—his family.

"I need you to know that this pains me," he said, causing Gyda to look up at him. "My heart breaks to do this. You must see that."

"I do," she said softly.

He raised his sword again. "I can take solace in that, at least."

The arc began softly above his head and whistled down, gaining speed. Gyda closed her eyes, but Abraxas forced himself not to. If he was going to kill her, he was going to force himself to watch.

Before the blade could land at her neck, it jolted out of his hands as an arrow pinged on the blade and sent it skittering on the floor. He whirled around, facing Evren as she lowered her bow.

Her black eyes held an ocean of emotion. A single tear slipped down her cheek. But she notched another arrow, her jaw firm.

"Step away from my heart," she hissed.

ABRAXAS TOOK a step back from Gyda's defeated form, arms raised. His boot crunched on shards of broken steel as he did, and Evren forced herself to watch his movements and not look at Gyda. She was breathing, that was all Evren could hope for.

Abraxas was nothing like she remembered. His face was a little more lined, and the streaks of silver at his temples had grown thicker. But the way he carried himself, the way he looked at her *like a threat* made her stomach churn.

That wasn't her friend. Gyda's heart was breaking with every breath, and Evren didn't know if it was Gyda's pain or her own. She forced her hands not to shake.

"Evren." He smiled at her, the same way he used to. Pushing a mug of water into her hands instead of ale. Watching over her as she crawled back from the brink of death. Chiding her recklessness while also secretly loving it.

He reached down for the sword and she hissed, "Don't."

He pulled away, frowning. "I thought you'd be happy to see me, or another Elder artifact."

"At the moment I'm a little torn," she murmured against her arrow.

Footfalls sounded behind her, causing Abraxas's attention to snap away from her. She edged closer to Gyda's slumped form as the rest of the group, whom she'd bolted away from when she'd felt Gyda's heart race faster, rounded the corner.

Sorin cried out, taking in the sight of Gyda, swordless and bloody. "What the hells did you do?"

"Now, Sorin," Abraxas said placatingly.

"No! Look at what you've done! Look at what you're doing. You've beaten Gyda. You nearly killed Sol. You locked us up after forcing us to see the horrors of Kleros. Horrors that you orchestrated."

Abraxas didn't deny it, and Sorin swore.

"Why?" he asked. "Why are we less important than your gods?"

Abraxas's eyes darkened. Evren was so close to Gyda now.

"I want to make you understand, but how can I when you come in and immediately assume the worse?" Abraxas asked. "What if Gyda attacked me first?"

Nerezza's fragile voice was stronger now as she stepped past Sorin. "But she didn't. They know it. Gyda loved you, they all did. You're the one that's changed."

Abraxas stared at Nerezza with unbridled hatred. Evren had never seen such venom in him before, even aimed at Keres. Nerezza stopped a few feet from him, looking weak where he looked strong, like a piece of gossamer thread clinging to a mountain.

Sahar was behind her, hand digging in her back, with Keres close behind. They hadn't pushed Nerezza for their soul back yet. They seemed to be waiting.

Nerezza drew back her shoulders. "End this, and I'll call off Serevadia."

Abraxas laughed bitterly. "Oh, will you? With what power? Gyda told me that your little pet called me Catarmon. It seems like even with the power of a god at your fingertips, you couldn't control even the most loyal of your people.

"They want war, Nerezza. Velcros has tasted blood and it is sweet. He won't stop until he's had it all. You can't change that now."

Nerezza paused, fingers brushing the edge of her veil. Evren reached Gyda and knelt beside her just as Nerezza started to speak again.

"I'm here, love," Evren whispered.

Gyda, gripping the dark hilt of her sword, shuddered as she sobbed.

"Maybe I can't change Serevadia," Nerezza mused thoughtfully. "But I can fix one mistake I've made."

Abraxas's expression darkened. "You wouldn't dare."

Nerezza sounded like she was smiling. "If I do anything, it is dare."

She flung her hand out, a riot of shadows and blood-red magic following her just as Abraxas grasped the sword.

The room spun as the shadows came to life, torn between the two elves. Evren grabbed onto Gyda as a whirlwind tore through the room. One circled Abraxas, bearing the Shadow Dancer's sword, the other swarmed around Nerezza. The magic from both sides clashed, a fierce mix that reminded Evren of a thunderstorm. Red arcs of lightning struck from the black clouds, hitting the walls with a resounding crack. Wicked daggers of darkness shot at Nerezza and spun away, inches from impaling her.

In the back, Sorin huddled with Sol and the worg, staring at Abraxas with horror and tears in his eyes. Keres gripped the wall, holding Sahar so she didn't blow away. When a volley of daggers headed her way, they took them for her, all nine puncturing their back. The screaming wind didn't drown out their cries of pain.

Evren huddled with Gyda, bow abandoned, one hand clasped around hers and the other going for the spell in her pocket. She wouldn't use it. Arke would be there any minute now. She was sure of it.

Evren dared peek over Gyda's shoulder. The battle of wills and magic wasn't going well. There was more black than red. Nerezza's knees were buckling. With every passing second, she was getting weaker, and Abraxas just seemed to be getting darker.

The look in his eyes gave her chills. That wasn't the man she knew and adored. That was a monster wearing his skin.

Nerezza fell to one knee and her veil slipped. It disappeared in the clouds above her head, and she looked over at Sahar. Black eyes, eight of them across her face. Torn lips, sunken cheeks, blackened ears. She was crying, all eight eyes bleeding black. But she smiled sorrowfully at Sahar.

"We're still sisters?" she asked. "Right?"

Sahar covered her mouth with her hand, staring at her with horror. But she didn't look away. She nodded and reached her hand out to Nerezza. The only thing holding her back was Keres, who was looking on grimly.

Keres and Nerezza nodded. She reached out and touched Sahar's hand.

"I'm so sorry," Nerezza said.

Her magic died in an instant, the whirlwind that had been protecting her vanishing. Two dozen razor sharp daggers flew into her body, one after the other, and she gasped.

Nerezza looked up at Abraxas, her dress turning blacker by the minute. He regarded her coldly, more daggers forming behind him.

"I . . ." she croaked, black blood dribbling down her chin. "Do not . . . apologize . . . to you."

"Pity," Abraxas said and sent the rest of the daggers into her body.

Nerezza's hand slid from Sahar's as her body hit the ground. Sahar wrenched herself free from Keres and ran to her, clutching her to her chest and sobbing.

Evren brought out the paper, and the motion drew Gyda's eyes. "What is that?"

Evren swallowed nervously. Abraxas wasn't looking at them at all, instead watching Sahar's grief unfold for a second time. He stepped closer to her; eyes darkly thoughtful.

"A way out," Evren whispered, unfolding the paper so Gyda could see.

Abraxas was a foot away from Sahar before Keres stepped between them. In a child's body, they didn't look imposing. Against the sword in Abraxas's hand, Evren feared the odds.

"I felt you," Abraxas said, looking Keres up and down. "No one to stop me from killing you now."

"I would say the same about you," Keres said with a grin. Too happy, too confident. Even Abraxas noticed and took a small step back to make room for his sword.

"Evren, dear, you should start on that escape plan now," Keres called over their shoulder. The dull glow in their eyes shifted, changed. They were suddenly an unfathomable prismatic shade, like looking into the facets of a diamond. "Things are about to get nasty."

Keres threw their hands to the side, palms facing the walls. Evren's ears popped as the air changed, and then a massive web of cracks spiraled from the center of both walls. They caved, groaning under the sudden pressure.

Abraxas yelled as he swung the sword, but in a puff of mist Keres was no longer there. He was right behind Abraxas, and a wave of ear cracking magic sent him flying to the opposite wall.

"Bad choice, letting me live after lovely Nezza." Keres tsked, raising a hand to the ceiling. It cracked too, a gush of water falling in. Sahar screamed, covering Nerezza's body. Abraxas spat saltwater from his mouth as he stood up.

"You'll drown them all?" he yelled at Keres.

Keres frowned. "You'd kill them all?"

That gave Abraxas pause, his eyes sliding over to where Sorin was trying to keep Sol dry. The water was rushing in, covering the whole floor and rising to their ankles. Abraxas looked away, ashamed.

Gyda's breath was hot on Evren's ear. "Do it."

Evren shook her head. "Not without Arke."

"Evren, none of us live if you don't do this."

She fought back a sob, turning to face her. "It'll kill you."

Outside of Gyda, the world didn't matter. The water was rising. The parchment was getting soaked between their hands. Keres was yelling, threatening to destroy the window next. Abraxas was threatening to cut Sahar's head off if they tried.

Evren looked past Gyda, to the doorway she'd entered through. Empty. No Arke. Just the rising waves lapping into the hallway.

Evren was weak. She couldn't do it. She crumbled the paper in her fist, shaking her head. She lived so long without Gyda. Doing this meant the end of her, the end of Arke. She was already losing one friend, how could she bear to lose another?

But then her eyes caught Sorin and Sol. Still alive, still breathing. Sahar off to the side, holding another dead friend. Evren squeezed her eyes shut. They didn't deserve to die. She loved them, too. If the roles were reversed and using this spell meant Evren's death, not Gyda's, she'd do it with only a moment's hesitation. Sacrifice was easy when it was just herself.

The fight raged beyond her eyelids. She couldn't tell if Abraxas or Keres was winning, only that this fight had been a long time coming and neither would give up. Keres, because they feared the Divines' return, and Abraxas, because he viewed Keres as an abomination.

Gyda's soft kiss on her lips opened her eyes. Evren's dagger tugged at her armor as Gyda tore it free and pulled away.

"Whatever happens, it was worth it," Gyda said. "All of it."

Evren's heart caught in her throat. She nodded numbly. It was. "I'll find you again, in this life or the next."

There was a decision made, easier now that Gyda held the

dagger. But the spell was Evren's. The cut was just a formality, a way of giving permission.

Gyda slashed Evren's palm open and pressed it against the wad of spell paper. Evren didn't fight the rush of magic in her veins, the strength awakening in her and the paper burning in her hands despite the water. She felt the shadows at Abraxas's command, felt them turn to her control, briefly and wildly.

They fought her. The binds of Arke's spell were just enough to wrangle them into submission. Barely.

Gyda's hair was turning white in front of her. Evren shook and held her.

"I love you," Evren said, as if it wasn't obvious, as if she wouldn't have let all of them drown in the vain hope that she could spare Gyda.

Gyda smiled. She parted her lips to reply, the words forming. Then the shadows enveloped them, and the whole world went black and cold.

Evren was falling.

Evren was alone.

27

Arke

Arke knew he'd lose the Wandering Sols eventually, but it still hurt like a bitch. More so because he expected it to be years down the line when they were too tired of adventures and heroics. Sol would want to go home and see if she could reclaim her honor. Evren and Gyda would likely find some ridiculously idyllic hut in the middle of nowhere and be sickeningly in love with each other. Sorin would want to sail again and try to drag Arke with him, and Arke would humor him because it was hard to tell the kid no.

He shook his head, sprinting down the black halls as fast as he could. He had to stop thinking of them as kids. By goblin standards they were, but they weren't goblins. Hell, he was barely a goblin at this point.

Still, he would miss them, assuming Evren wasn't so dumb as to not use his spell. First of its kind, manipulating existing arcane energy to transfer multiple people miles away. He was sure he got it right. At least enough where they came out the other side alive and with all their limbs. And hopefully somewhere safe. He figured just about anywhere was safer than here.

It was a spell that would've put his name in the history books. It would've cemented his place in the Greyreach Conclave along with all the taller human and elven mages who didn't believe he could do something worth stepping into their halls. Well, the jokes on them! Or it would've been.

The floor shook beneath his feet. Stone and sprinkles of water showered from the ceiling. His claws dug into his spellbook as he ran.

Arke had given up a lot for that chance. The Conclave would've been a way to raise Goblinkin from the dirt into the light of civilization, like they deserved. He could've shown the whole world what they were capable of, that they weren't just raiders and thieves.

But he'd gotten distracted. Attached. To Sorin and his bubbling laughter, the way he made Arke feel welcome without needing to prove himself. To Sol, who mirrored him in more ways than either of them were comfortable with and who deserved far better than the hand fate had dealt her. To Gyda, who had treated him with respect and never doubted him from the moment they met. To Evren, who'd accidentally ripped at the hole leaving his brother had left in his chest and made him lash out at first. They were too similar, Arke and Evren. Loners forced into a party of misfits and growing to care about them against all odds.

Evren was good. She understood that she was their only ticket out. She'd take the spell and use it, curse him later when she was alone, but she'd be alive. So would Sorin and Sol, maybe even Sahar.

But not Abraxas.

A wave of water rushed down the hallway, and Arke immediately took the stairs. The briny water rushed down like a waterfall and nearly swept him away, but he dug into the banister and kept going.

Abraxas hurt more than any of them. It would've been easier if he'd died, and Arke hated himself for thinking like that. But now what? Arke had given up his family for power. He'd given up staying in Orenlion with Neri for the Wandering Sols. How much more would he be sacrificing?

How much longer did he have?

He was soaked from the waist up, shivering and cursingas he fell away from the stairs and turned down another hallway. The water mostly continued down the next set of stairs, but some trailed after him in a slower flow. He shook his legs dry as he ran.

Everything Arke had done led to this. A grave at the bottom of Sorin's fucking ocean, and for what? There was still an army out there. Tolk and his people were still trapped and nowhere to be found. A quarter of his friends were dead or dying.

He'd abandoned Tolk for power.

He'd given up his name for power.

He would've given up more for Neri, if she'd asked.

Would he see her again? Did they share an afterlife? Did Arke even believe in an afterlife? Fuck, he had no clue. There had only been one constant in his life, one voice that whispered to him ever since he was able to crawl.

Unnethen.

There was power in a name, just as much as there was power in a word. Everyone in Terevas knew this and kept their true names secret. Even Sahar, obviously practicing Vernesian culture, kept to this rule. Sahar was not her True Name.

Arke didn't have a True Name anymore. He'd given it up for a chance at life in the rest of Eith. He'd sold it, and his right as King, for a greater purpose.

Well, that purpose was draining into the fucking ocean now.

He stopped short of the next stairway. It dipped down into

several feet of water, which was rising and swallowing the steps as he watched.

The end of the line.

Arke gritted his teeth, thumbing through his spells. He could try to freeze the water to walk on it, but it wouldn't last long. He wouldn't be able to freeze enough to walk far, or enough to stop the water from rising. He didn't have that kind of power.

He growled as he snapped his spellbook shut.

Fuck Abraxas. Fuck Serevadia. Fuck the hellsdamned Divines and everything that had anything to do with them.

This was *not* how he was going to die.

The water was rising faster now. What the fuck did Abraxas do? Arke's spell wouldn't have caused this. Likely Keres. Fuck them too.

Arke closed his eyes and tried to ignore the rising water. "Unnethen!" he called. "I know you're there! I'm ready to make a deal!"

A musical voice tinkled in his ear, as if someone was leaning over his shoulder. "Are you now?"

Arke knew better than to turn around. As far as Fey went, Unnethen was relatively calm. Looking upon her form would change that quickly.

"I need your help," he said, defeated. There was no lie in his voice. Arke couldn't lie to her.

"You do seem to be in a bind," she mused. "But what happened to never asking for my help ever again?"

"Lot's changed. My friend has lost his mind. Pretty sure another is dead. I need to get Tolk and my people out of here."

"Hmm," she hummed noncommittally. "And if Tolk wasn't here?"

Arke froze. "He is."

"They're taking him out." Arke could imagine her admiring her nails now, sharpening them into fine points sharp enough to kill. "I'm afraid the water is too high to retrieve him."

Arke squashed down his frustration. "Not for you."

"No, but for you it is. Did you forget, dear, how rude you were to me the last time we talked?"

Arke winced. He hadn't forgotten. The last time he'd talked with her, he'd been furious about having to leave Tolk without even saying goodbye. It had been another one of her rules as a part of their deal. Power came at a price, and that meant breaking his brother's heart by sneaking out in the middle of the night after telling him that Arke hated him.

Arke couldn't lie to Unnethen, but he'd lied plenty of times *for* her, and hated it each time.

The water lapped his toes, bitingly cold, but he didn't back away. "What do you want as an apology?"

"A piece of glass."

Arke's heart jolted, his hand immediately going to the mirror shard in his pocket. It was the only glass he had, the only one Unnethen would want. But Neri . . .

He took it out and tossed it over his shoulder. Unnethen giggled with delight. The water was at his ankles now.

"Happy?"

"For now."

"Help me," he said. "Another deal, Unnethen. Get me through this and to my brother and you can have me. All of me."

"All of you? Arke, I already have your name. That's all I need."

"I know," he said softly. With his name she had power over him. The past year with the Wandering Sols had been a rebellion she'd humored. She'd *let* him walk away, and that above all made him want to gouge her eyes out. "Eith is in danger. We could fix that, but I need Tolk first."

"Abraxas Kain seeks to destroy the Aether that holds back

the Divines." Unnethen sniffed in distaste. "I do despise those creatures."

"So, you'll help me?"

"Why else would I be here? He's not the first to toy with the Aether. If you want to stop him from burning the world down, and ruining everything we Fey have built, then you'll need to understand more."

"I don't know what the Aether is," he growled.

"I can teach you. For now, think of it as the ties that bind the unnatural away from Eith, and Abraxas Kain seeks to cut those ties and destroy the natural order. This won't do. We know this."

"Why haven't you done anything before?" The water was up to his waist now. He was growing uncomfortably numb and weightless, the current pushing him back.

"Because I needed you to invite me, obviously. I need a deal."

The sound of rushing water roared in his ears. He breathed deeply. This could save Sorin and Tolk, and everyone else he hated to love. Fuck, he wished he didn't care at all. Hellsdamn his heart.

"What do you need?" he asked.

"You." Her voice made him grow colder. "When this is done and you live, you come with me forever."

"Like, after this escape?"

"No, dear, after you kill Abraxas Kain."

Arke's heart sank. So, he wasn't dead. Why couldn't the elf just die and spare them some pain? Arke didn't want to kill him.

He also really didn't want to live with Unnethen. That would mean giving up every dream he had. Studying at the Conclave, sailing with Sorin, having a life with Tolk again, reshaping how Eith viewed goblins. All of it, gone with a snap of his fingers.

Unnethen could command him to do this, but that was the

point of the deal. She wanted consent. She wanted him to hurt for her help. *That* was the true cost of the deal.

The water tickled his chin.

"Okay," he said finally. "My life is fuckin' yours."

"Excellent."

In a rush, the water fell away from him. He fell to the ground, dripping and shivering, spellbook miraculously dry, as usual. The water parted for him, raging against the walls Unnethen pressed it back. The stairs, and the hallways beyond, were clear and waiting for him.

He clamored down the stairs, splashing through the puddles left over and pointedly ignoring the thrashing sea around him. Unnethen's presence tickled the back of his neck, her soft voice humming a melody as she followed.

Each twist and turn looked the same. A hallway underwater, a tunnel of magic carved for him. His skin was sticky with drying saltwater. He hummed the same melody as Unnethen to keep going.

He didn't dare think of Sorin or Neri. None of them. It hurt so much worse when he did.

At last, Unnethen's tunnel ended at a pair of massive doors. They fell open before Arke could reach them, twin slabs of obsidian crashing onto the dry ocean floor that carpeted the bottom of Serevadia's bridge.

He stepped forward. The soldiers marching stopped to look at him. Dozens of them that he could see, and more that he couldn't see. All bound in silvery armor, holding weapons laced with Light. One by one they all turned to him, a lone goblin standing in the wreckage of an ancient palace slowly filling with water.

And then they started to laugh.

Arke couldn't quell the rage inside him. Even in Serevadia he was seen as nothing dangerous.

"Tolk is in there?" Arke whispered to Unnethen. They wouldn't be able to see her unless she let them.

"Yes."

He flipped open his spellbook, and her tinkling laughter joined the army's. She wasn't laughing at Arke, but at them.

"They don't think you're a threat." She giggled. "How quaint."

Arke tore a page from his book. "Let's change their minds, shall we?"

THE END

Thank you for reading WHERE THE LIGHT DIES.

The Blood of Eith series continues next with
WHERE THE SKY BURNS
available at
www.GillianGrant.com

Keep reading for a excerpt from
WHERE THE SKY BURNS…

EXCERPT OF WHERE THE SKY BURNS
THE BLOOD OF EITH, BOOK FIVE

Prologue: Evren

Heavy, moist dirt clogged Evren's nose and mouth. It caked under her fingernails as she crawled her way up, up, ever upward. It slid through the folds of her armor, chilling her skin faintly like the memories of shadowy tendrils that belonged to someone who'd once been a friend.

Two lost friends. One lost love. And yet she was still living.

Her fingers broke through thick mud first, and then hit open air. She dug them in like claws, meeting slime and gunk of newly wetted earth, and pulled herself up inch by agonizing inch. The soil didn't want to give her up. It kept a loving, cold grip around her torso, around her legs, and tugged her down with every inch she gained.

Peace would not be gained by surrender, not to the earth nor to her own grief. There was work to be done to make up for everything she'd lost.

With a surge of strength, Evren pulled her head and chest free of the ground, gasping and spitting up soil. The sky was dark, and clouds choked away any signs of starlight. The wind was sweet and cold on her skin as she heaved lungfuls of air. The gritty taste of dirt caked her tongue, overwhelming the salt and shadow she'd left.

No.

Evren forced those brand-new memories away. She had to focus on the present. She could ignore what happened, if only briefly, to survive this.

Her hands sunk up to her wrists in mud as she heaved herself out of her would-be grave. The mud made wet sucking sounds as her legs left and she crawled away. Every breath that rattled in her lungs she told herself she deserved. Every blink of her eyes made the world clearer. Every beat of their heart—

No.

Getting a few feet away from the hole, Evren collapsed on the ground. The mud eagerly pooled into her armor and hair again. A part of her screamed about her bowstring and how she'd have to clean and replace it. The arrows too. But she couldn't bring herself to care.

There was night. There was air in her lungs. There was an unfathomable ache in her chest. And she was alone.

A cry gurgled from her throat as she sat up. She looked around wildly for holes like hers. She saw nothing but mud and grass. She combed through the mud, torn between wanting to find a hand and terrified if she found one still and cold.

Where were the Wandering Sols? The spell had worked. She *felt* it take her from one place and dump her in another. But what of the others? The spell hadn't forgotten about them. Arke would've made sure they all made it out. He wouldn't have messed it up.

It had to have been a fault on Evren's side.

She wasn't sure how long she dug. Hours, perhaps. Her arms screamed with every shove of mud. Her frustration bubbled into a boil when every precious inch she cleared away filled back up in a manner of minutes. She was getting nowhere, and soon her digging became a frantic clawing.

Nothing. Nothing. Nothing

Evren's arms gave out just as a sob finally tore free from her chest. She slumped on her knees, cradling her head in her cold, slimy hands as hot tears cut tracks through the crusted earth on her face. There was no primal urge to scream. No need to kick the ground and rage. Her cries left her exhausted. With every new wave of tears she sank deeper into herself and the knowledge that they were gone, and it was her fault.

Inevitably, her mind returned to the floor of the Boreal Sea. To a palace made of obsidian and a room filling with water. Sorin clutching Sol's unconscious body as tight as he could, wide eyes begging Evren to get them out alive. Sahar still reaching for Nerezza's body, torn and mangled beyond recognition by Divine magic and weapons both. Keres facing off against Abraxas not in triumph and in strength but in desperation as they kept his attention away from Evren. The shattered remains of Gyda's sword glinting in the blue light, winking as blood seeped from the cut on Evren's hand. Soft kisses on Evren's lips. *It was worth it.* Arke pressing the spell into her hands,

"I'm sorry, but I left him once. I can't do it again."

Evren had left Arke. That he knew it would happen and prepared for it didn't make it better. If he'd casted the spell, he would've done it right.

Evren tore her hands through her grimy hair, heaving another pathetic sob. It was all for nothing. Nerezza's death. Gyda and Arke's sacrifice. If she hadn't managed to save Sorin, Sol, and Sahar, then she was useless. She'd failed them, all of them.

Abraxas most of all.

Evren hated the guilt that gnawed at her when she thought of him. Even more, she hated the wave of disgust when she remembered how he'd looked having Gyda at his mercy.

People changed, she knew that. But she never expected him to fall so far.

When there were no more tears left to shed, no more mud to rake through, and the ache in her chest turned to a dull throb that wouldn't stop beating, Evren forced herself to her feet. In every direction a night blanketed world spread out before her. Shrouded and still, like it was holding its breath and waiting for something.

Waiting for her.

She could've taken the time to examine the ground and fauna to figure out where she was. But Evren had no energy to do so. A heart that didn't belong to her tugged north, perhaps out of memory or habit, and she followed. Her feet drug tracks across the muddy grave she'd dug herself out of, and the air smelled like death as she left it behind.

~

Check out WHERE THE SKY BURNS today at
www.GillianGrant.com

ACKNOWLEDGMENTS

I don't know what it says about me that this was one of my easiest to write, or that Abraxas as a POV character spoke to me in ways Evren never did. A fallen hero was always something I wanted to write, and i'm honestly so proud of how its turned out. Without these lovely people though, it would still be a pile of wordy mush.

- As always, Laura, Charity, Stef, for being an amazing team.
- My ARC team, always patient and thoughtful.
- My friends and family.
- Special shout out to my cats, who enforced breaks when I would've gone on writing without taking care of myself.
- And, always, to my readers. This world is nothing without you.

ABOUT THE AUTHOR

Gillian Grant was born in Texas and grew up enthralled with fantasy stories of all kinds. As she got older she often traveled with her family and imagined wild adventures while exploring the mountains of Colorado and the glens of Scotland. Back home in Texas she took her love of fantasy to the next level and sat a group of friends down to play Dungeons and Dragons. From there, they built the world her first novel, *Where The Shadows Beckon* was set in. When she's not writing Gillian is normally juggling too many D&D campaigns, grooming dogs, and imagining her next adventure. She still lives in Texas with her two cats.

www.GillianGrant.com

facebook.com/GillianGrantAuthor

instagram.com/gilliangrantauthor

bookbub.com/profile/gillian-grant

amazon.com/Gillian-Grant/e/B09J94DBHP